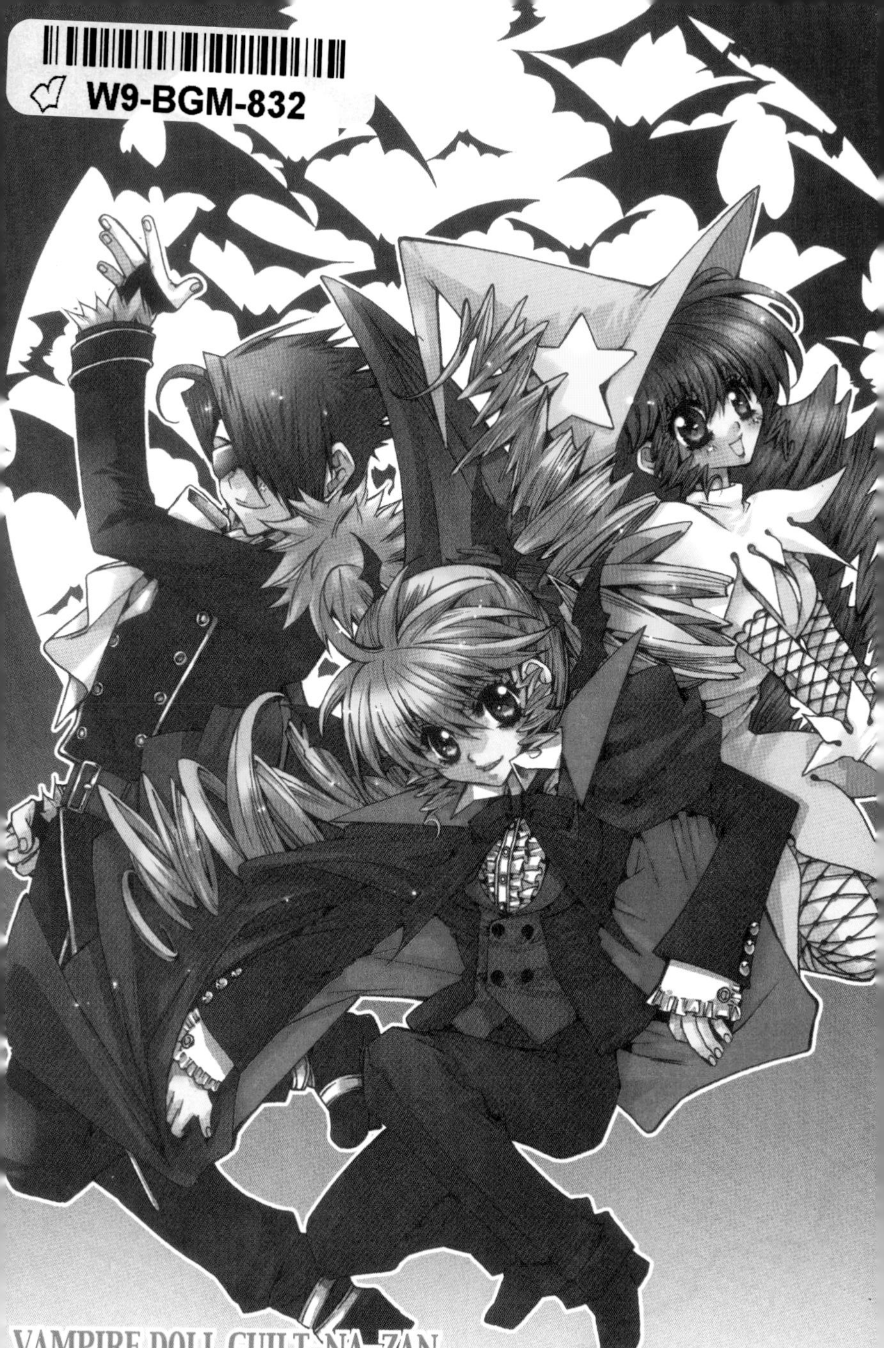

VAMPIRE DOLL GUILT-NA-ZAN

CONTENTS

Vampire Doll
Guilt-na-Zaan

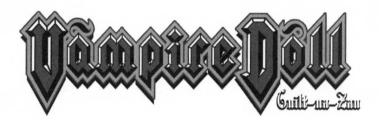

VOLUME 4

CREATED BY
ERIKA KARI

TOKYOPOP®

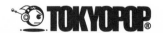

HAMBURG // LONDON // LOS ANGELES // TOKYO

Vampire Doll: Guilt-na-Zan Volume 4
Created by Erika Kari

Translation - Yoohae Yang
English Adaptation - Patricia Duffield
Retouch and Lettering - Star Print Brokers
Production Artist - Bowen Park
Graphic Designer - Fawn Lau

Editor - Alexis Kirsch
Digital Imaging Manager - Chris Buford
Pre-Production Supervisor - Erika Terriquez
Production Manager - Elisabeth Brizzi
Managing Editor - Vy Nguyen
Creative Director - Anne Marie Horne
Editor-in-Chief - Rob Tokar
Publisher - Mike Kiley
President and C.O.O. - John Parker
C.E.O. and Chief Creative Officer - Stuart Levy

A  Manga

TOKYOPOP Inc.
5900 Wilshire Blvd. Suite 2000
Los Angeles, CA 90036

E-mail: info@TOKYOPOP.com
Come visit us online at www.TOKYOPOP.com

ISBN: 978-1-4278-0459-4

First TOKYOPOP printing: October 2007
10 9 8 7 6 5 4 3 2 1
Printed in the USA

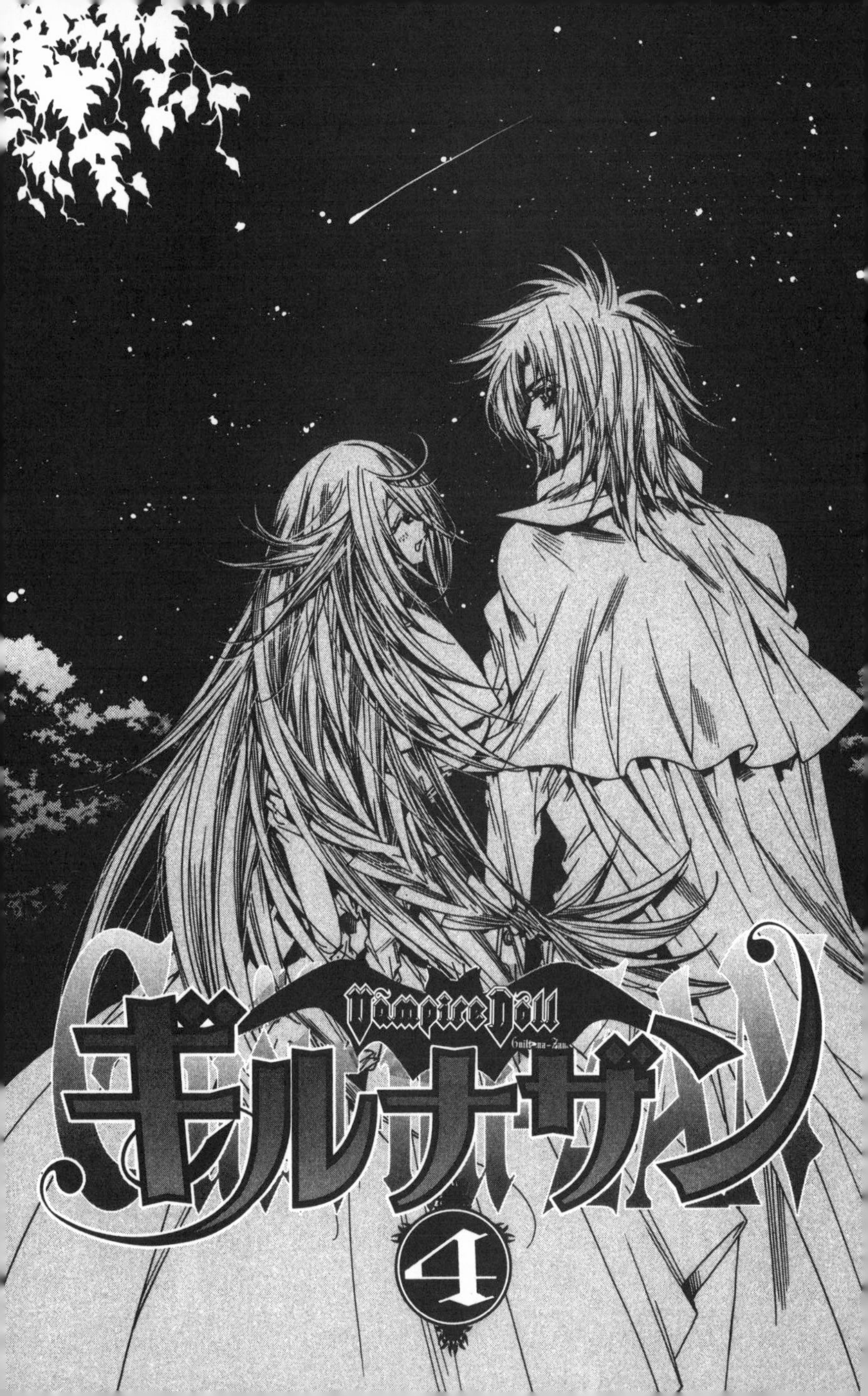
Vampire Doll
ギルナザン
4

VAMPIRE DOLL GUILT-NA-ZAN

MAIN CHARACTERS

STORY SO FAR:

IN DAYS OF OLD, EUROPE'S MOST FEARFUL VAMPIRE WAS GUILT-NA-ZAN. OVER A CENTURY AFTER BEING SEALED AWAY BY THE EXORCIST KYOEISAI YOTOBARI, THE LEGEND HAS BEEN REVIVED AS A GIRL BY KYOEISAI'S POWERFUL DESCENDANT, KYOJI. NOW, GUILT-NA-ZAN LIVES AS A MAID FOR THE YOTOBARI FAMILY WHILE OCCASIONALLY BEING USED AS A MONSTER HUNTER. THE HARDSHIPS OF GUILT-NA-ZAN CONTINUE...

GUILT-NA

LONG AGO, HE WAS KNOWN AS THE LORD OF VAMPIRES, THE MOST FEARED OF ALL HIS KIND. KYOJI RESURRECTED HIM INTO THE FIGURE OF A WAX DOLL. NOW HE MUST OBEY KYOJI.

GUILT-NA-ZAN

THIS IS WHAT GUILT-NA ORIGINALLY LOOKED LIKE. BY SUCKING 1CC OF TONAE'S BLOOD, HE CAN TRANSFORM INTO HIMSELF-- BUT ONLY FOR TEN MINUTES!

KYOJI

A VERY SKILLED BUT LAZY EXORCIST, HE SPENDS MOST DAYS MAKING FUN OF GUILT-NA.

VINCENT

ORIGINALLY A BAT, VINCENT IS A SERVANT OF GUILT-NA-ZAN. HE'S TOO NICE TO BE CALLED A MONSTER.

TONAE

SHE IS KYOJI'S YOUNGER SISTER. LIKE VINCENT, SHE IS PURE AND SOMEWHAT SPACEY.

DANTE

THIS IS NOT HIS ORIGINAL FORM, FOR MARIYA IMPLANTED THIS MONSTER'S SOUL INTO A WAX DOLL. HE NOW HAS HUGE CLAWS AND IS MARIYA'S SERVANT.

MARIYA

A MASTER WAX-DOLL MAKER AND KYOJI'S MENTOR, MARIYA FOUND DANTE IN THE COUNTRY OF W, WHICH NO LONGER EXISTS. HE SPEAKS IN THE HIROSHIMA DIALECT, AND HIS AGE IS A MYSTERY.

DUNE

HE FEEDS BY ABSORBING NEGATIVE ENERGY FROM HUMANS AND IS CURRENTLY LIVING AND WORKING AT MITSUHACHI ACADEMY.

#25『Starry Starry Night CHAPTER 4 "Hush-a-bye my dear."』

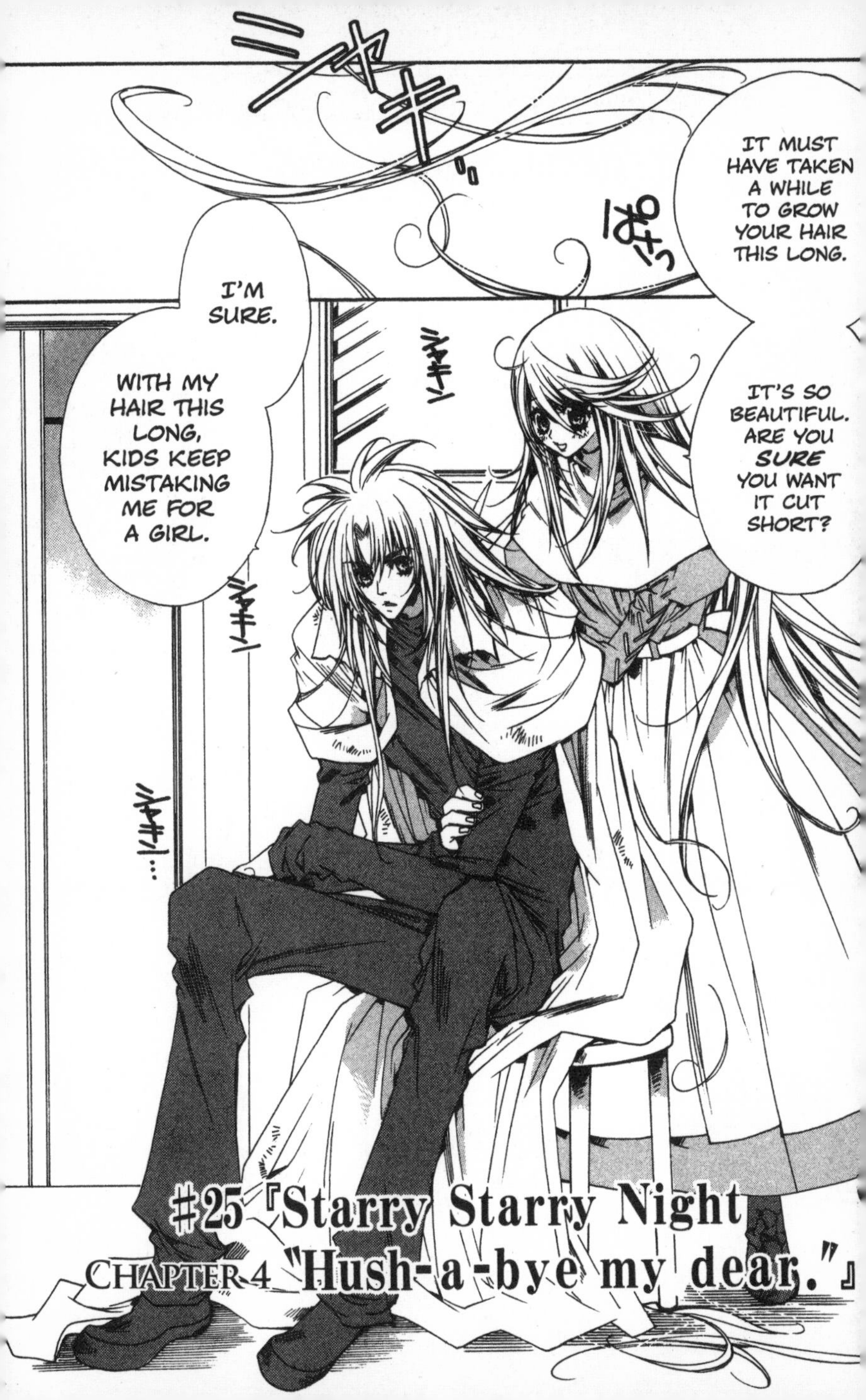
シャキ
ぱさっ
IT MUST HAVE TAKEN A WHILE TO GROW YOUR HAIR THIS LONG.
IT'S SO BEAUTIFUL. ARE YOU *SURE* YOU WANT IT CUT SHORT?
I'M SURE.
WITH MY HAIR THIS LONG, KIDS KEEP MISTAKING ME FOR A GIRL.
シャキン
シャキン
シャキン…

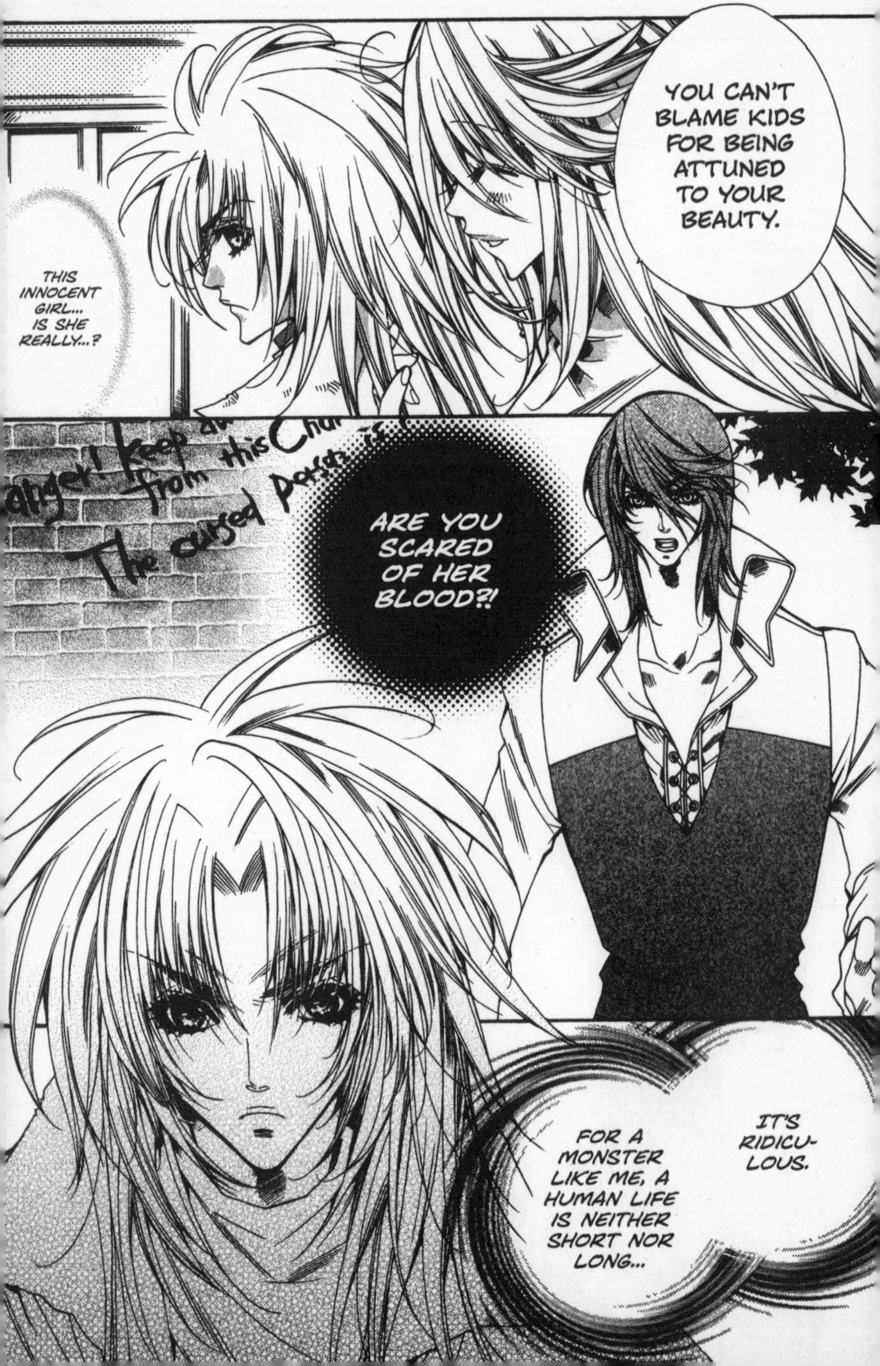
YOU CAN'T BLAME KIDS FOR BEING ATTUNED TO YOUR BEAUTY.
THIS INNOCENT GIRL... IS SHE REALLY...?
ARE YOU SCARED OF HER BLOOD?!
IT'S RIDICU-LOUS.
FOR A MONSTER LIKE ME, A HUMAN LIFE IS NEITHER SHORT NOR LONG...

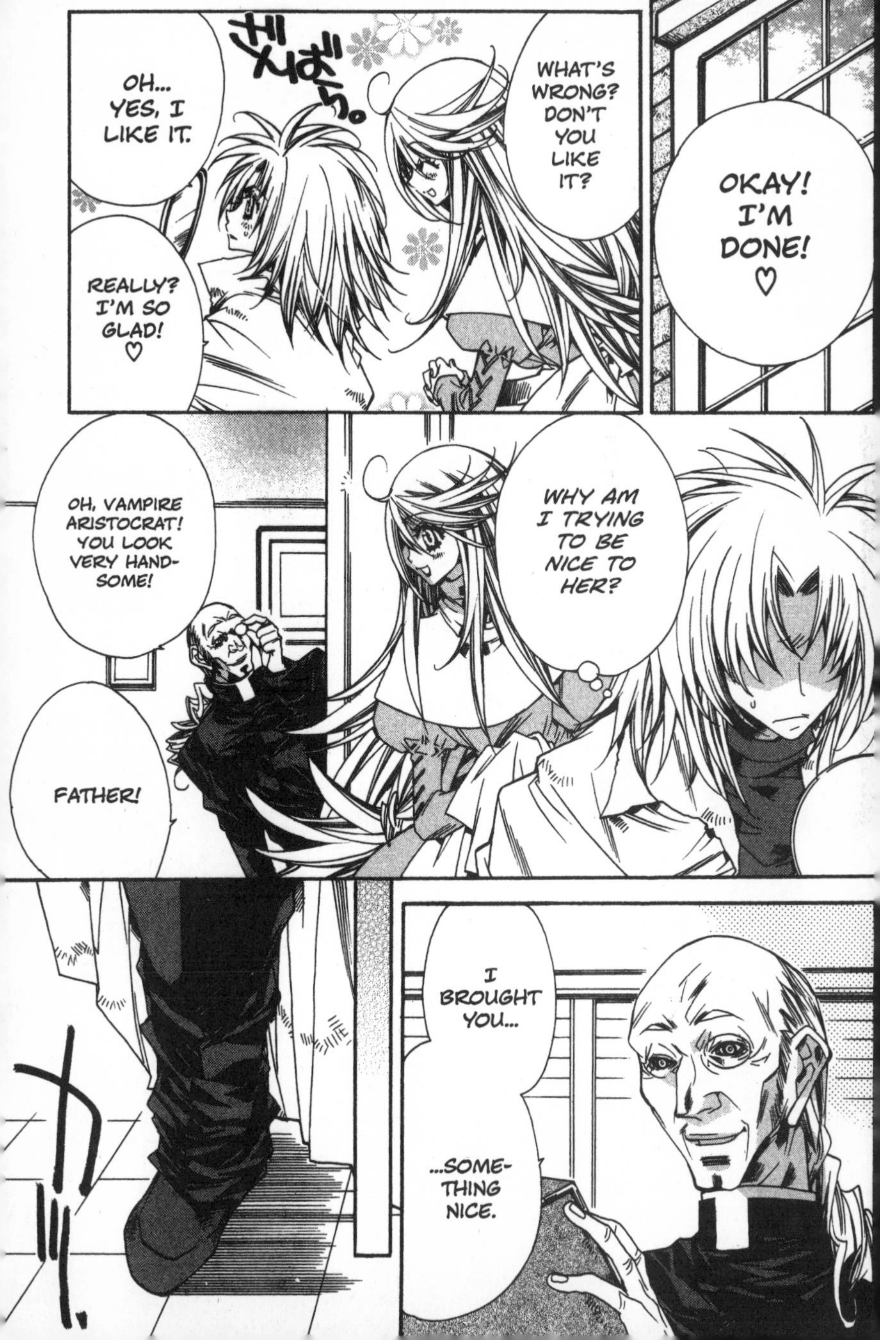
OKAY! I'M DONE! ♡
WHAT'S WRONG? DON'T YOU LIKE IT?
OH... YES, I LIKE IT.
REALLY? I'M SO GLAD! ♡
WHY AM I TRYING TO BE NICE TO HER?
OH, VAMPIRE ARISTOCRAT! YOU LOOK VERY HAND-SOME!
FATHER!
I BROUGHT YOU...
...SOME-THING NICE.

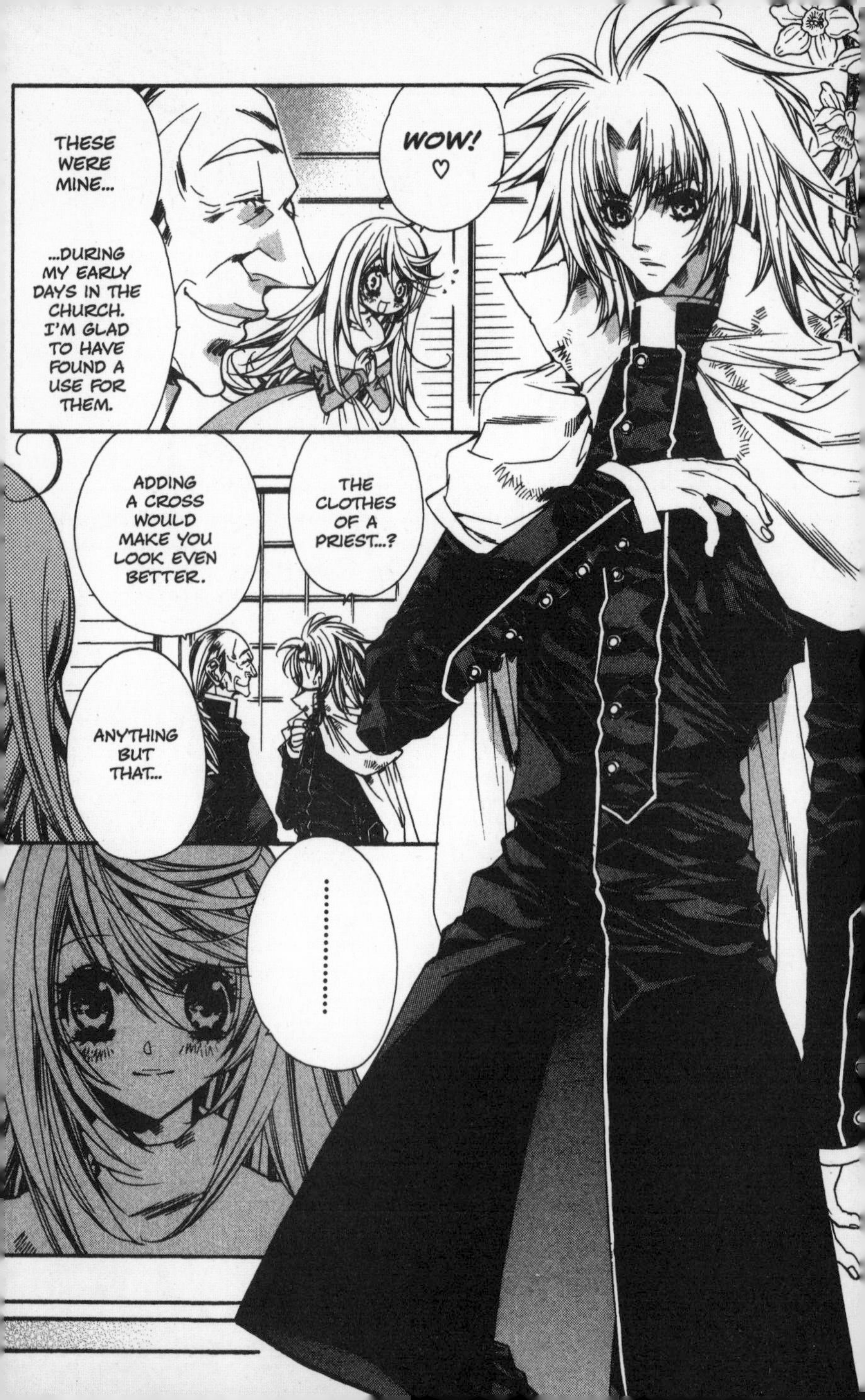
WOW! ♡
THESE WERE MINE...
...DURING MY EARLY DAYS IN THE CHURCH. I'M GLAD TO HAVE FOUND A USE FOR THEM.
THE CLOTHES OF A PRIEST...?
ADDING A CROSS WOULD MAKE YOU LOOK EVEN BETTER.
ANYTHING BUT THAT...
....

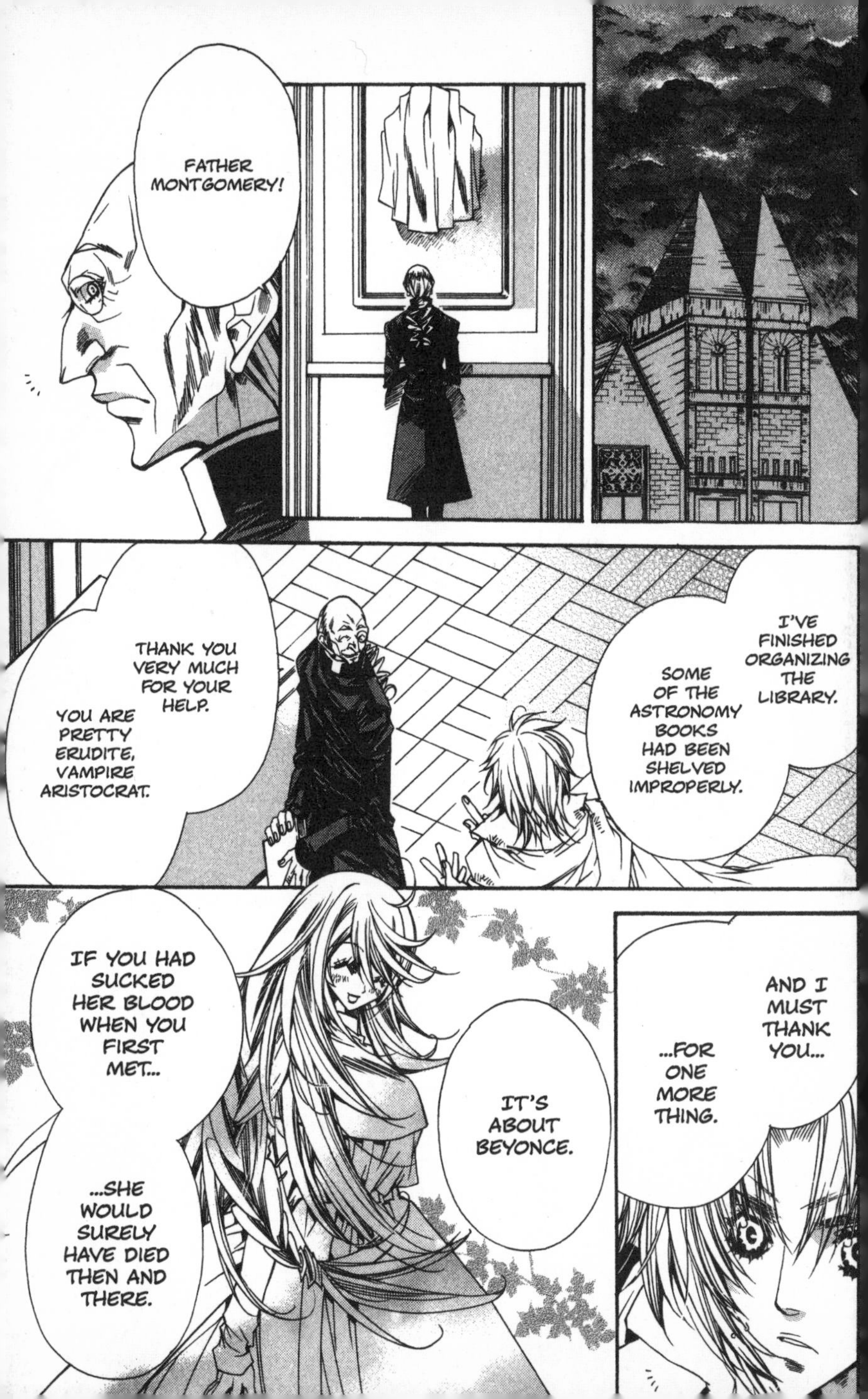
FATHER MONTGOMERY!
I'VE FINISHED ORGANIZING THE LIBRARY.
SOME OF THE ASTRONOMY BOOKS HAD BEEN SHELVED IMPROPERLY.
THANK YOU VERY MUCH FOR YOUR HELP.
YOU ARE PRETTY ERUDITE, VAMPIRE ARISTOCRAT.
AND I MUST THANK YOU...
...FOR ONE MORE THING.
IT'S ABOUT BEYONCE.
IF YOU HAD SUCKED HER BLOOD WHEN YOU FIRST MET...
...SHE WOULD SURELY HAVE DIED THEN AND THERE.

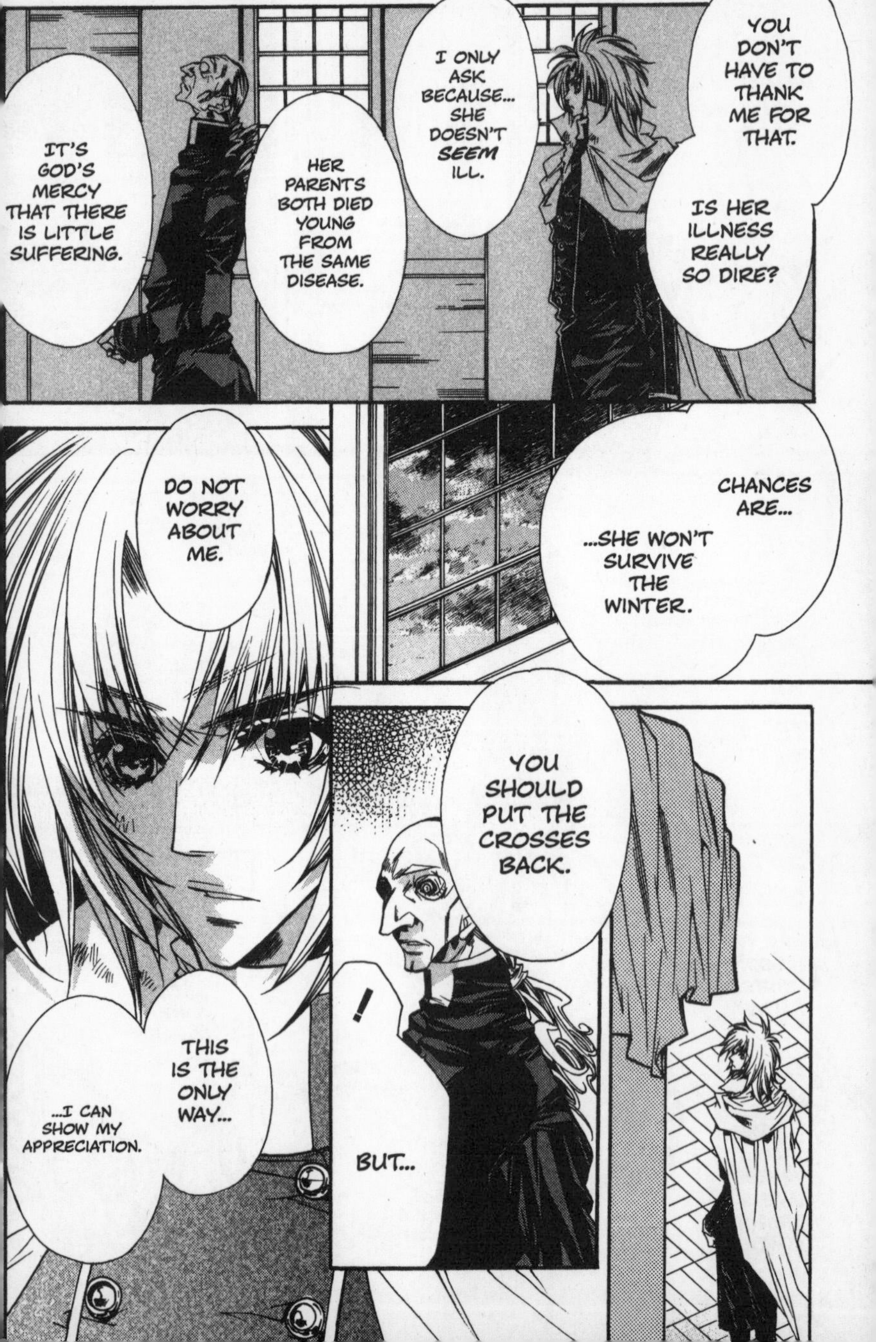

YOU DON'T HAVE TO THANK ME FOR THAT.
IS HER ILLNESS REALLY SO DIRE?
I ONLY ASK BECAUSE... SHE DOESN'T *SEEM* ILL.
HER PARENTS BOTH DIED YOUNG FROM THE SAME DISEASE.
IT'S GOD'S MERCY THAT THERE IS LITTLE SUFFERING.
CHANCES ARE...
...SHE WON'T SURVIVE THE WINTER.
YOU SHOULD PUT THE CROSSES BACK.
!
BUT...
DO NOT WORRY ABOUT ME.
THIS IS THE ONLY WAY...
...I CAN SHOW MY APPRECIATION.

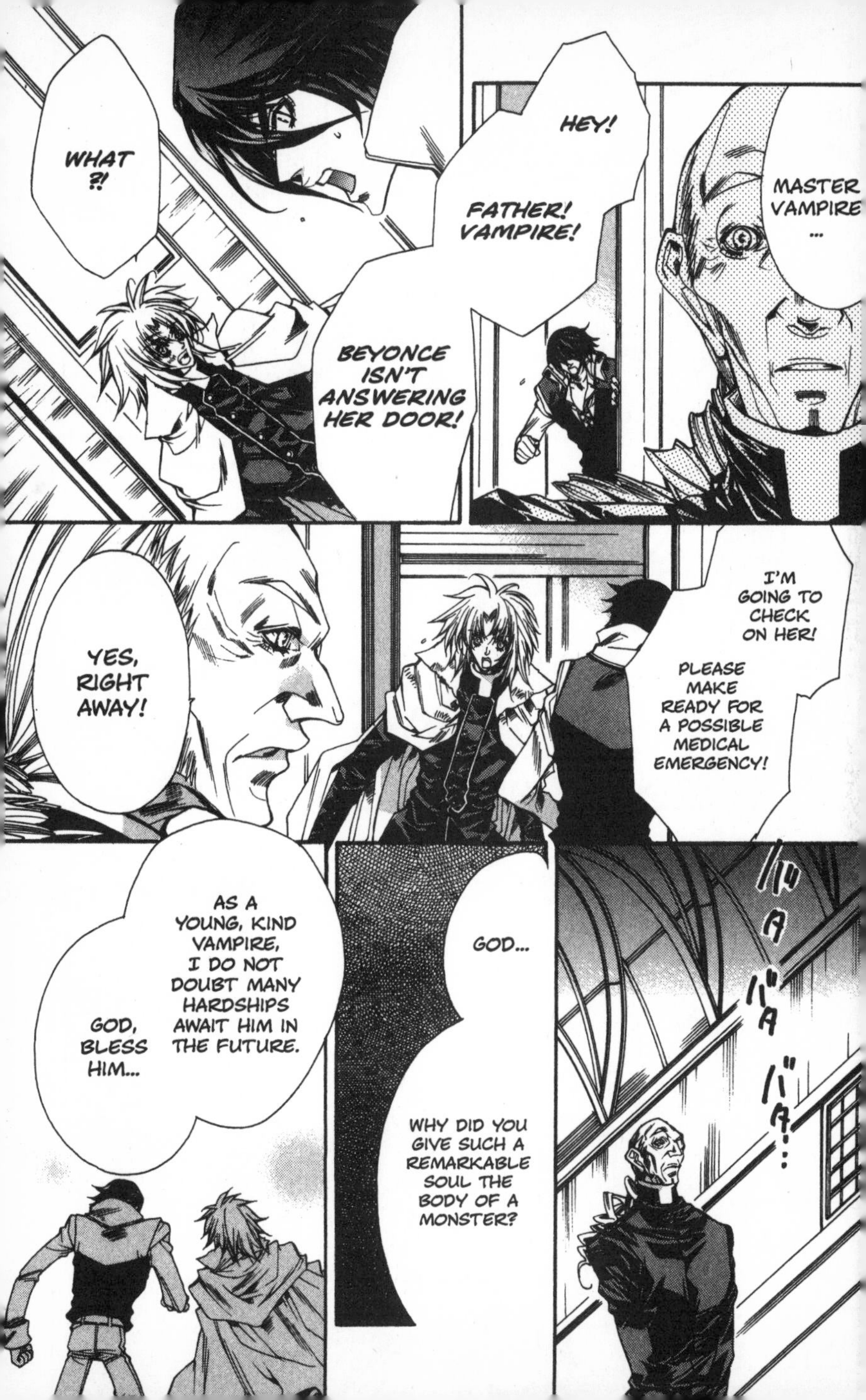
MASTER VAMPIRE ...
HEY!
FATHER! VAMPIRE!
BEYONCE ISN'T ANSWERING HER DOOR!
WHAT ?!
I'M GOING TO CHECK ON HER!
PLEASE MAKE READY FOR A POSSIBLE MEDICAL EMERGENCY!
YES, RIGHT AWAY!
GOD...
WHY DID YOU GIVE SUCH A REMARKABLE SOUL THE BODY OF A MONSTER?
AS A YOUNG, KIND VAMPIRE, I DO NOT DOUBT MANY HARDSHIPS AWAIT HIM IN THE FUTURE.
GOD, BLESS HIM...

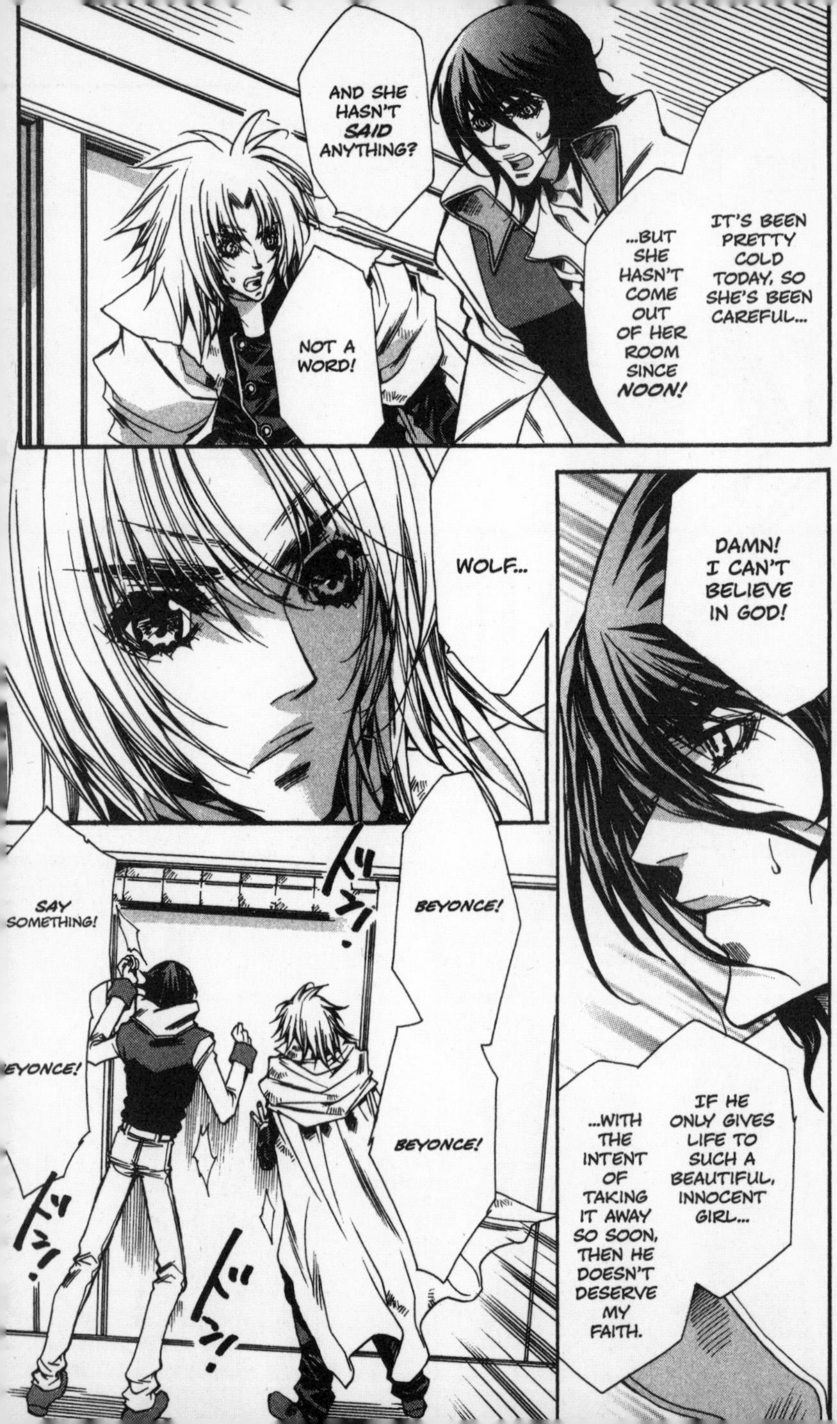

IT'S BEEN PRETTY COLD TODAY, SO SHE'S BEEN CAREFUL...
...BUT SHE HASN'T COME OUT OF HER ROOM SINCE *NOON!*
AND SHE HASN'T *SAID* ANYTHING?
NOT A WORD!
DAMN! I CAN'T BELIEVE IN GOD!
IF HE ONLY GIVES LIFE TO SUCH A BEAUTIFUL, INNOCENT GIRL...
...WITH THE INTENT OF TAKING IT AWAY SO SOON, THEN HE DOESN'T DESERVE MY FAITH.
WOLF...
BEYONCE!
BEYONCE!
SAY SOMETHING!
EYONCE!

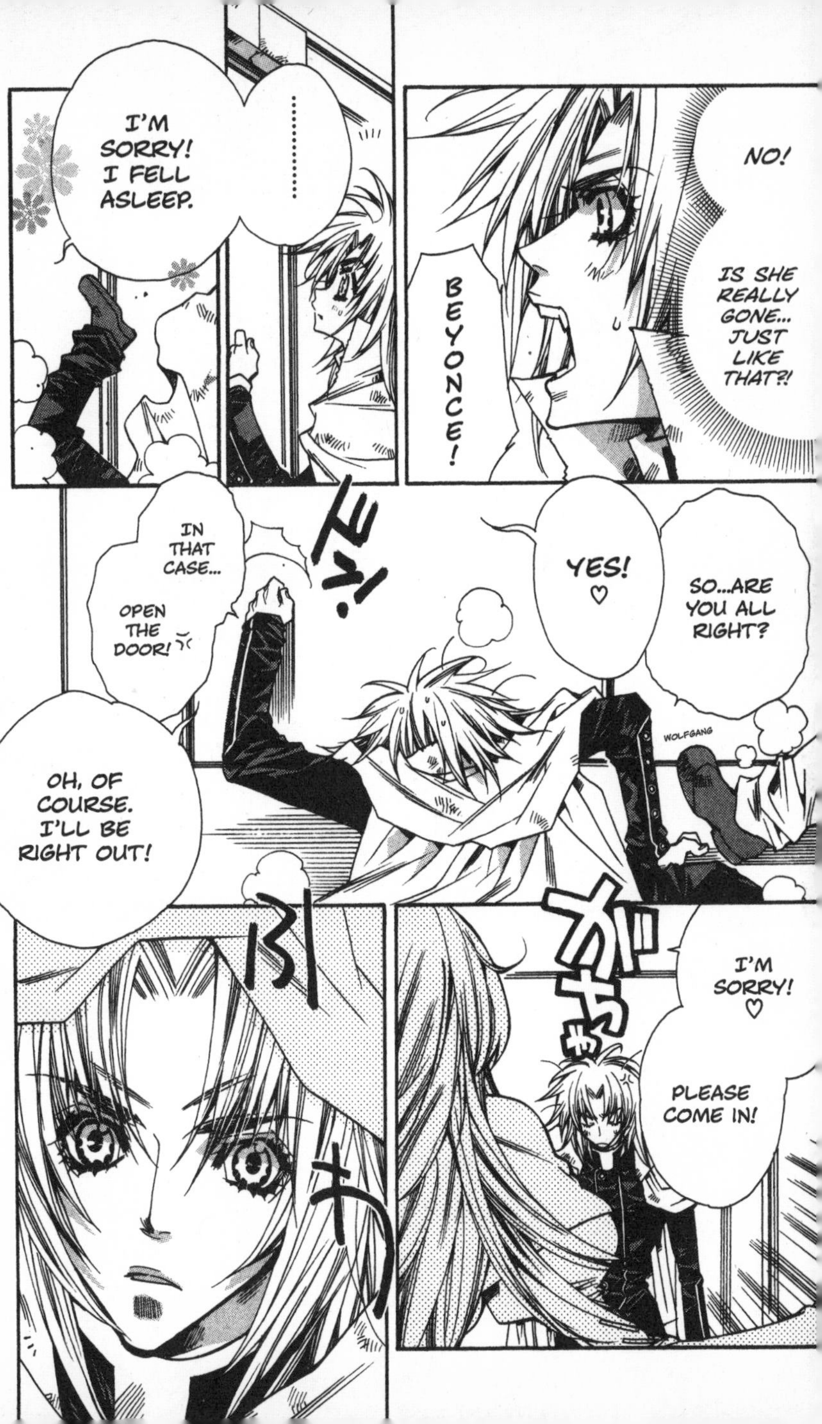
NO!
IS SHE REALLY GONE... JUST LIKE THAT?!
BEYONCE!
......
I'M SORRY! I FELL ASLEEP.
SO...ARE YOU ALL RIGHT?
YES! ♡
WOLFGANG
IN THAT CASE... OPEN THE DOOR!
OH, OF COURSE. I'LL BE RIGHT OUT!
I'M SORRY! ♡
PLEASE COME IN!
がちゃ

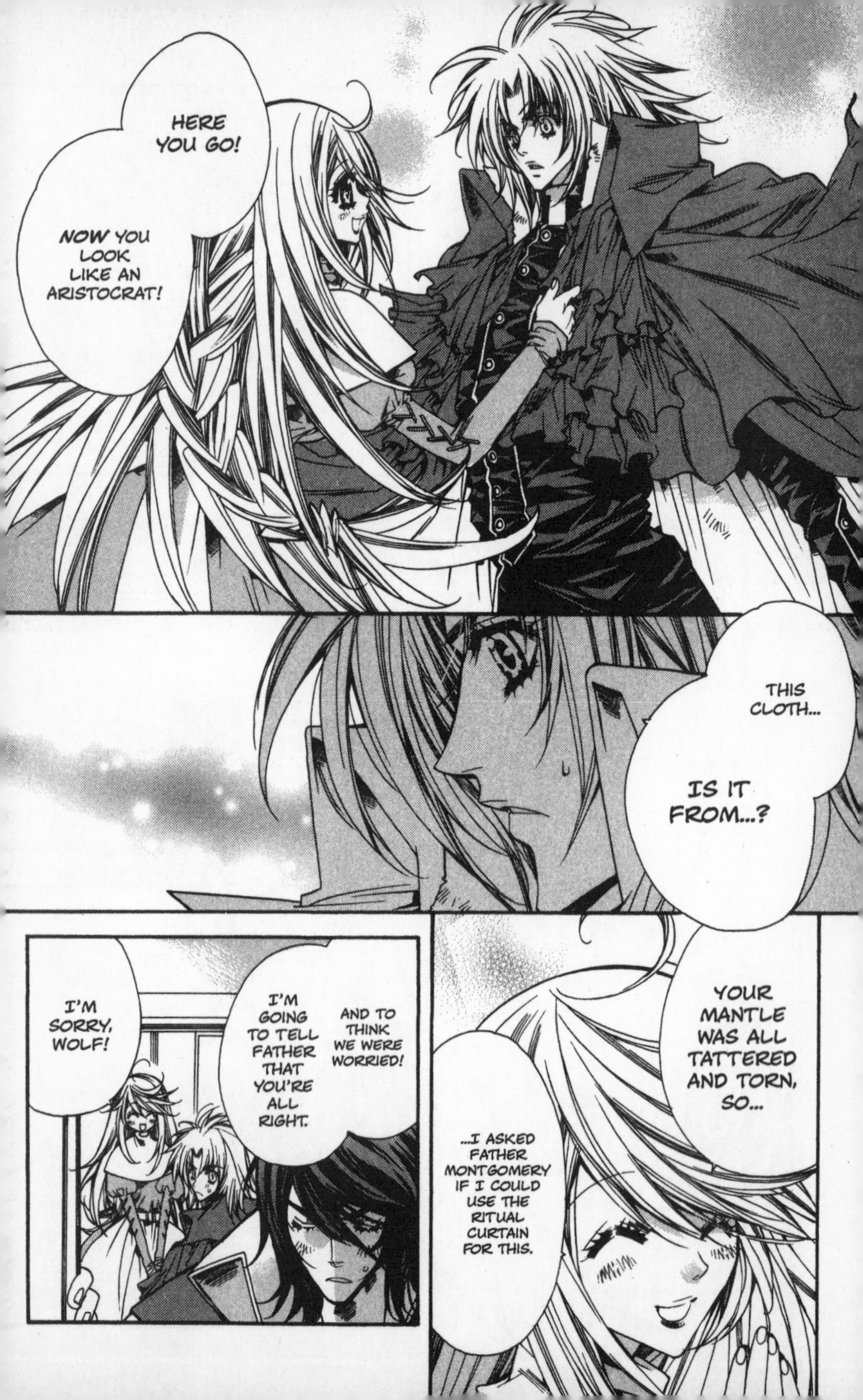
HERE YOU GO!
NOW YOU LOOK LIKE AN ARISTOCRAT!
THIS CLOTH...
IS IT FROM...?
YOUR MANTLE WAS ALL TATTERED AND TORN, SO...
...I ASKED FATHER MONTGOMERY IF I COULD USE THE RITUAL CURTAIN FOR THIS.
AND TO THINK WE WERE WORRIED!
I'M GOING TO TELL FATHER THAT YOU'RE ALL RIGHT.
I'M SORRY, WOLF!

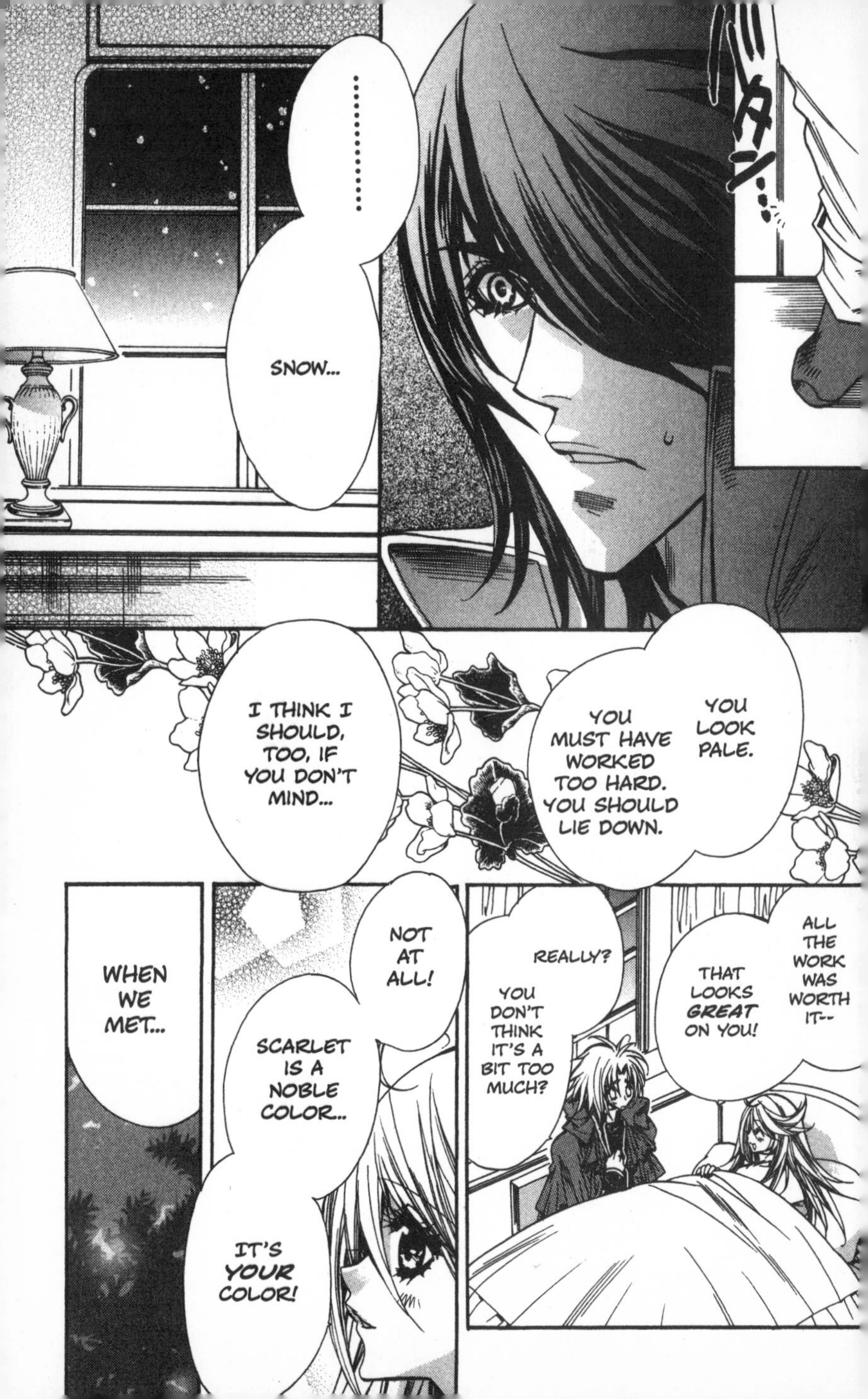

......
SNOW...
YOU LOOK PALE.
YOU MUST HAVE WORKED TOO HARD. YOU SHOULD LIE DOWN.
I THINK I SHOULD, TOO, IF YOU DON'T MIND...
ALL THE WORK WAS WORTH IT--
THAT LOOKS GREAT ON YOU!
REALLY?
YOU DON'T THINK IT'S A BIT TOO MUCH?
NOT AT ALL!
SCARLET IS A NOBLE COLOR...
IT'S YOUR COLOR!
WHEN WE MET...

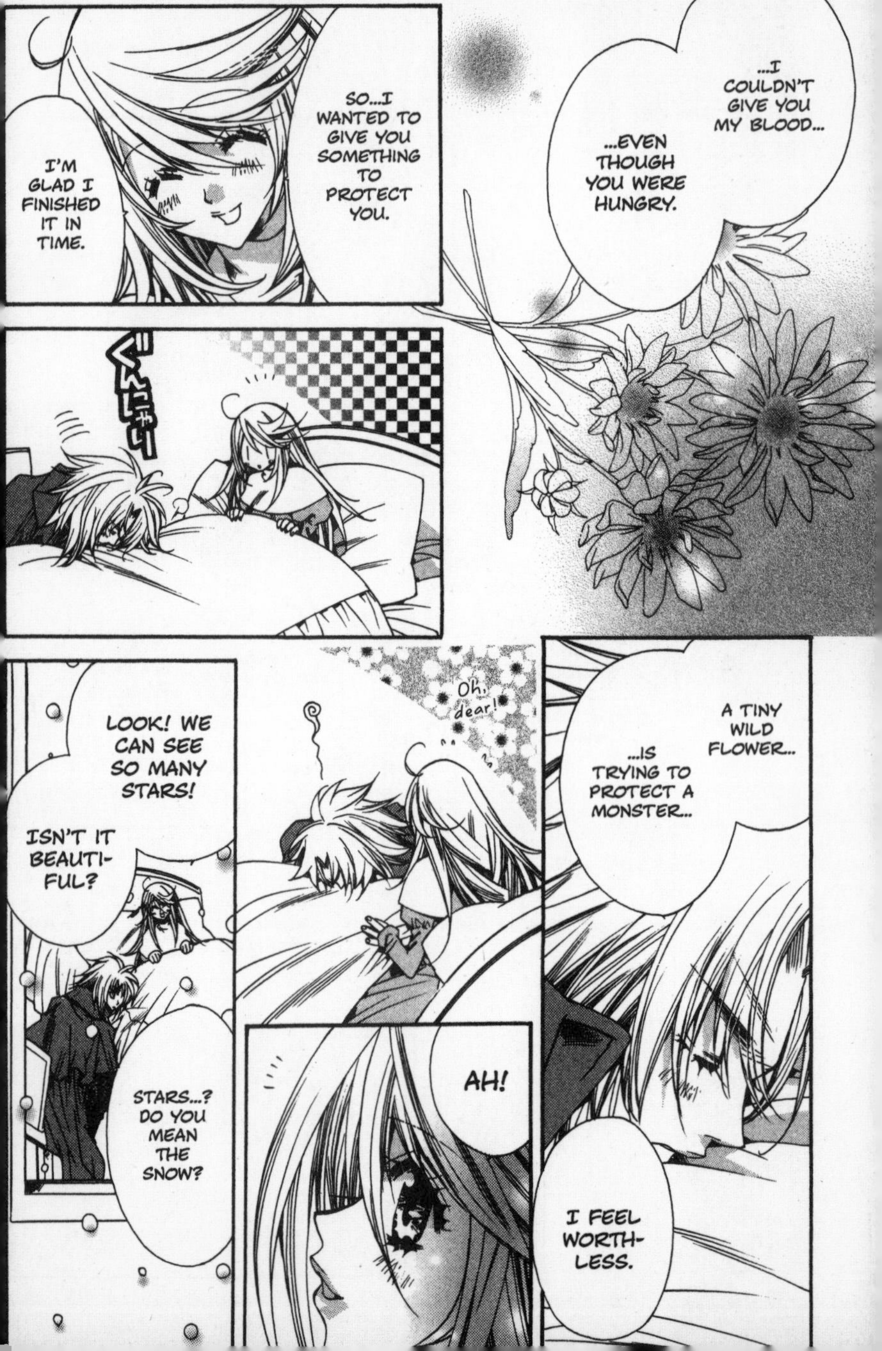
...I COULDN'T GIVE YOU MY BLOOD...
...EVEN THOUGH YOU WERE HUNGRY.
SO...I WANTED TO GIVE YOU SOMETHING TO PROTECT YOU.
I'M GLAD I FINISHED IT IN TIME.
ぐんにゃり
A TINY WILD FLOWER...
...IS TRYING TO PROTECT A MONSTER...
I FEEL WORTH-LESS.
Oh, dear!
AH!
LOOK! WE CAN SEE SO MANY STARS!
ISN'T IT BEAUTI-FUL?
STARS...? DO YOU MEAN THE SNOW?

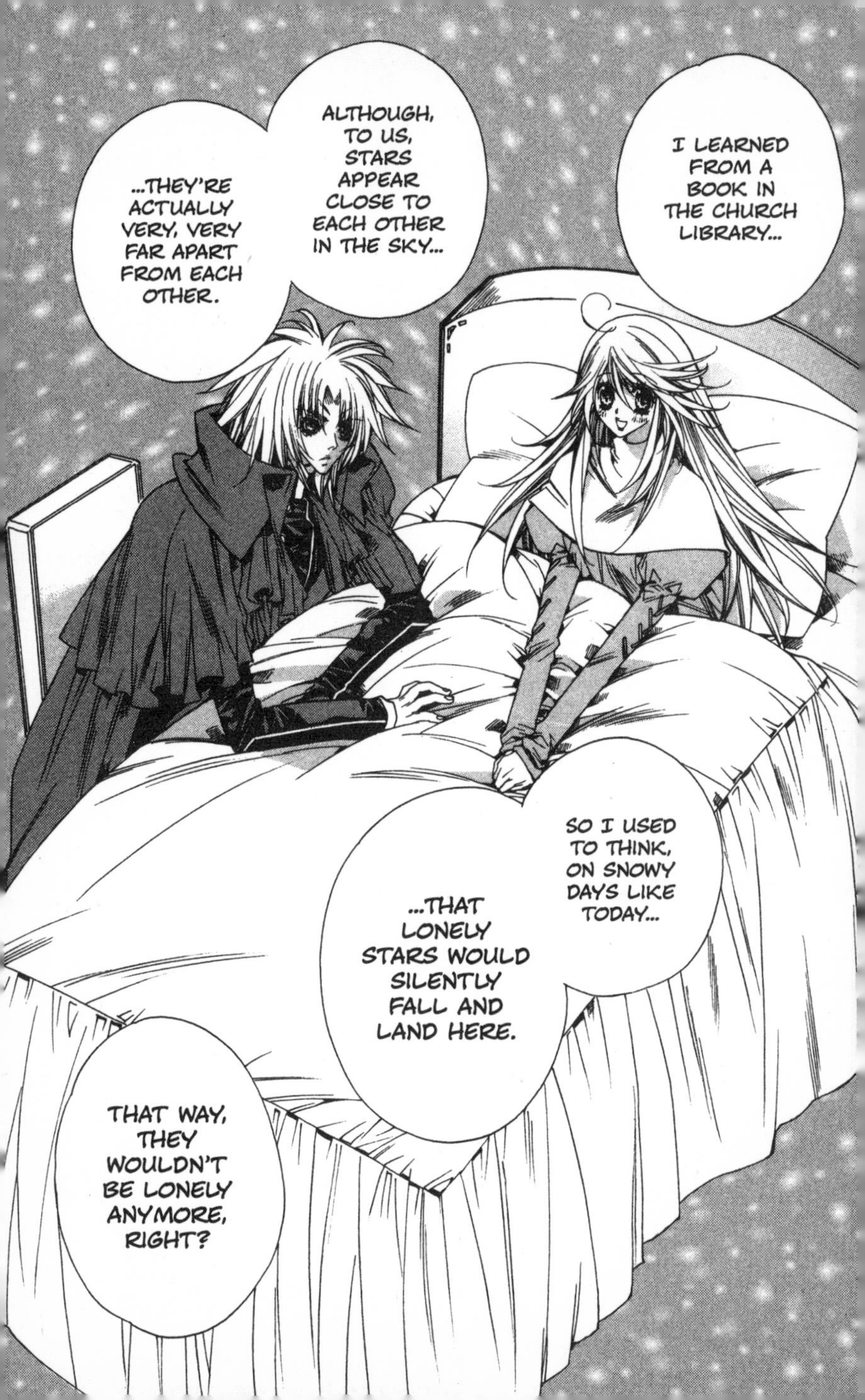
I LEARNED FROM A BOOK IN THE CHURCH LIBRARY...
ALTHOUGH, TO US, STARS APPEAR CLOSE TO EACH OTHER IN THE SKY...
...THEY'RE ACTUALLY VERY, VERY FAR APART FROM EACH OTHER.
SO I USED TO THINK, ON SNOWY DAYS LIKE TODAY...
...THAT LONELY STARS WOULD SILENTLY FALL AND LAND HERE.
THAT WAY, THEY WOULDN'T BE LONELY ANYMORE, RIGHT?

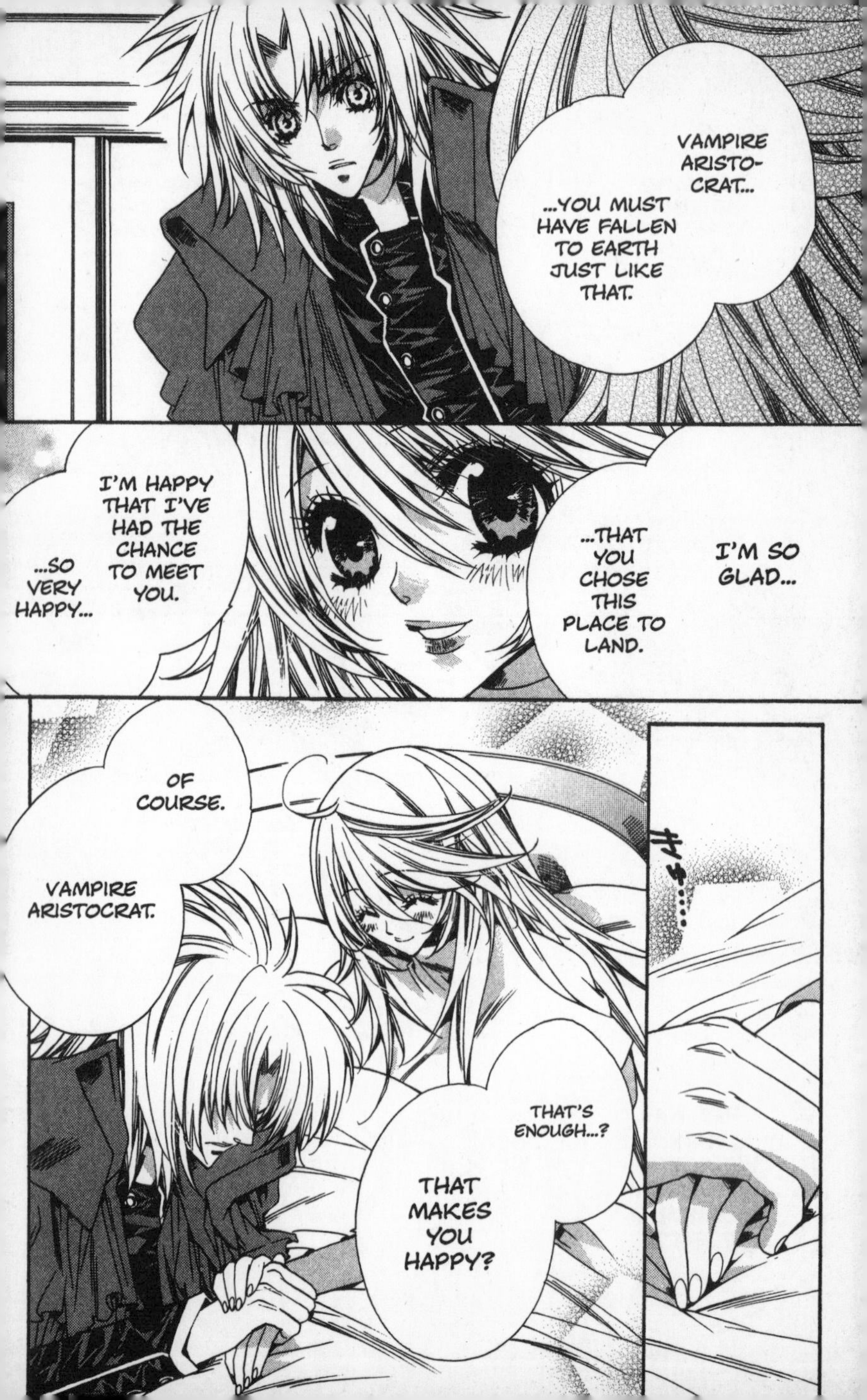
VAMPIRE ARISTO-CRAT...
...YOU MUST HAVE FALLEN TO EARTH JUST LIKE THAT.
I'M SO GLAD...
...THAT YOU CHOSE THIS PLACE TO LAND.
I'M HAPPY THAT I'VE HAD THE CHANCE TO MEET YOU.
...SO VERY HAPPY...
THAT'S ENOUGH...?
THAT MAKES YOU HAPPY?
OF COURSE.
VAMPIRE ARISTOCRAT.

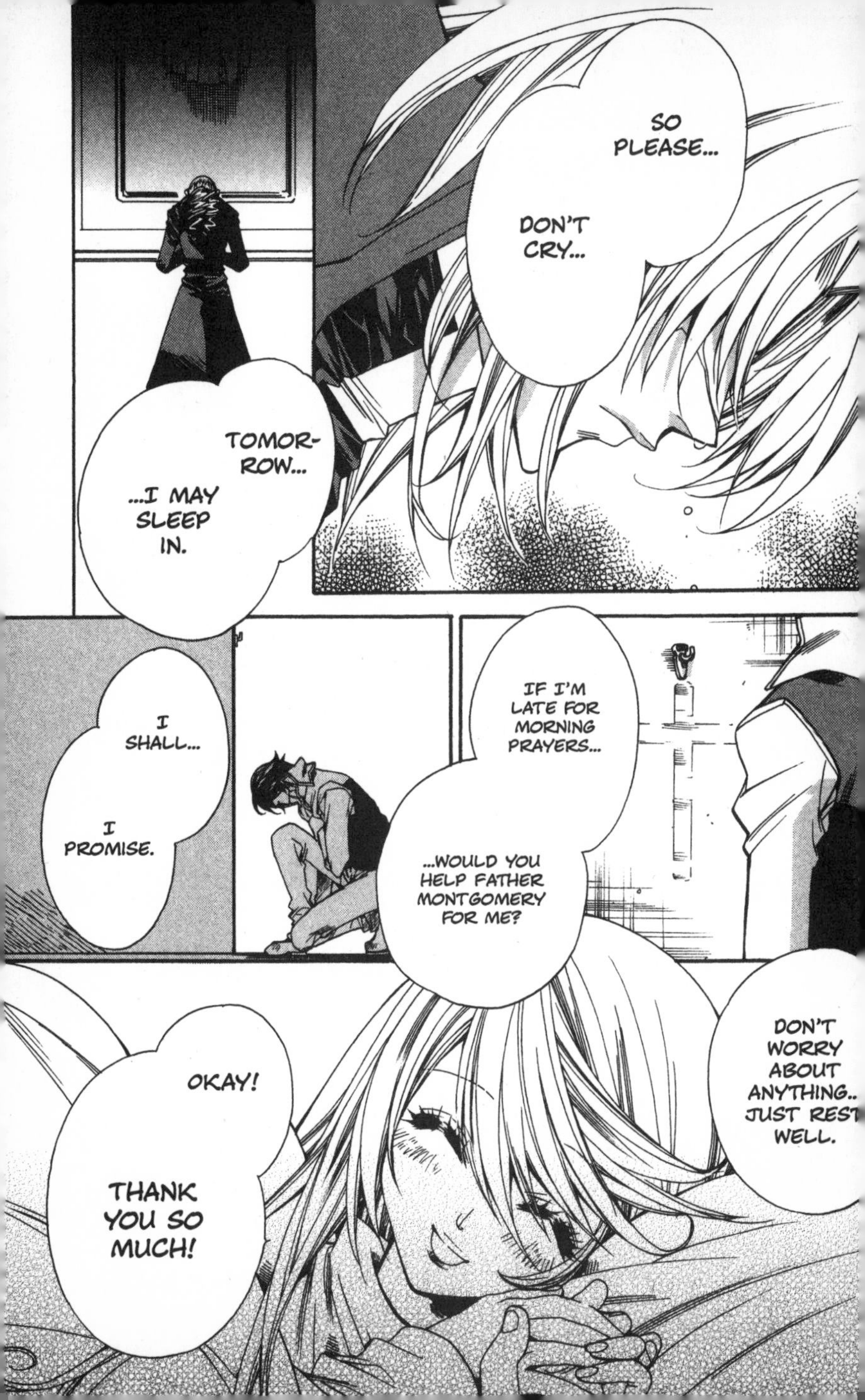
SO PLEASE...
DON'T CRY...
TOMORROW...
...I MAY SLEEP IN.
IF I'M LATE FOR MORNING PRAYERS...
...WOULD YOU HELP FATHER MONTGOMERY FOR ME?
I SHALL...
I PROMISE.
DON'T WORRY ABOUT ANYTHING.. JUST REST WELL.
OKAY!
THANK YOU SO MUCH!

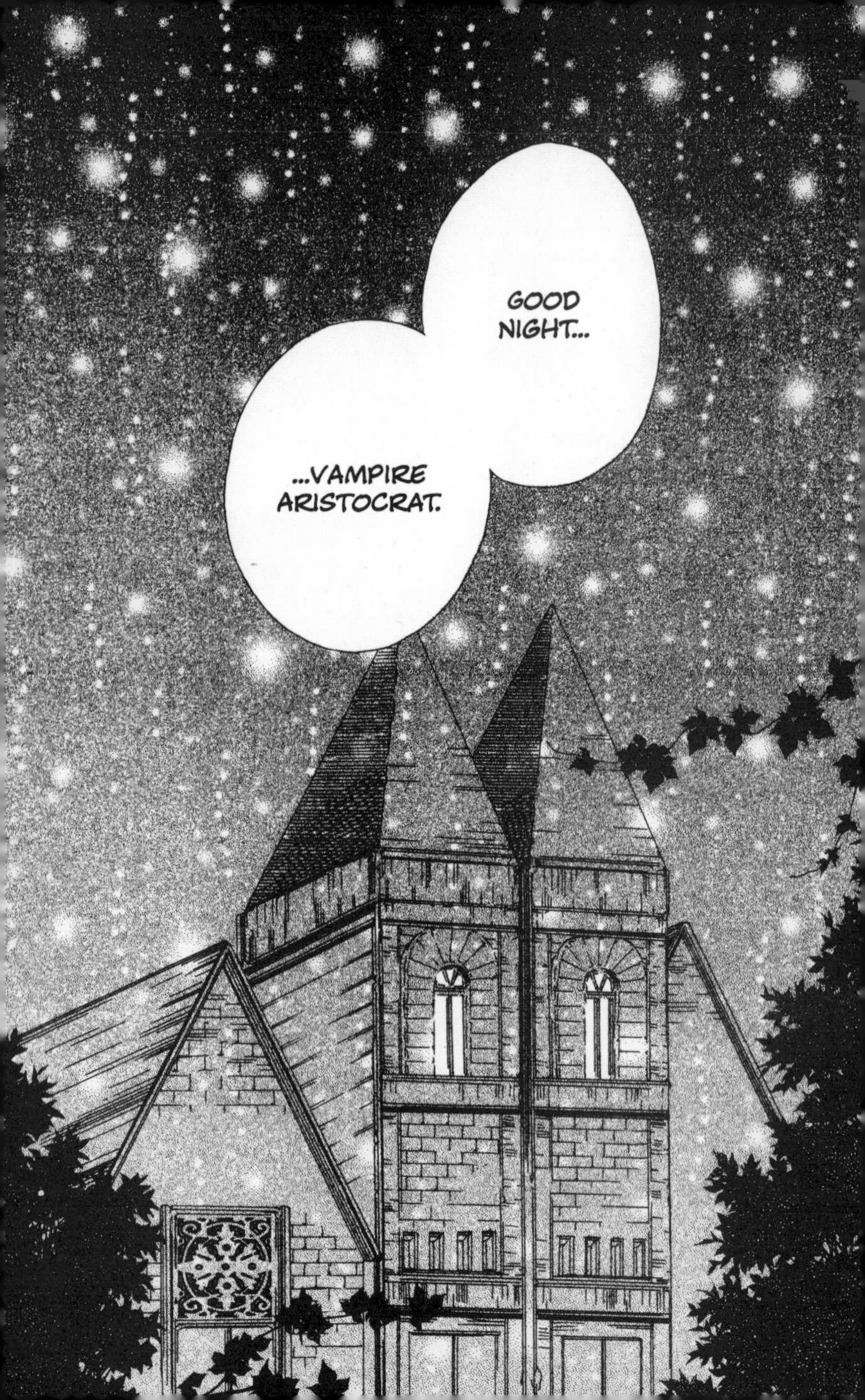
GOOD NIGHT...
...VAMPIRE ARISTOCRAT.

♯26『Starry Starry Night
Chapter 5 "I'll Remember You"』

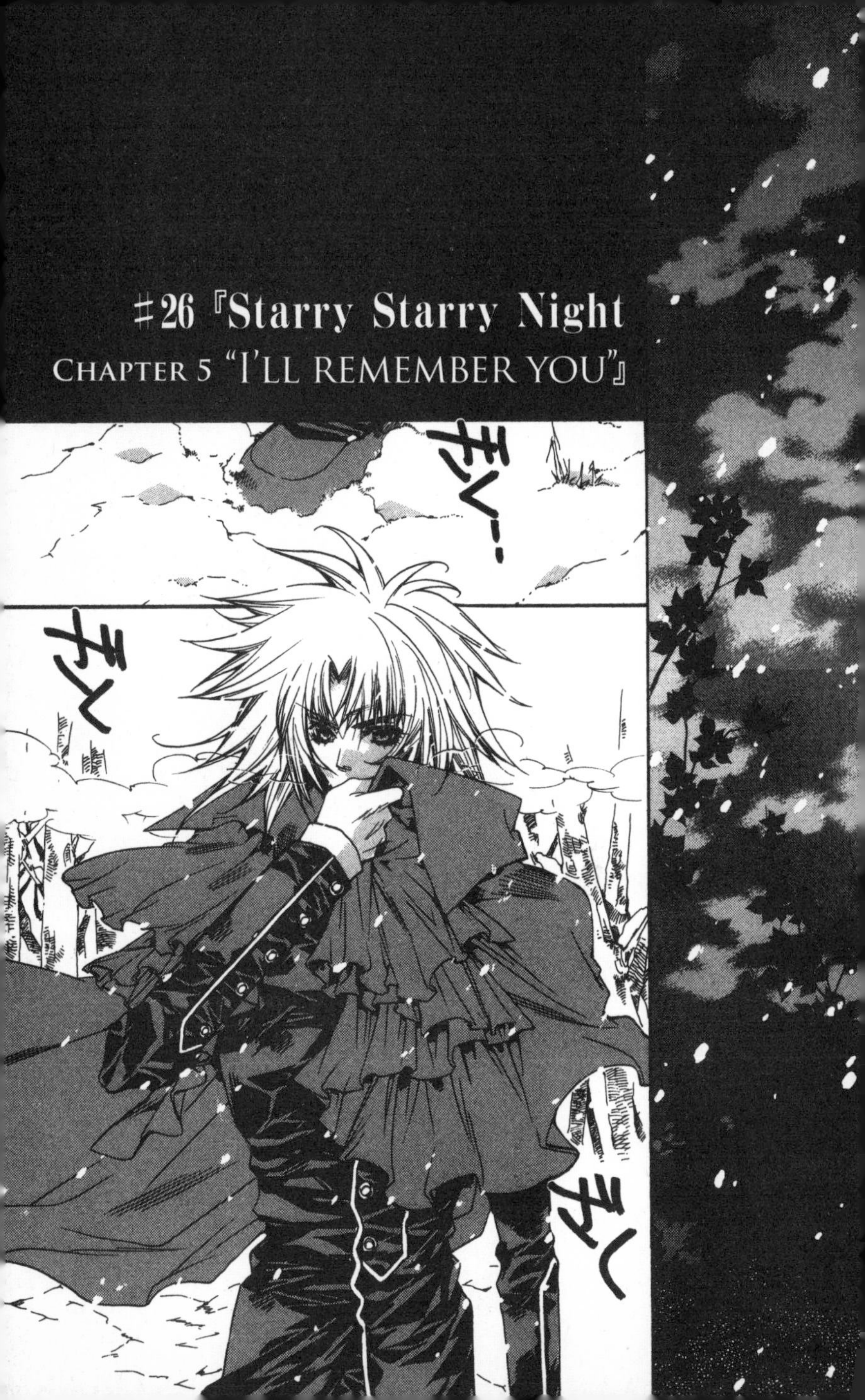

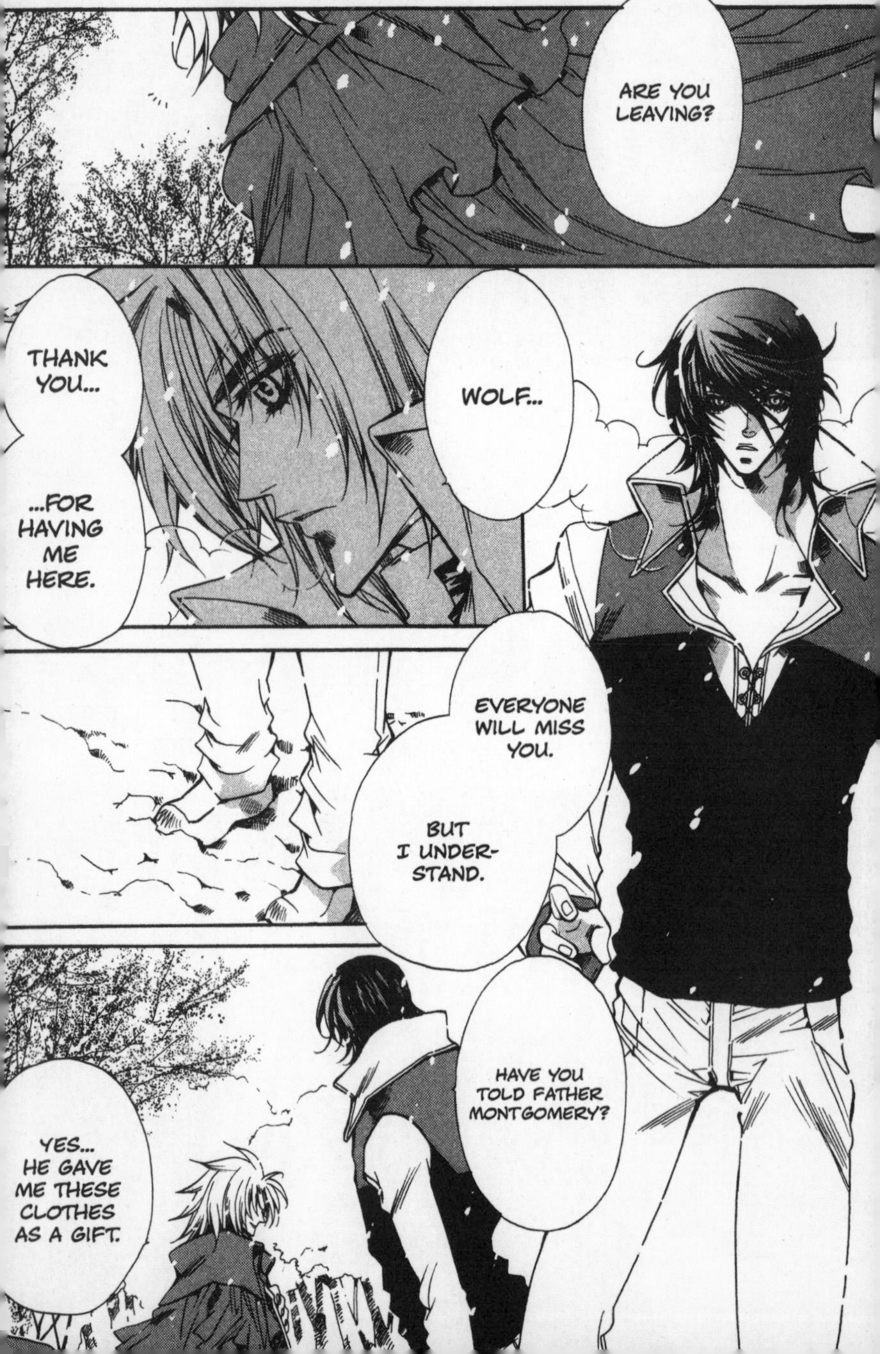
ARE YOU LEAVING?
WOLF...
THANK YOU...
...FOR HAVING ME HERE.
EVERYONE WILL MISS YOU.
BUT I UNDER-STAND.
HAVE YOU TOLD FATHER MONTGOMERY?
YES... HE GAVE ME THESE CLOTHES AS A GIFT.

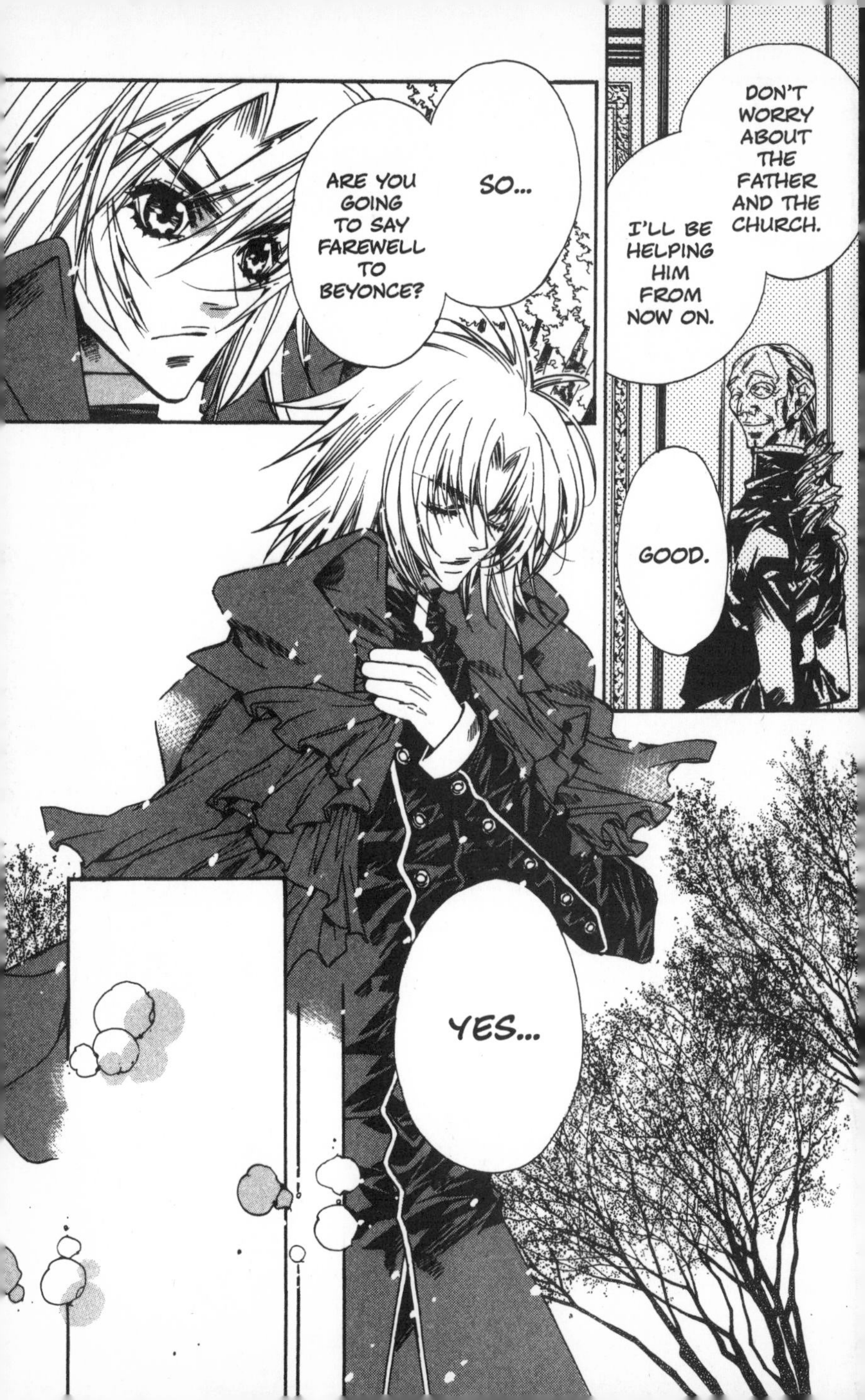
DON'T WORRY ABOUT THE FATHER AND THE CHURCH.
I'LL BE HELPING HIM FROM NOW ON.
GOOD.
SO...
ARE YOU GOING TO SAY FAREWELL TO BEYONCE?
YES...

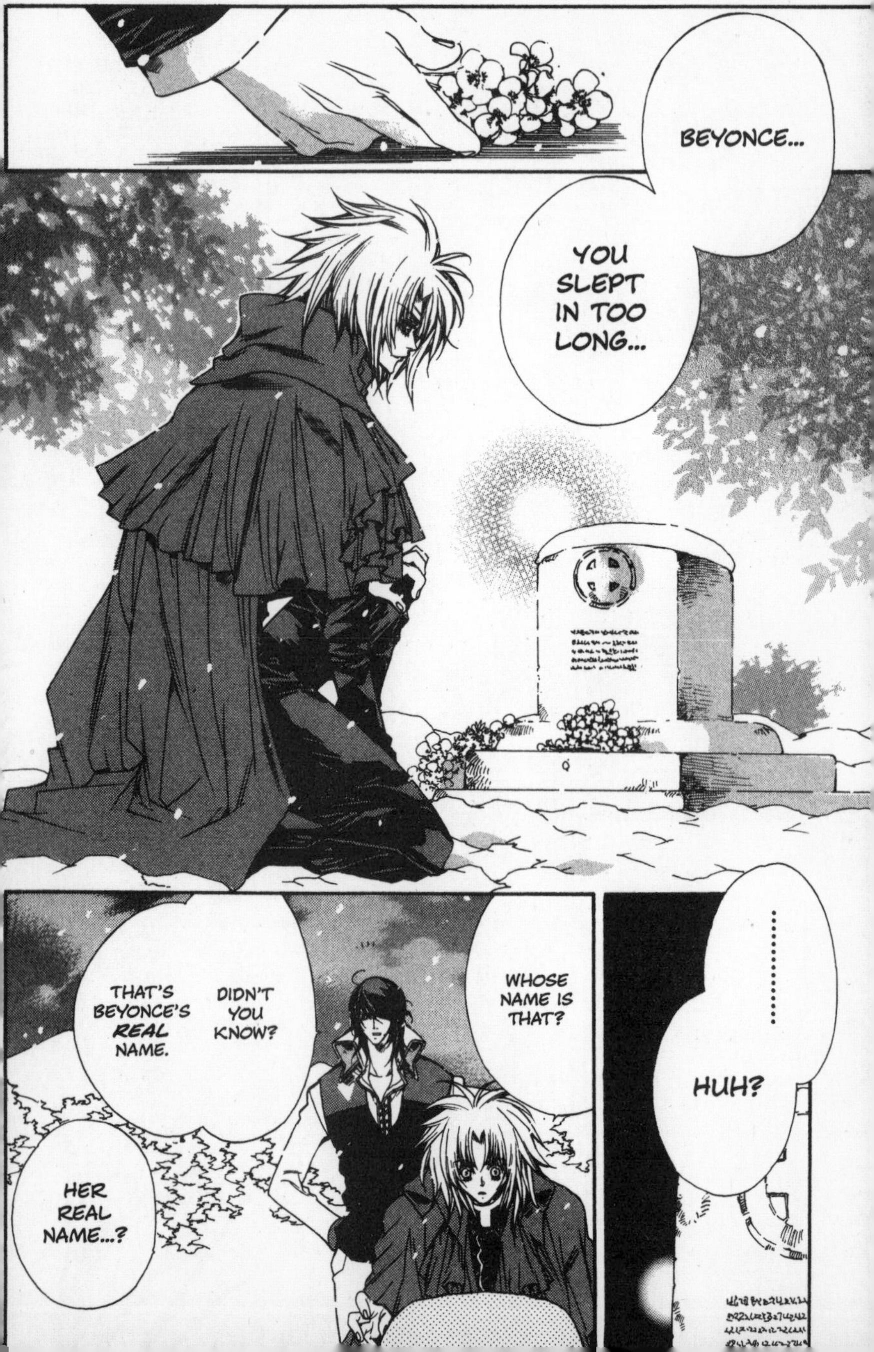
BEYONCE...
YOU SLEPT IN TOO LONG...
......
HUH?
WHOSE NAME IS THAT?
DIDN'T YOU KNOW?
THAT'S BEYONCE'S *REAL* NAME.
HER REAL NAME...?

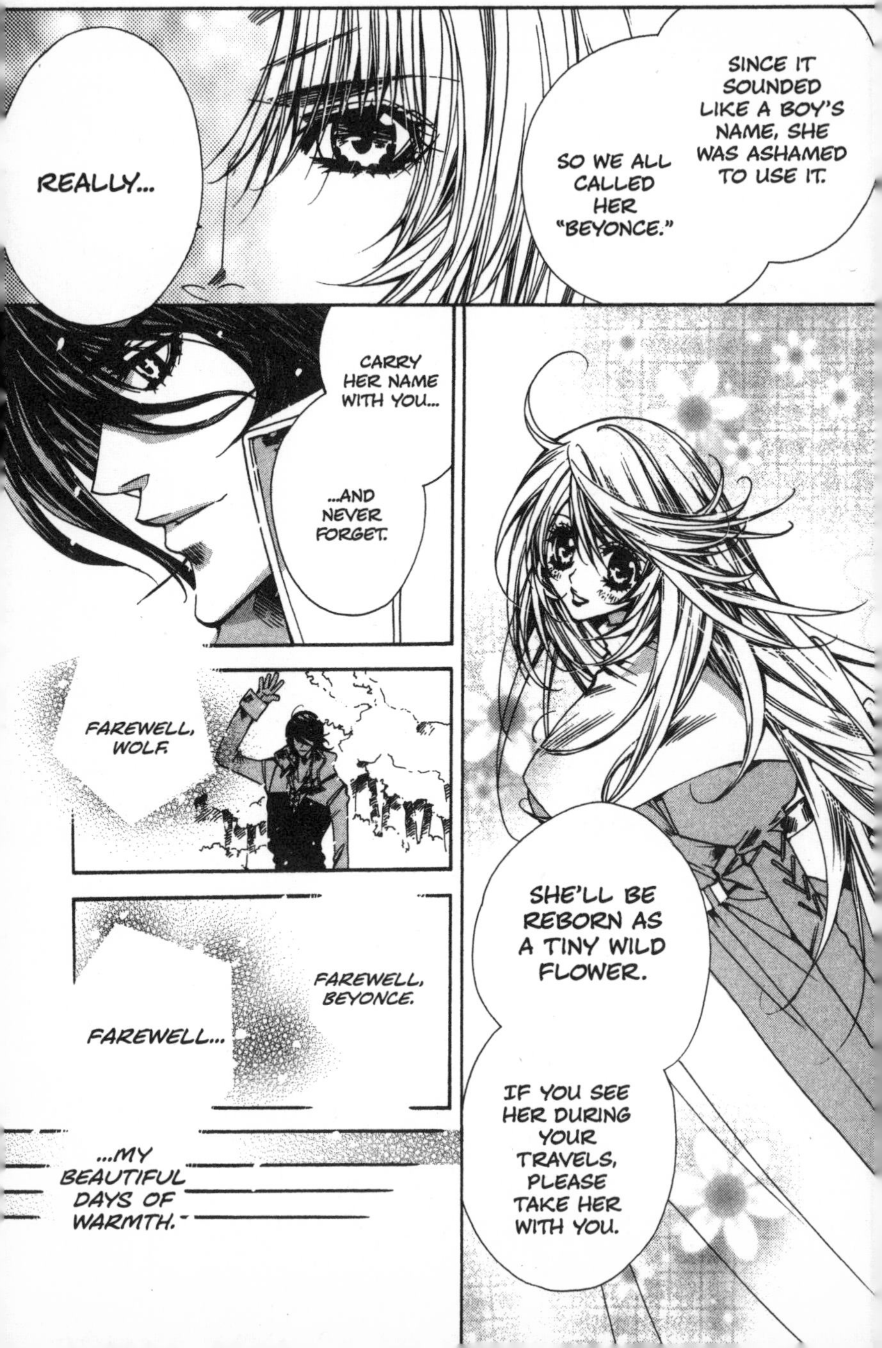
SINCE IT SOUNDED LIKE A BOY'S NAME, SHE WAS ASHAMED TO USE IT.
SO WE ALL CALLED HER "BEYONCE."
REALLY...
SHE'LL BE REBORN AS A TINY WILD FLOWER.
IF YOU SEE HER DURING YOUR TRAVELS, PLEASE TAKE HER WITH YOU.
CARRY HER NAME WITH YOU...
...AND NEVER FORGET.
FAREWELL, WOLF.
FAREWELL, BEYONCE.
FAREWELL...
...MY BEAUTIFUL DAYS OF WARMTH.

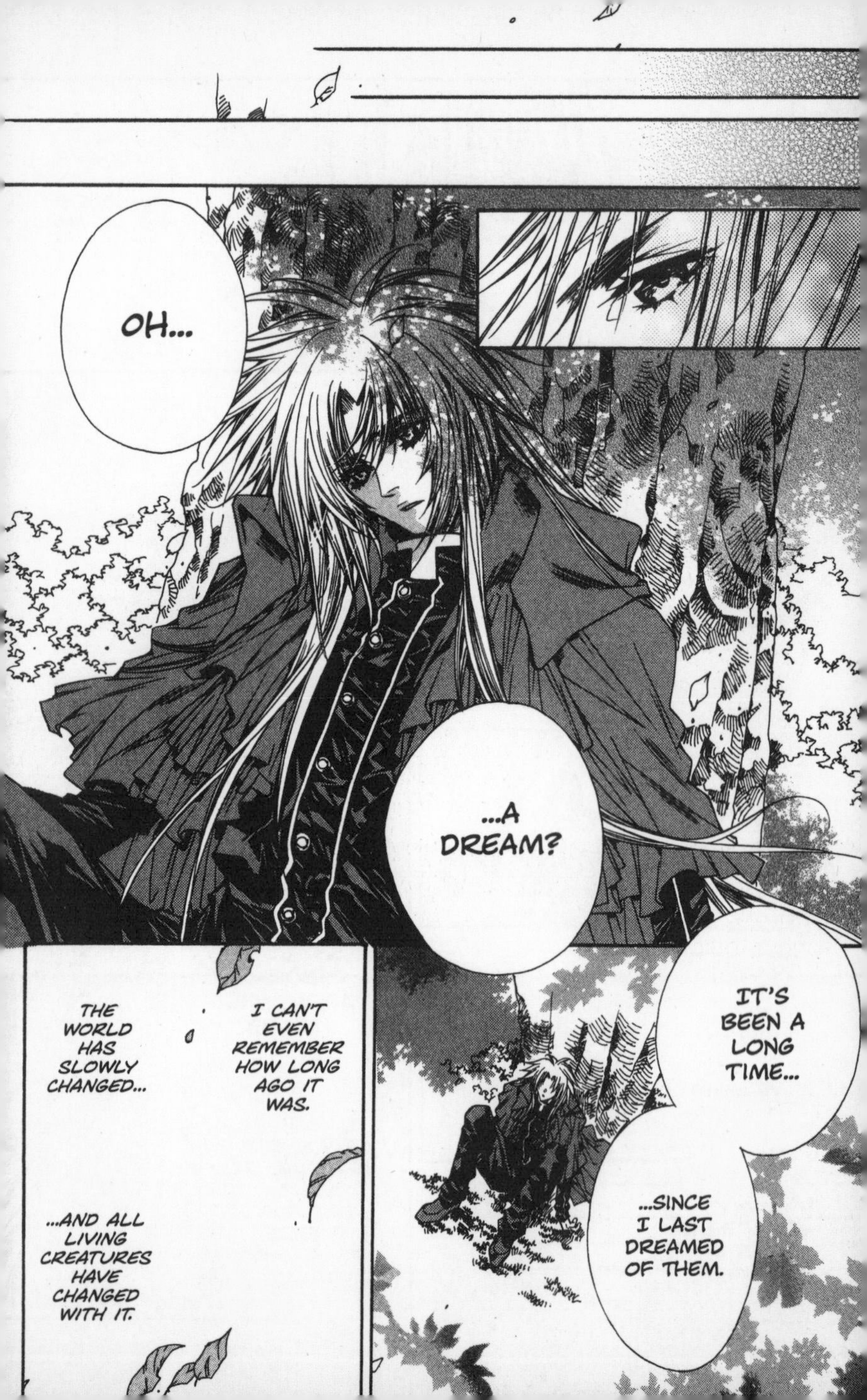
OH...
...A DREAM?
IT'S BEEN A LONG TIME...
...SINCE I LAST DREAMED OF THEM.
I CAN'T EVEN REMEMBER HOW LONG AGO IT WAS.
THE WORLD HAS SLOWLY CHANGED...
...AND ALL LIVING CREATURES HAVE CHANGED WITH IT.

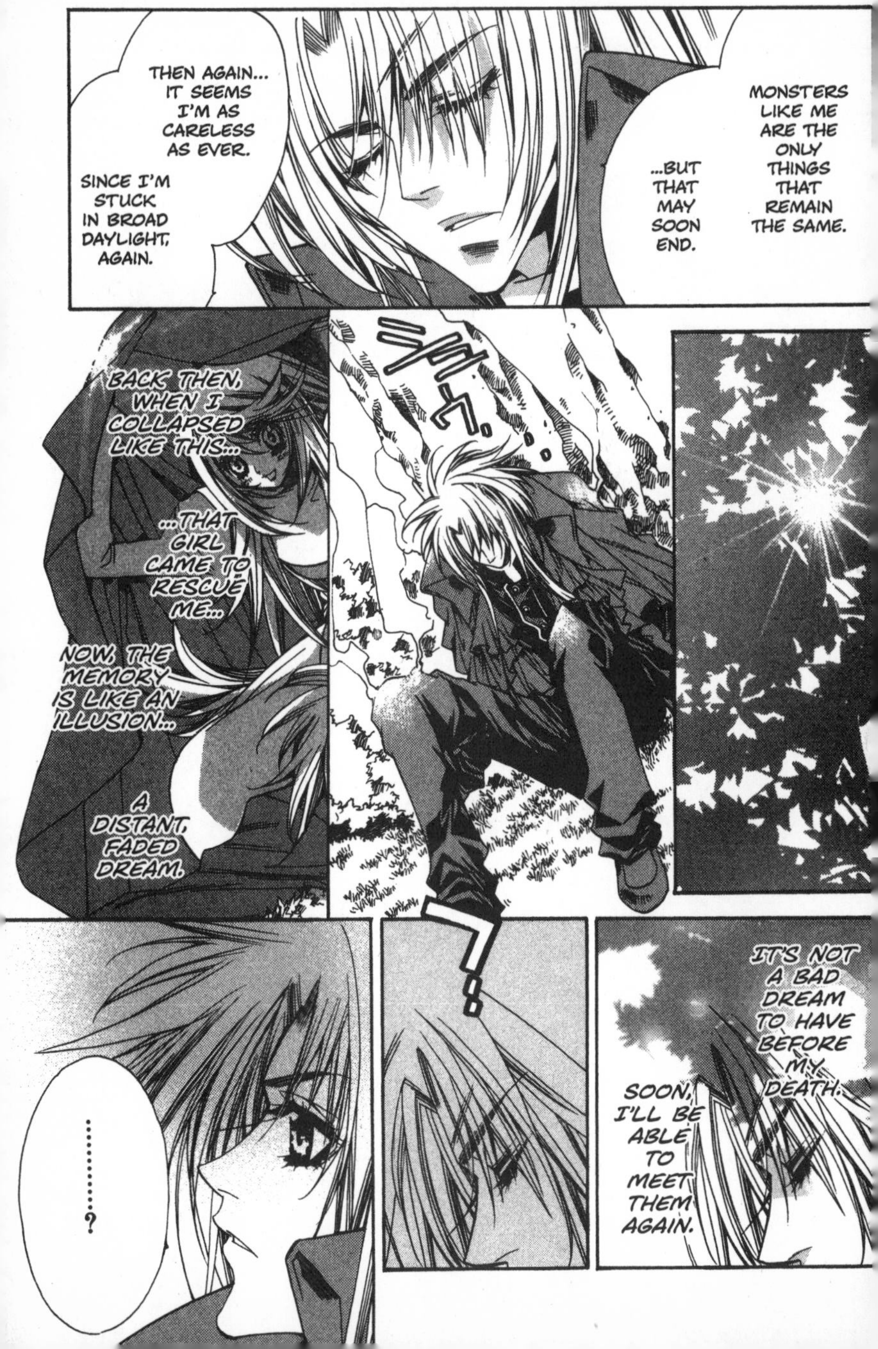
MONSTERS LIKE ME ARE THE ONLY THINGS THAT REMAIN THE SAME.
...BUT THAT MAY SOON END.
THEN AGAIN... IT SEEMS I'M AS CARELESS AS EVER.
SINCE I'M STUCK IN BROAD DAYLIGHT, AGAIN.
BACK THEN, WHEN I COLLAPSED LIKE THIS...
...THAT GIRL CAME TO RESCUE ME...
NOW, THE MEMORY IS LIKE AN ILLUSION...
A DISTANT, FADED DREAM.
IT'S NOT A BAD DREAM TO HAVE BEFORE MY DEATH.
SOON, I'LL BE ABLE TO MEET THEM AGAIN.
......?

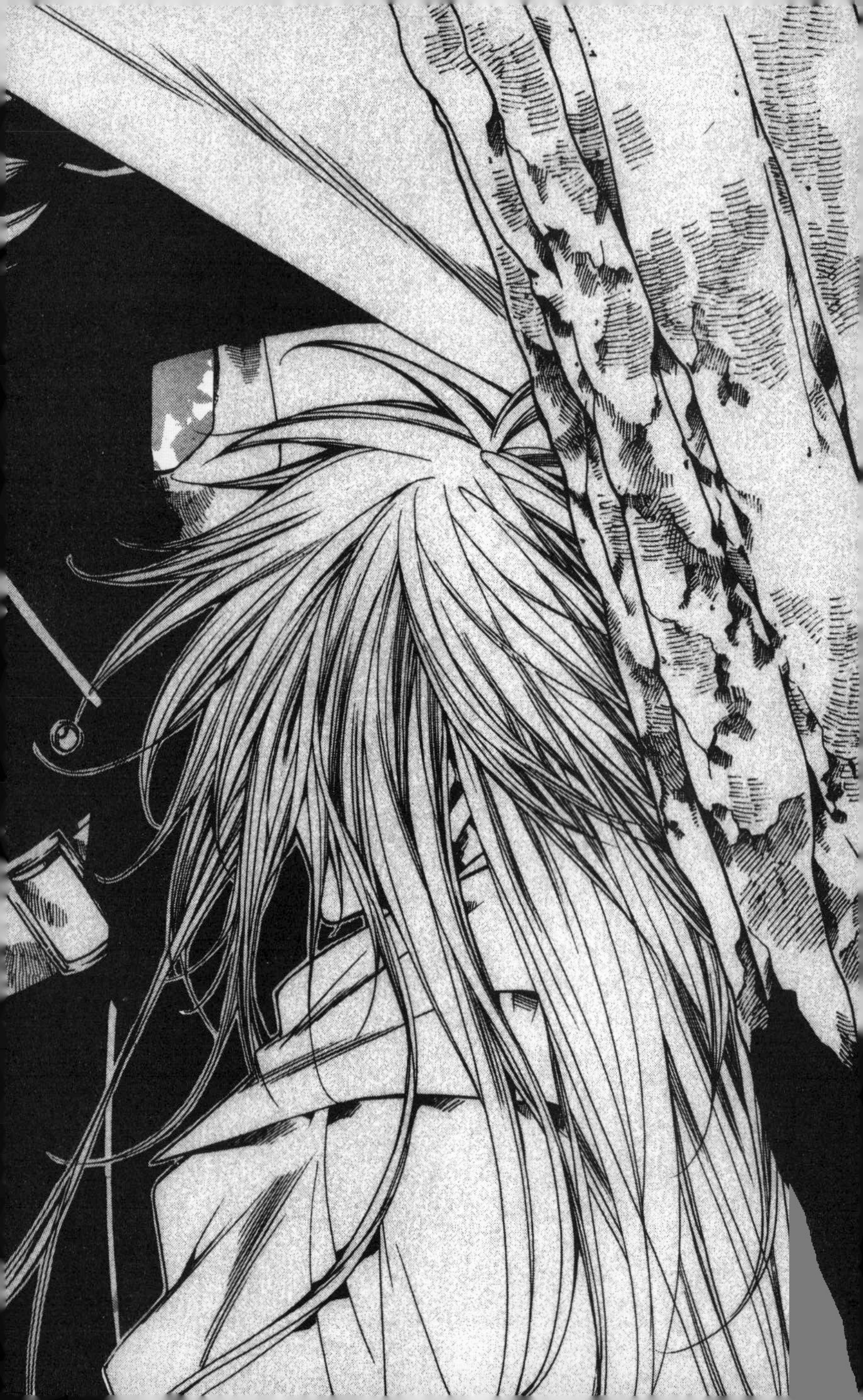

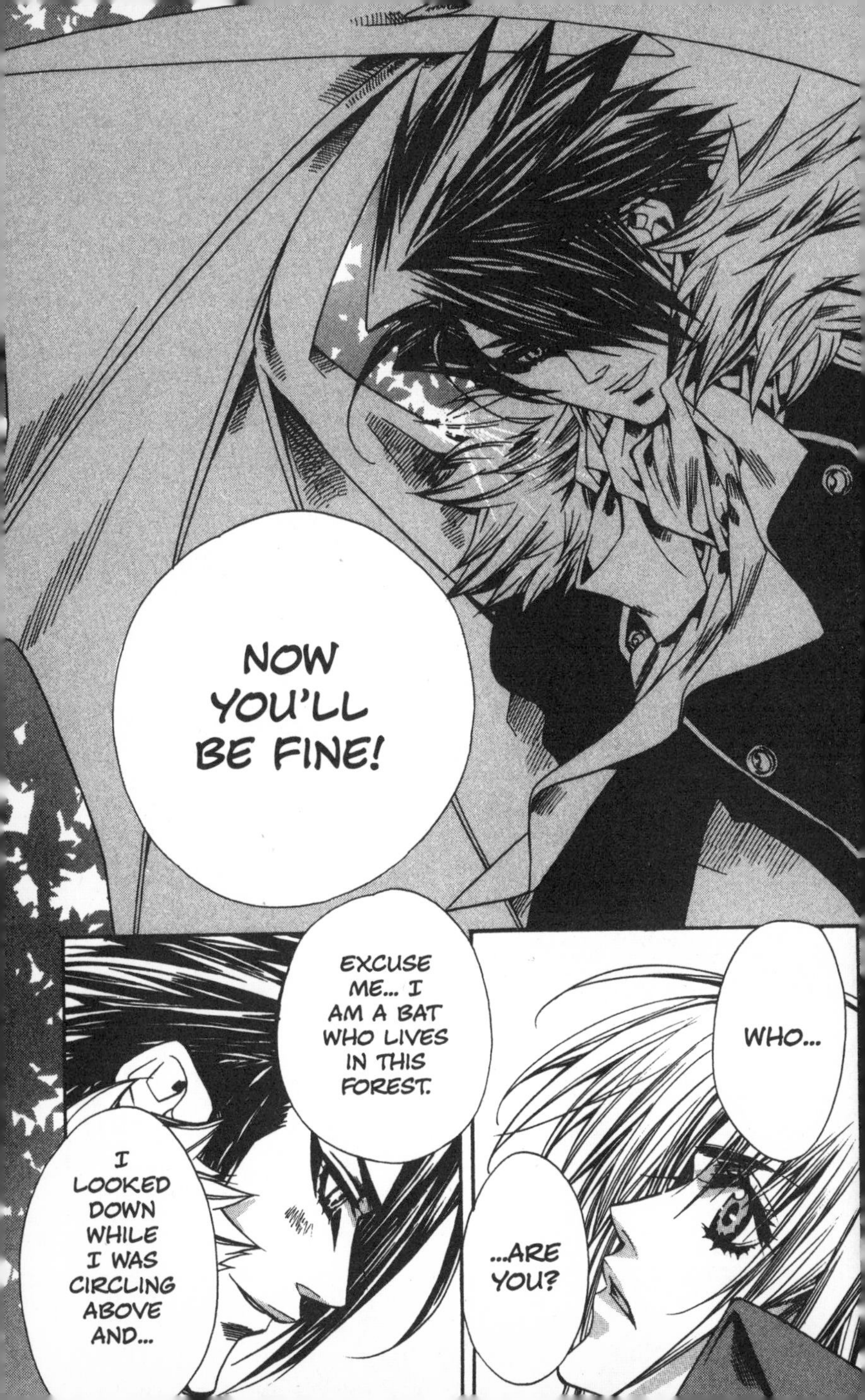
NOW YOU'LL BE FINE!
WHO...
...ARE YOU?
EXCUSE ME... I AM A BAT WHO LIVES IN THIS FOREST.
I LOOKED DOWN WHILE I WAS CIRCLING ABOVE AND...

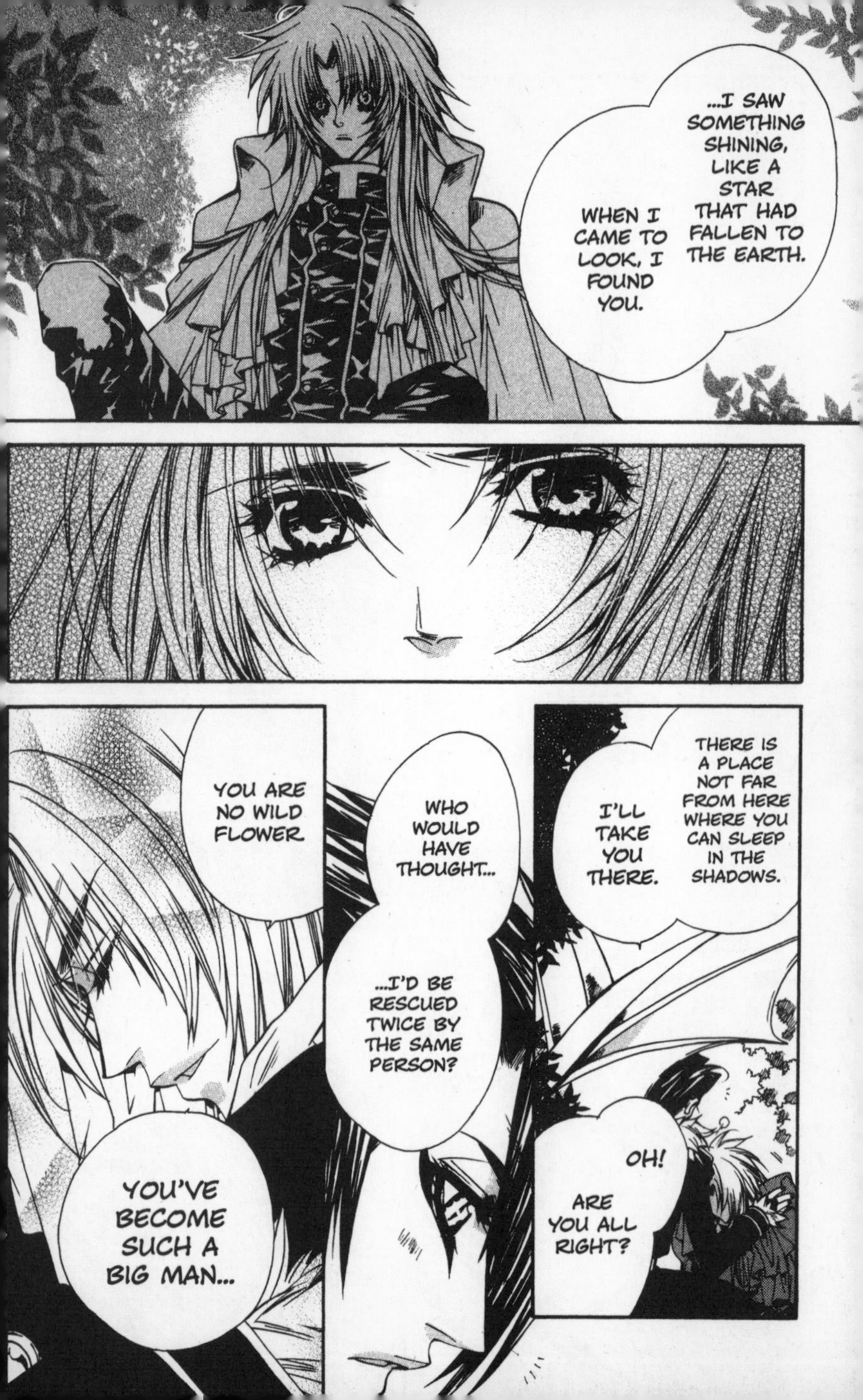
...I SAW SOMETHING SHINING, LIKE A STAR THAT HAD FALLEN TO THE EARTH.
WHEN I CAME TO LOOK, I FOUND YOU.
THERE IS A PLACE NOT FAR FROM HERE WHERE YOU CAN SLEEP IN THE SHADOWS.
I'LL TAKE YOU THERE.
OH!
ARE YOU ALL RIGHT?
WHO WOULD HAVE THOUGHT...
...I'D BE RESCUED TWICE BY THE SAME PERSON?
YOU ARE NO WILD FLOWER
YOU'VE BECOME SUCH A BIG MAN...

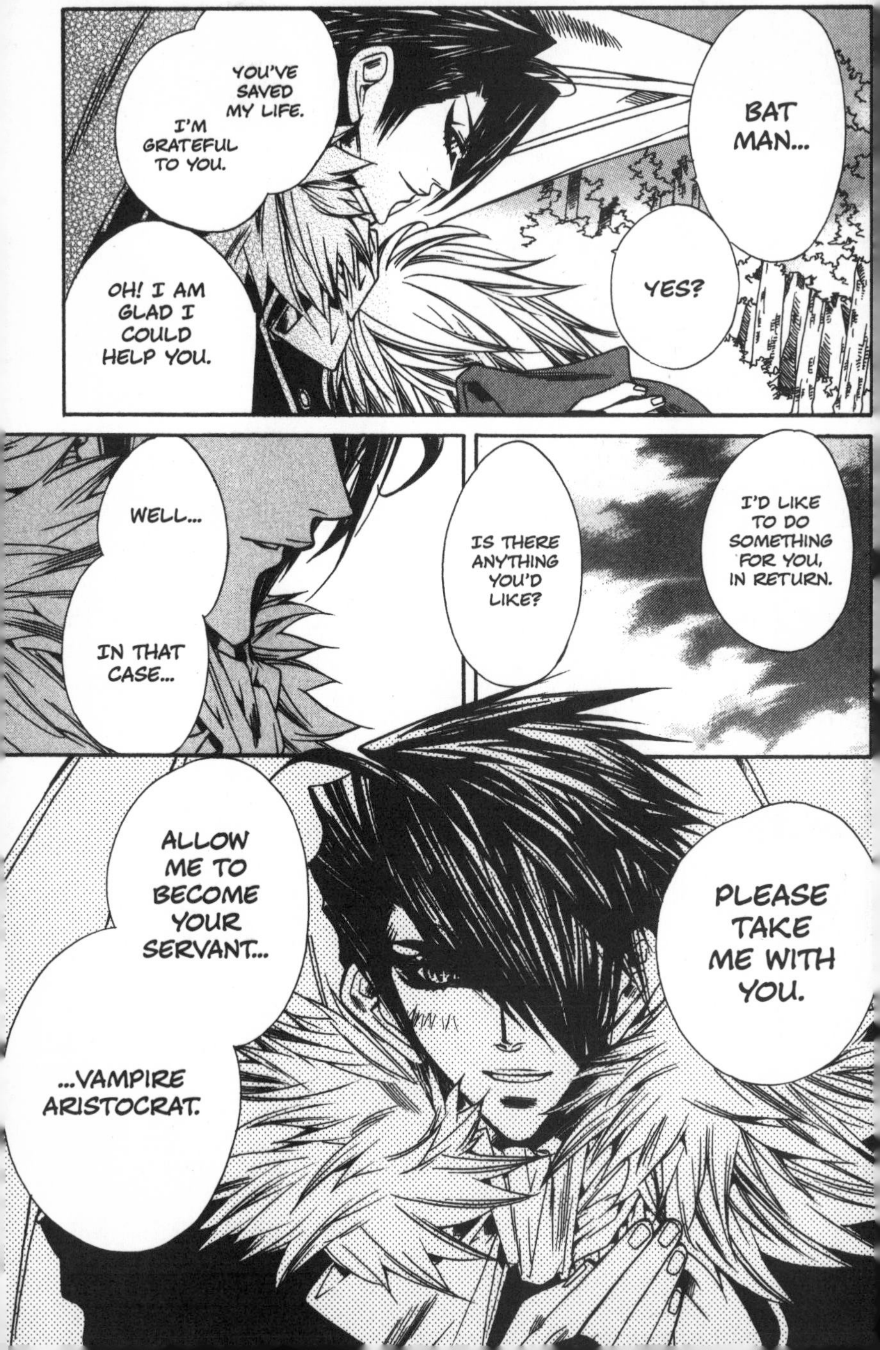
BAT MAN...
YES?
YOU'VE SAVED MY LIFE. I'M GRATEFUL TO YOU.
OH! I AM GLAD I COULD HELP YOU.
I'D LIKE TO DO SOMETHING FOR YOU, IN RETURN.
IS THERE ANYTHING YOU'D LIKE?
WELL...
IN THAT CASE...
PLEASE TAKE ME WITH YOU.
ALLOW ME TO BECOME YOUR SERVANT...
...VAMPIRE ARISTOCRAT.

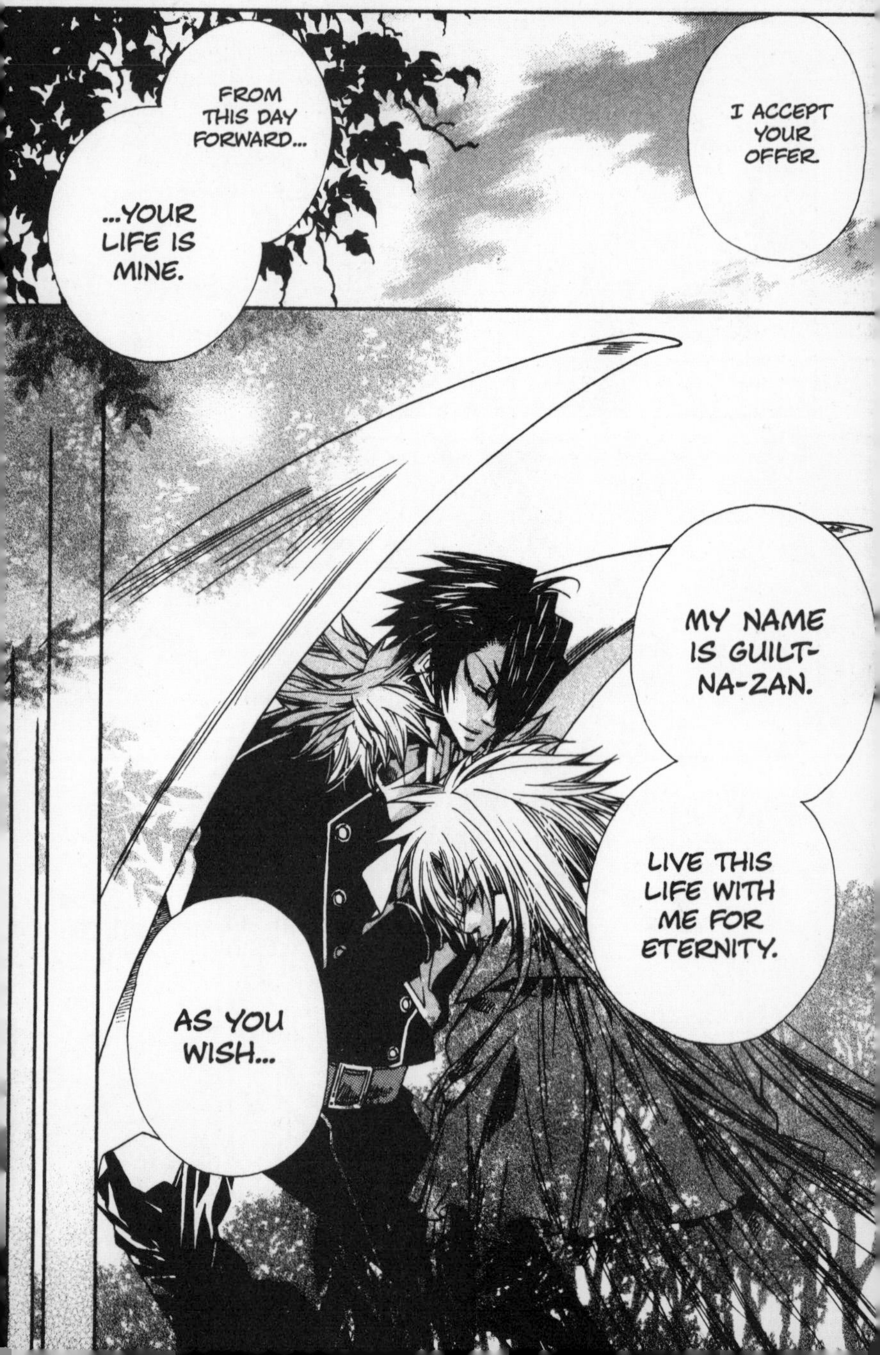
I ACCEPT YOUR OFFER
FROM THIS DAY FORWARD...
...YOUR LIFE IS MINE.
MY NAME IS GUILT-NA-ZAN.
LIVE THIS LIFE WITH ME FOR ETERNITY.
AS YOU WISH...

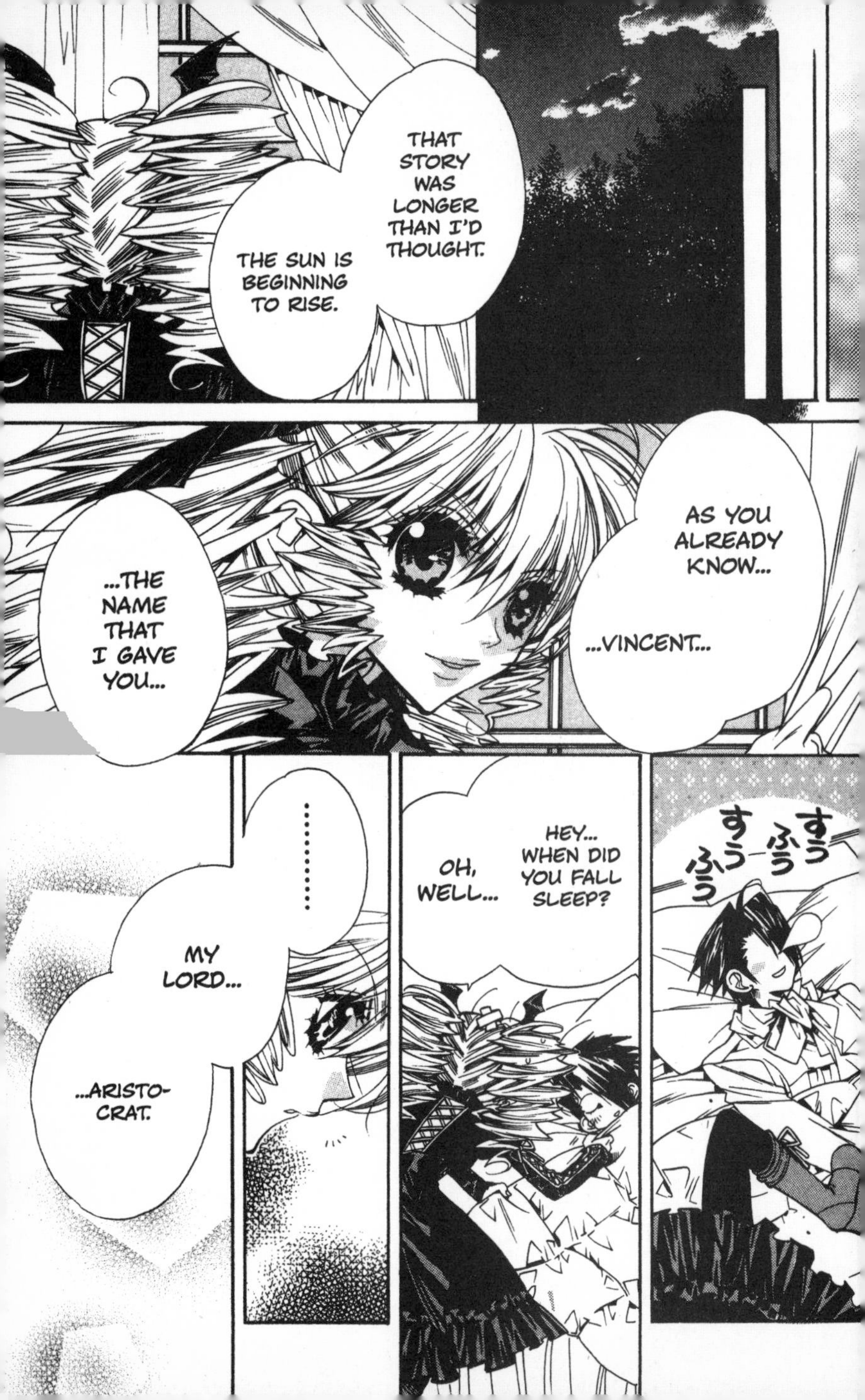
THAT STORY WAS LONGER THAN I'D THOUGHT.
THE SUN IS BEGINNING TO RISE.
AS YOU ALREADY KNOW...
...VINCENT...
...THE NAME THAT I GAVE YOU...
すうふう
すうふう
HEY... WHEN DID YOU FALL SLEEP?
OH, WELL...
....
MY LORD...
...ARISTO-CRAT.

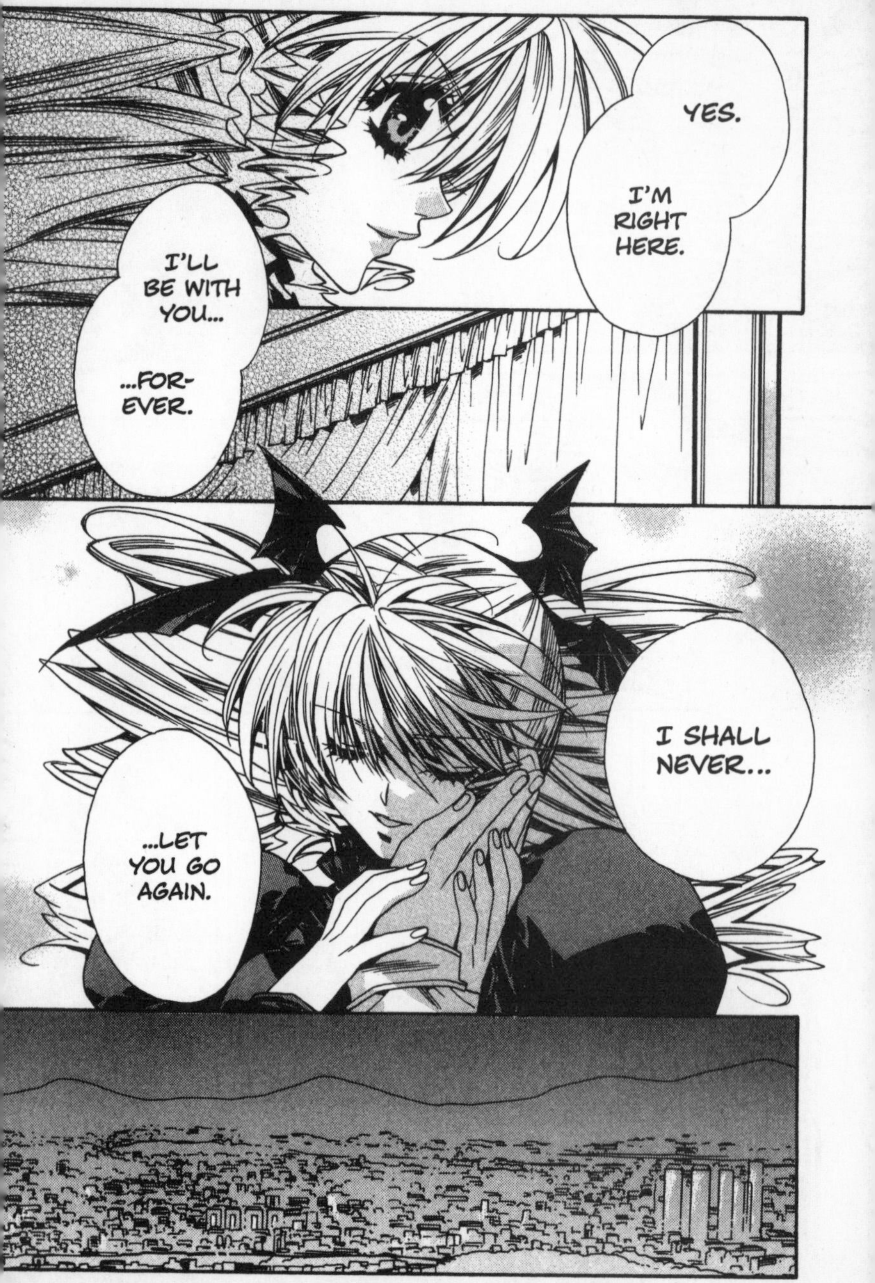
YES.
I'M RIGHT HERE.
I'LL BE WITH YOU...
...FOR-EVER.
I SHALL NEVER...
...LET YOU GO AGAIN.

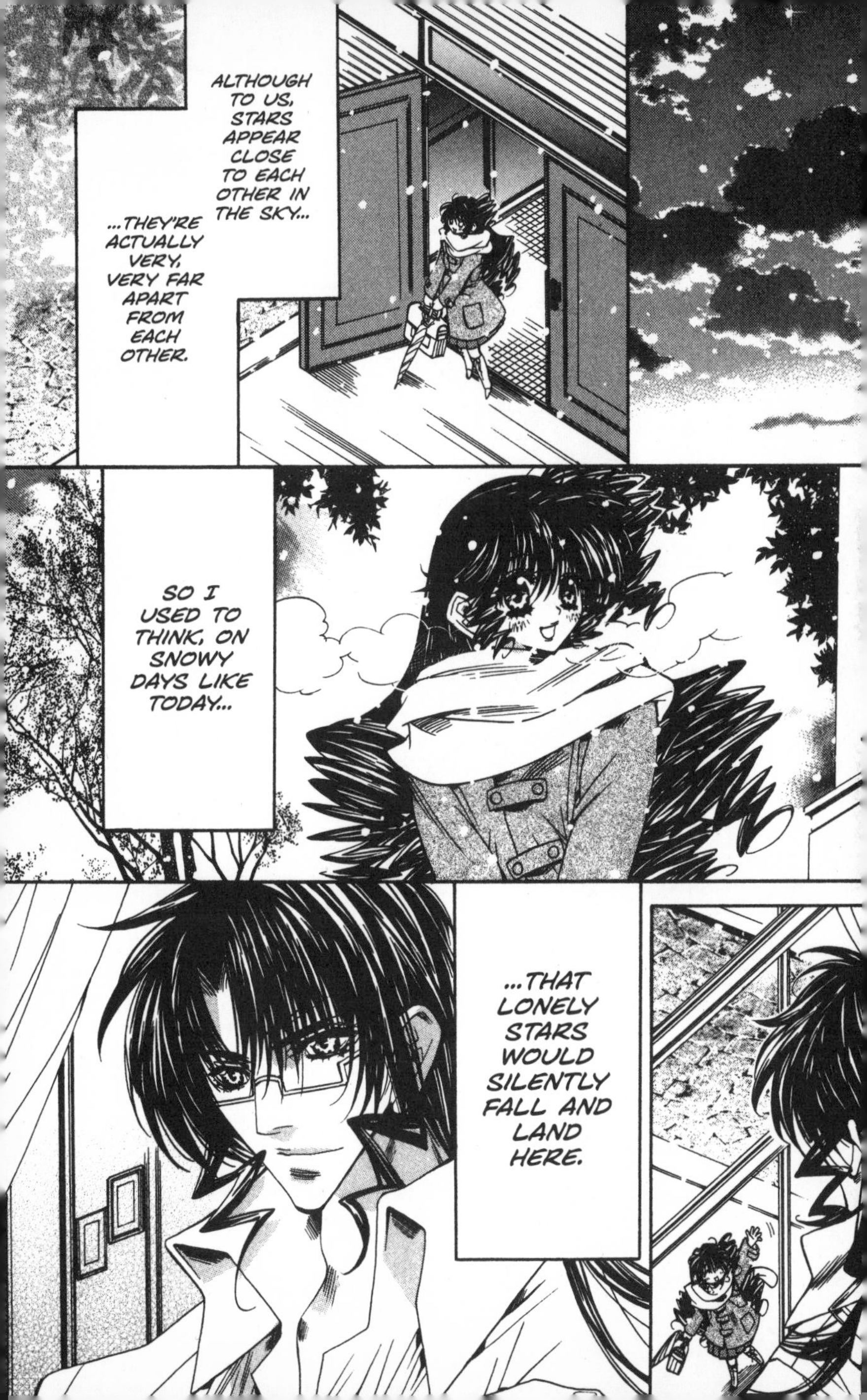
ALTHOUGH TO US, STARS APPEAR CLOSE TO EACH OTHER IN THE SKY...
...THEY'RE ACTUALLY VERY, VERY FAR APART FROM EACH OTHER.
SO I USED TO THINK, ON SNOWY DAYS LIKE TODAY...
...THAT LONELY STARS WOULD SILENTLY FALL AND LAND HERE.

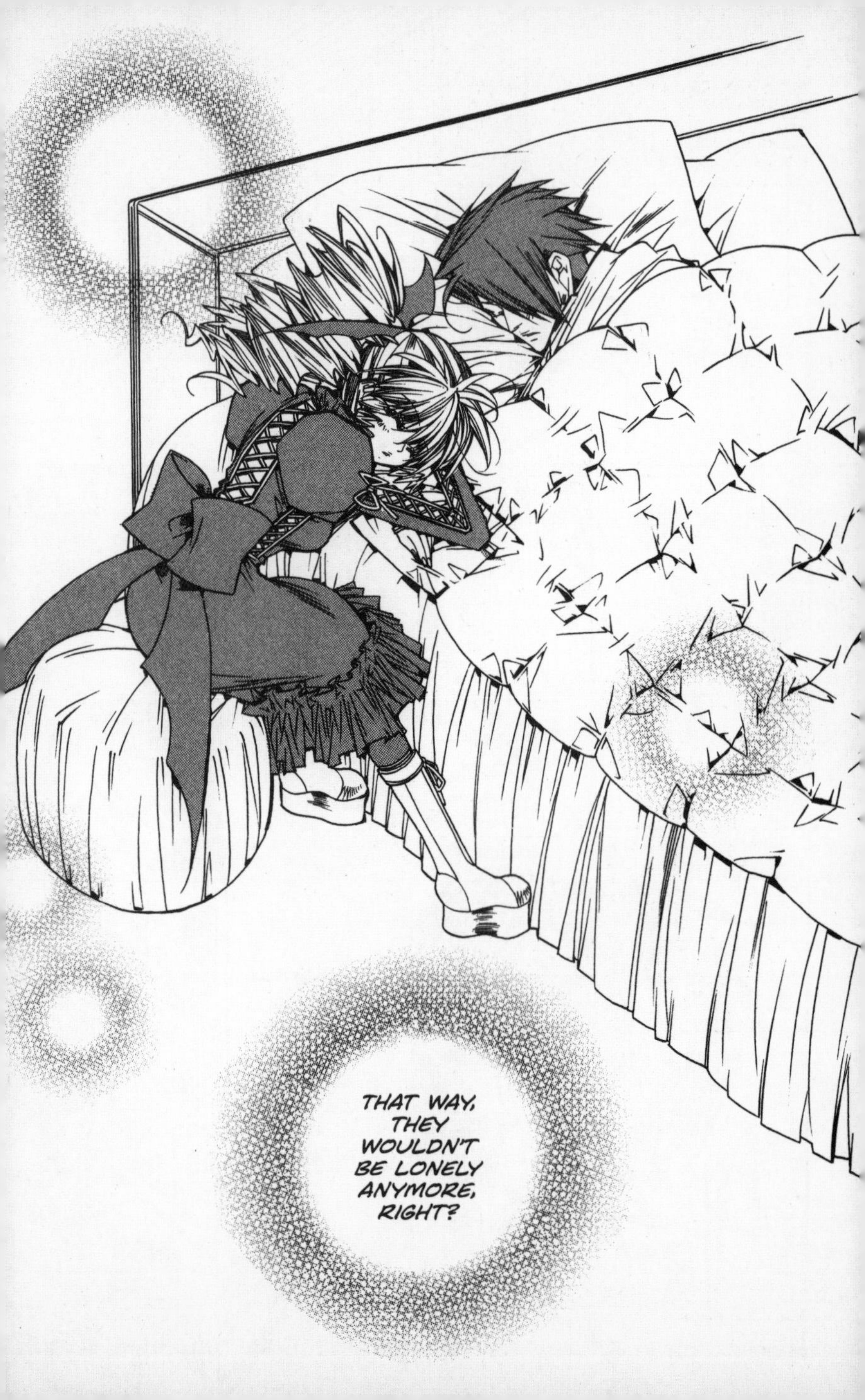
THAT WAY, THEY WOULDN'T BE LONELY ANYMORE, RIGHT?

BONUS COMIC STRIP

VAMPIRE DOLL

REFLECTIONS

Starry Starry Night

Q.

WHAT KIND OF LIFE DID WOLFGANG HAVE AFTER GUILT-NA-ZAN LEFT?

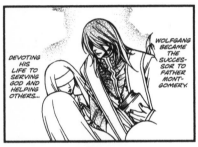

WOLFGANG BECAME THE SUCCES-SOR TO FATHER MONT-GOMERY.
DEVOTING HIS LIFE TO SERVING GOD AND HELPING OTHERS...
...HE BECAME THE LEGENDARY "ST. WOLFGANG" AND WAS QUOTED AS SAYING THINGS LIKE THIS...
"NO MATTER THE PASSAGE OF YEARS..."
"...I SHALL ETERNALLY PRAY FOR THE HAPPINESS OF MY INHUMAN FRIEND."
A BUMPKIN LIKE HIM DIDN'T HAVE TO BE SO ELOQUENT.
"SHUT UP!"

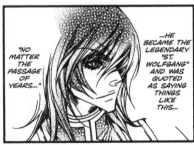

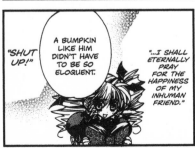

BAT "INNOCENT HEART " VINCENT

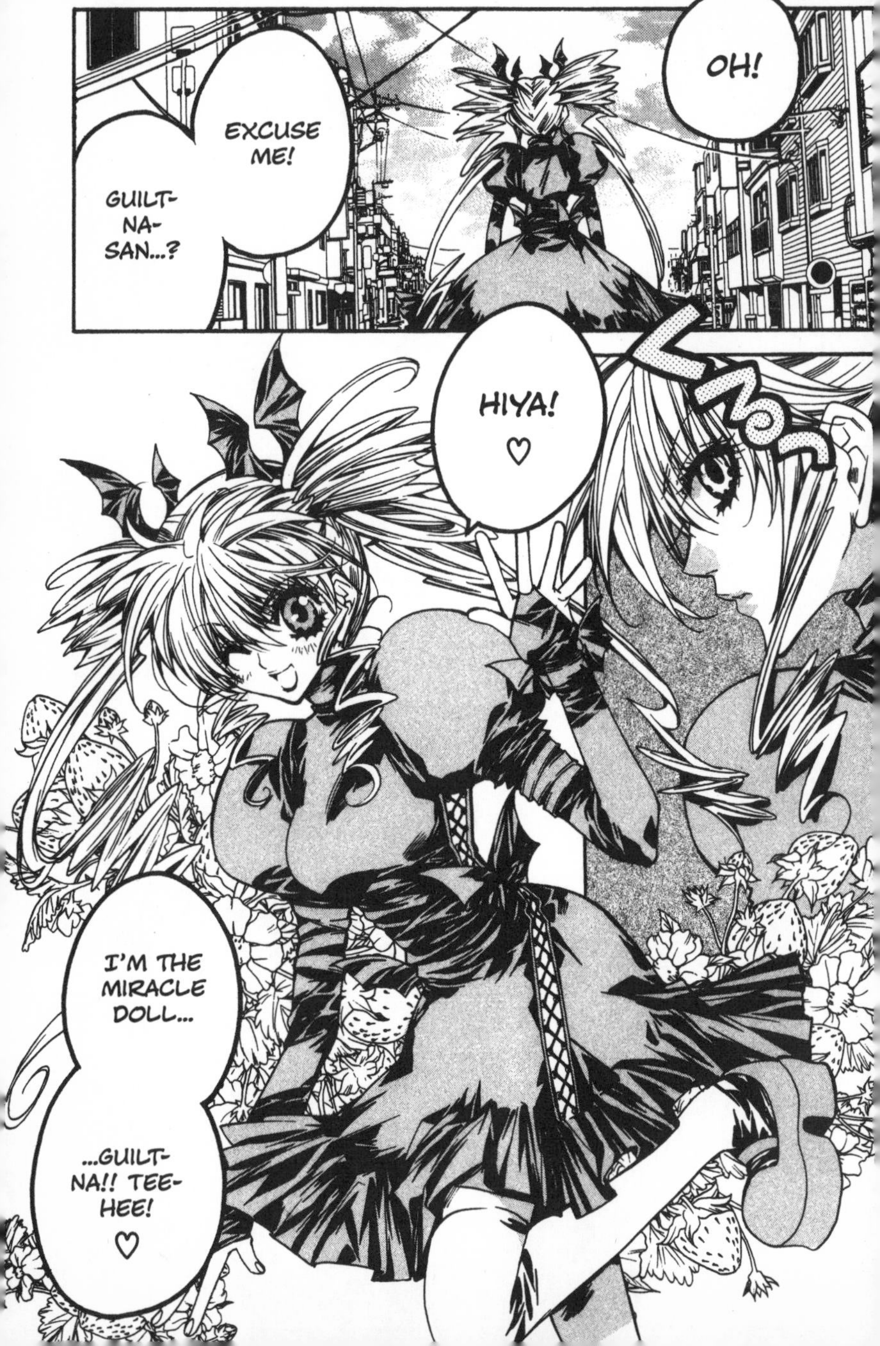

OH!
EXCUSE ME!
GUILT-NA-SAN...?
HIYA! ♡
I'M THE MIRACLE DOLL...
...GUILT-NA!! TEE-HEE! ♡

♯27 "Fake to Fake"
PART 1

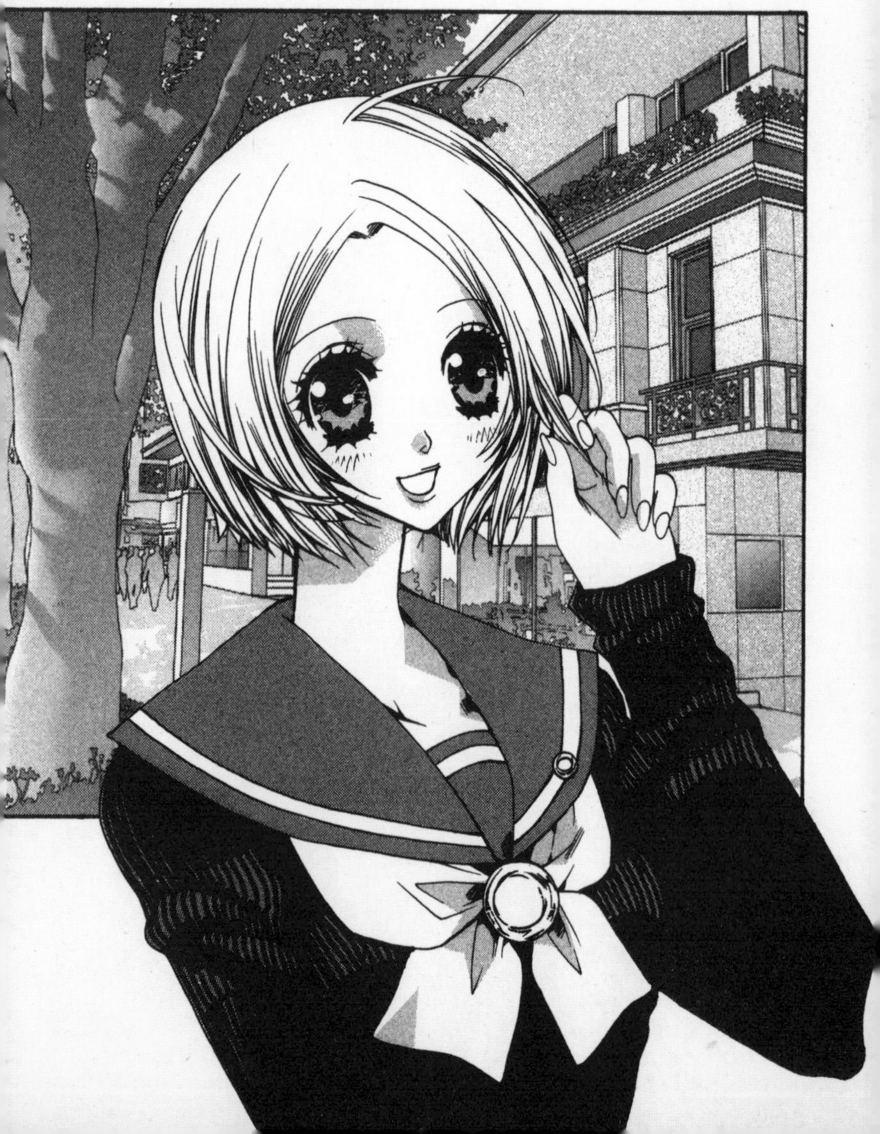

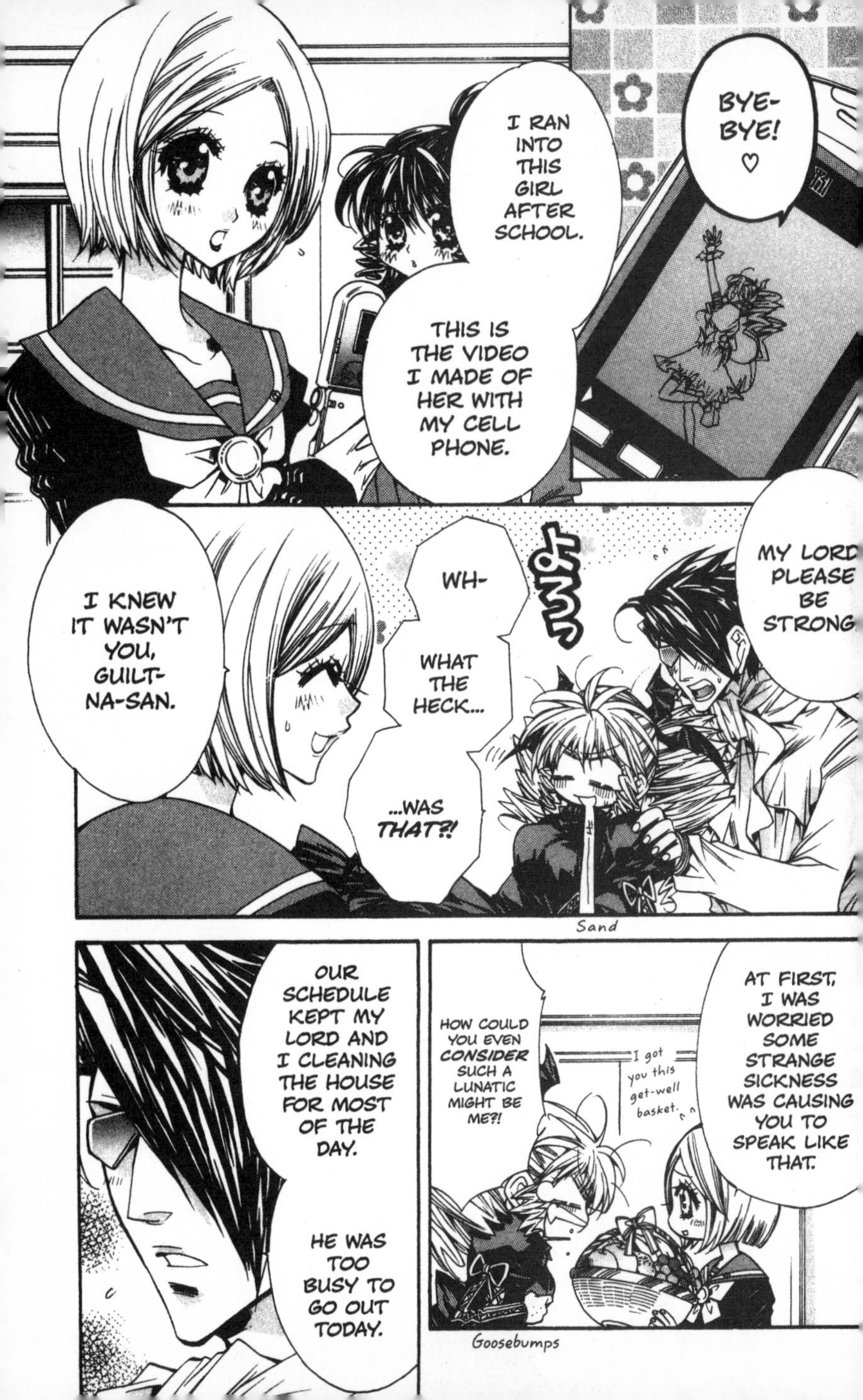
BYE-BYE! ♡
I RAN INTO THIS GIRL AFTER SCHOOL.
THIS IS THE VIDEO I MADE OF HER WITH MY CELL PHONE.
MY LORD PLEASE BE STRONG
よろっ
WH-
WHAT THE HECK...
...WAS THAT?!
I KNEW IT WASN'T YOU, GUILT-NA-SAN.
Sand
AT FIRST, I WAS WORRIED SOME STRANGE SICKNESS WAS CAUSING YOU TO SPEAK LIKE THAT.
I got you this get-well basket.
HOW COULD YOU EVEN CONSIDER SUCH A LUNATIC MIGHT BE ME?!
Goosebumps
OUR SCHEDULE KEPT MY LORD AND I CLEANING THE HOUSE FOR MOST OF THE DAY.
HE WAS TOO BUSY TO GO OUT TODAY.

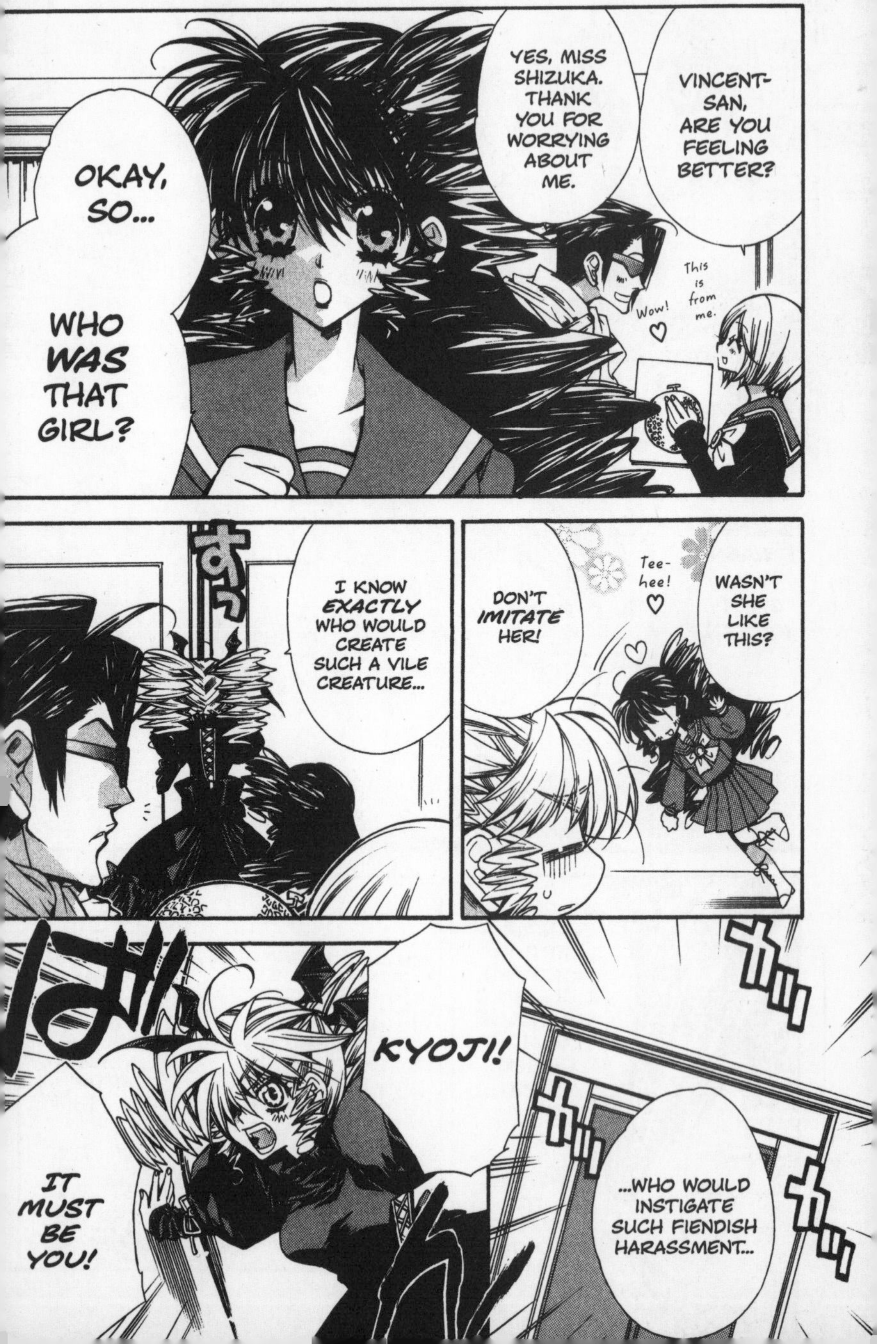
VINCENT-SAN, ARE YOU FEELING BETTER?
YES, MISS SHIZUKA. THANK YOU FOR WORRYING ABOUT ME.
This is from me.
Wow! ♡
OKAY, SO...
WHO *WAS* THAT GIRL?
WASN'T SHE LIKE THIS?
Tee-hee! ♡
DON'T *IMITATE* HER!
すっ
I KNOW *EXACTLY* WHO WOULD CREATE SUCH A VILE CREATURE...
カッ
...WHO WOULD INSTIGATE SUCH FIENDISH HARASSMENT...
カッ
カッ
ば!!
KYOJI!
IT MUST BE YOU!

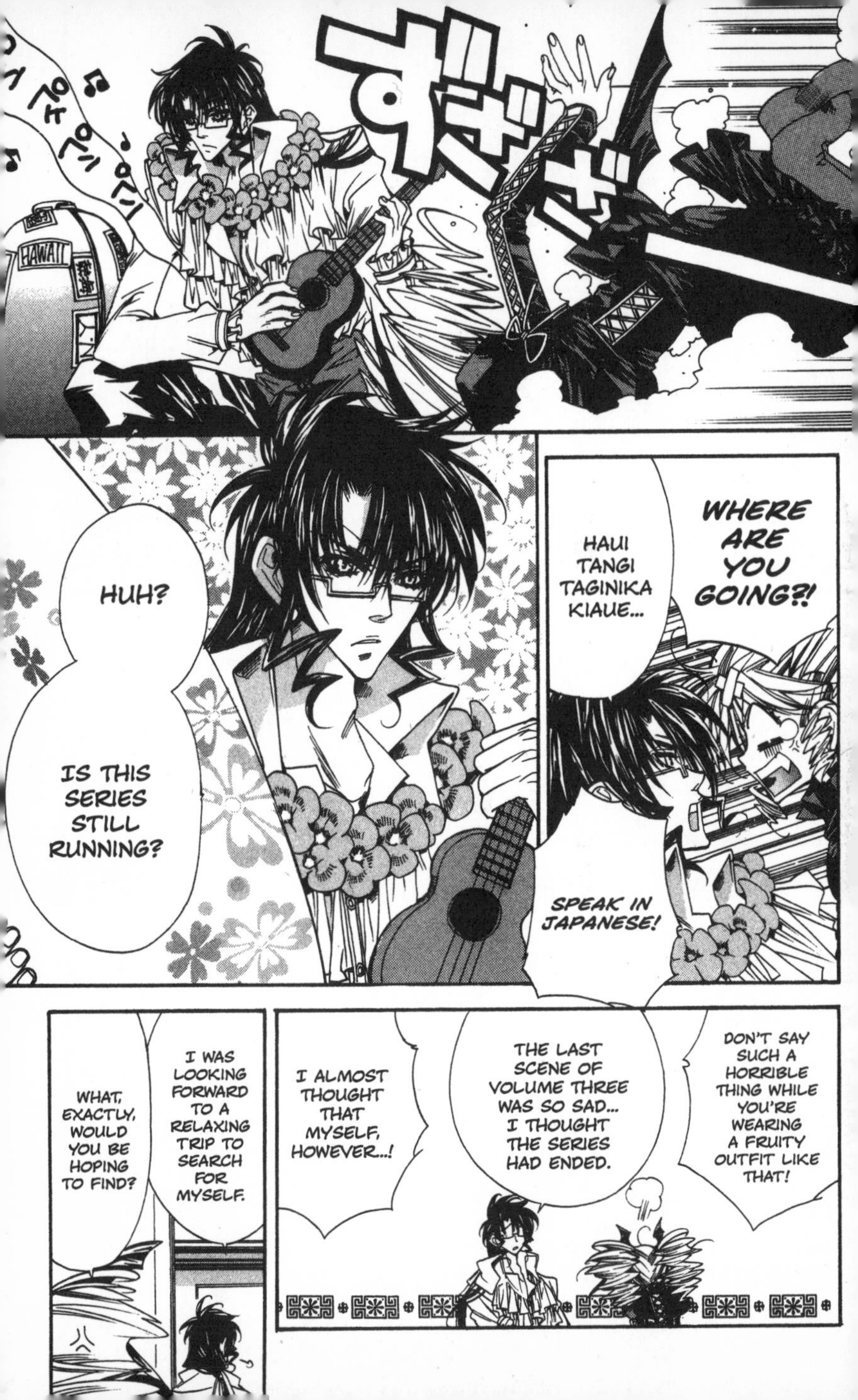

HAWAII
WHERE ARE YOU GOING?!
HAUI TANGI TAGINIKA KIAUE...
SPEAK IN JAPANESE!
HUH?
IS THIS SERIES STILL RUNNING?
DON'T SAY SUCH A HORRIBLE THING WHILE YOU'RE WEARING A FRUITY OUTFIT LIKE THAT!
THE LAST SCENE OF VOLUME THREE WAS SO SAD... I THOUGHT THE SERIES HAD ENDED.
I ALMOST THOUGHT THAT MYSELF, HOWEVER...!
I WAS LOOKING FORWARD TO A RELAXING TRIP TO SEARCH FOR MYSELF.
WHAT, EXACTLY, WOULD YOU BE HOPING TO FIND?

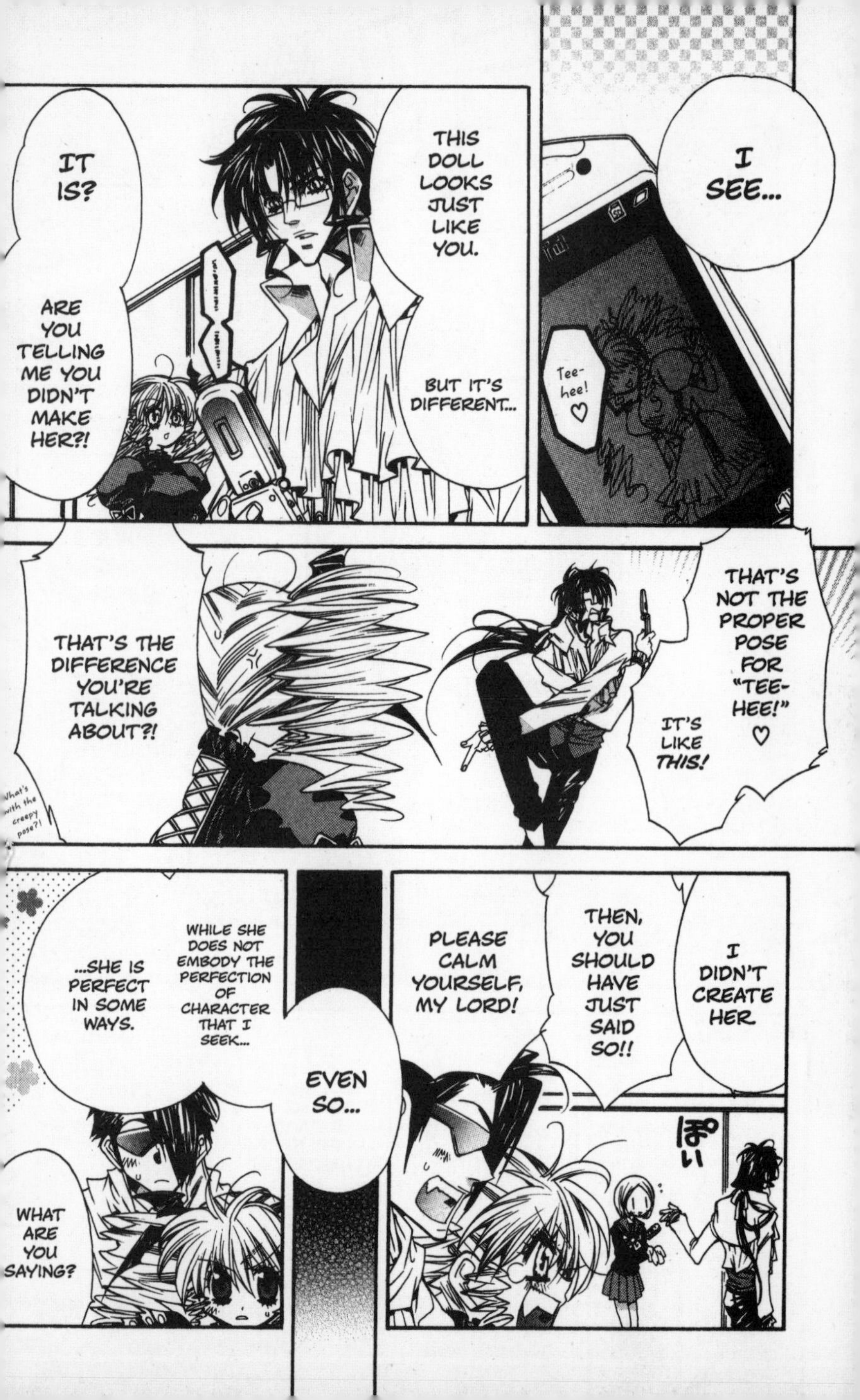
I SEE...
Tee-hee! ♡
THIS DOLL LOOKS JUST LIKE YOU.
BUT IT'S DIFFERENT...
IT IS?
ARE YOU TELLING ME YOU DIDN'T MAKE HER?!
THAT'S NOT THE PROPER POSE FOR "TEE-HEE!" ♡
IT'S LIKE THIS!
THAT'S THE DIFFERENCE YOU'RE TALKING ABOUT?!
What's with the creepy pose?!
I DIDN'T CREATE HER
THEN, YOU SHOULD HAVE JUST SAID SO!!
PLEASE CALM YOURSELF, MY LORD!
ぽい
EVEN SO...
WHILE SHE DOES NOT EMBODY THE PERFECTION OF CHARACTER THAT I SEEK...
...SHE IS PERFECT IN SOME WAYS.
WHAT ARE YOU SAYING?

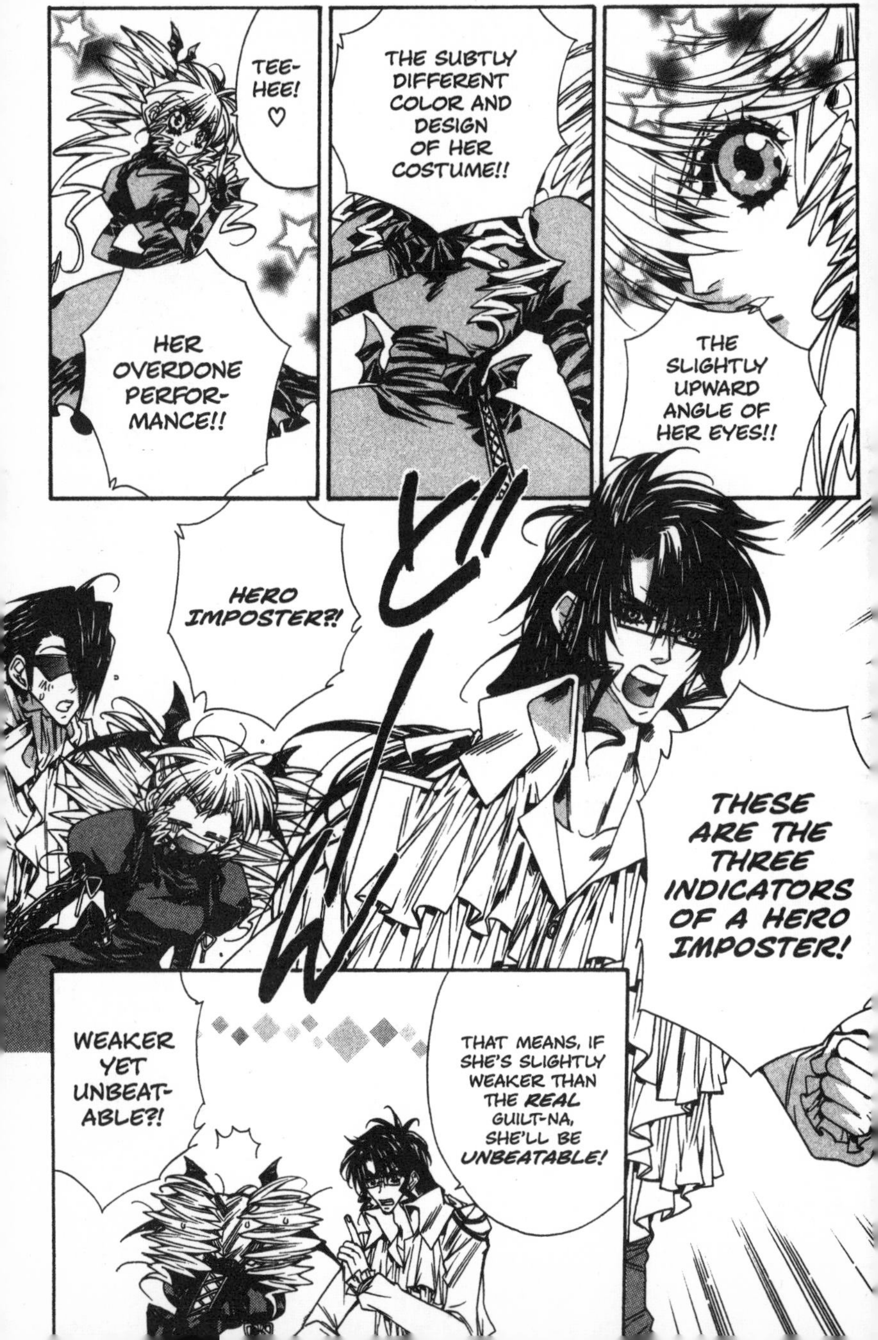
THE SLIGHTLY UPWARD ANGLE OF HER EYES!!
THE SUBTLY DIFFERENT COLOR AND DESIGN OF HER COSTUME!!
TEE-HEE! ♡
HER OVERDONE PERFORMANCE!!
THESE ARE THE THREE INDICATORS OF A HERO IMPOSTER!
HERO IMPOSTER?!
THAT MEANS, IF SHE'S SLIGHTLY WEAKER THAN THE REAL GUILT-NA, SHE'LL BE UNBEATABLE!
WEAKER YET UNBEATABLE?!

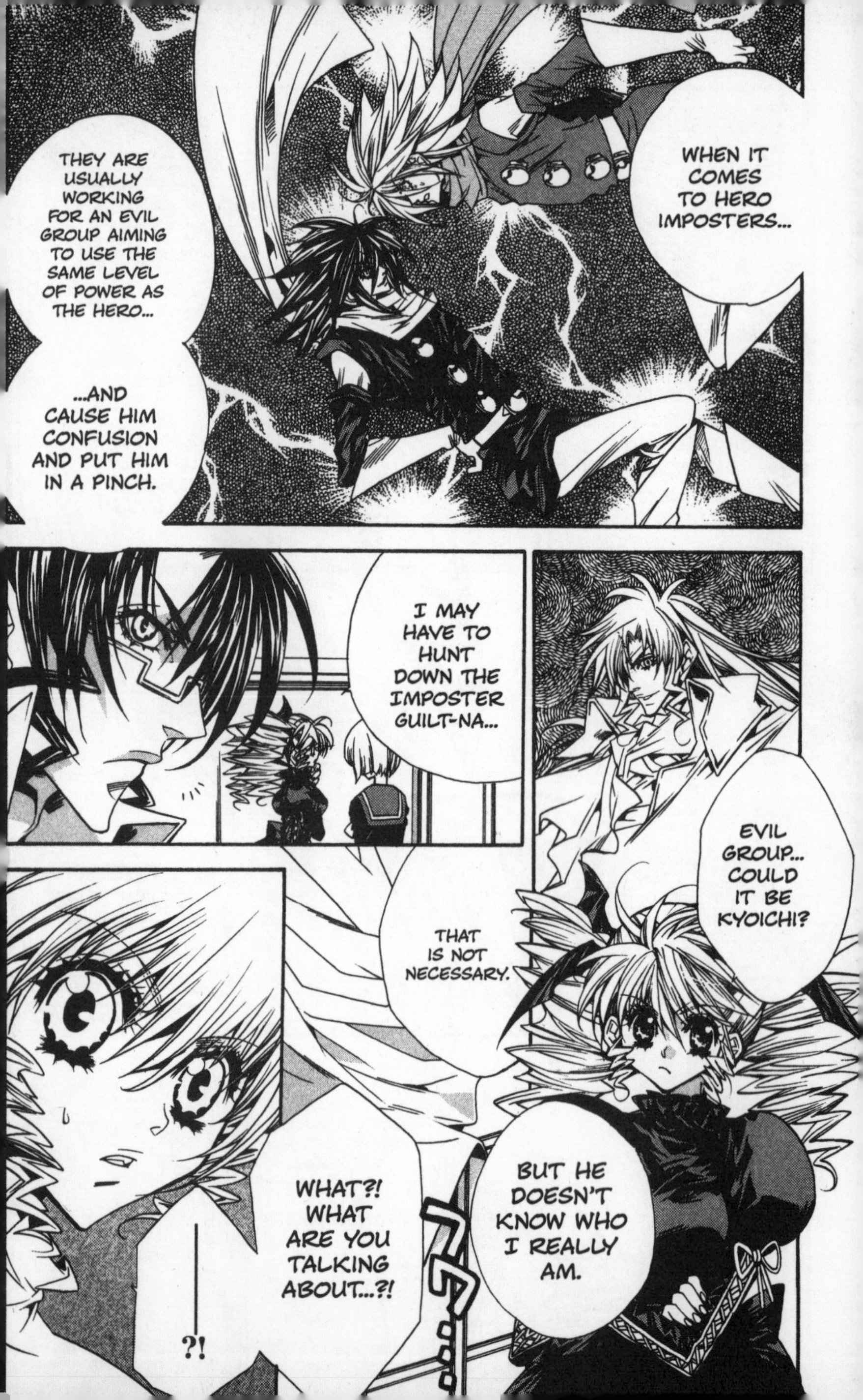
WHEN IT COMES TO HERO IMPOSTERS...
THEY ARE USUALLY WORKING FOR AN EVIL GROUP AIMING TO USE THE SAME LEVEL OF POWER AS THE HERO...
...AND CAUSE HIM CONFUSION AND PUT HIM IN A PINCH.
I MAY HAVE TO HUNT DOWN THE IMPOSTER GUILT-NA...
EVIL GROUP... COULD IT BE KYOICHI?
BUT HE DOESN'T KNOW WHO I REALLY AM.
THAT IS NOT NECESSARY.
WHAT?! WHAT ARE YOU TALKING ABOUT...?!
——?!

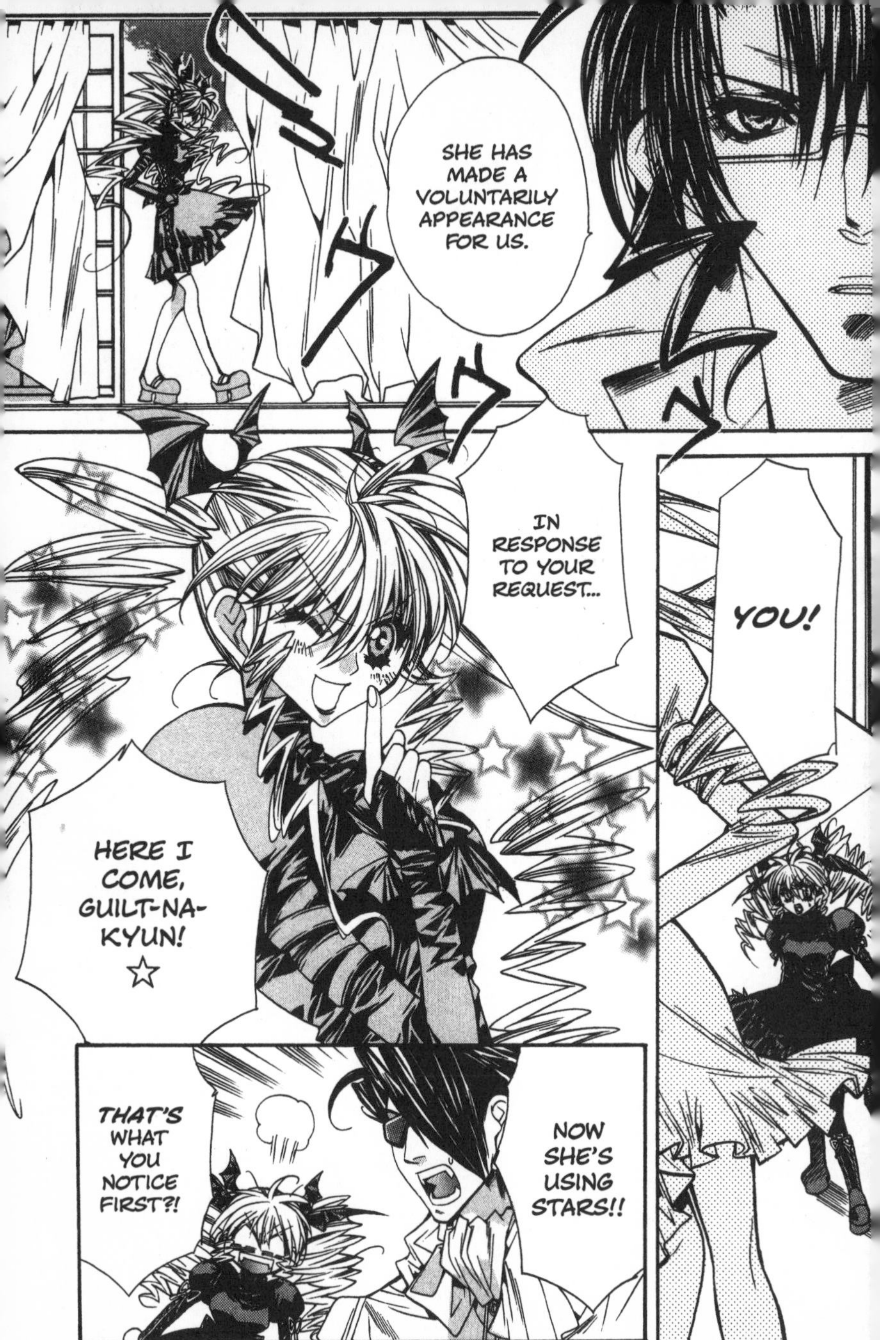
SHE HAS MADE A VOLUNTARILY APPEARANCE FOR US.
YOU!
IN RESPONSE TO YOUR REQUEST...
HERE I COME, GUILT-NA-KYUN! ☆
NOW SHE'S USING STARS!!
THAT'S WHAT YOU NOTICE FIRST?!

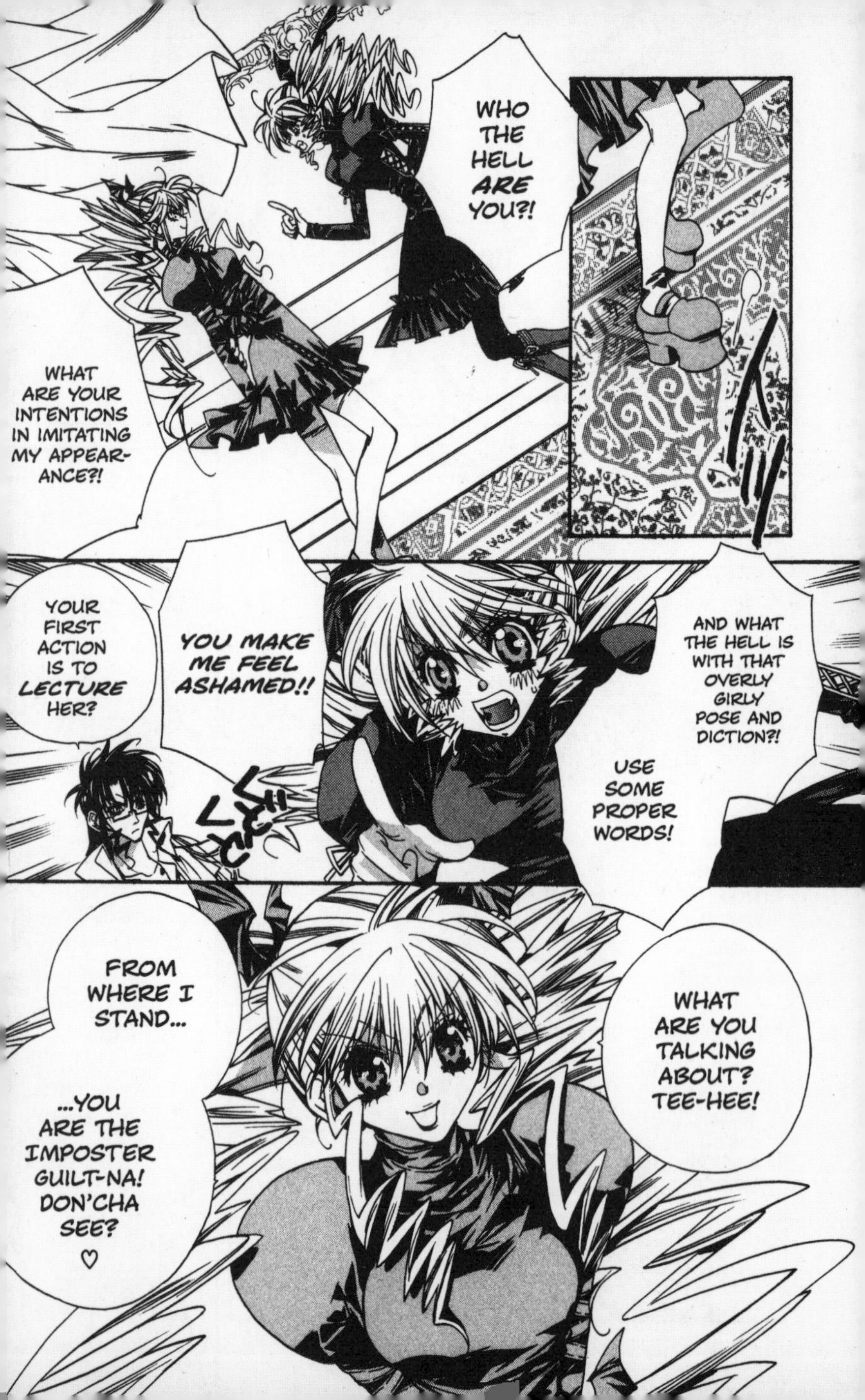
WHO THE HELL ARE YOU?!
WHAT ARE YOUR INTENTIONS IN IMITATING MY APPEARANCE?!
AND WHAT THE HELL IS WITH THAT OVERLY GIRLY POSE AND DICTION?!
USE SOME PROPER WORDS!
YOU MAKE ME FEEL ASHAMED!!
YOUR FIRST ACTION IS TO LECTURE HER?
WHAT ARE YOU TALKING ABOUT? TEE-HEE!
FROM WHERE I STAND...
...YOU ARE THE IMPOSTER GUILT-NA! DON'CHA SEE? ♡

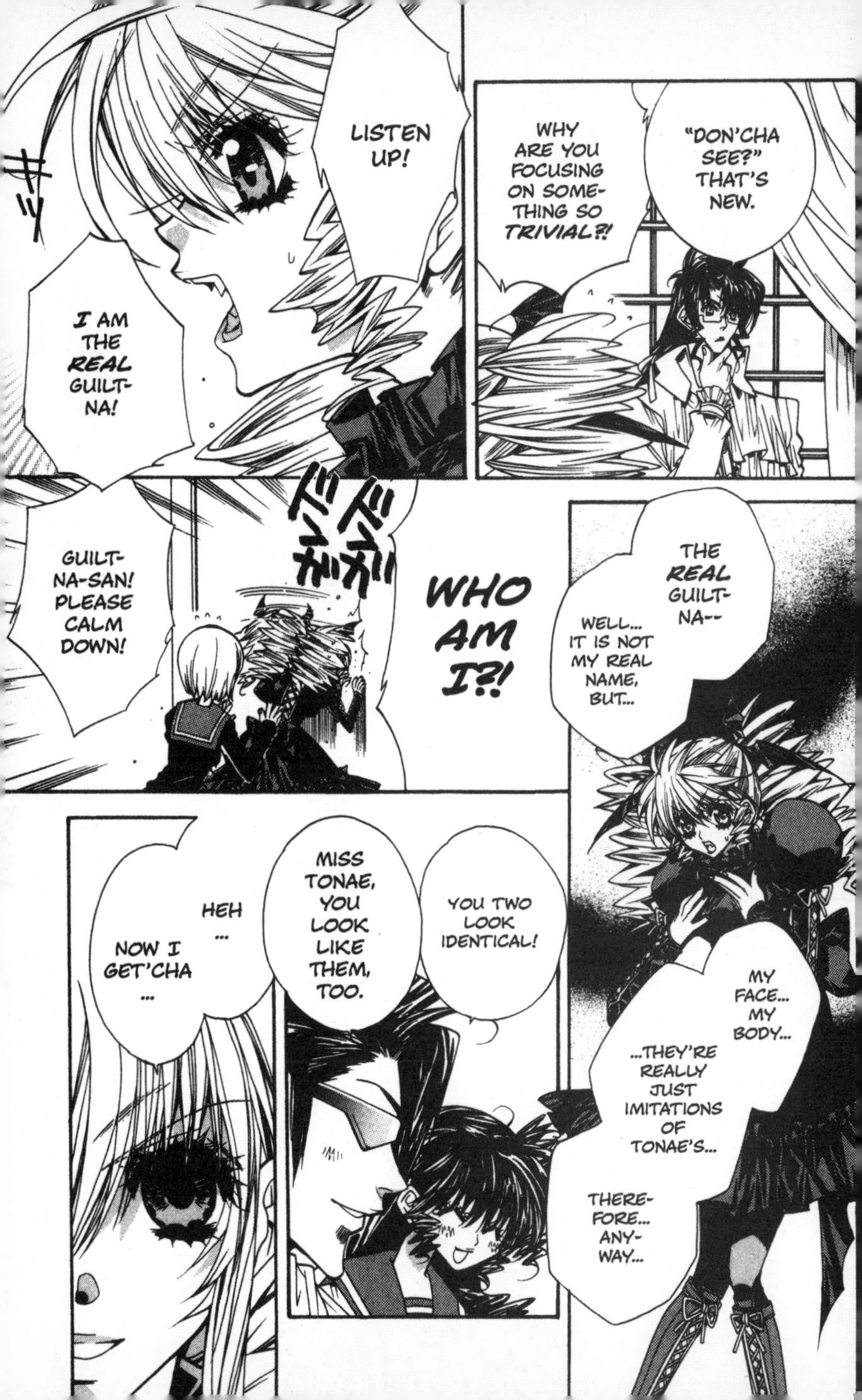
"DON'CHA SEE?" THAT'S NEW.
WHY ARE YOU FOCUSING ON SOMETHING SO *TRIVIAL*?!
LISTEN UP!
I AM THE *REAL* GUILTNA!
THE *REAL* GUILTNA--
WELL... IT IS NOT MY REAL NAME, BUT...
MY FACE... MY BODY...
...THEY'RE REALLY JUST IMITATIONS OF TONAE'S...
THEREFORE... ANYWAY...
WHO AM I?!
GUILTNA-SAN! PLEASE CALM DOWN!
YOU TWO LOOK IDENTICAL!
MISS TONAE, YOU LOOK LIKE THEM, TOO.
HEH...
NOW I GET'CHA...

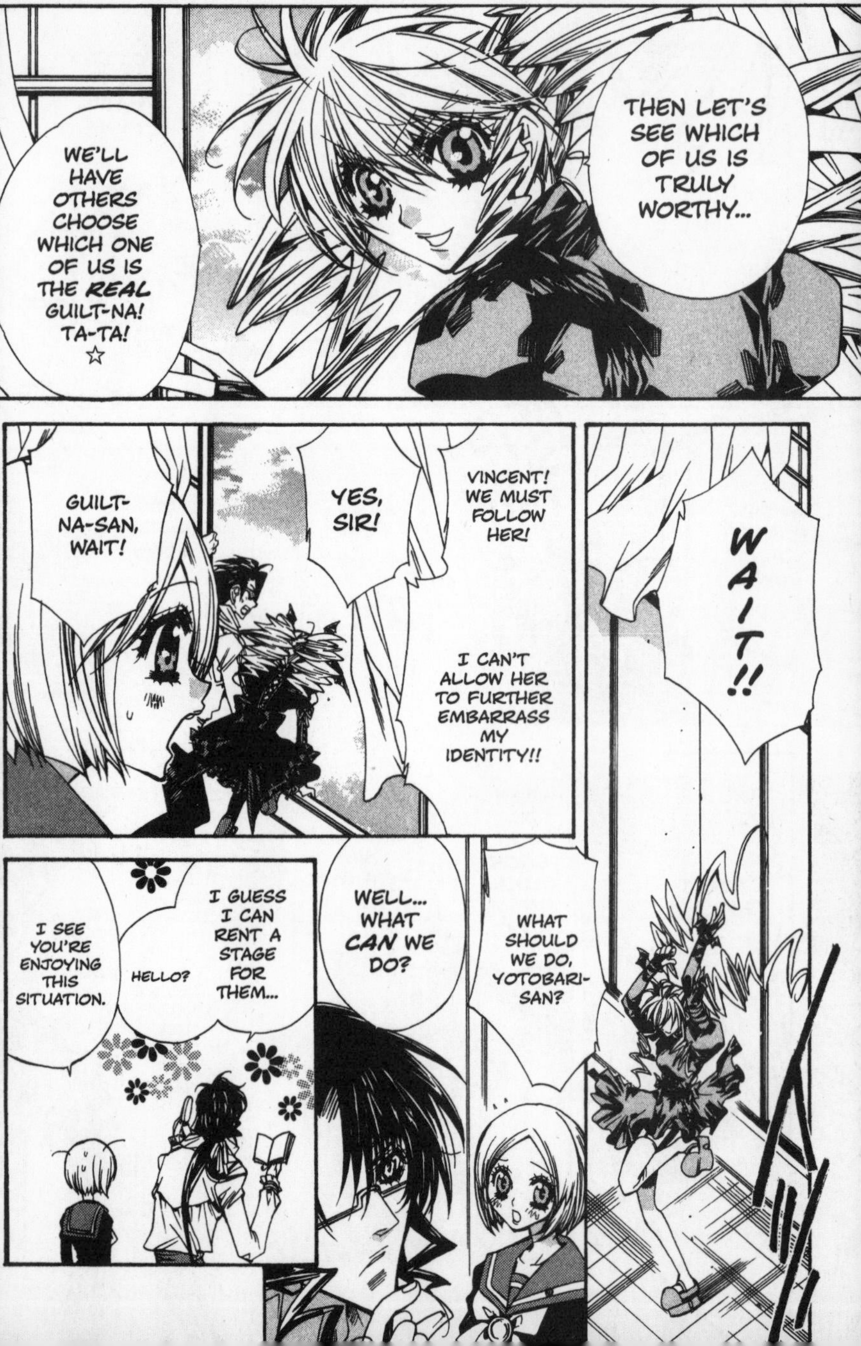
THEN LET'S SEE WHICH OF US IS TRULY WORTHY...
WE'LL HAVE OTHERS CHOOSE WHICH ONE OF US IS THE *REAL* GUILT-NA! TA-TA! ☆
WAIT!!
VINCENT! WE MUST FOLLOW HER!
I CAN'T ALLOW HER TO FURTHER EMBARRASS MY IDENTITY!!
YES, SIR!
GUILT-NA-SAN, WAIT!
WHAT SHOULD WE DO, YOTOBARI-SAN?
WELL... WHAT *CAN* WE DO?
I GUESS I CAN RENT A STAGE FOR THEM...
HELLO?
I SEE YOU'RE ENJOYING THIS SITUATION.

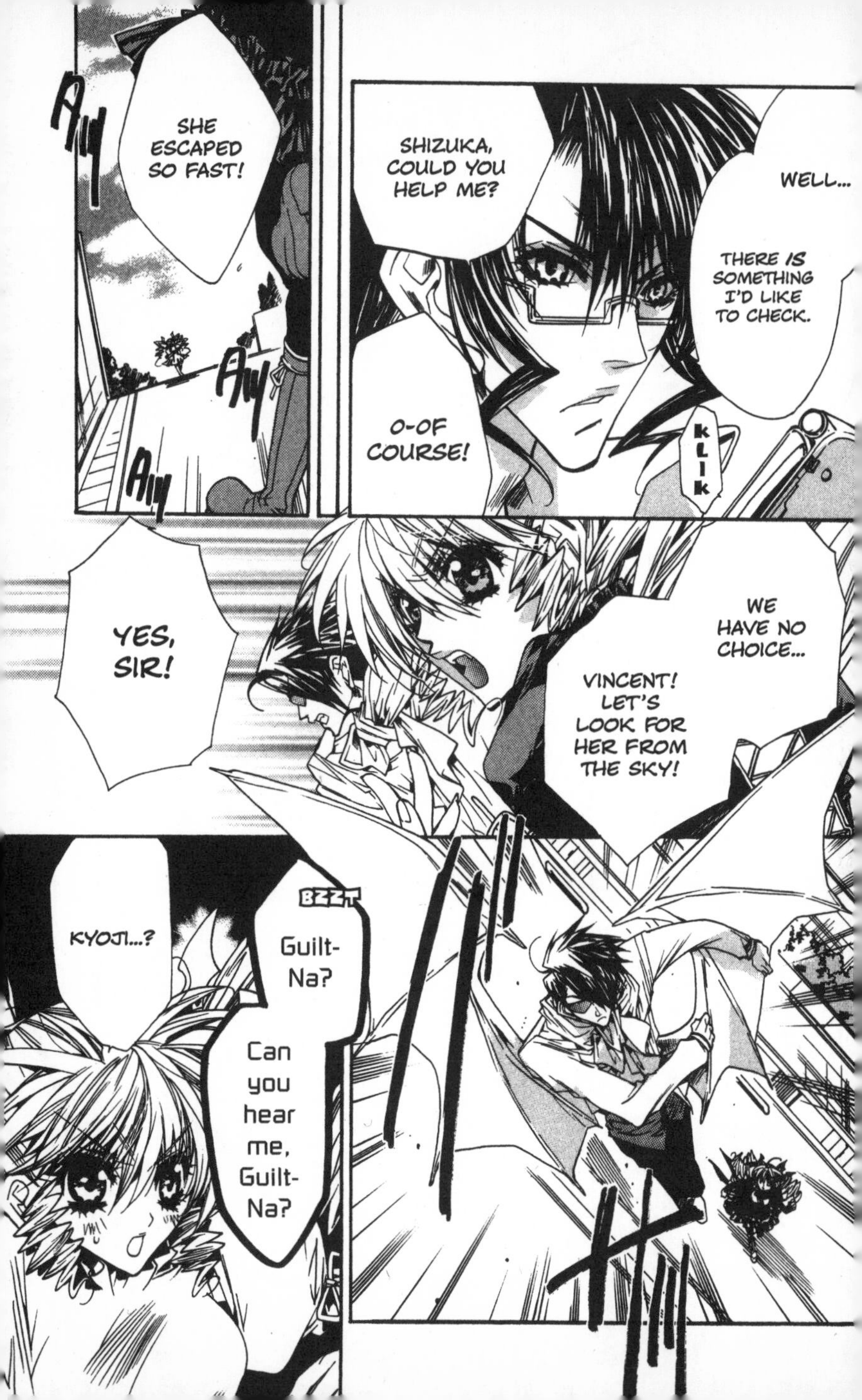
WELL...
THERE IS SOMETHING I'D LIKE TO CHECK.
SHIZUKA, COULD YOU HELP ME?
KLIK
O-OF COURSE!
SHE ESCAPED SO FAST!
WE HAVE NO CHOICE...
VINCENT! LET'S LOOK FOR HER FROM THE SKY!
YES, SIR!
BZZT
Guilt-Na?
Can you hear me, Guilt-Na?
KYOJI...?

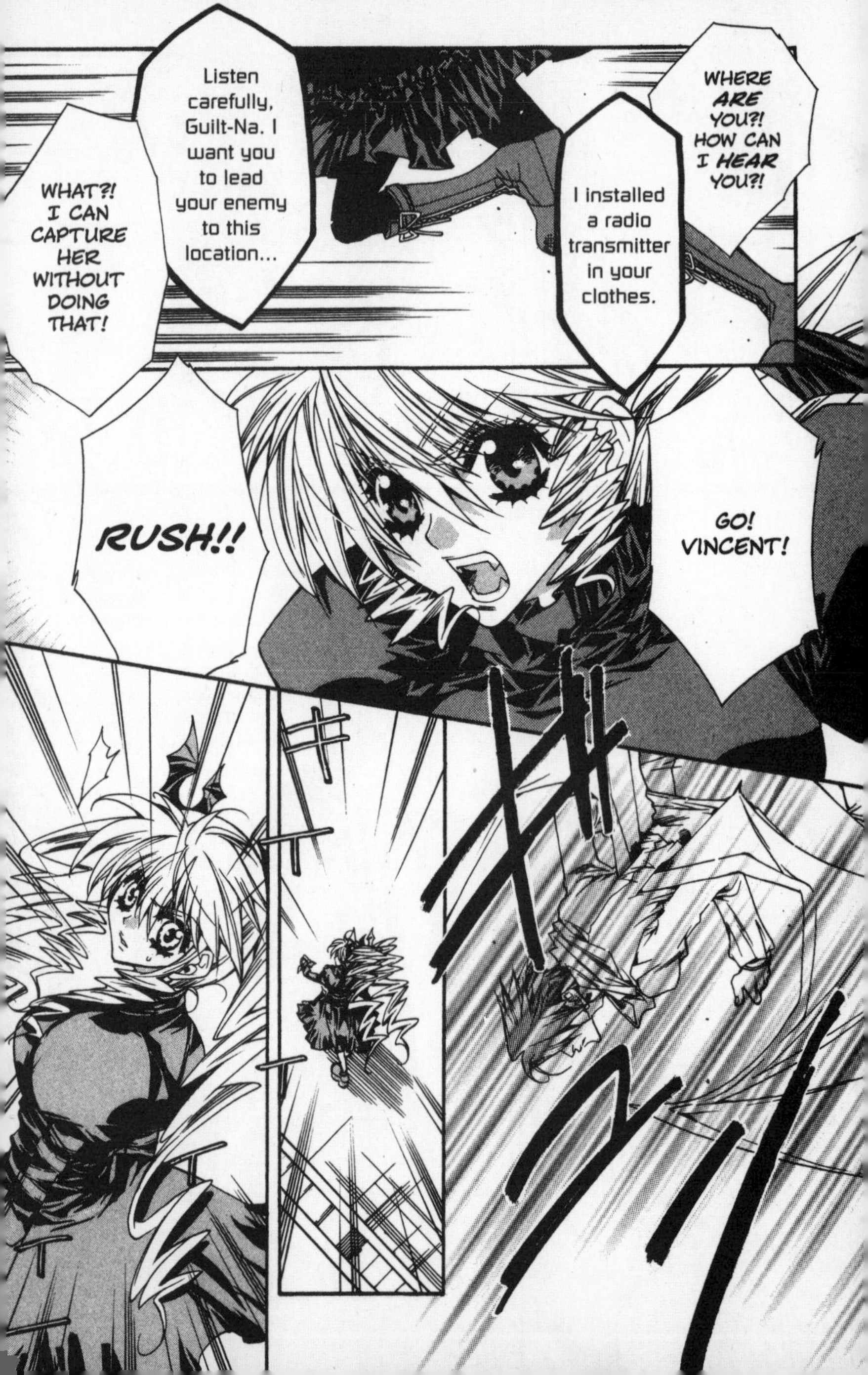
WHERE ARE YOU?! HOW CAN I HEAR YOU?!
I installed a radio transmitter in your clothes.
Listen carefully, Guilt-Na. I want you to lead your enemy to this location...
WHAT?! I CAN CAPTURE HER WITHOUT DOING THAT!
GO! VINCENT!
RUSH!!

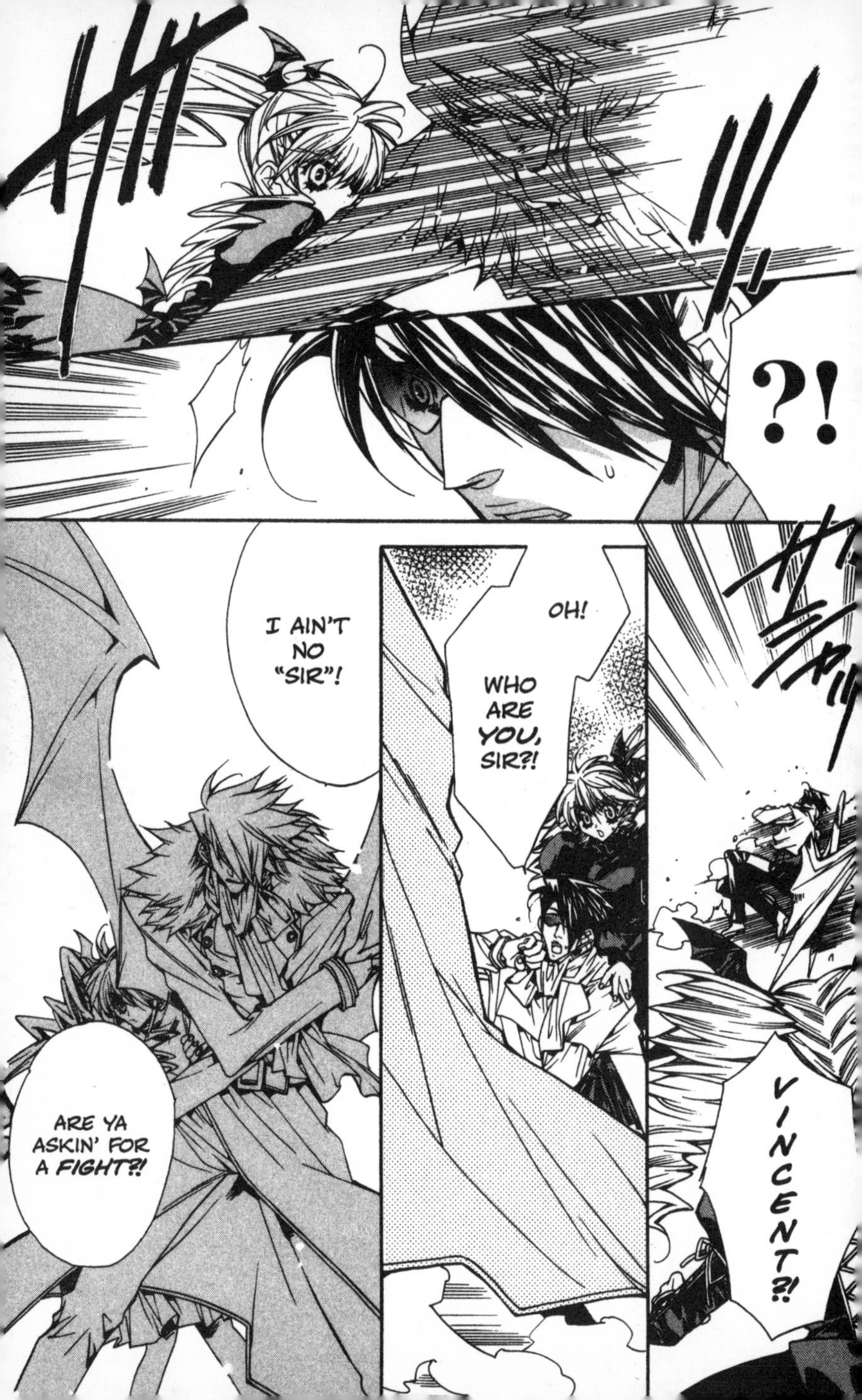
?!
VINCENT?!
OH!
WHO ARE YOU, SIR?!
I AIN'T NO "SIR"!
ARE YA ASKIN' FOR A FIGHT?!

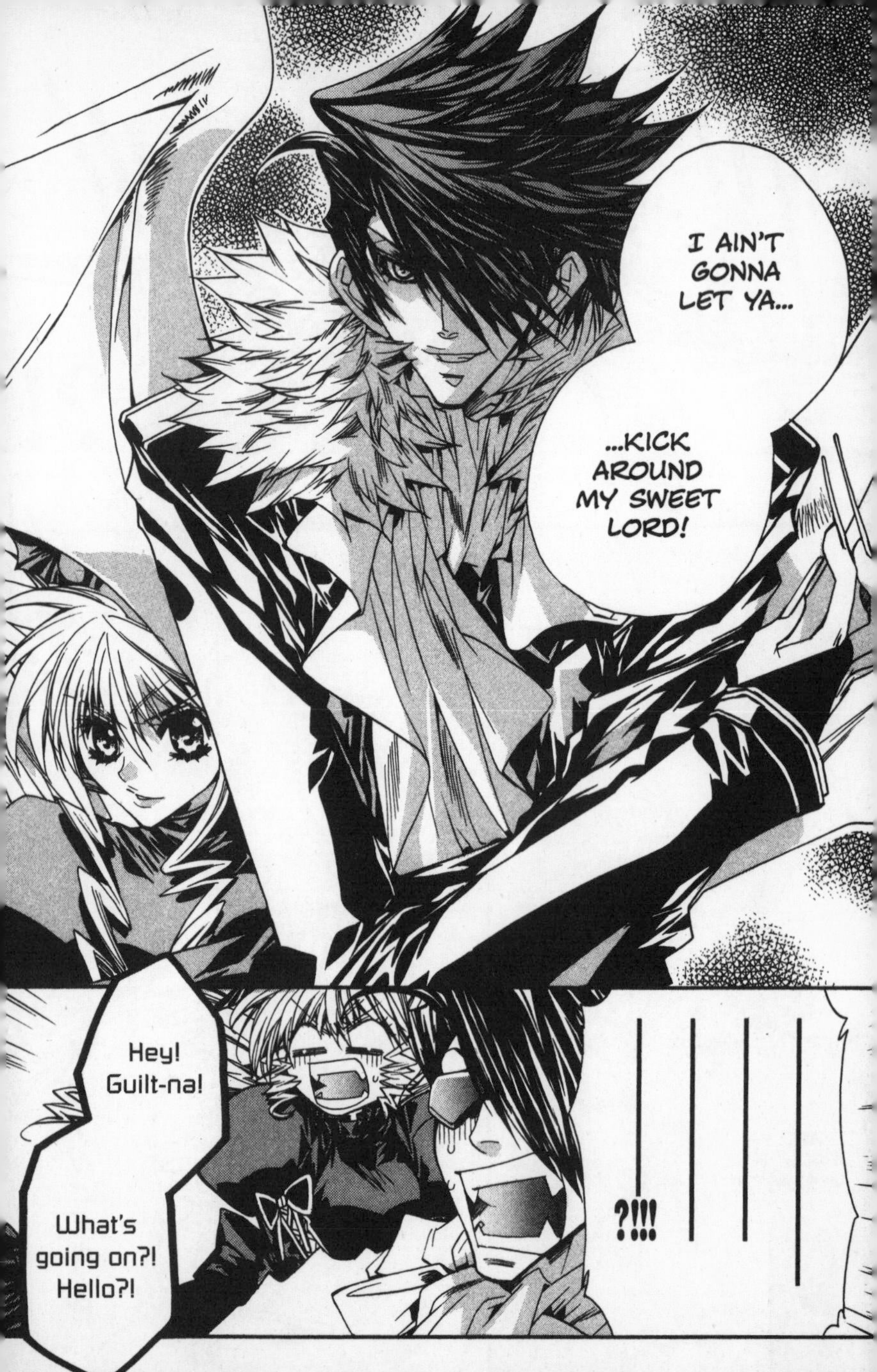
I AIN'T GONNA LET YA...
...KICK AROUND MY SWEET LORD!
?!!!
Hey! Guilt-na!
What's going on?! Hello?!

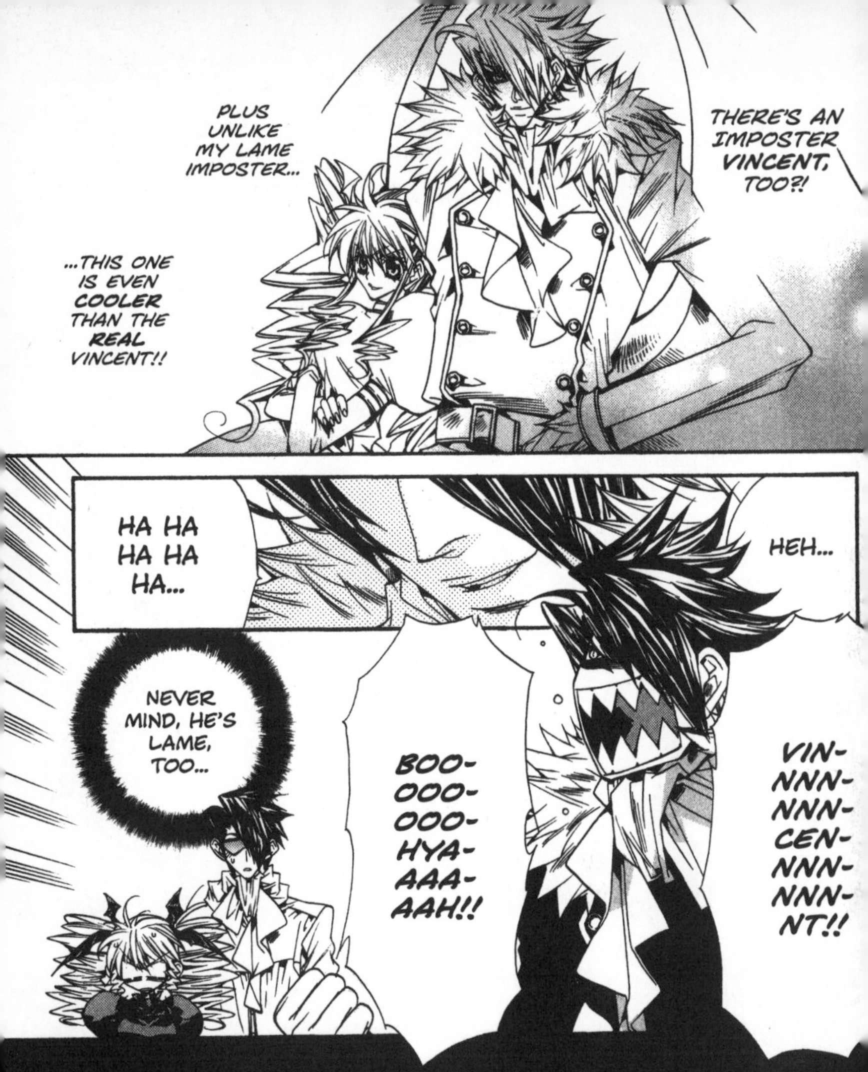
THERE'S AN IMPOSTER VINCENT, TOO?!
PLUS UNLIKE MY LAME IMPOSTER...
...THIS ONE IS EVEN COOLER THAN THE REAL VINCENT!!
HEH...
HA HA HA HA HA...
VIN-NNN-NNN-CEN-NNN-NNN-NT!!
BOO-OOO-OOO-HYA-AAA-AAH!!
NEVER MIND, HE'S LAME, TOO...

♯28 "Fake to Fake"
PART 2

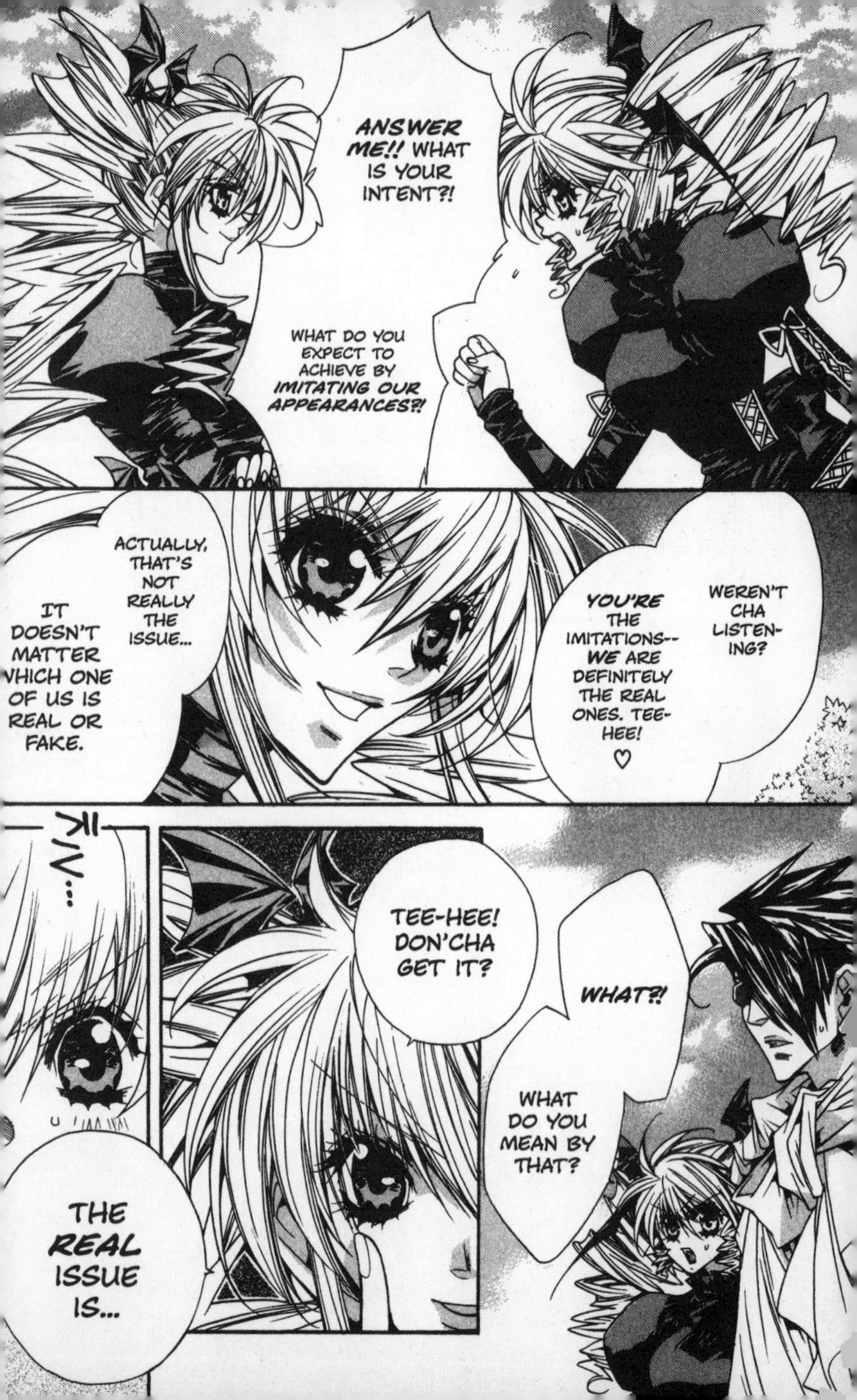
ANSWER ME!! WHAT IS YOUR INTENT?!
WHAT DO YOU EXPECT TO ACHIEVE BY IMITATING OUR APPEARANCES?!
WEREN'T CHA LISTENING?
YOU'RE THE IMITATIONS-- WE ARE DEFINITELY THE REAL ONES. TEE-HEE! ♡
ACTUALLY, THAT'S NOT REALLY THE ISSUE...
IT DOESN'T MATTER WHICH ONE OF US IS REAL OR FAKE.
TEE-HEE! DON'CHA GET IT?
WHAT?!
WHAT DO YOU MEAN BY THAT?
KIV...
THE REAL ISSUE IS...

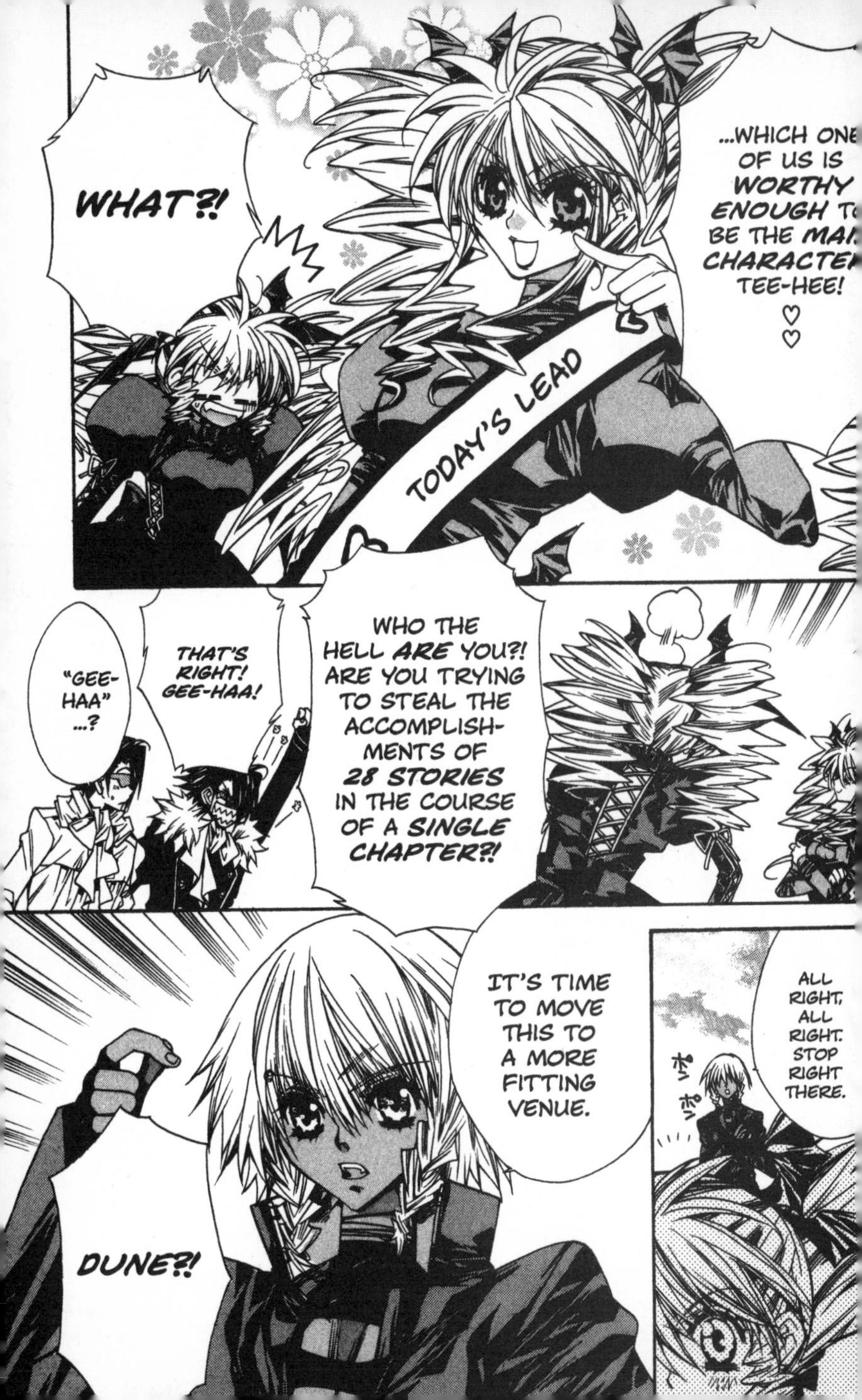
...WHICH ONE OF US IS WORTHY ENOUGH T BE THE MAI CHARACTE TEE-HEE! ♡ ♡
WHAT?!
TODAY'S LEAD
WHO THE HELL ARE YOU?! ARE YOU TRYING TO STEAL THE ACCOMPLISHMENTS OF 28 STORIES IN THE COURSE OF A SINGLE CHAPTER?!
THAT'S RIGHT! GEE-HAA!
"GEE-HAA" ...?
ALL RIGHT, ALL RIGHT. STOP RIGHT THERE.
IT'S TIME TO MOVE THIS TO A MORE FITTING VENUE.
DUNE?!

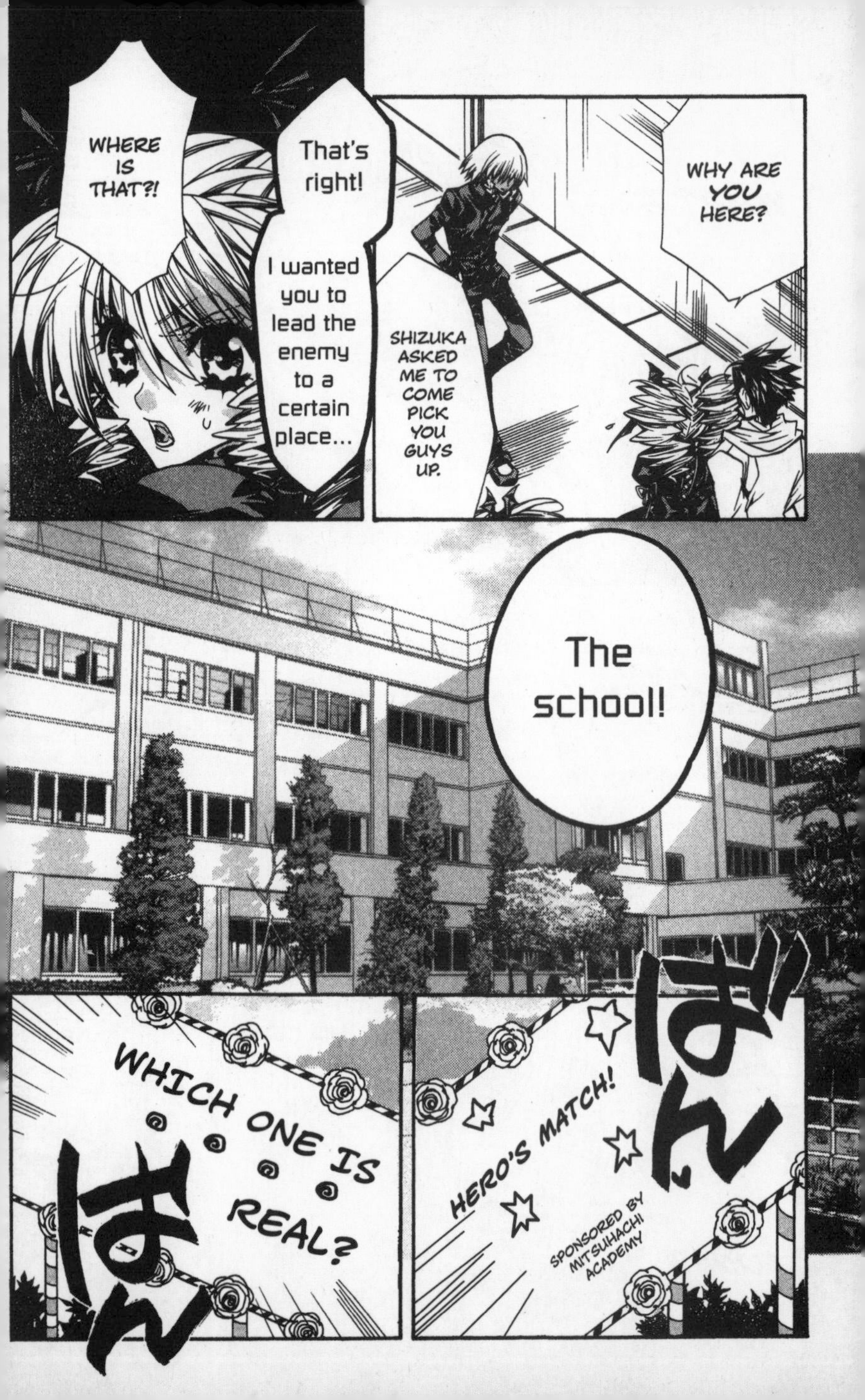
WHY ARE YOU HERE?
SHIZUKA ASKED ME TO COME PICK YOU GUYS UP.
That's right!
I wanted you to lead the enemy to a certain place...
WHERE IS THAT?!
The school!
ばん
HERO'S MATCH!
SPONSORED BY MITSUHACHI ACADEMY
WHICH ONE IS REAL?

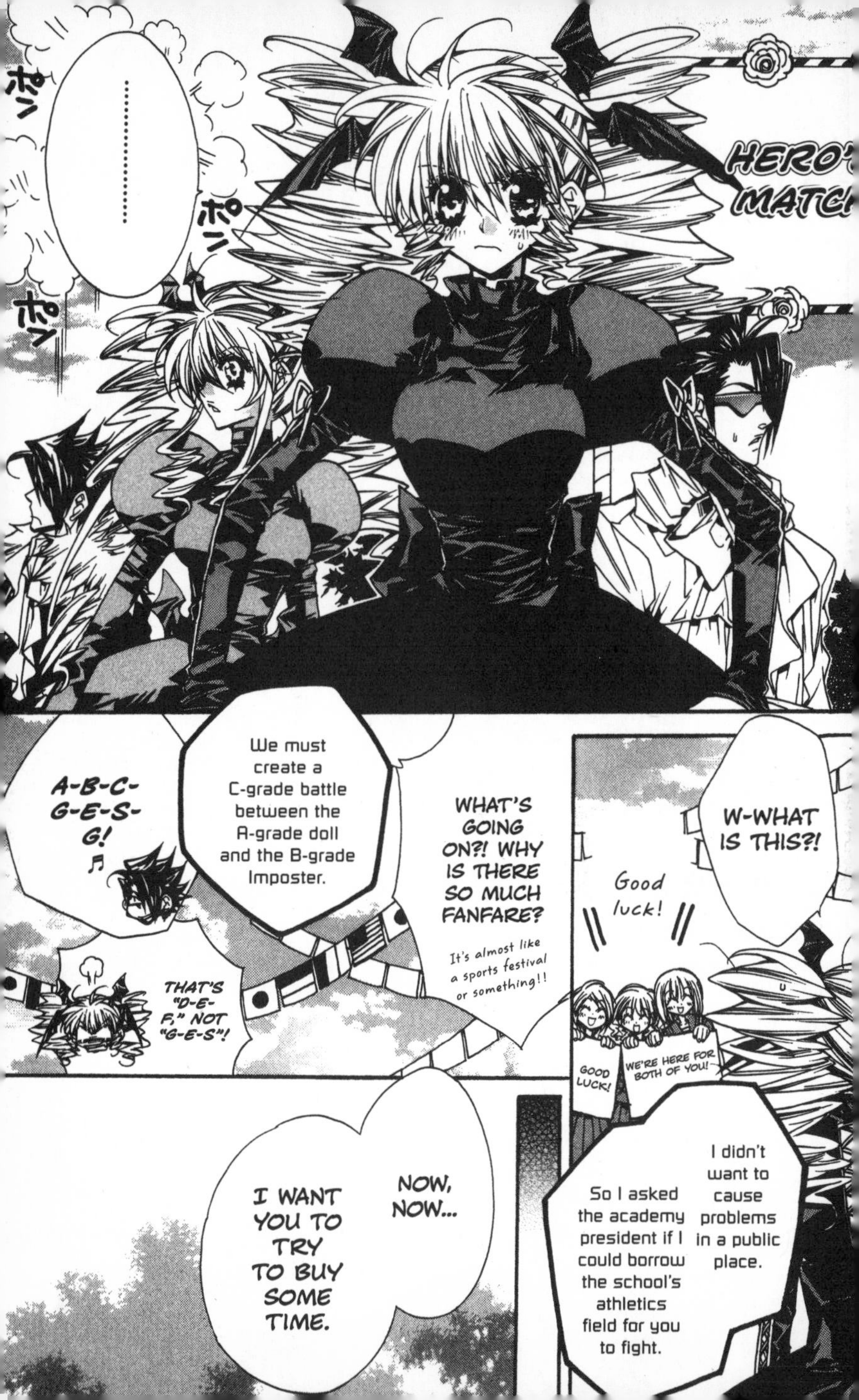

HERO'
MATC
ポン
ポン
ポン
......
W-WHAT IS THIS?!
Good luck!
WE'RE HERE FOR BOTH OF YOU!
GOOD LUCK!
WHAT'S GOING ON?! WHY IS THERE SO MUCH FANFARE?
It's almost like a sports festival or something!!
We must create a C-grade battle between the A-grade doll and the B-grade Imposter.
A-B-C-G-E-S-G! ♪
THAT'S "D-E-F," NOT "G-E-S"!
I didn't want to cause problems in a public place.
So I asked the academy president if I could borrow the school's athletics field for you to fight.
NOW, NOW...
I WANT YOU TO TRY TO BUY SOME TIME.

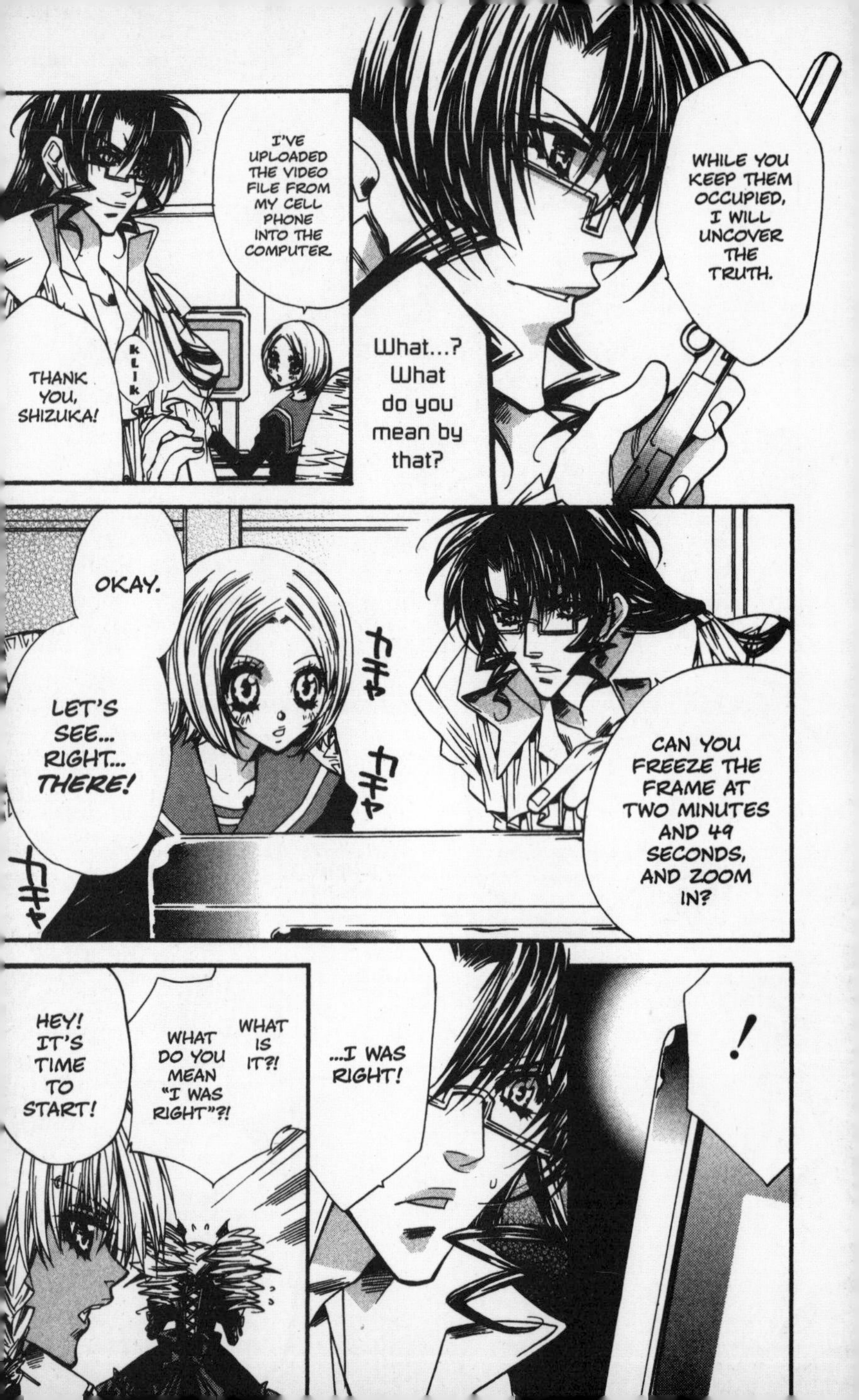
WHILE YOU KEEP THEM OCCUPIED, I WILL UNCOVER THE TRUTH.
What...? What do you mean by that?
I'VE UPLOADED THE VIDEO FILE FROM MY CELL PHONE INTO THE COMPUTER.
KLIK
THANK YOU, SHIZUKA!
CAN YOU FREEZE THE FRAME AT TWO MINUTES AND 49 SECONDS, AND ZOOM IN?
カチャ
カチャ
OKAY.
LET'S SEE... RIGHT... THERE!
カチャ
!
...I WAS RIGHT!
WHAT IS IT?!
WHAT DO YOU MEAN "I WAS RIGHT"?!
HEY! IT'S TIME TO START!

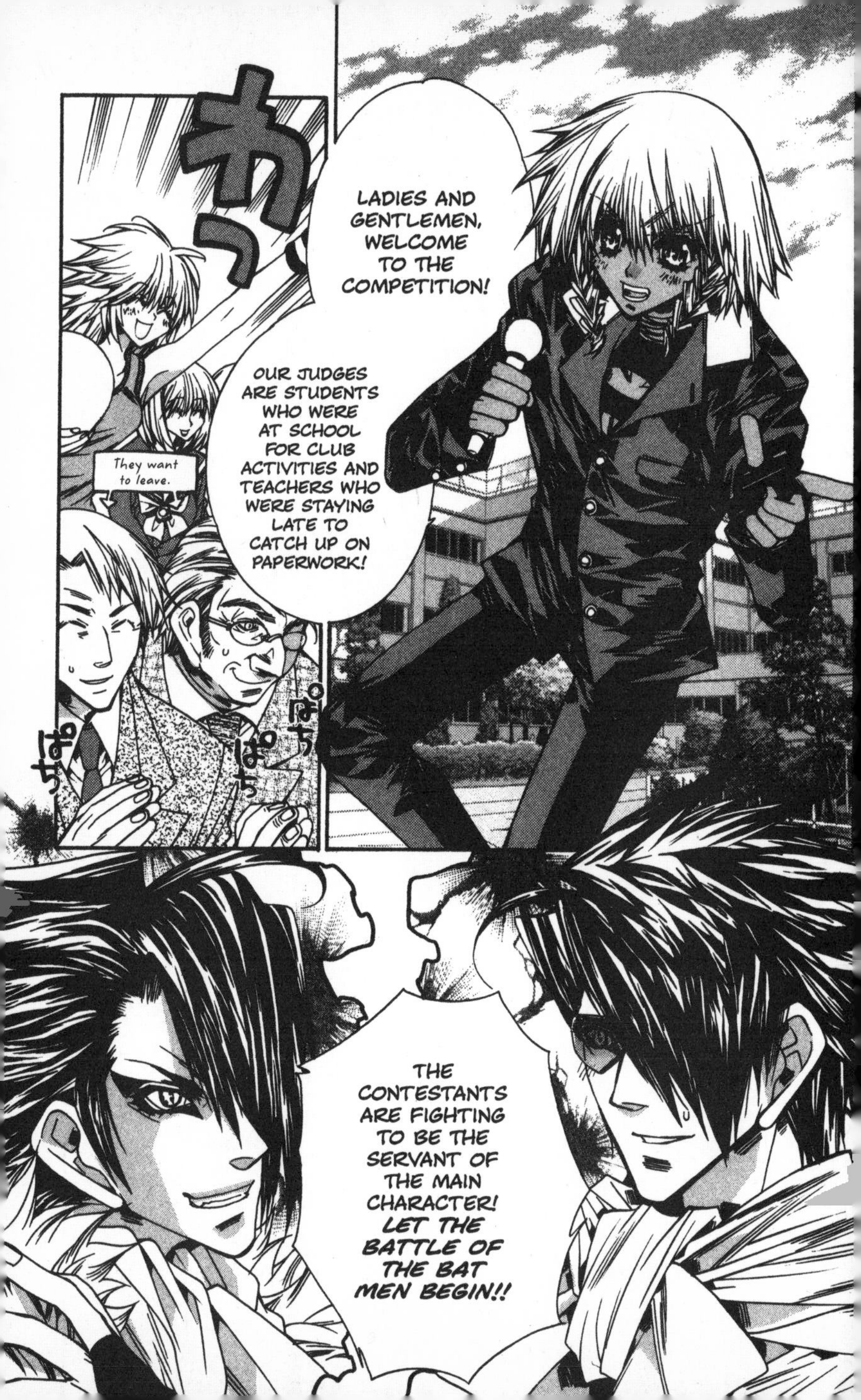
LADIES AND GENTLEMEN, WELCOME TO THE COMPETITION!
OUR JUDGES ARE STUDENTS WHO WERE AT SCHOOL FOR CLUB ACTIVITIES AND TEACHERS WHO WERE STAYING LATE TO CATCH UP ON PAPERWORK!
わっ
They want to leave.
ぱちぱち
ぱちぱち
THE CONTESTANTS ARE FIGHTING TO BE THE SERVANT OF THE MAIN CHARACTER! *LET THE BATTLE OF THE BAT MEN BEGIN!!*

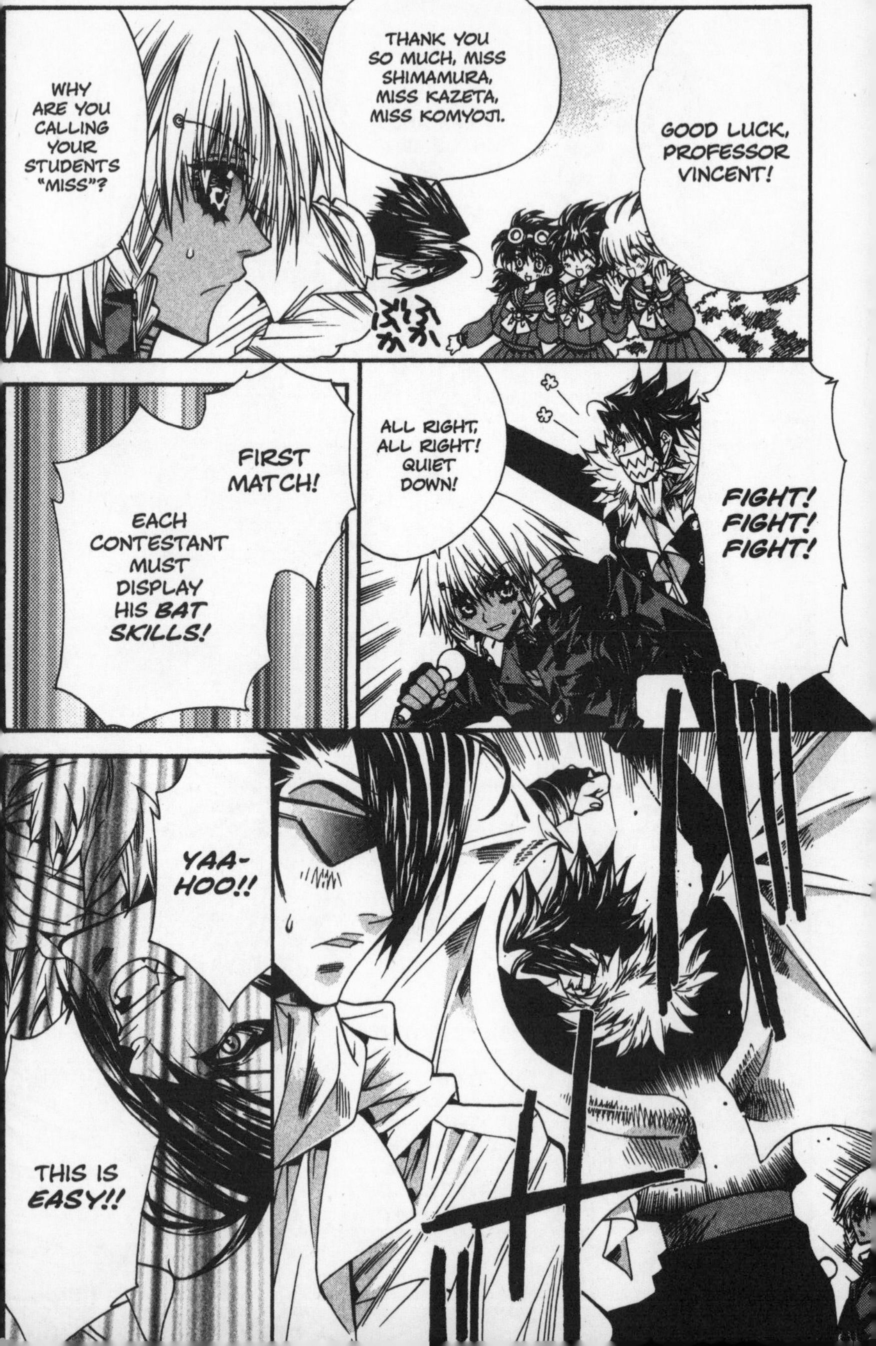
GOOD LUCK, PROFESSOR VINCENT!
THANK YOU SO MUCH, MISS SHIMAMURA, MISS KAZETA, MISS KOMYOJI.
WHY ARE YOU CALLING YOUR STUDENTS "MISS"?
FIGHT! FIGHT! FIGHT!
ALL RIGHT, ALL RIGHT! QUIET DOWN!
FIRST MATCH!
EACH CONTESTANT MUST DISPLAY HIS BAT SKILLS!
YAA-HOO!!
THIS IS EASY!!

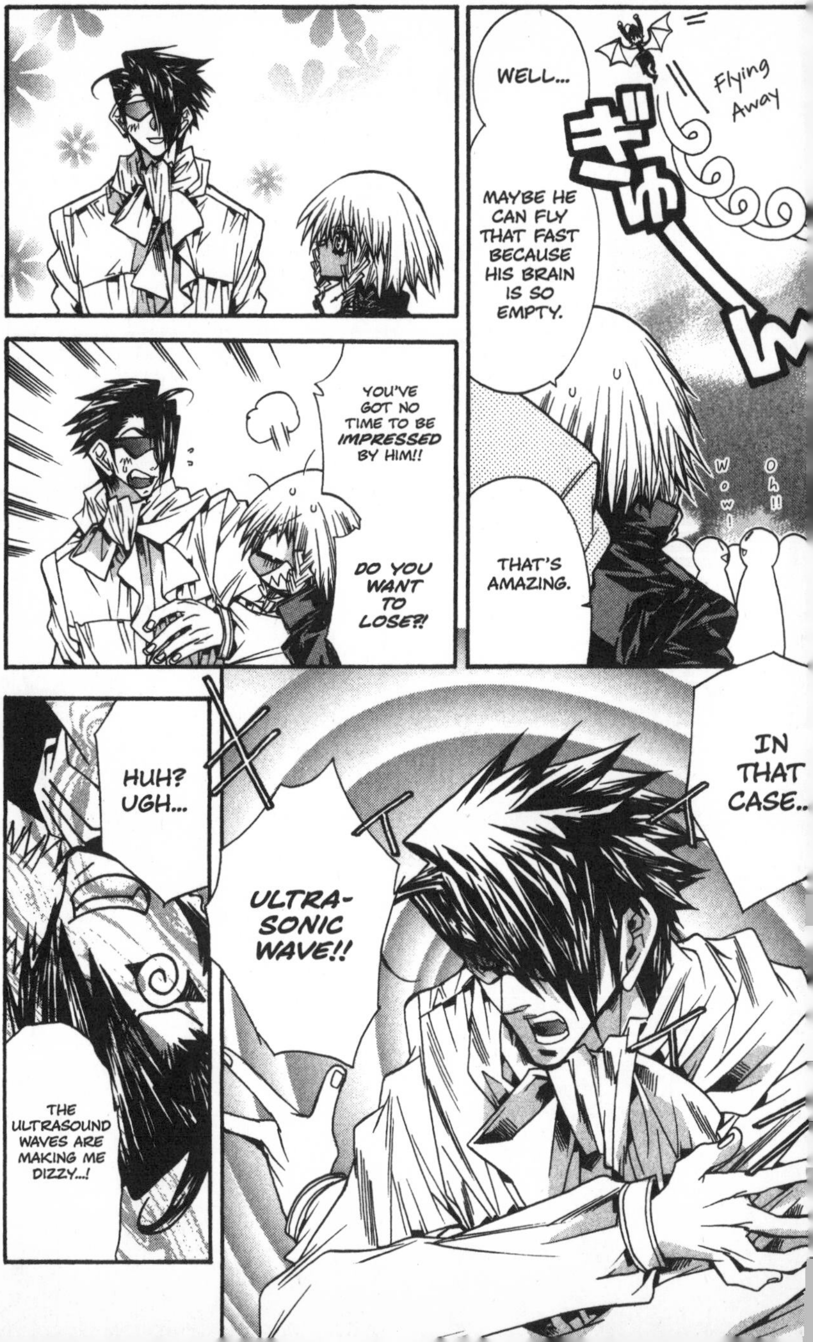
WELL...
Flying Away
ぎゅーん
MAYBE HE CAN FLY THAT FAST BECAUSE HIS BRAIN IS SO EMPTY.
Oh!!
Wow!
THAT'S AMAZING.
YOU'VE GOT NO TIME TO BE *IMPRESSED* BY HIM!!
DO YOU WANT TO LOSE?!
IN THAT CASE...
ULTRA-SONIC WAVE!!
HUH? UGH...
THE ULTRASOUND WAVES ARE MAKING ME DIZZY...!

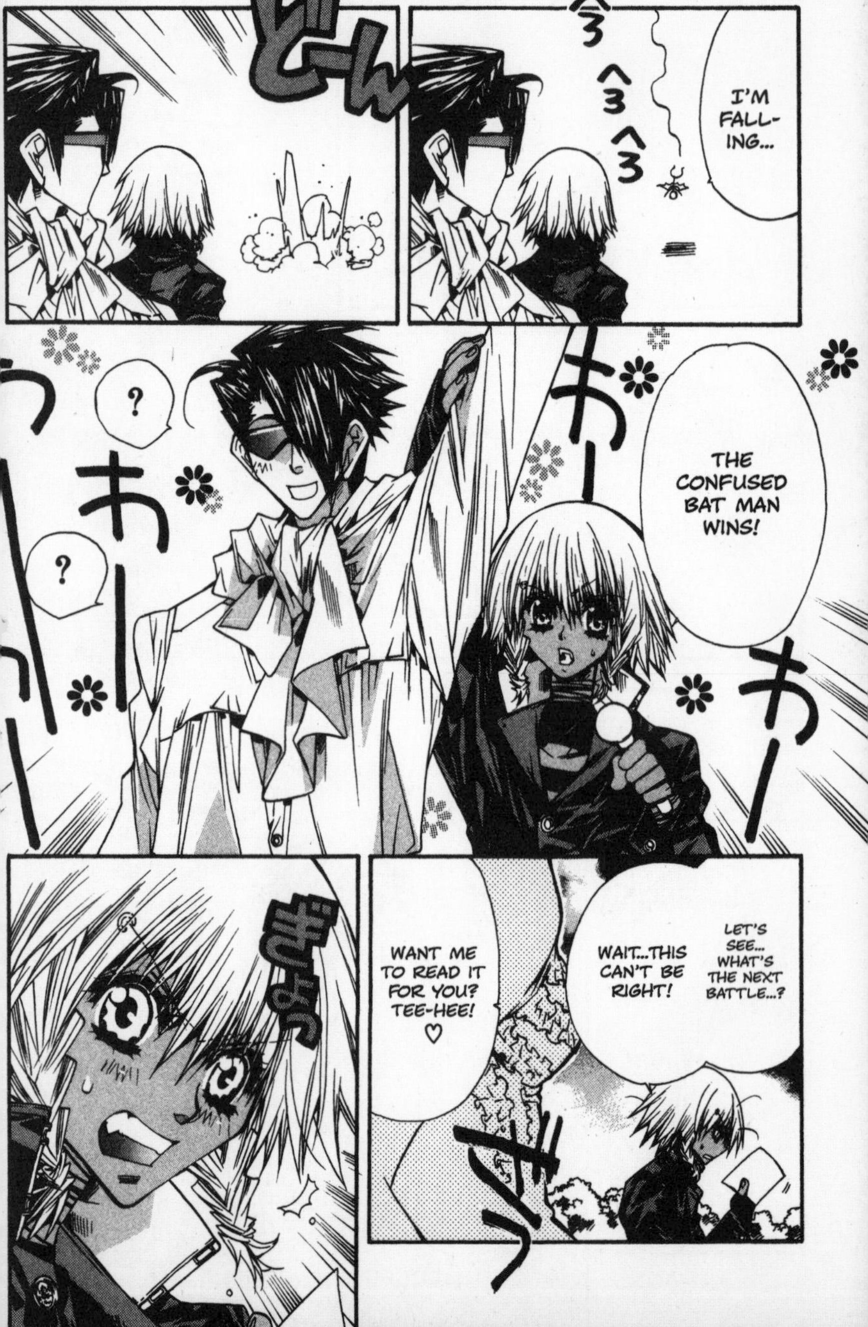
I'M FALLING...
どーん
THE CONFUSED BAT MAN WINS!
?
?
LET'S SEE... WHAT'S THE NEXT BATTLE...?
WAIT...THIS CAN'T BE RIGHT!
WANT ME TO READ IT FOR YOU? TEE-HEE! ♡
ぎょっ

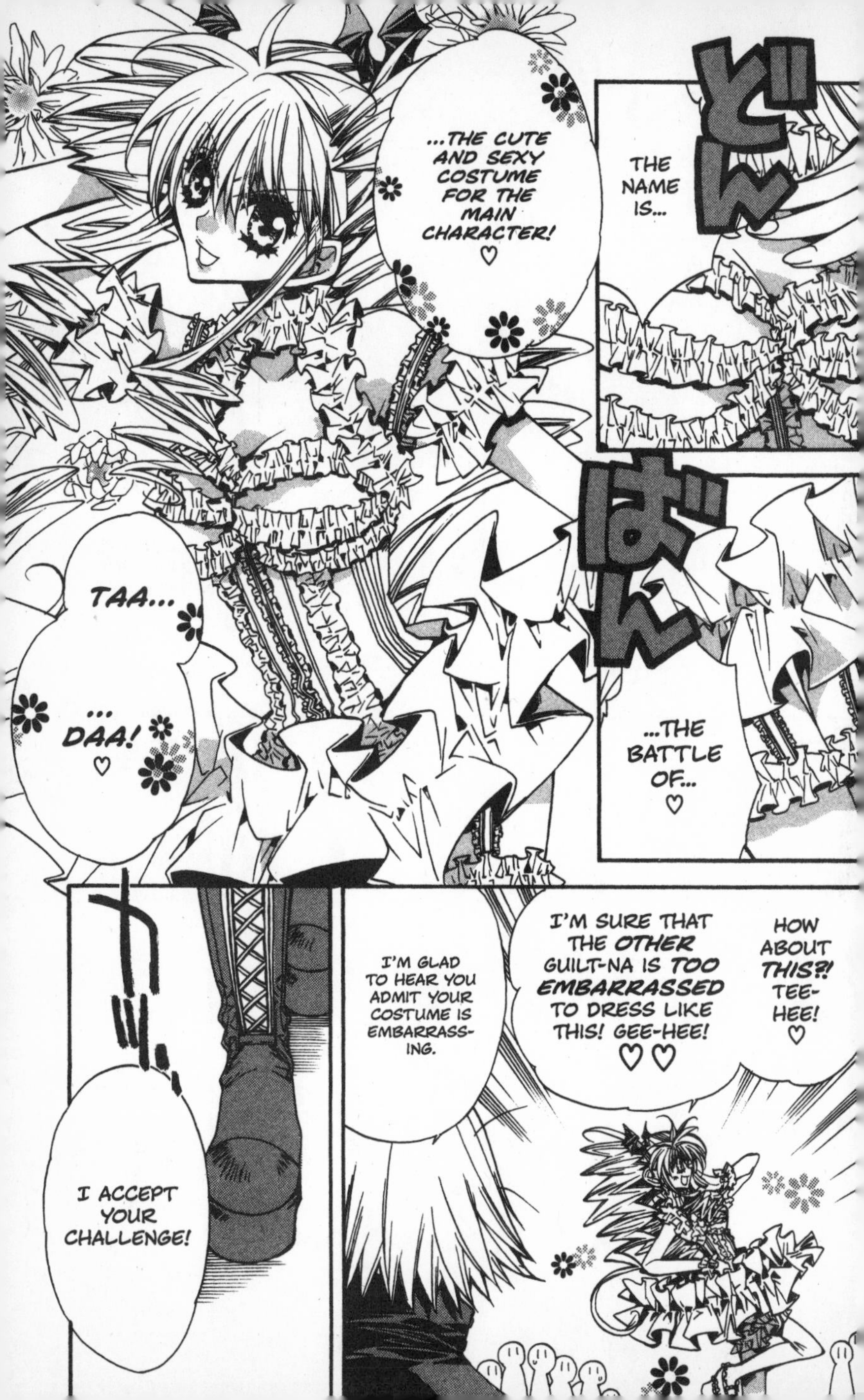
どん
THE NAME IS...
ばん
...THE BATTLE OF... ♡
...THE CUTE AND SEXY COSTUME FOR THE MAIN CHARACTER! ♡
TAA... ...DAA! ♡
HOW ABOUT THIS?! TEE-HEE! ♡
I'M SURE THAT THE OTHER GUILT-NA IS TOO EMBARRASSED TO DRESS LIKE THIS! GEE-HEE! ♡♡
I'M GLAD TO HEAR YOU ADMIT YOUR COSTUME IS EMBARRASS-ING.
I ACCEPT YOUR CHALLENGE!

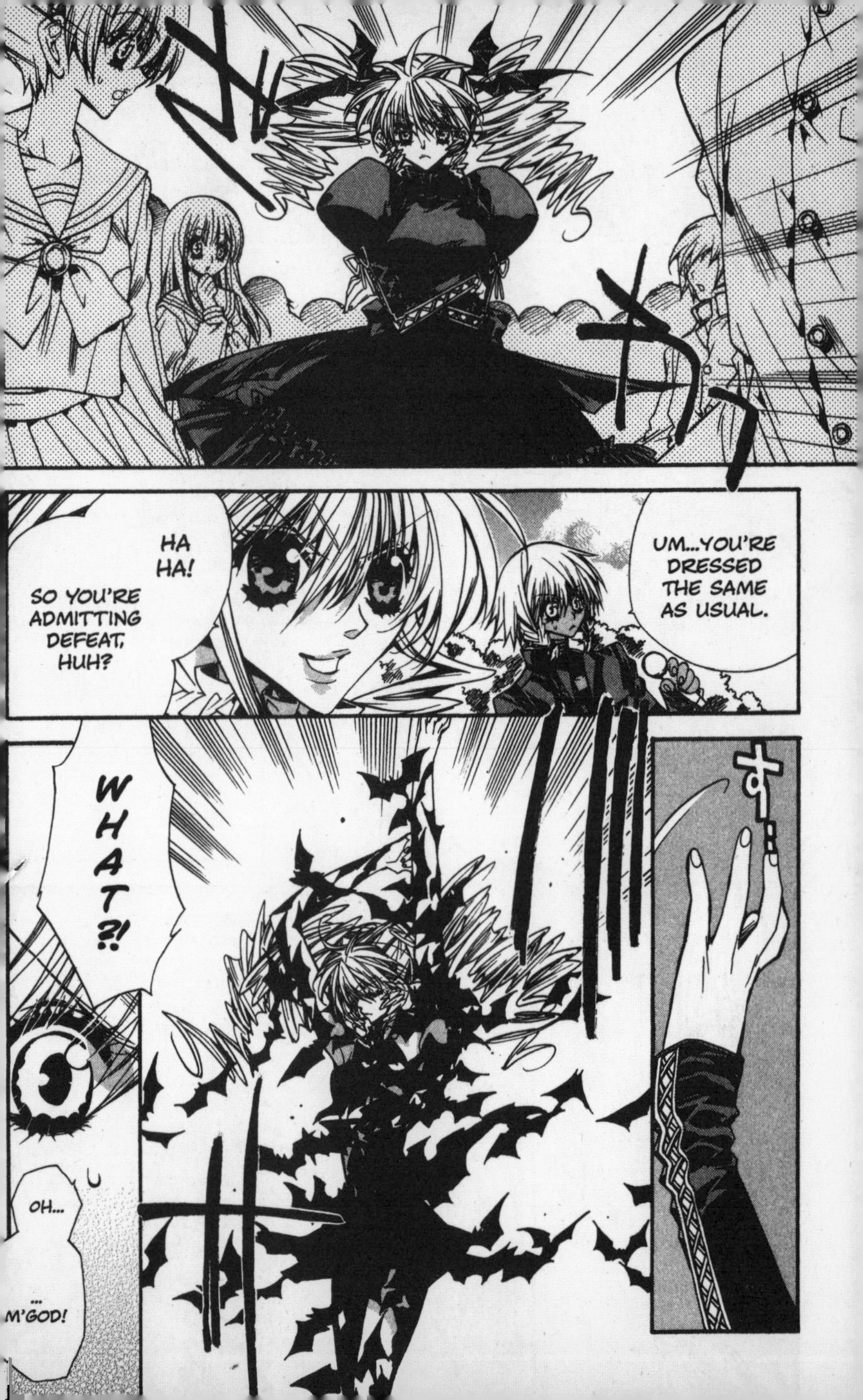
UM...YOU'RE DRESSED THE SAME AS USUAL.
HA HA!
SO YOU'RE ADMITTING DEFEAT, HUH?
WHAT?!
OH...
...M'GOD!

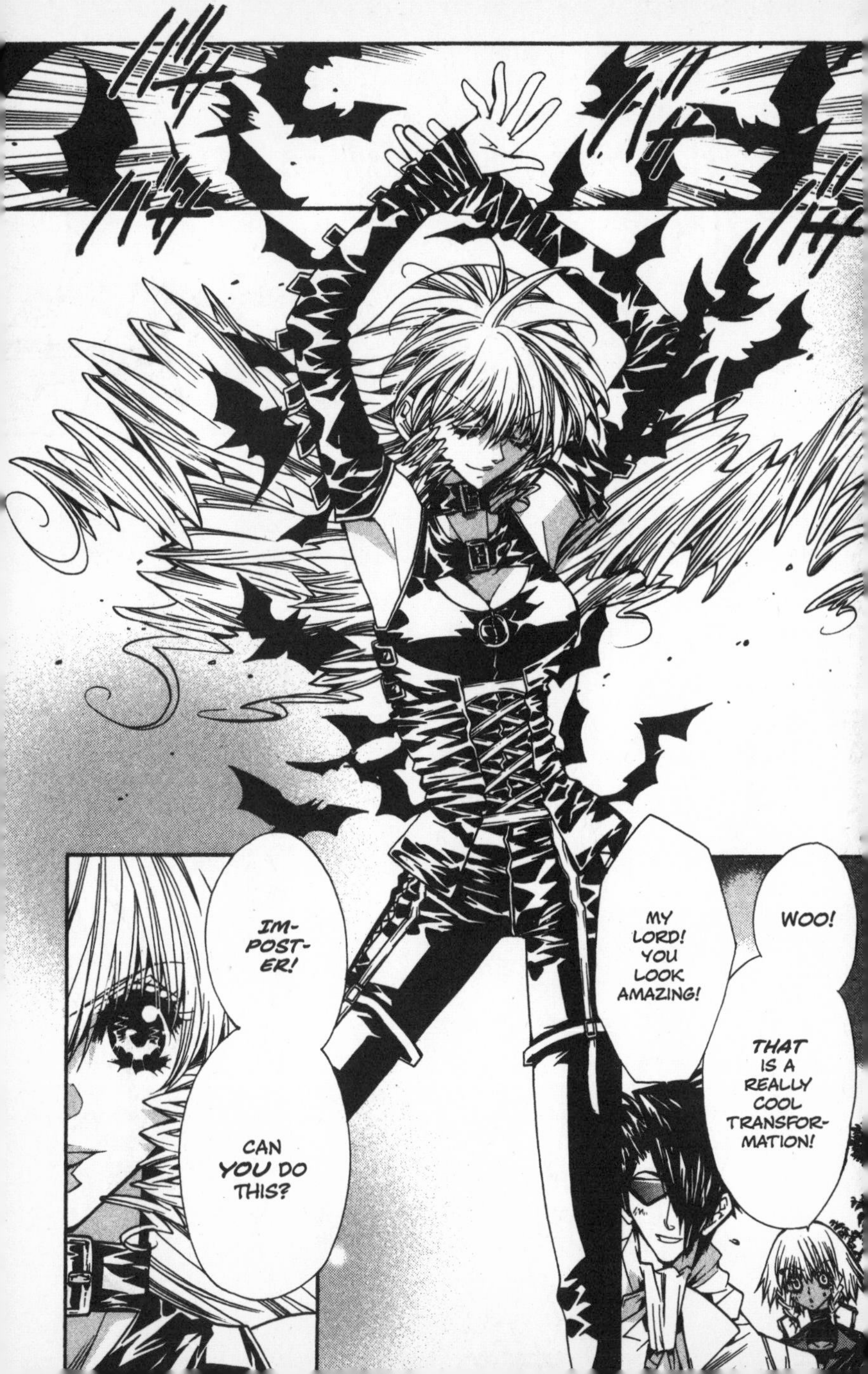
IM-POSTER!
CAN YOU DO THIS?
WOO!
THAT IS A REALLY COOL TRANSFORMATION!
MY LORD! YOU LOOK AMAZING!

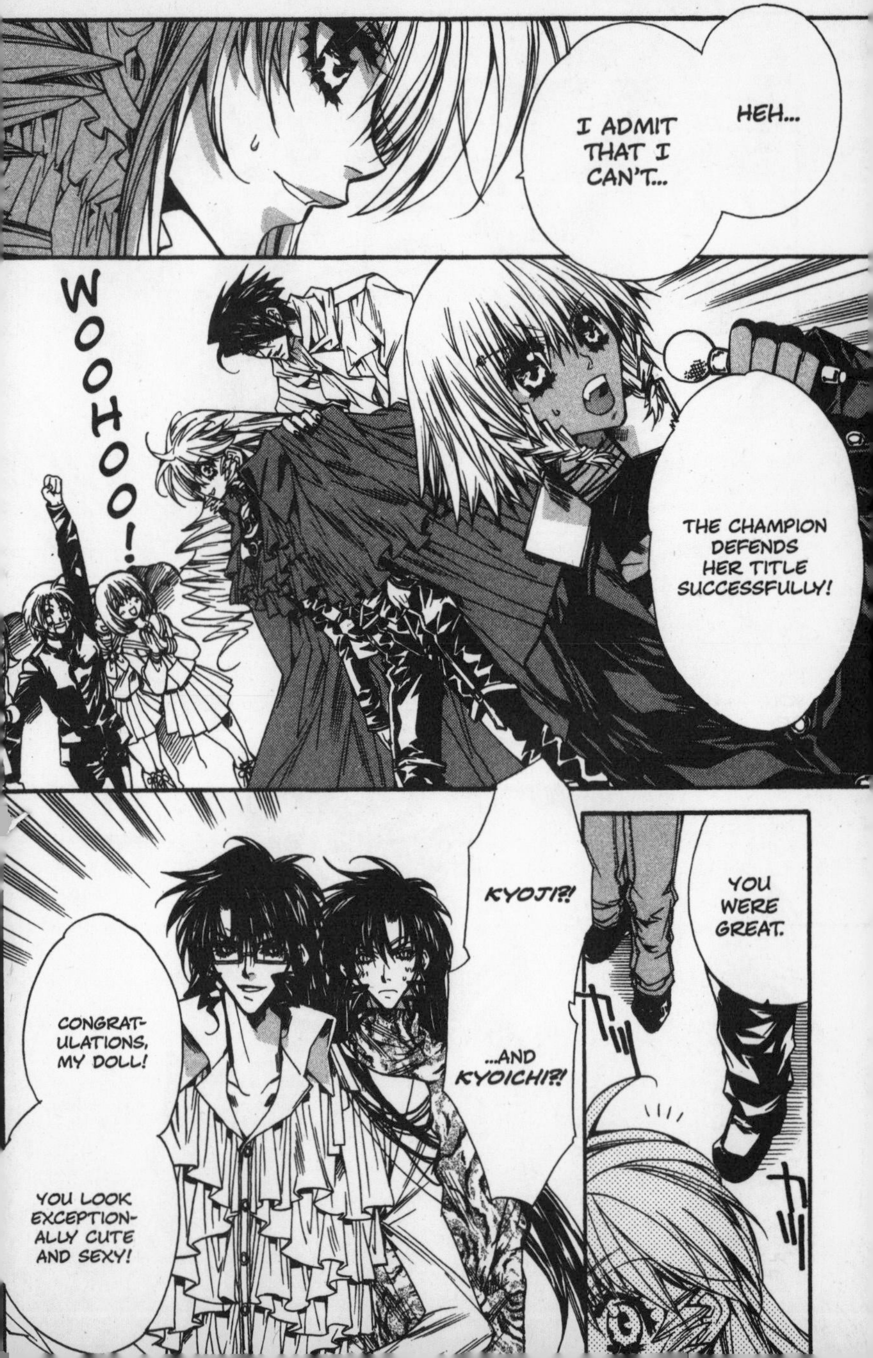
HEH...
I ADMIT THAT I CAN'T...
THE CHAMPION DEFENDS HER TITLE SUCCESSFULLY!
WOOHOO!
YOU WERE GREAT.
KYOJI?!
...AND KYOICHI?!
CONGRAT-ULATIONS, MY DOLL!
YOU LOOK EXCEPTION-ALLY CUTE AND SEXY!

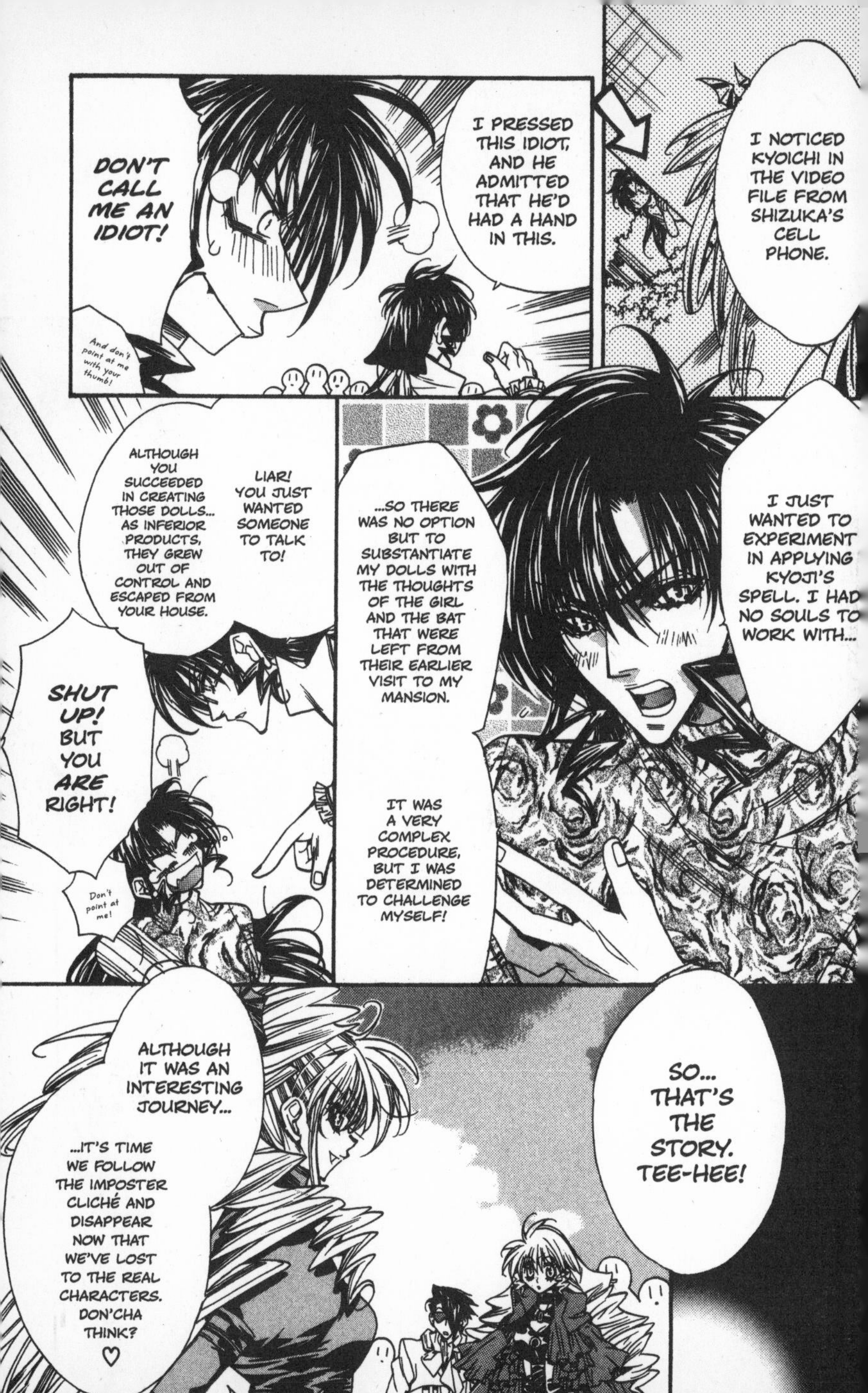
I NOTICED KYOICHI IN THE VIDEO FILE FROM SHIZUKA'S CELL PHONE.
I PRESSED THIS IDIOT, AND HE ADMITTED THAT HE'D HAD A HAND IN THIS.
DON'T CALL ME AN IDIOT!
And don't point at me with your thumb!
I JUST WANTED TO EXPERIMENT IN APPLYING KYOJI'S SPELL. I HAD NO SOULS TO WORK WITH...
...SO THERE WAS NO OPTION BUT TO SUBSTANTIATE MY DOLLS WITH THE THOUGHTS OF THE GIRL AND THE BAT THAT WERE LEFT FROM THEIR EARLIER VISIT TO MY MANSION.
IT WAS A VERY COMPLEX PROCEDURE, BUT I WAS DETERMINED TO CHALLENGE MYSELF!
LIAR! YOU JUST WANTED SOMEONE TO TALK TO!
ALTHOUGH YOU SUCCEEDED IN CREATING THOSE DOLLS... AS INFERIOR PRODUCTS, THEY GREW OUT OF CONTROL AND ESCAPED FROM YOUR HOUSE.
SHUT UP! BUT YOU ARE RIGHT!
Don't point at me!
SO... THAT'S THE STORY. TEE-HEE!
ALTHOUGH IT WAS AN INTERESTING JOURNEY...
...IT'S TIME WE FOLLOW THE IMPOSTER CLICHÉ AND DISAPPEAR NOW THAT WE'VE LOST TO THE REAL CHARACTERS. DON'CHA THINK? ♡

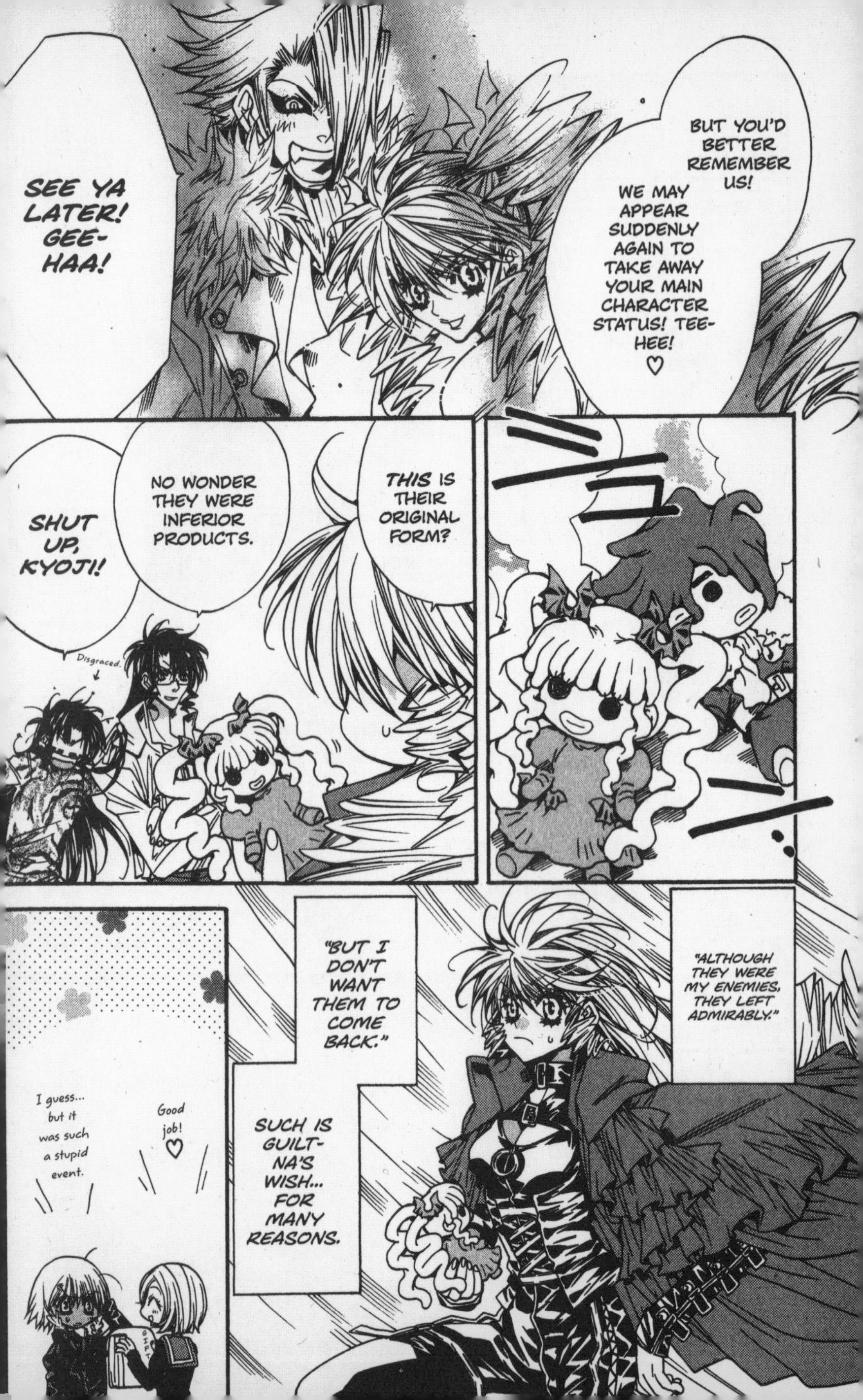

BUT YOU'D BETTER REMEMBER US!
WE MAY APPEAR SUDDENLY AGAIN TO TAKE AWAY YOUR MAIN CHARACTER STATUS! TEE-HEE! ♡
SEE YA LATER! GEE-HAA!
THIS IS THEIR ORIGINAL FORM?
NO WONDER THEY WERE INFERIOR PRODUCTS.
SHUT UP, KYOJI!
Disgraced.
"ALTHOUGH THEY WERE MY ENEMIES, THEY LEFT ADMIRABLY."
"BUT I DON'T WANT THEM TO COME BACK."
SUCH IS GUILT-NA'S WISH... FOR MANY REASONS.
Good job! ♡
I guess... but it was such a stupid event.
GIFT

BONUS COMIC STRI

VAMPIRE DOLL REFLECTIONS

Fake to Fake

Q.
WHAT WOULD HAPPEN IF THE IMPOSTER CHARACTER TRANSFORMED?
I AM KNOWN AS...THE LORD OF VAMPIRES...
GUINO LENAZAN!
じゃーん
HIS NAME MAY BE STUPID, BUT HIS LOOKS CERTAINLY ARE ABOVE B-GRADE.
MY COSTUME IS MADE OF PURE SATIN!
テッカテッカ
NOW YOU LOOK LIKE A FAKE!!

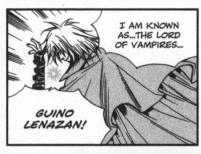

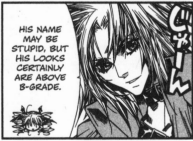

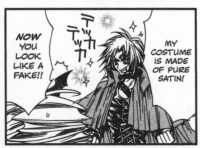

GUILTNA "FAKE" DOLL

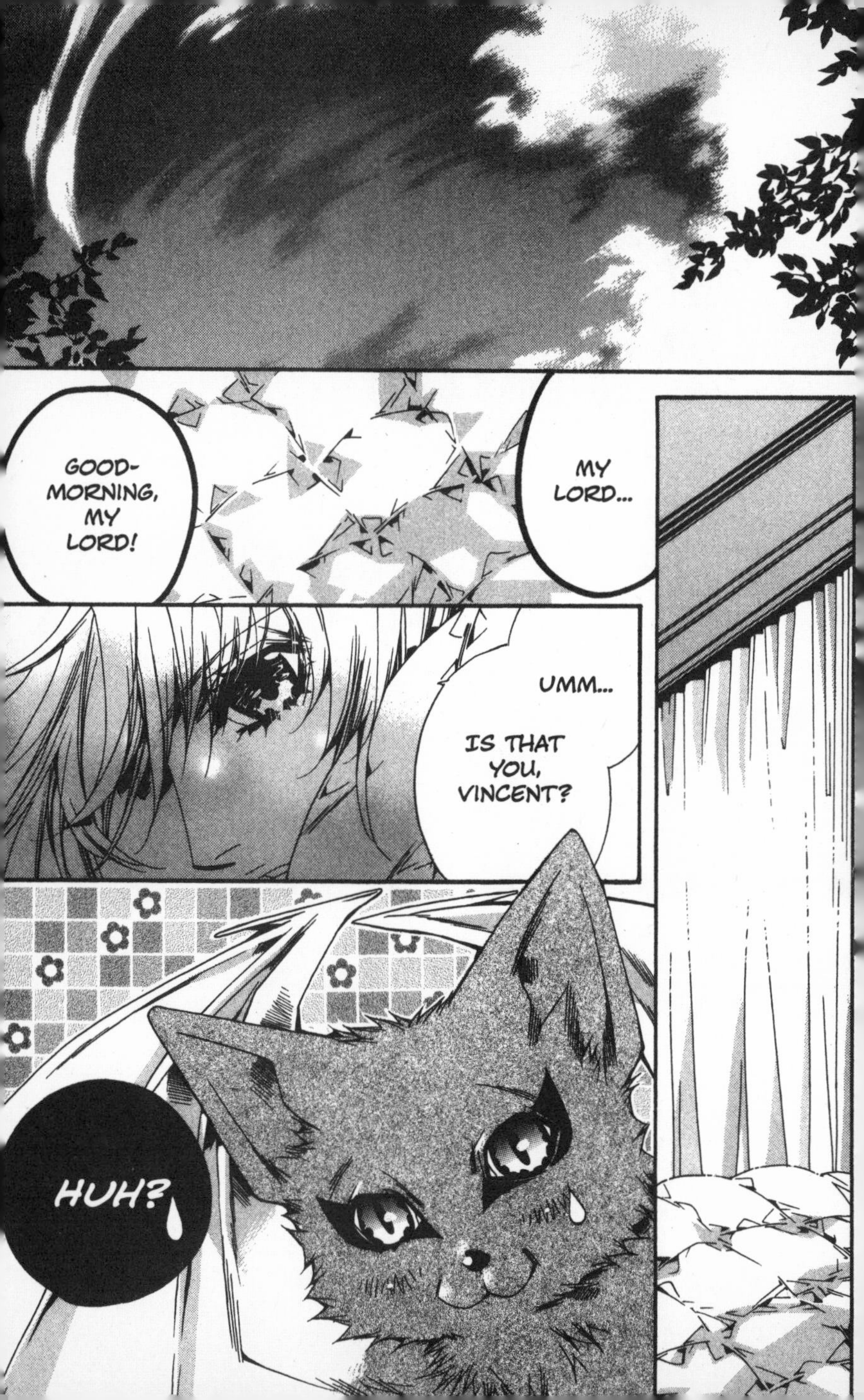
MY LORD...
GOOD-MORNING, MY LORD!
UMM...
IS THAT YOU, VINCENT?
HUH?

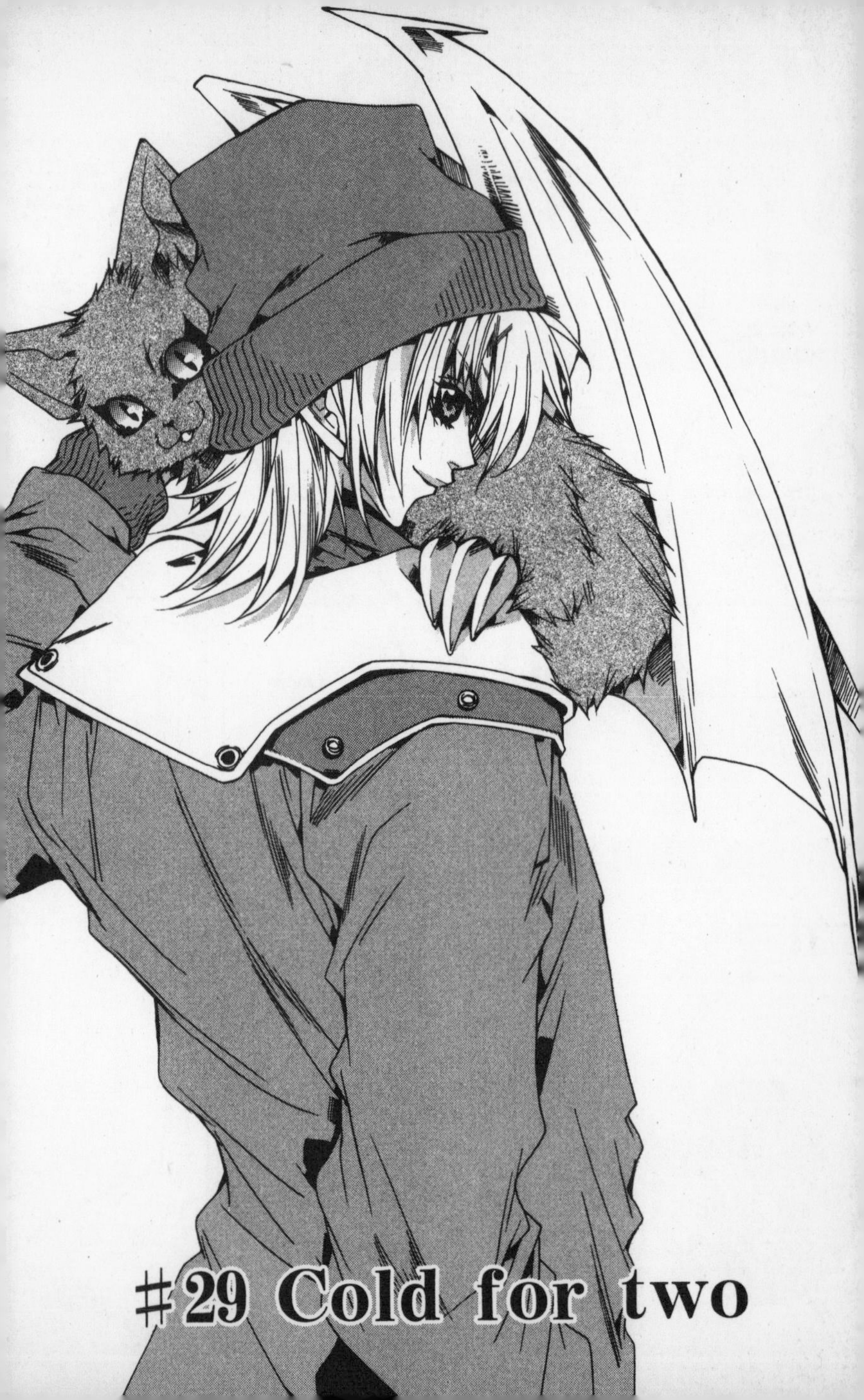

#29 Cold for two

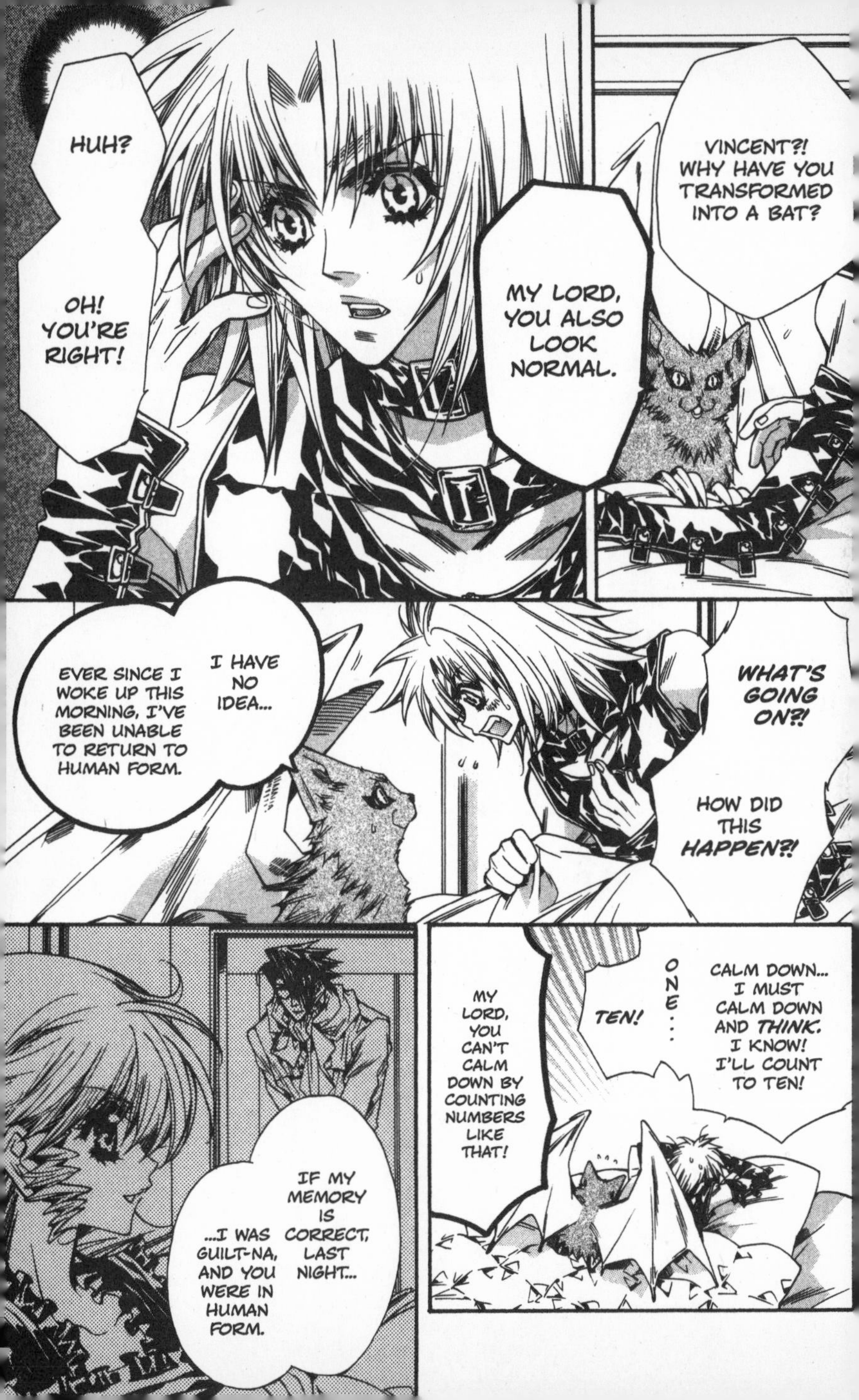
VINCENT?! WHY HAVE YOU TRANSFORMED INTO A BAT?
MY LORD, YOU ALSO LOOK NORMAL.
HUH?
OH! YOU'RE RIGHT!
WHAT'S GOING ON?!
HOW DID THIS HAPPEN?!
I HAVE NO IDEA...
EVER SINCE I WOKE UP THIS MORNING, I'VE BEEN UNABLE TO RETURN TO HUMAN FORM.
CALM DOWN... I MUST CALM DOWN AND THINK. I KNOW! I'LL COUNT TO TEN!
ONE...
TEN!
MY LORD, YOU CAN'T CALM DOWN BY COUNTING NUMBERS LIKE THAT!
IF MY MEMORY IS CORRECT, LAST NIGHT...
...I WAS GUILT-NA, AND YOU WERE IN HUMAN FORM.

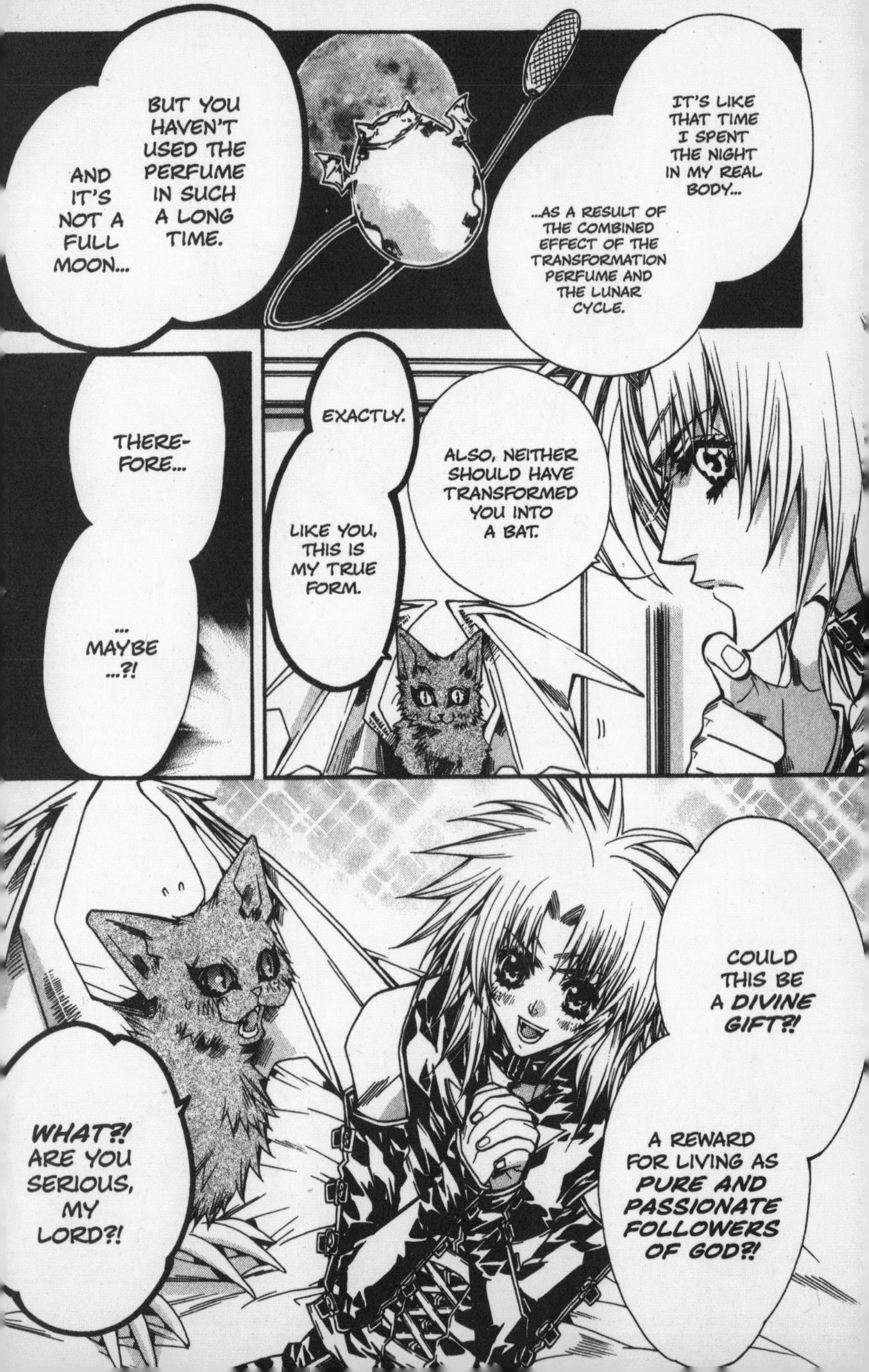

IT'S LIKE THAT TIME I SPENT THE NIGHT IN MY REAL BODY...
...AS A RESULT OF THE COMBINED EFFECT OF THE TRANSFORMATION PERFUME AND THE LUNAR CYCLE.
BUT YOU HAVEN'T USED THE PERFUME IN SUCH A LONG TIME.
AND IT'S NOT A FULL MOON...
ALSO, NEITHER SHOULD HAVE TRANSFORMED YOU INTO A BAT.
EXACTLY.
LIKE YOU, THIS IS MY TRUE FORM.
THERE-FORE...
...MAYBE...?!
COULD THIS BE A *DIVINE GIFT?!*
A REWARD FOR LIVING AS *PURE AND PASSIONATE FOLLOWERS OF GOD?!*
WHAT?! ARE YOU SERIOUS, MY LORD?!

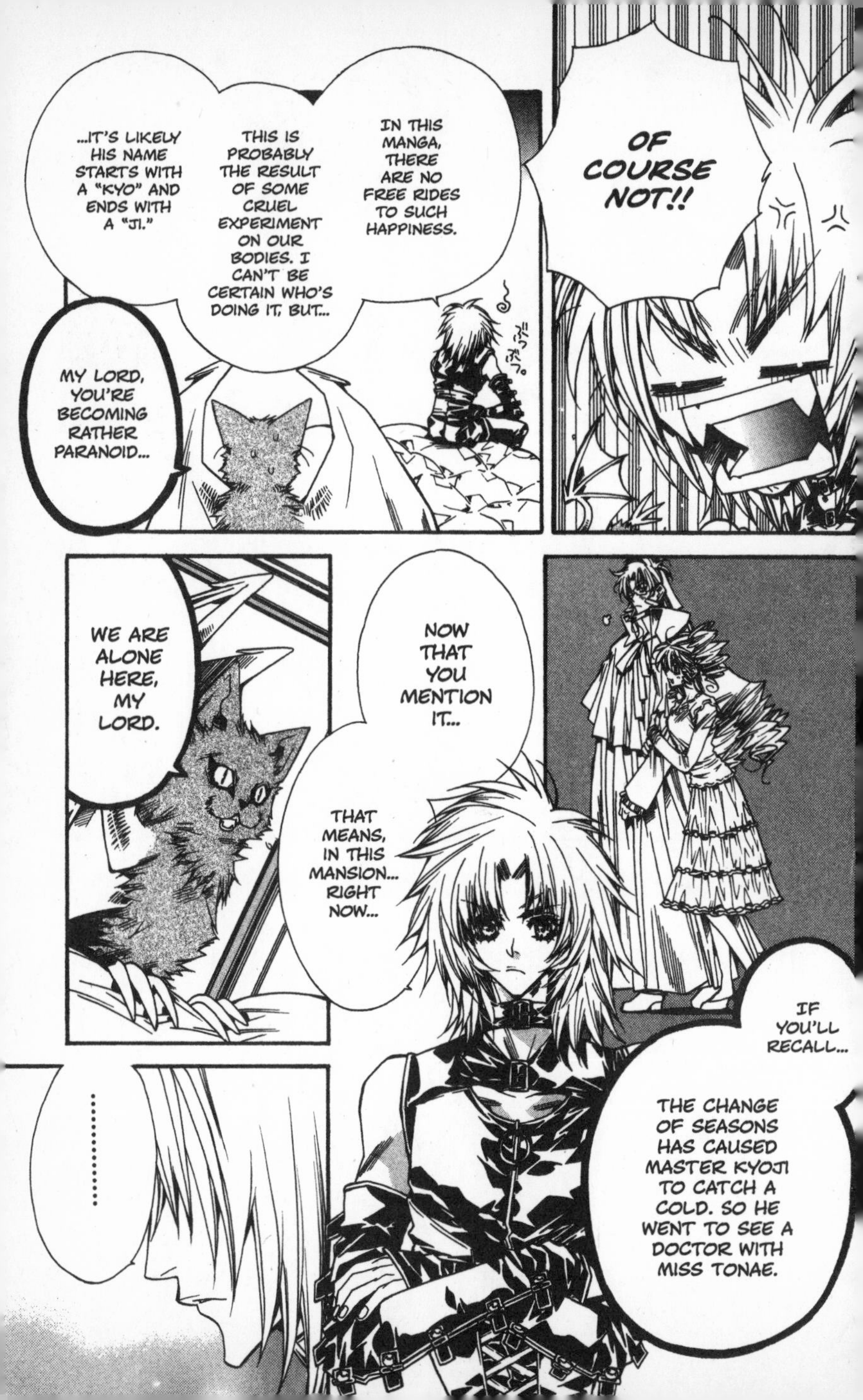
OF COURSE NOT!!
IN THIS MANGA, THERE ARE NO FREE RIDES TO SUCH HAPPINESS.
THIS IS PROBABLY THE RESULT OF SOME CRUEL EXPERIMENT ON OUR BODIES. I CAN'T BE CERTAIN WHO'S DOING IT, BUT...
...IT'S LIKELY HIS NAME STARTS WITH A "KYO" AND ENDS WITH A "JI."
ぶつぶつ。
MY LORD, YOU'RE BECOMING RATHER PARANOID...
IF YOU'LL RECALL...
THE CHANGE OF SEASONS HAS CAUSED MASTER KYOJI TO CATCH A COLD. SO HE WENT TO SEE A DOCTOR WITH MISS TONAE.
NOW THAT YOU MENTION IT...
THAT MEANS, IN THIS MANSION... RIGHT NOW...
WE ARE ALONE HERE, MY LORD.
......

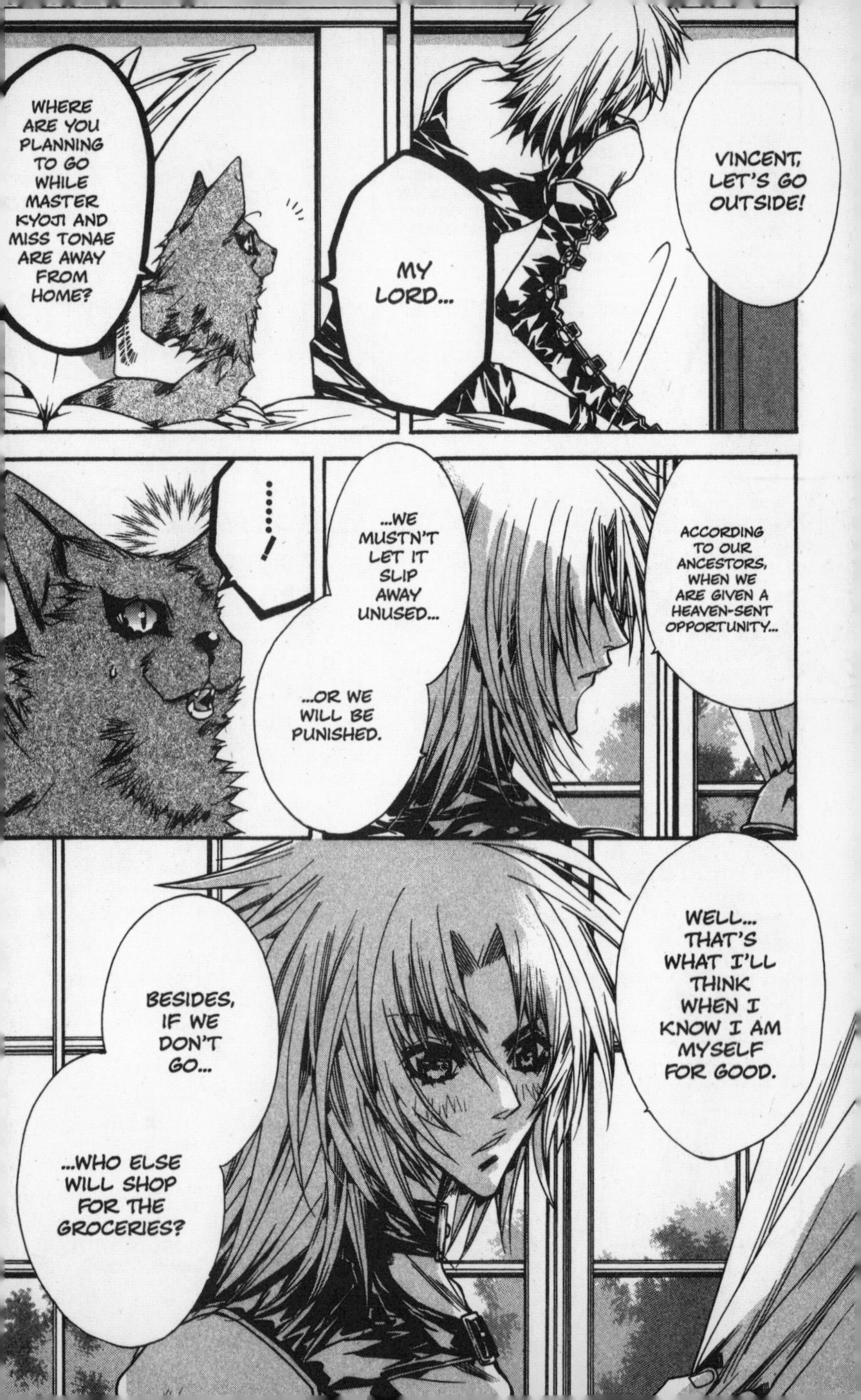
VINCENT, LET'S GO OUTSIDE!
MY LORD...
WHERE ARE YOU PLANNING TO GO WHILE MASTER KYOJI AND MISS TONAE ARE AWAY FROM HOME?
ACCORDING TO OUR ANCESTORS, WHEN WE ARE GIVEN A HEAVEN-SENT OPPORTUNITY...
...WE MUSTN'T LET IT SLIP AWAY UNUSED...
...OR WE WILL BE PUNISHED.
......!
WELL... THAT'S WHAT I'LL THINK WHEN I KNOW I AM MYSELF FOR GOOD.
BESIDES, IF WE DON'T GO...
...WHO ELSE WILL SHOP FOR THE GROCERIES?

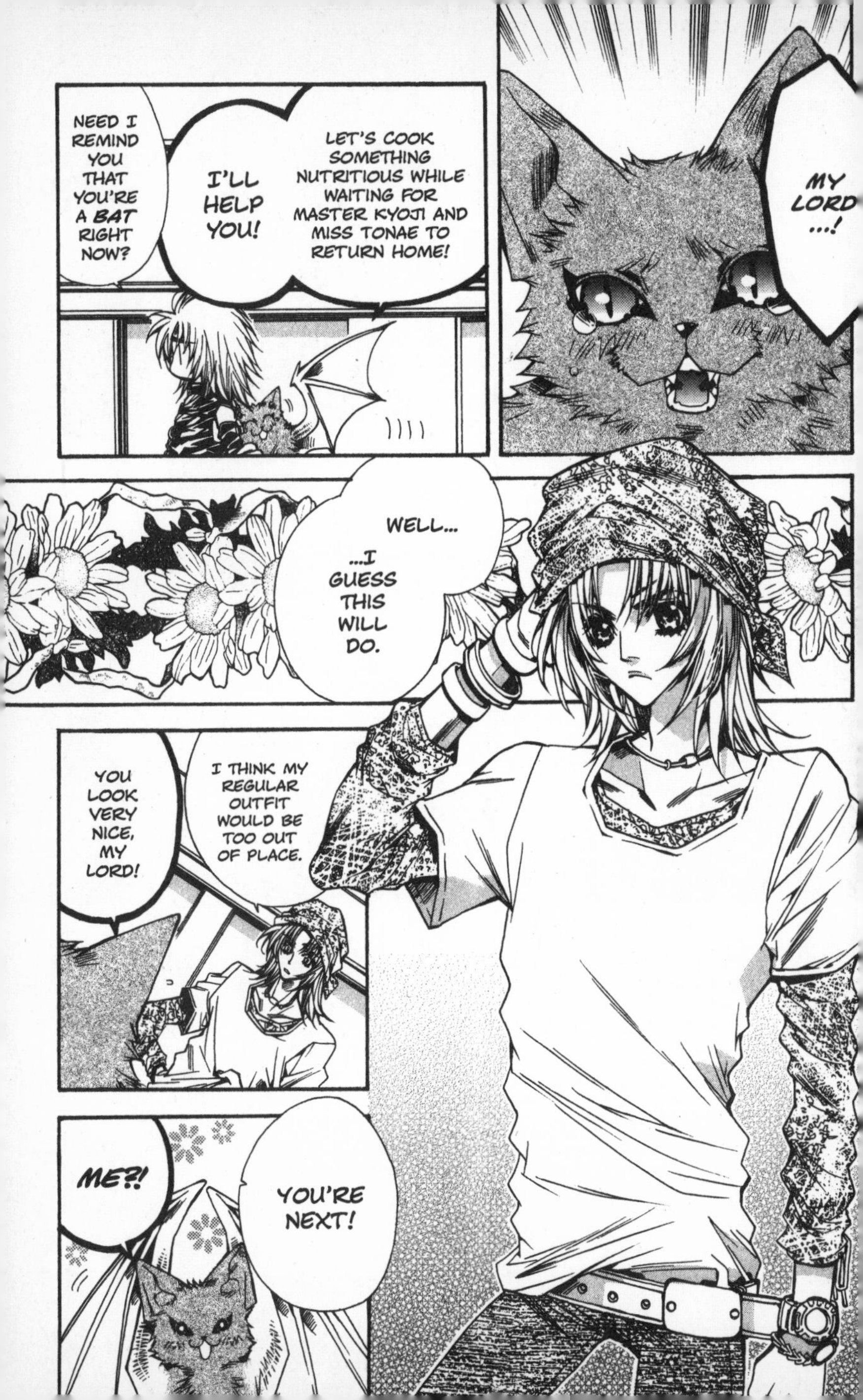
MY LORD ...!
LET'S COOK SOMETHING NUTRITIOUS WHILE WAITING FOR MASTER KYOJI AND MISS TONAE TO RETURN HOME!
I'LL HELP YOU!
NEED I REMIND YOU THAT YOU'RE A *BAT* RIGHT NOW?
WELL...
...I GUESS THIS WILL DO.
I THINK MY REGULAR OUTFIT WOULD BE TOO OUT OF PLACE.
YOU LOOK VERY NICE, MY LORD!
YOU'RE NEXT!
ME?!

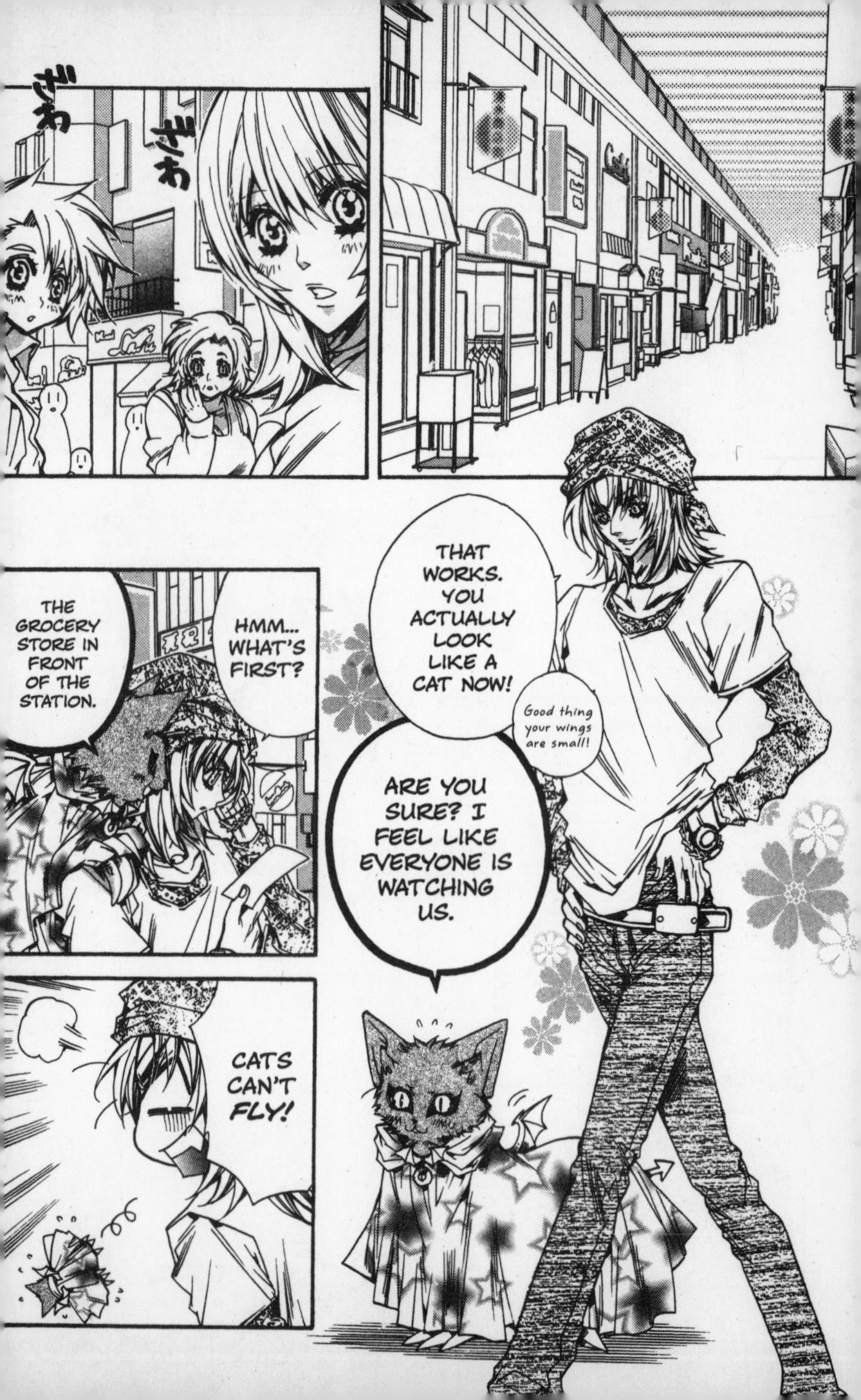
ざわ
ざわ
THAT WORKS. YOU ACTUALLY LOOK LIKE A CAT NOW!
Good thing your wings are small!
ARE YOU SURE? I FEEL LIKE EVERYONE IS WATCHING US.
HMM... WHAT'S FIRST?
THE GROCERY STORE IN FRONT OF THE STATION.
CATS CAN'T FLY!

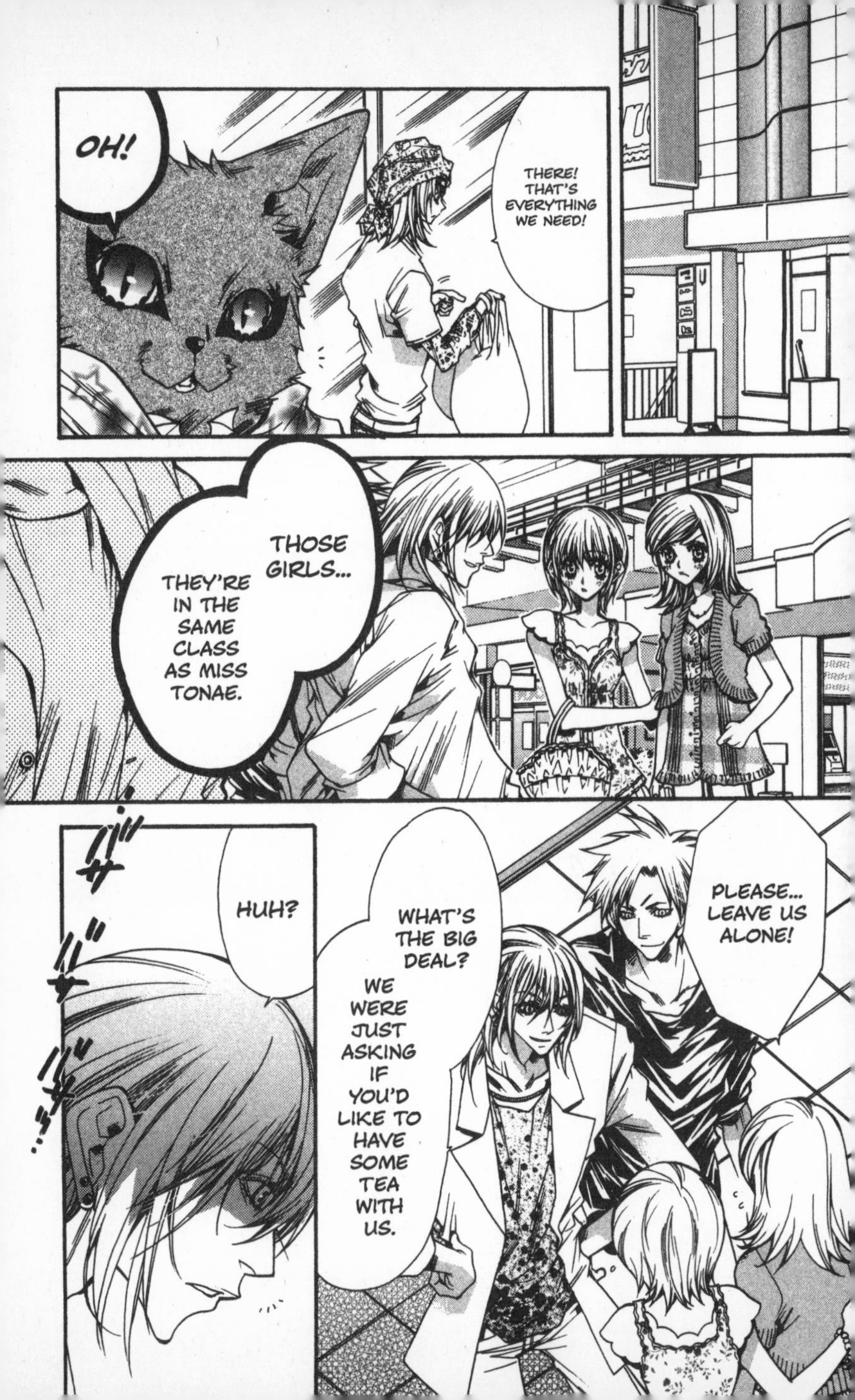
THERE! THAT'S EVERYTHING WE NEED!
OH!
THOSE GIRLS...
THEY'RE IN THE SAME CLASS AS MISS TONAE.
PLEASE... LEAVE US ALONE!
WHAT'S THE BIG DEAL?
WE WERE JUST ASKING IF YOU'D LIKE TO HAVE SOME TEA WITH US.
HUH?

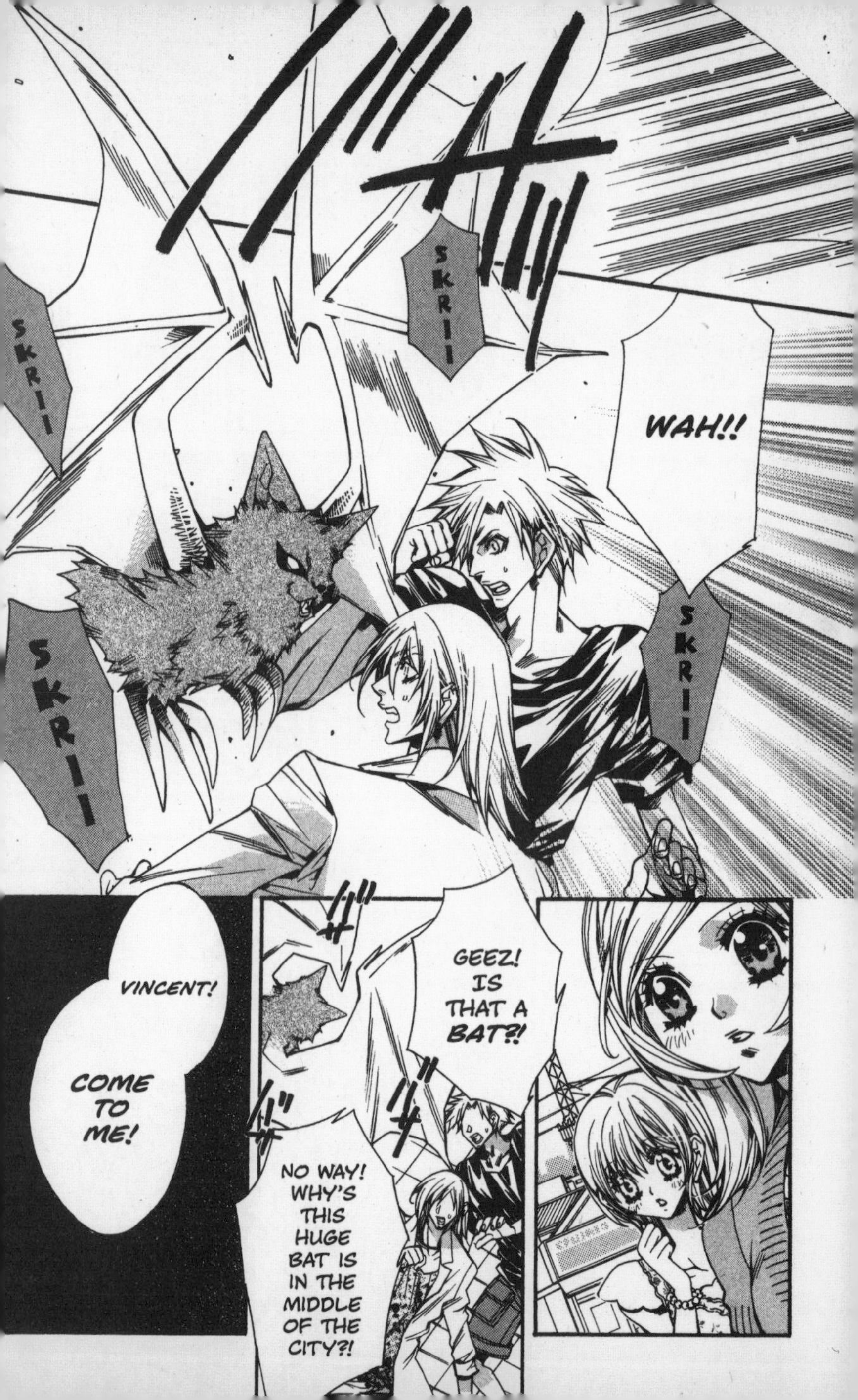
SKRII
WAH!!
SKRII
SKRII
SKRIII
GEEZ! IS THAT A BAT?!
NO WAY! WHY'S THIS HUGE BAT IS IN THE MIDDLE OF THE CITY?!
VINCENT!
COME TO ME!

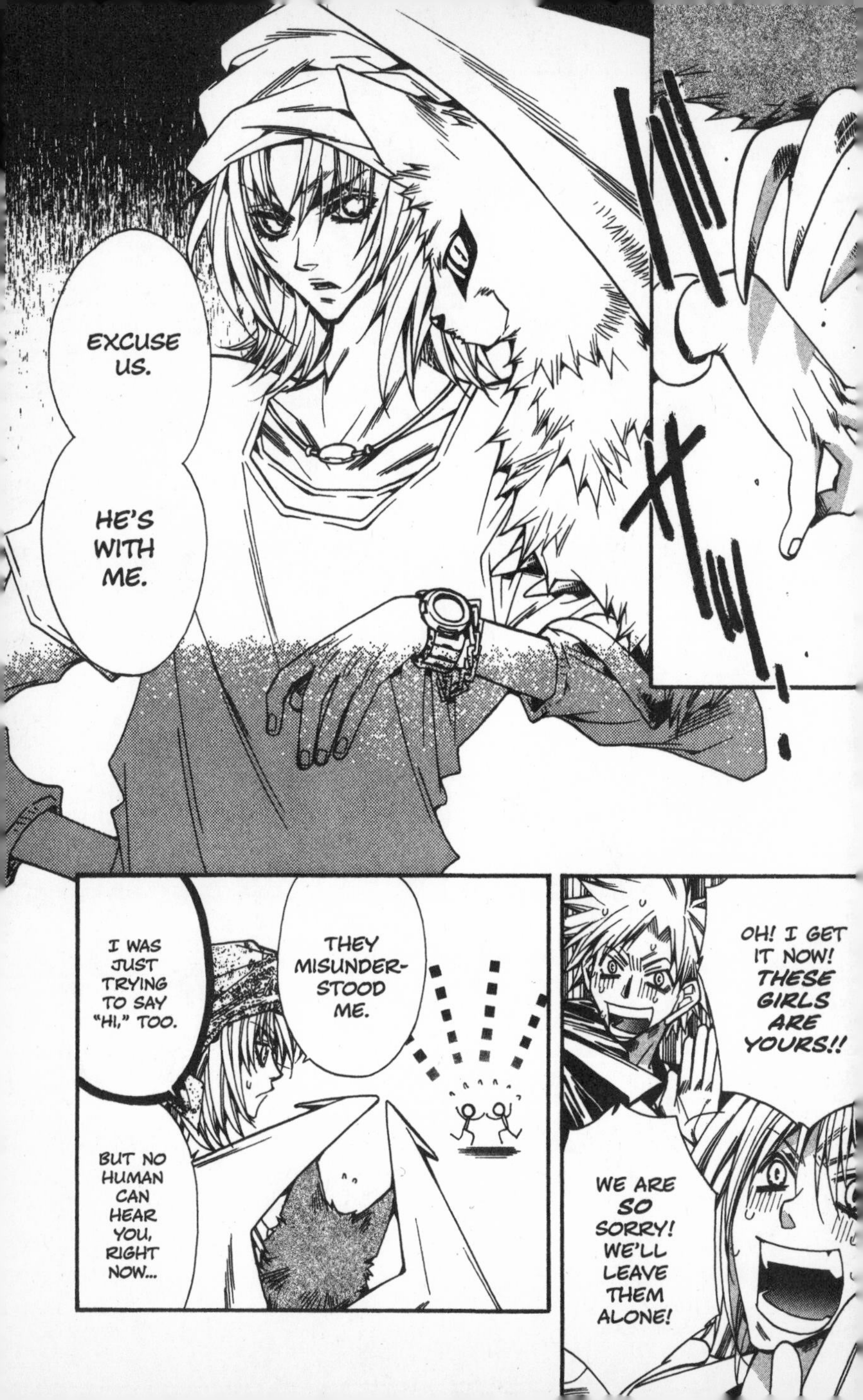
EXCUSE US.
HE'S WITH ME.
OH! I GET IT NOW! THESE GIRLS ARE YOURS!!
WE ARE SO SORRY! WE'LL LEAVE THEM ALONE!
THEY MISUNDER-STOOD ME.
I WAS JUST TRYING TO SAY "HI," TOO.
BUT NO HUMAN CAN HEAR YOU, RIGHT NOW...

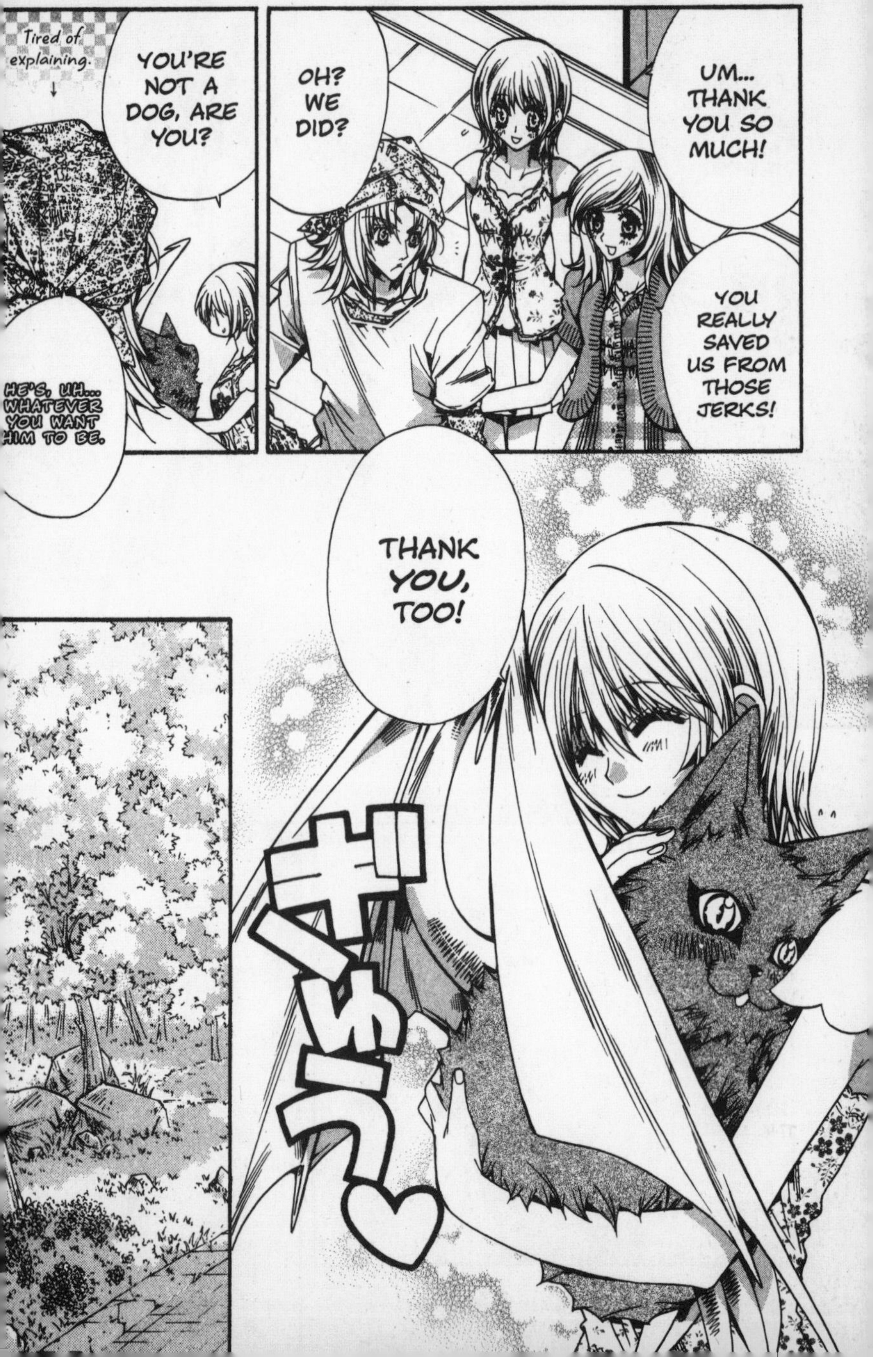
UM... THANK YOU SO MUCH!
YOU REALLY SAVED US FROM THOSE JERKS!
OH? WE DID?
Tired of explaining.
YOU'RE NOT A DOG, ARE YOU?
HE'S, UH... WHATEVER YOU WANT HIM TO BE.
THANK YOU, TOO!

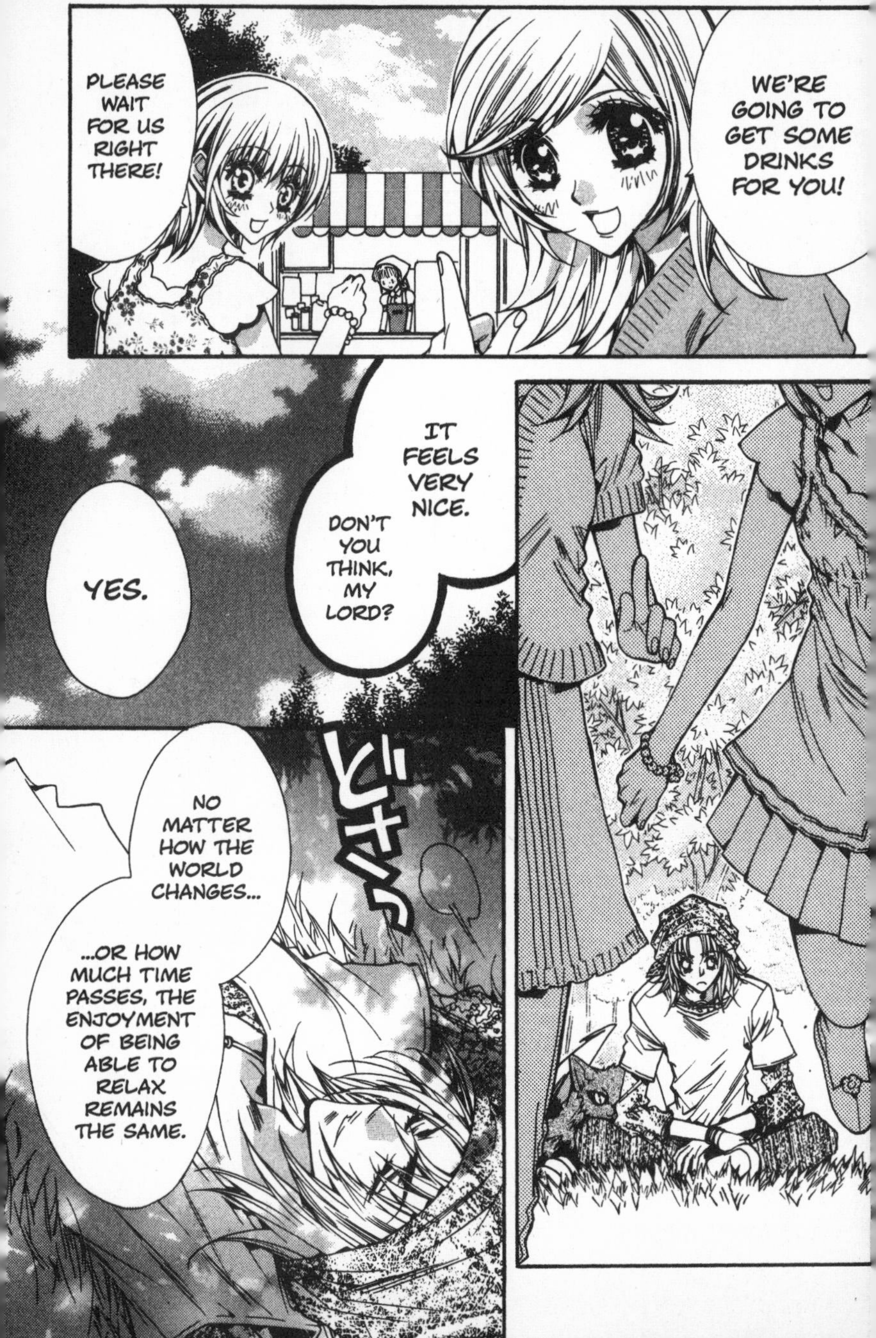
WE'RE GOING TO GET SOME DRINKS FOR YOU!
PLEASE WAIT FOR US RIGHT THERE!
IT FEELS VERY NICE.
DON'T YOU THINK, MY LORD?
YES.
どさっ
NO MATTER HOW THE WORLD CHANGES...
...OR HOW MUCH TIME PASSES, THE ENJOYMENT OF BEING ABLE TO RELAX REMAINS THE SAME.

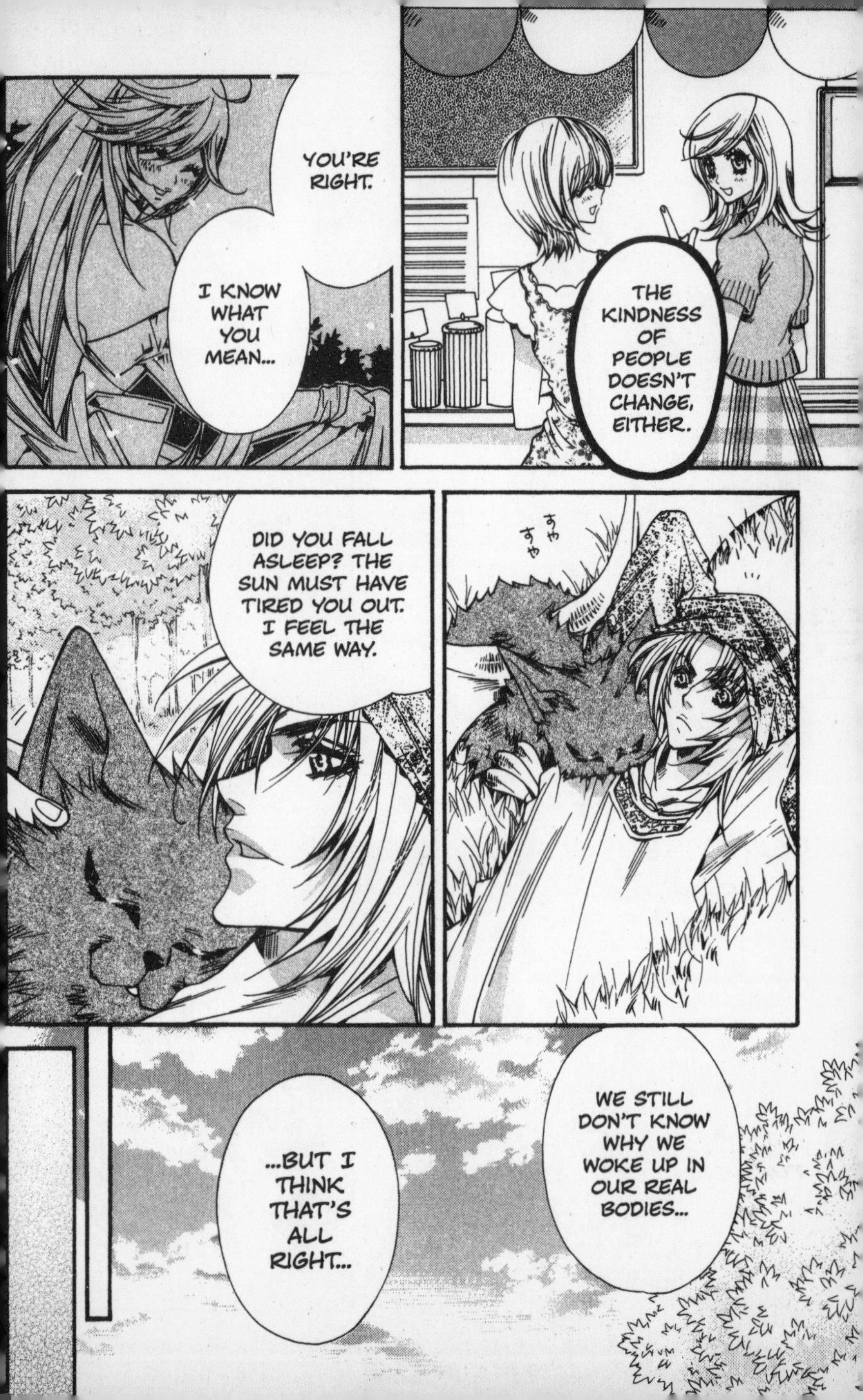
THE KINDNESS OF PEOPLE DOESN'T CHANGE, EITHER.
YOU'RE RIGHT.
I KNOW WHAT YOU MEAN...
すや すや
...
DID YOU FALL ASLEEP? THE SUN MUST HAVE TIRED YOU OUT. I FEEL THE SAME WAY.
WE STILL DON'T KNOW WHY WE WOKE UP IN OUR REAL BODIES...
...BUT I THINK THAT'S ALL RIGHT...

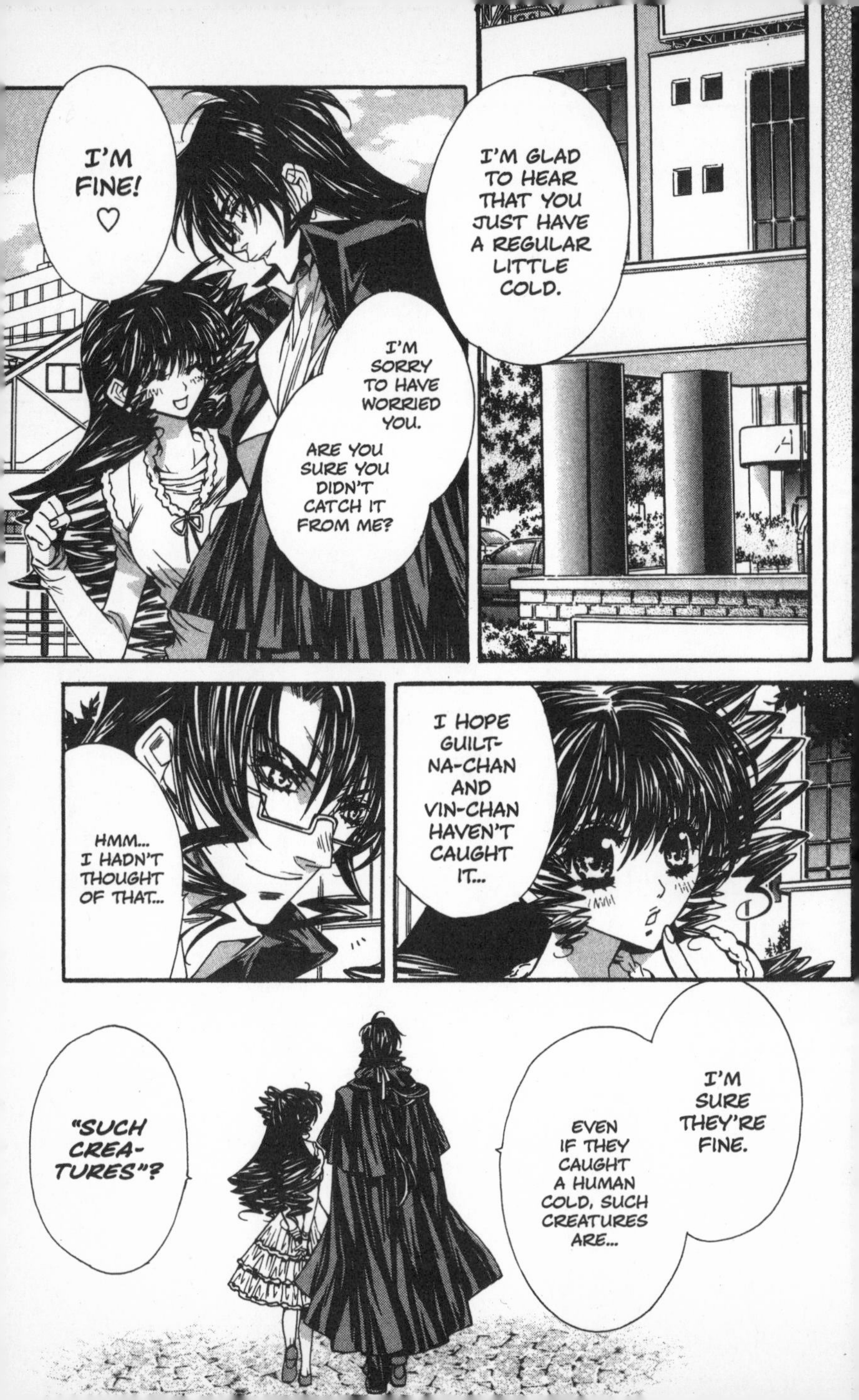
I'M GLAD TO HEAR THAT YOU JUST HAVE A REGULAR LITTLE COLD.
I'M FINE! ♡
I'M SORRY TO HAVE WORRIED YOU.
ARE YOU SURE YOU DIDN'T CATCH IT FROM ME?
I HOPE GUILT-NA-CHAN AND VIN-CHAN HAVEN'T CAUGHT IT...
HMM... I HADN'T THOUGHT OF THAT...
I'M SURE THEY'RE FINE.
EVEN IF THEY CAUGHT A HUMAN COLD, SUCH CREATURES ARE...
"SUCH CREA-TURES"?

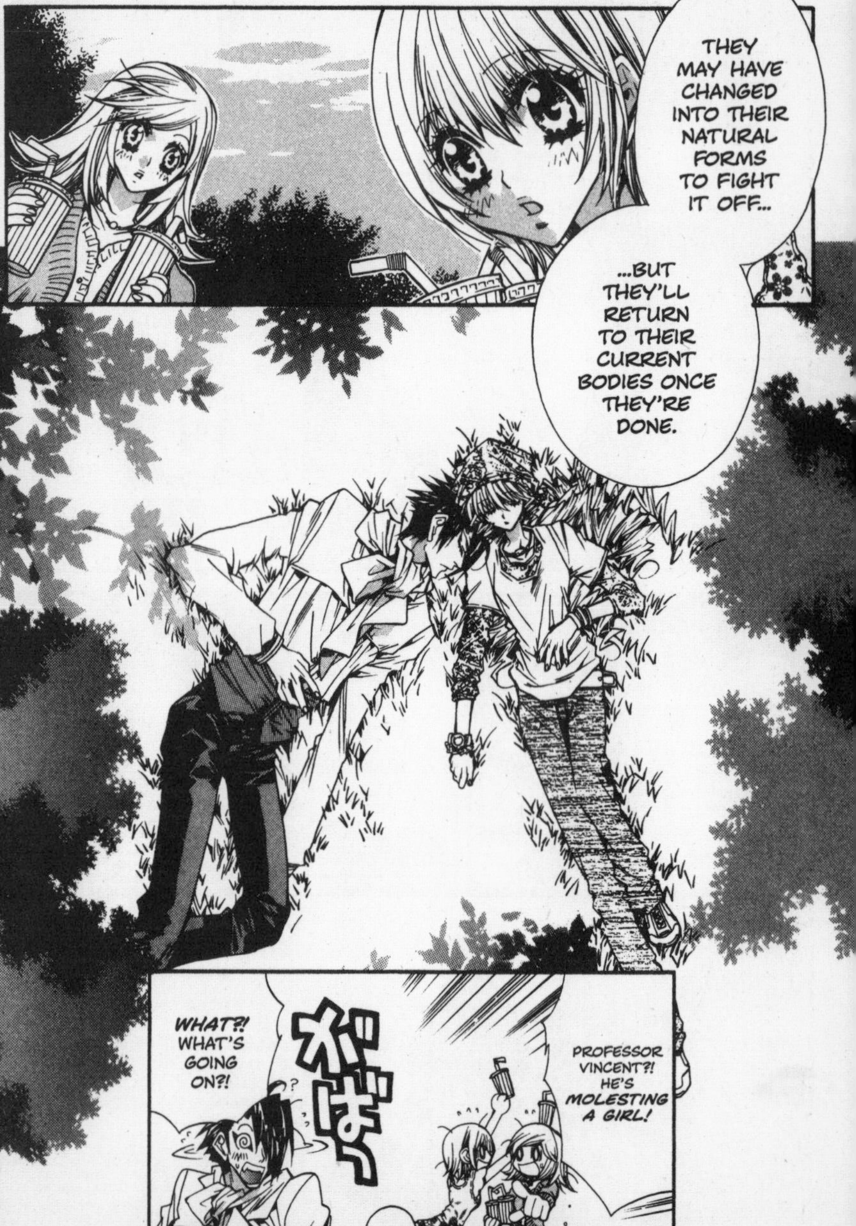
THEY MAY HAVE CHANGED INTO THEIR NATURAL FORMS TO FIGHT IT OFF...
...BUT THEY'LL RETURN TO THEIR CURRENT BODIES ONCE THEY'RE DONE.
PROFESSOR VINCENT?! HE'S MOLESTING A GIRL!
がばっ
WHAT?! WHAT'S GOING ON?!
Z.

BONUS COMIC STRIP

VAMPIRE DOLL

REFLECTIONS

Cold for tow

Q.
HOW DOES VINCENT EAT WHEN HE'S IN HIS BAT FORM?
THANK YOU FOR THIS FOOD! ♡
Napkin.
VINCENT
Ah!
VINCENT
FORGET THAT AND HURRY UP! I HAVE TO FINISH THE DISHES!
Aw!

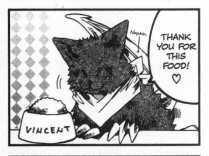

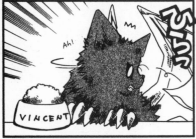

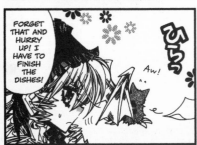

GUILTNA "CASUAL STYLE" ZAN

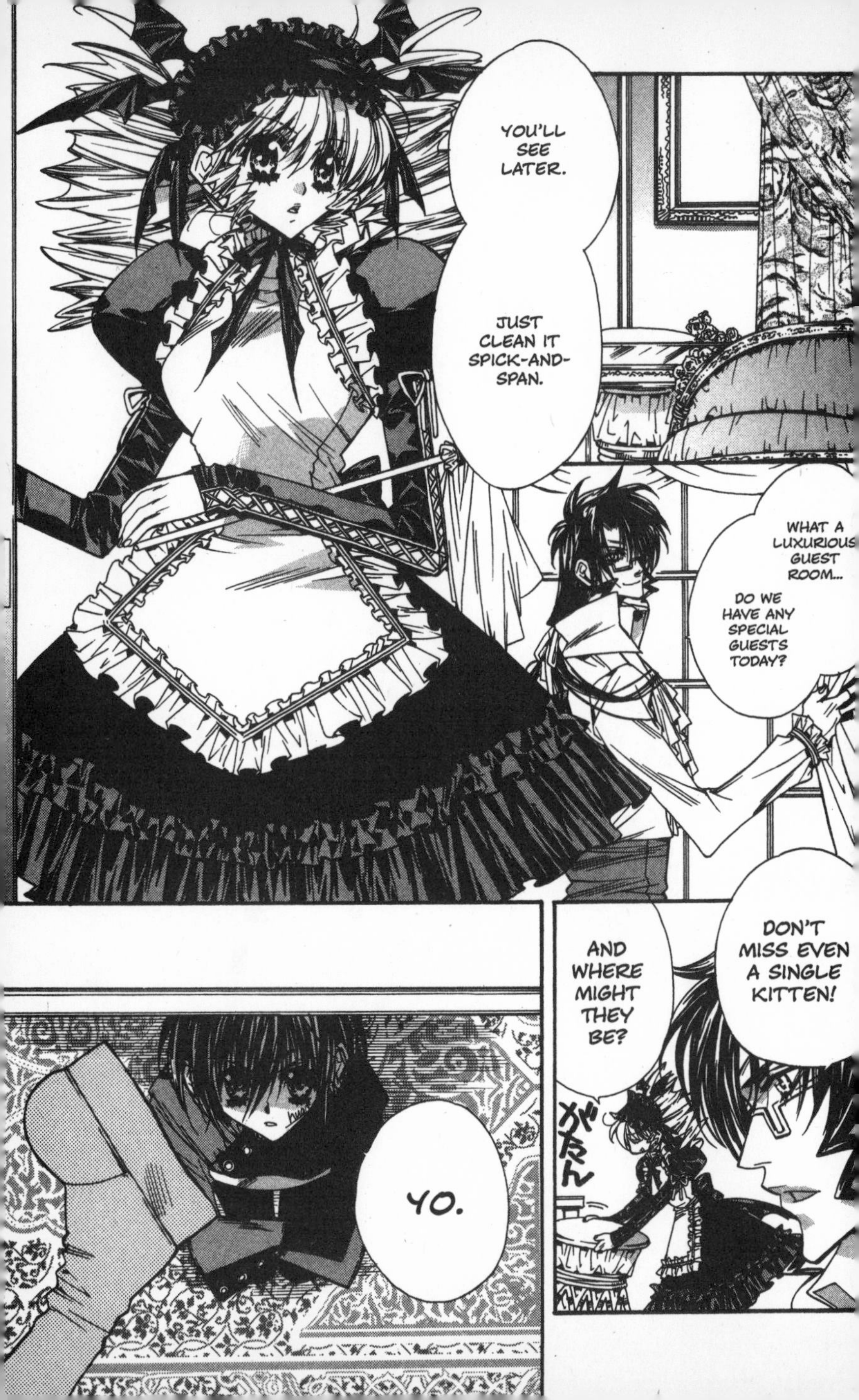
WHAT A LUXURIOUS GUEST ROOM...
DO WE HAVE ANY SPECIAL GUESTS TODAY?
YOU'LL SEE LATER.
JUST CLEAN IT SPICK-AND-SPAN.
DON'T MISS EVEN A SINGLE KITTEN!
AND WHERE MIGHT THEY BE?
がたん
YO.

#30 How Great Thou Art

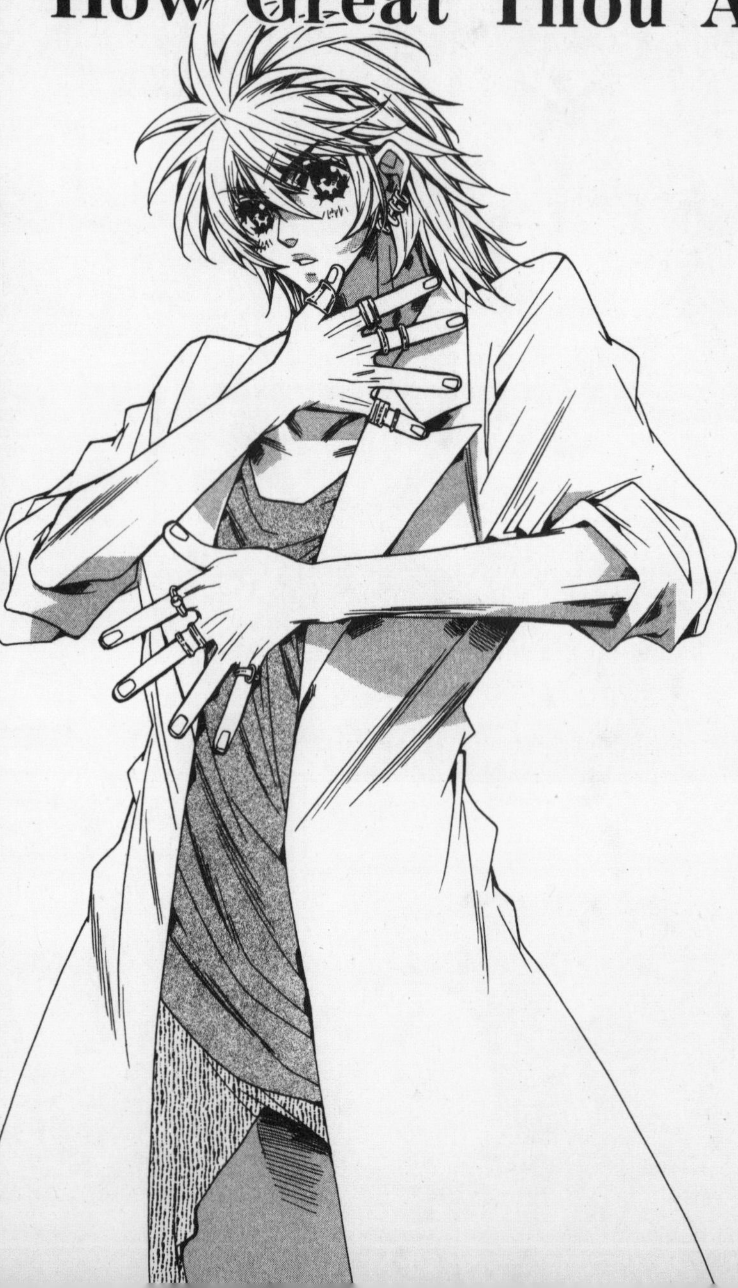

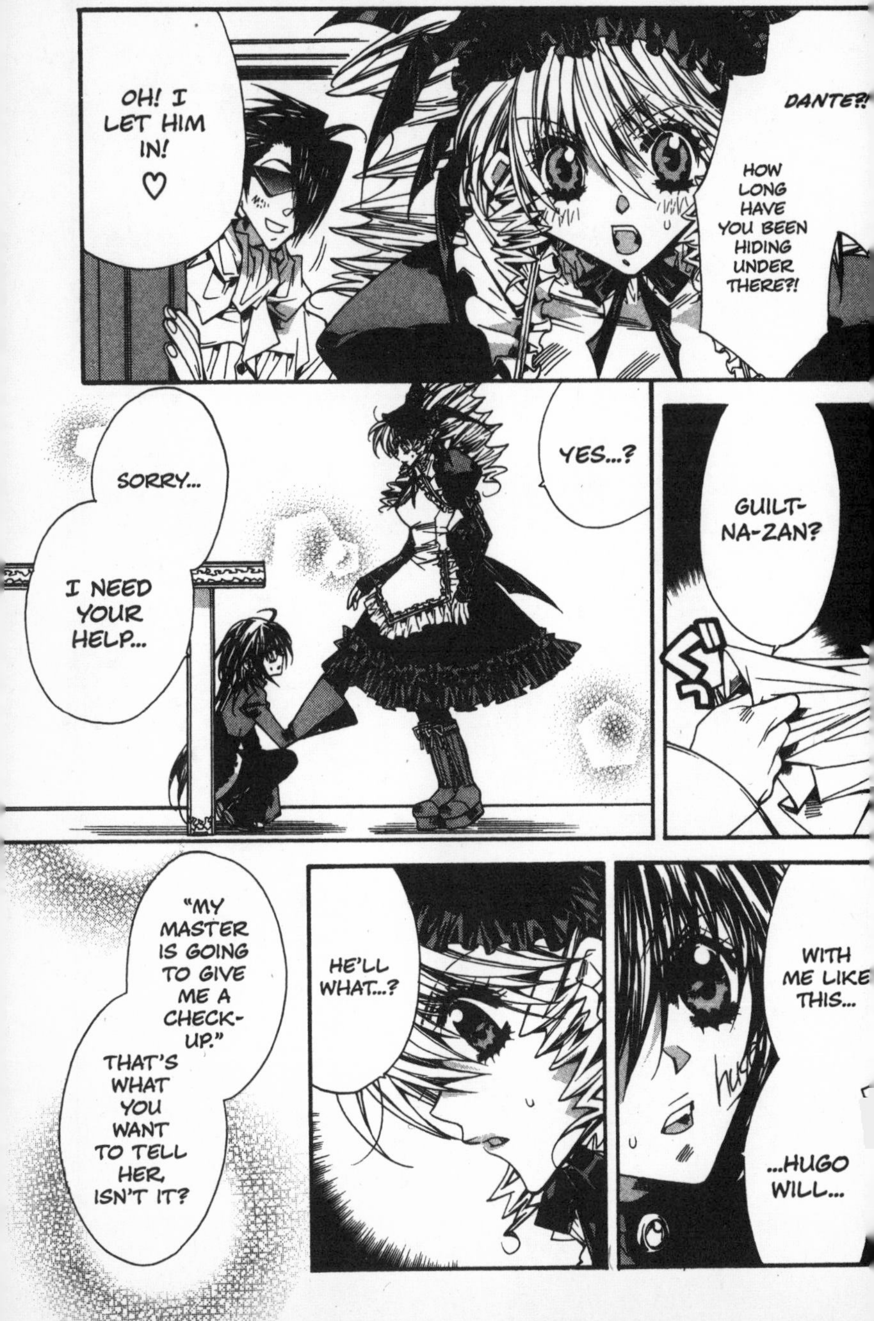
DANTE?!
HOW LONG HAVE YOU BEEN HIDING UNDER THERE?!
OH! I LET HIM IN! ♡
GUILT-NA-ZAN?
YES...?
SORRY...
I NEED YOUR HELP...
WITH ME LIKE THIS...
...HUGO WILL...
HE'LL WHAT...?
"MY MASTER IS GOING TO GIVE ME A CHECK-UP." THAT'S WHAT YOU WANT TO TELL HER, ISN'T IT?

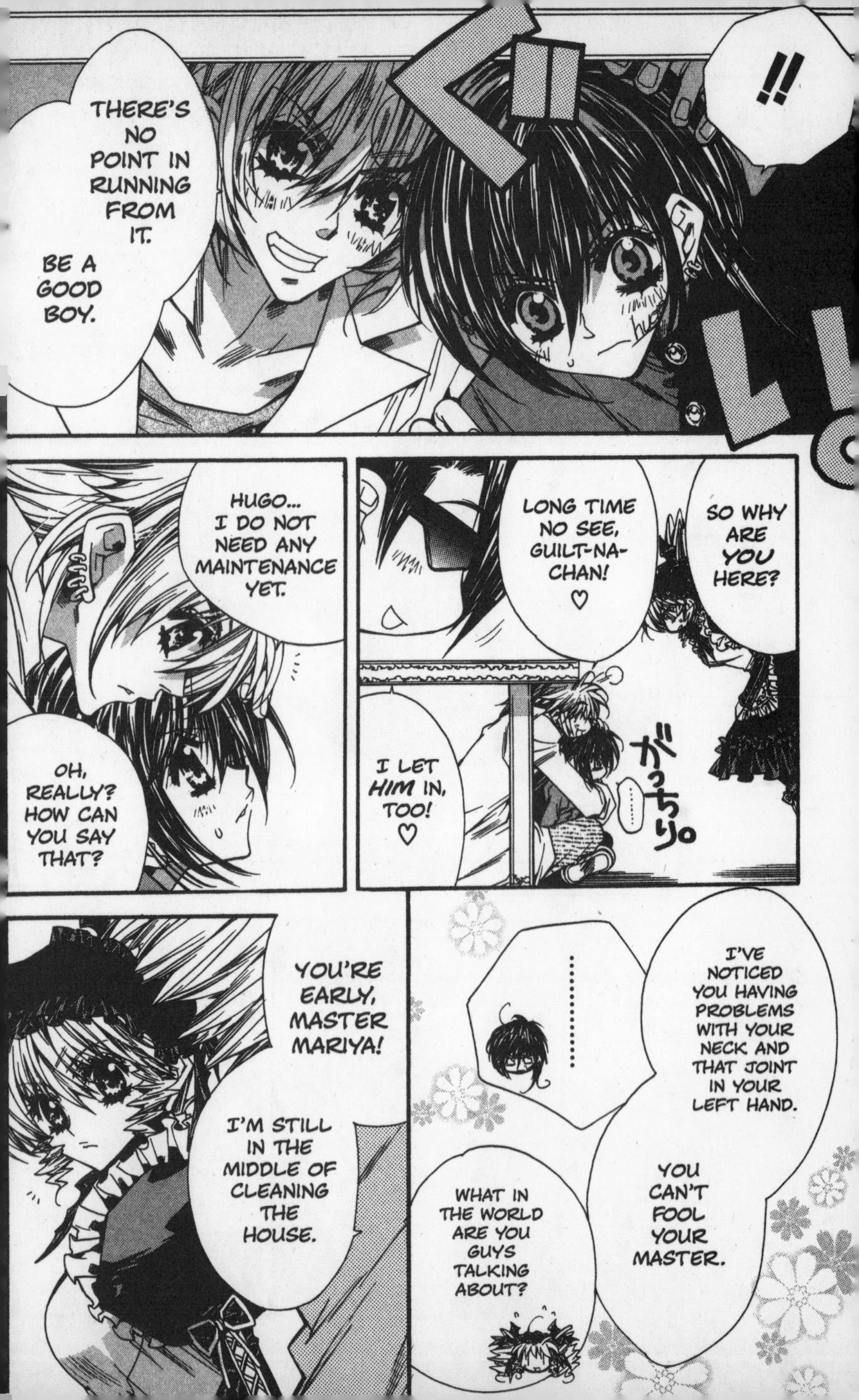
!!
THERE'S NO POINT IN RUNNING FROM IT.
BE A GOOD BOY.
SO WHY ARE YOU HERE?
LONG TIME NO SEE, GUILT-NA-CHAN! ♡
I LET HIM IN, TOO! ♡
......
がっちり。
HUGO... I DO NOT NEED ANY MAINTENANCE YET.
OH, REALLY? HOW CAN YOU SAY THAT?
I'VE NOTICED YOU HAVING PROBLEMS WITH YOUR NECK AND THAT JOINT IN YOUR LEFT HAND.
......
YOU CAN'T FOOL YOUR MASTER.
WHAT IN THE WORLD ARE YOU GUYS TALKING ABOUT?
YOU'RE EARLY, MASTER MARIYA!
I'M STILL IN THE MIDDLE OF CLEANING THE HOUSE.

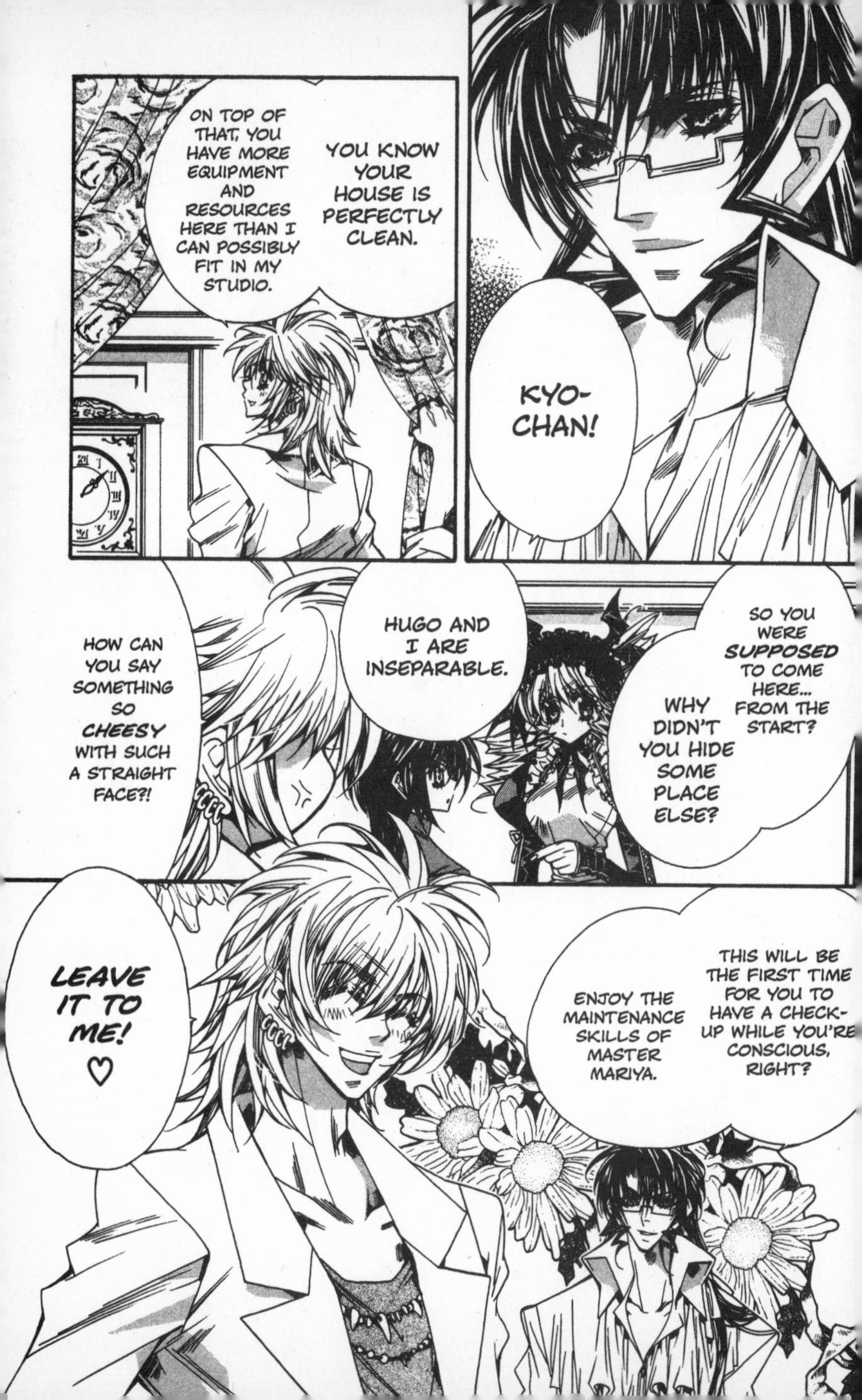
KYO-CHAN!
YOU KNOW YOUR HOUSE IS PERFECTLY CLEAN.
ON TOP OF THAT, YOU HAVE MORE EQUIPMENT AND RESOURCES HERE THAN I CAN POSSIBLY FIT IN MY STUDIO.
SO YOU WERE SUPPOSED TO COME HERE... FROM THE START?
WHY DIDN'T YOU HIDE SOME PLACE ELSE?
HUGO AND I ARE INSEPARABLE.
HOW CAN YOU SAY SOMETHING SO CHEESY WITH SUCH A STRAIGHT FACE?!
THIS WILL BE THE FIRST TIME FOR YOU TO HAVE A CHECK-UP WHILE YOU'RE CONSCIOUS, RIGHT?
ENJOY THE MAINTENANCE SKILLS OF MASTER MARIYA.
LEAVE IT TO ME! ♡

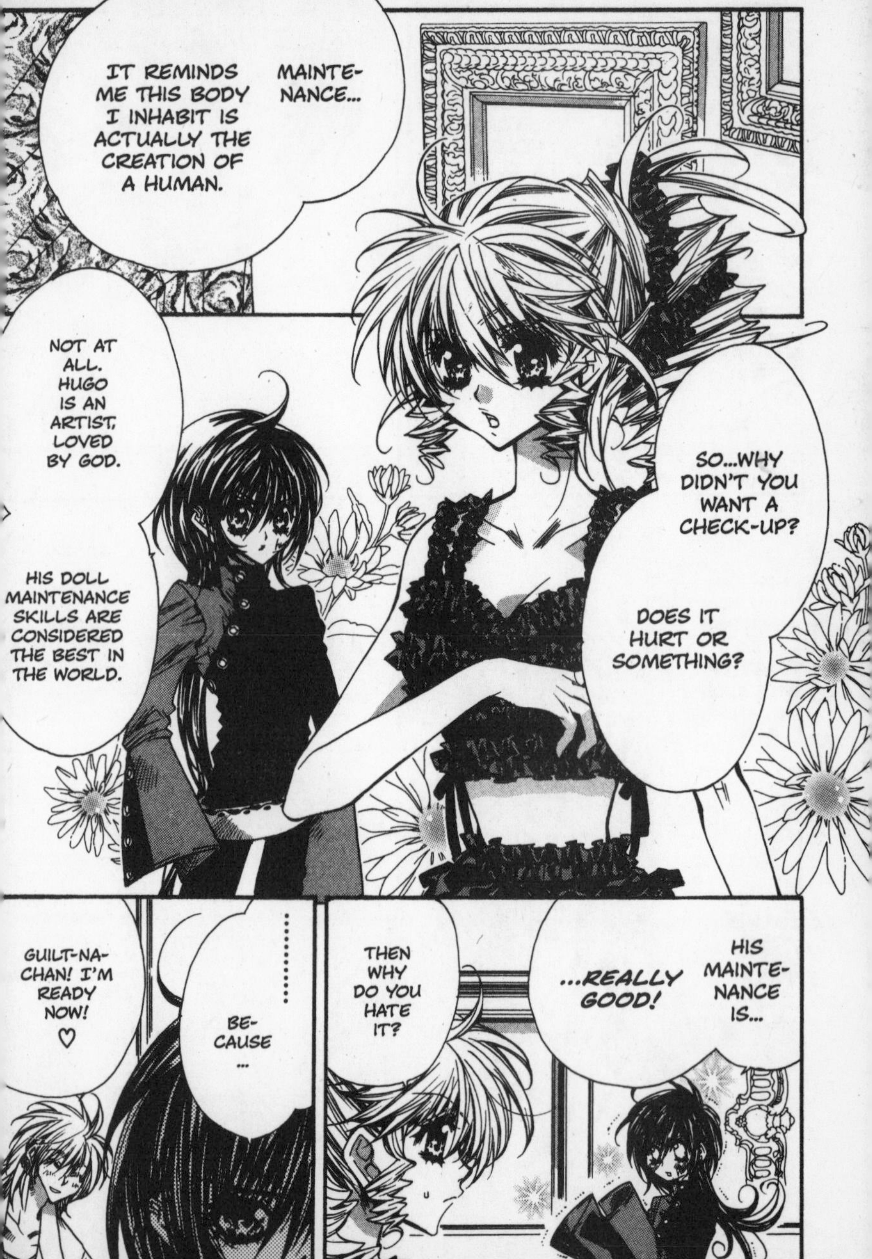
MAINTE-NANCE...
IT REMINDS ME THIS BODY I INHABIT IS ACTUALLY THE CREATION OF A HUMAN.
SO...WHY DIDN'T YOU WANT A CHECK-UP?
DOES IT HURT OR SOMETHING?
NOT AT ALL. HUGO IS AN ARTIST, LOVED BY GOD.
HIS DOLL MAINTENANCE SKILLS ARE CONSIDERED THE BEST IN THE WORLD.
HIS MAINTE-NANCE IS...
...REALLY GOOD!
THEN WHY DO YOU HATE IT?
......
BE-CAUSE ...
GUILT-NA-CHAN! I'M READY NOW! ♡

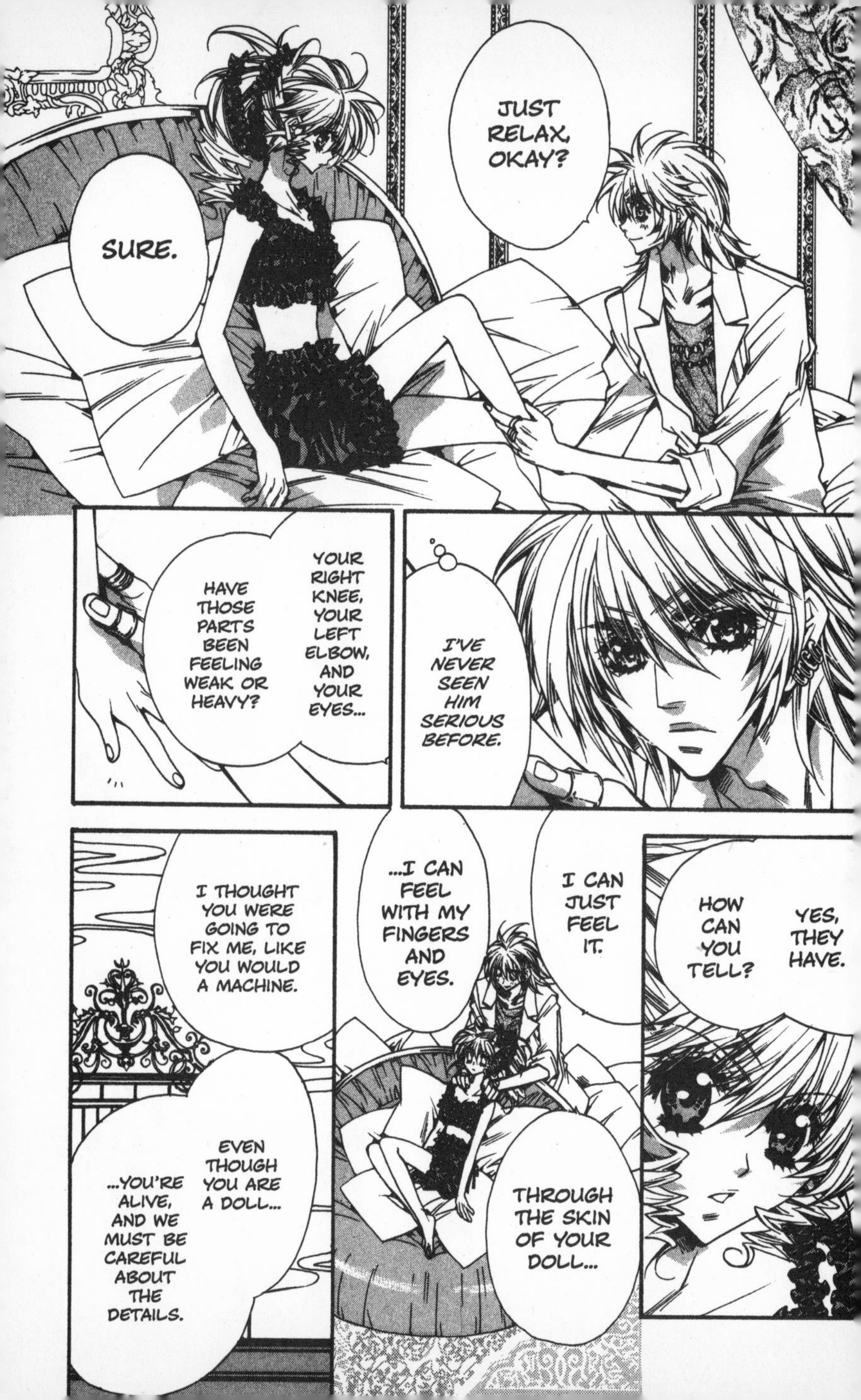
JUST RELAX, OKAY?
SURE.
I'VE NEVER SEEN HIM SERIOUS BEFORE.
YOUR RIGHT KNEE, YOUR LEFT ELBOW, AND YOUR EYES...
HAVE THOSE PARTS BEEN FEELING WEAK OR HEAVY?
YES, THEY HAVE.
HOW CAN YOU TELL?
I CAN JUST FEEL IT.
...I CAN FEEL WITH MY FINGERS AND EYES.
THROUGH THE SKIN OF YOUR DOLL...
I THOUGHT YOU WERE GOING TO FIX ME, LIKE YOU WOULD A MACHINE.
EVEN THOUGH YOU ARE A DOLL...
...YOU'RE ALIVE, AND WE MUST BE CAREFUL ABOUT THE DETAILS.

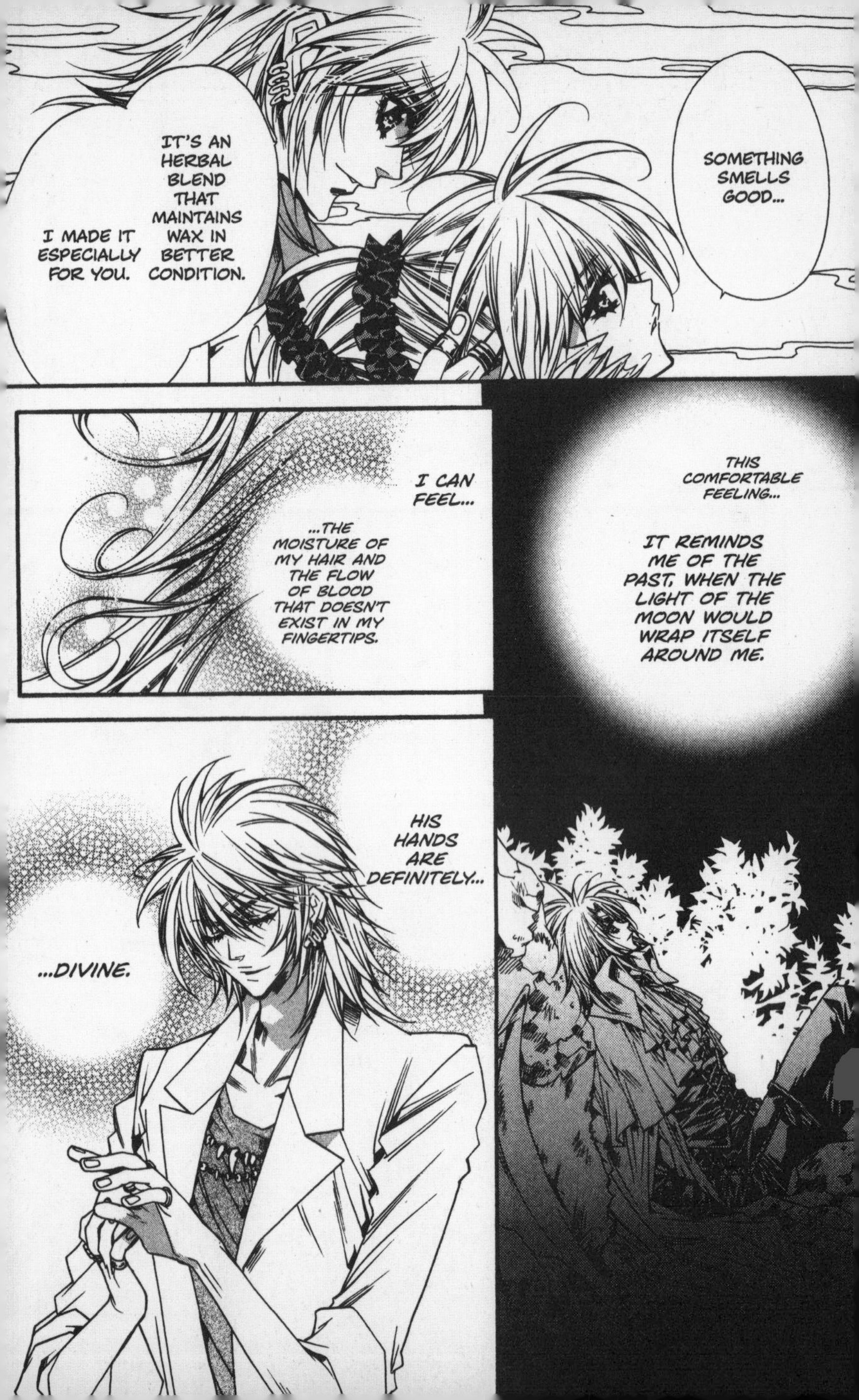
SOMETHING SMELLS GOOD...
IT'S AN HERBAL BLEND THAT MAINTAINS WAX IN BETTER CONDITION.
I MADE IT ESPECIALLY FOR YOU.
THIS COMFORTABLE FEELING...
IT REMINDS ME OF THE PAST, WHEN THE LIGHT OF THE MOON WOULD WRAP ITSELF AROUND ME.
I CAN FEEL...
...THE MOISTURE OF MY HAIR AND THE FLOW OF BLOOD THAT DOESN'T EXIST IN MY FINGERTIPS.
HIS HANDS ARE DEFINITELY...
...DIVINE.

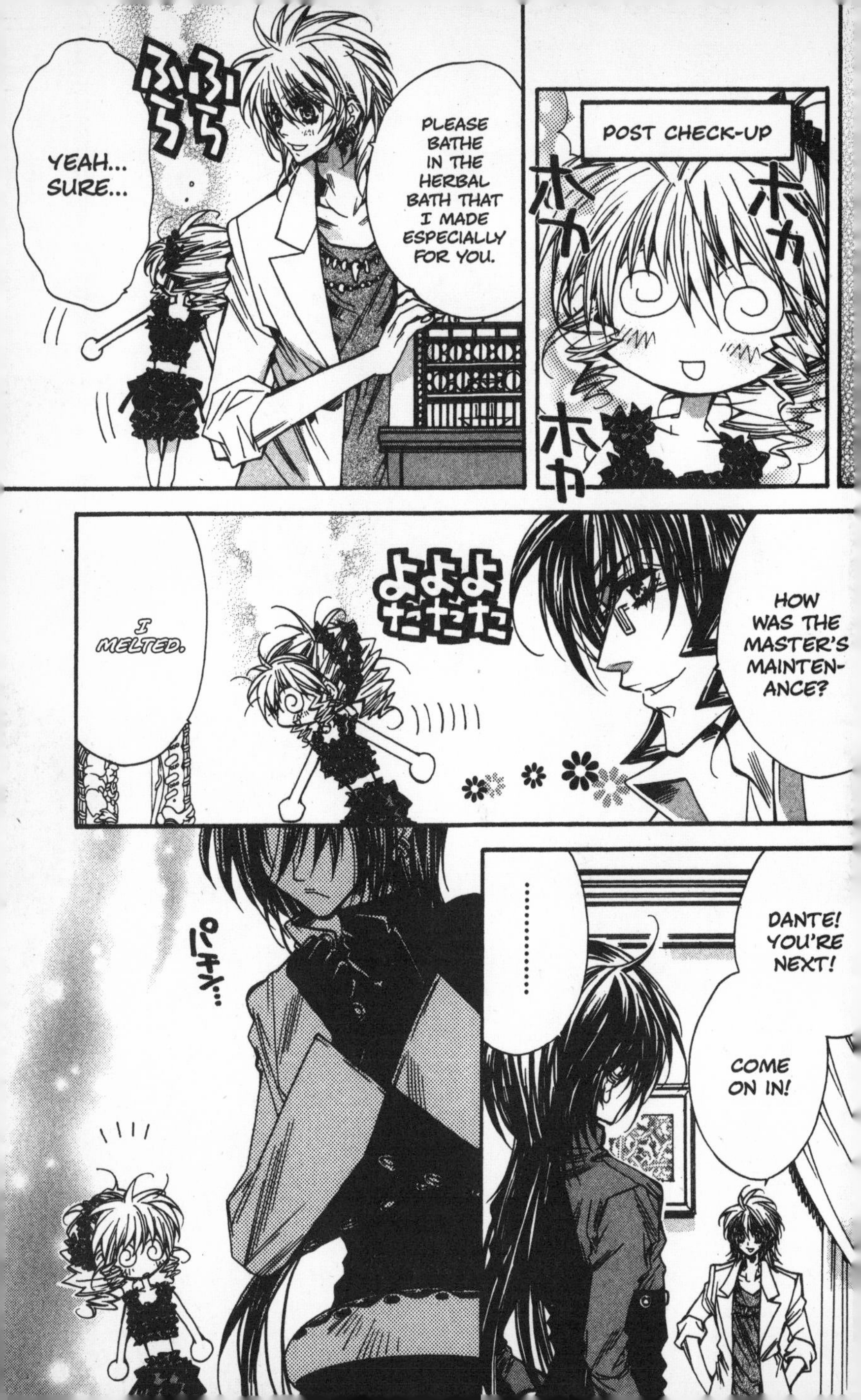
POST CHECK-UP
ホカホカ
ホカ
PLEASE BATHE IN THE HERBAL BATH THAT I MADE ESPECIALLY FOR YOU.
YEAH... SURE...
ふらふら
HOW WAS THE MASTER'S MAINTENANCE?
I MELTED.
DANTE! YOU'RE NEXT!
COME ON IN!
......

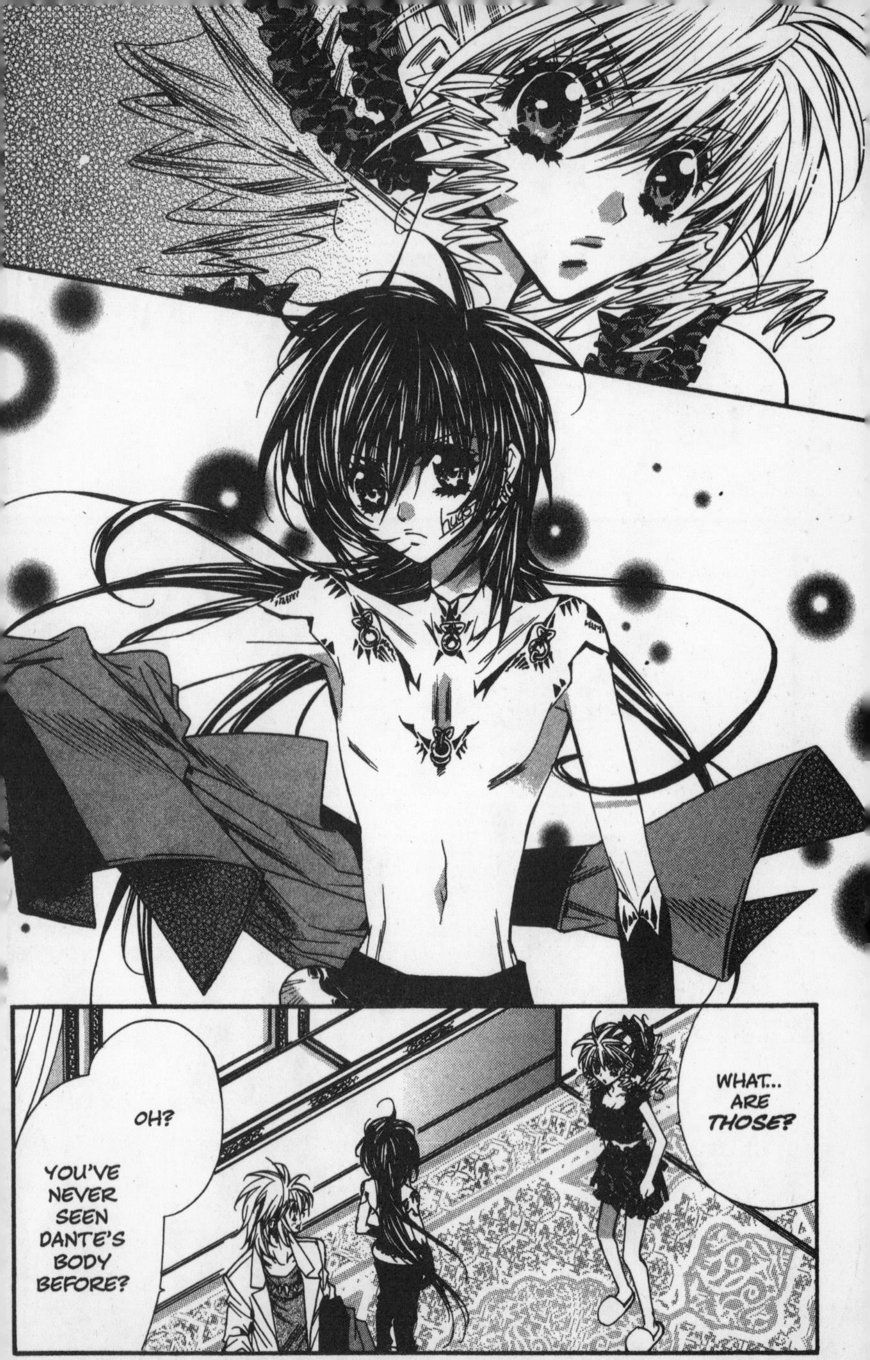
WHAT... ARE *THOSE?*
OH?
YOU'VE NEVER SEEN DANTE'S BODY BEFORE?

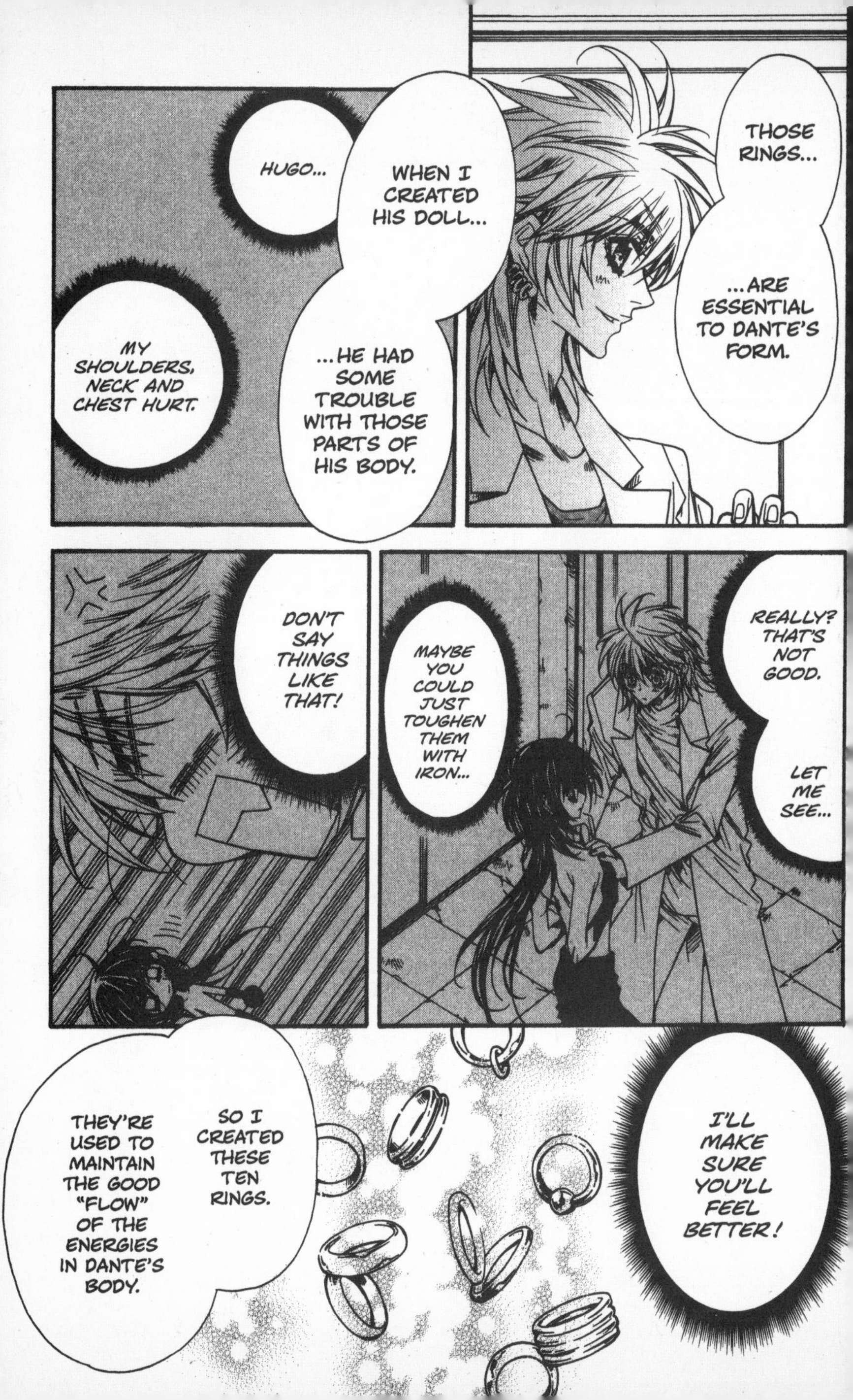
THOSE RINGS...
...ARE ESSENTIAL TO DANTE'S FORM.
WHEN I CREATED HIS DOLL...
...HE HAD SOME TROUBLE WITH THOSE PARTS OF HIS BODY.
HUGO...
MY SHOULDERS, NECK AND CHEST HURT.
REALLY? THAT'S NOT GOOD.
LET ME SEE...
MAYBE YOU COULD JUST TOUGHEN THEM WITH IRON...
DON'T SAY THINGS LIKE THAT!
I'LL MAKE SURE YOU'LL FEEL BETTER!
SO I CREATED THESE TEN RINGS.
THEY'RE USED TO MAINTAIN THE GOOD "FLOW" OF THE ENERGIES IN DANTE'S BODY.

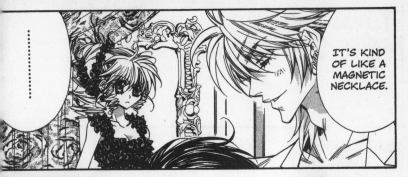

IT'S KIND OF LIKE A MAGNETIC NECKLACE.
......
GUILT-NA?
DID YOU NOTICE?
YES.
ALTHOUGH MASTER MARIYA CREATED IT, HE IS UNAWARE OF ITS POWER.
THAT HOOP...
...IS A SEALING DEVICE THAT LIMITS POWER.
HE'S NOT AN EXORCIST OR A MEDIUM.
HE IS AN *ARTIST.*
IT'S PROBABLY QUITE DIFFICULT TO KEEP DANTE'S POWER PROPERLY BALANCED IN THAT BODY.
ONCE THOSE RINGS LOSE THEIR EFFECTIVENESS, HE WON'T BE ABLE TO CONTROL HIS POWER.

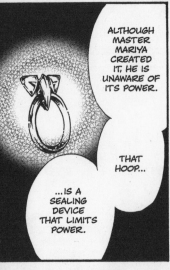

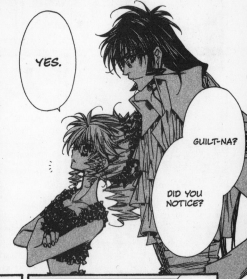

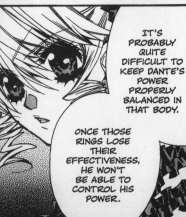

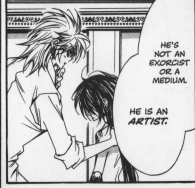

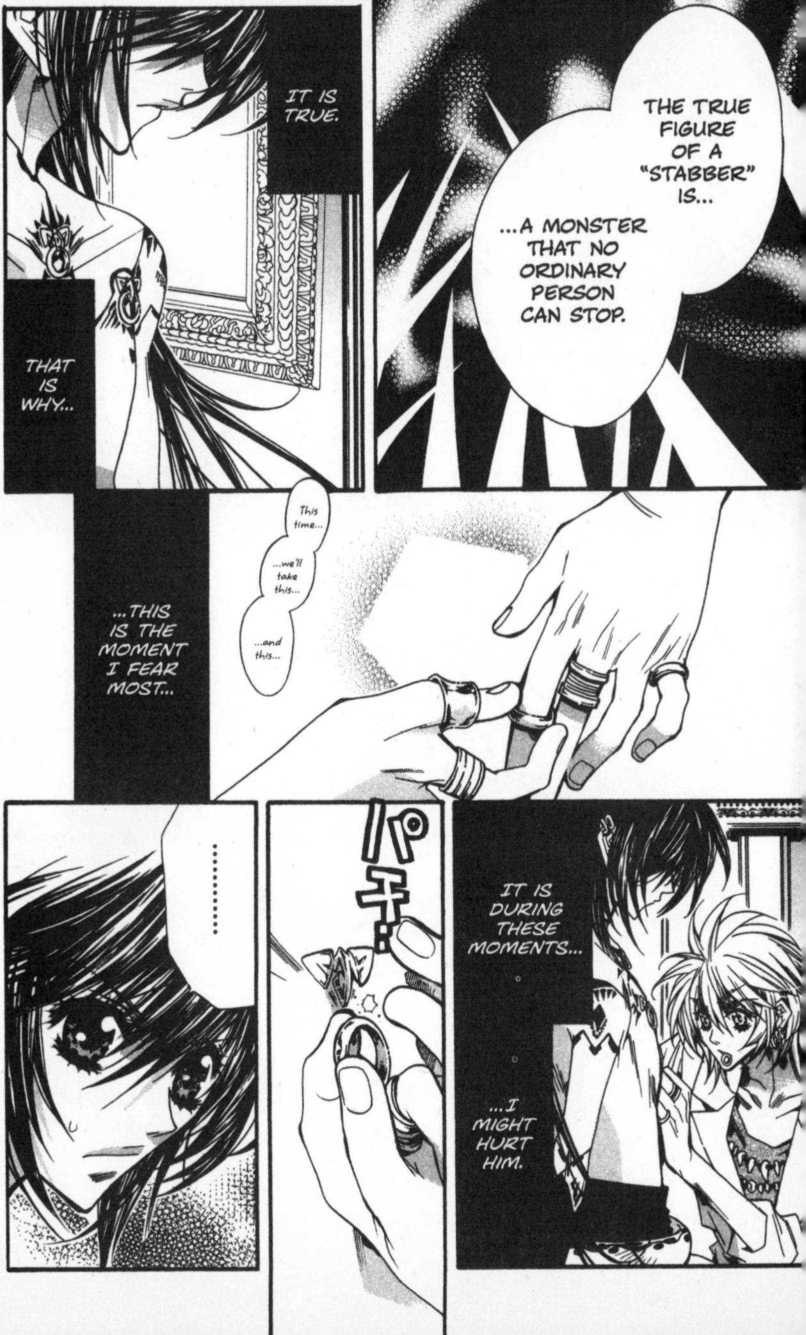
THE TRUE FIGURE OF A "STABBER" IS...
...A MONSTER THAT NO ORDINARY PERSON CAN STOP.
IT IS TRUE.
THAT IS WHY...
This time...
...we'll take this...
...and this...
...THIS IS THE MOMENT I FEAR MOST...
IT IS DURING THESE MOMENTS...
...I MIGHT HURT HIM.
パチ!
....

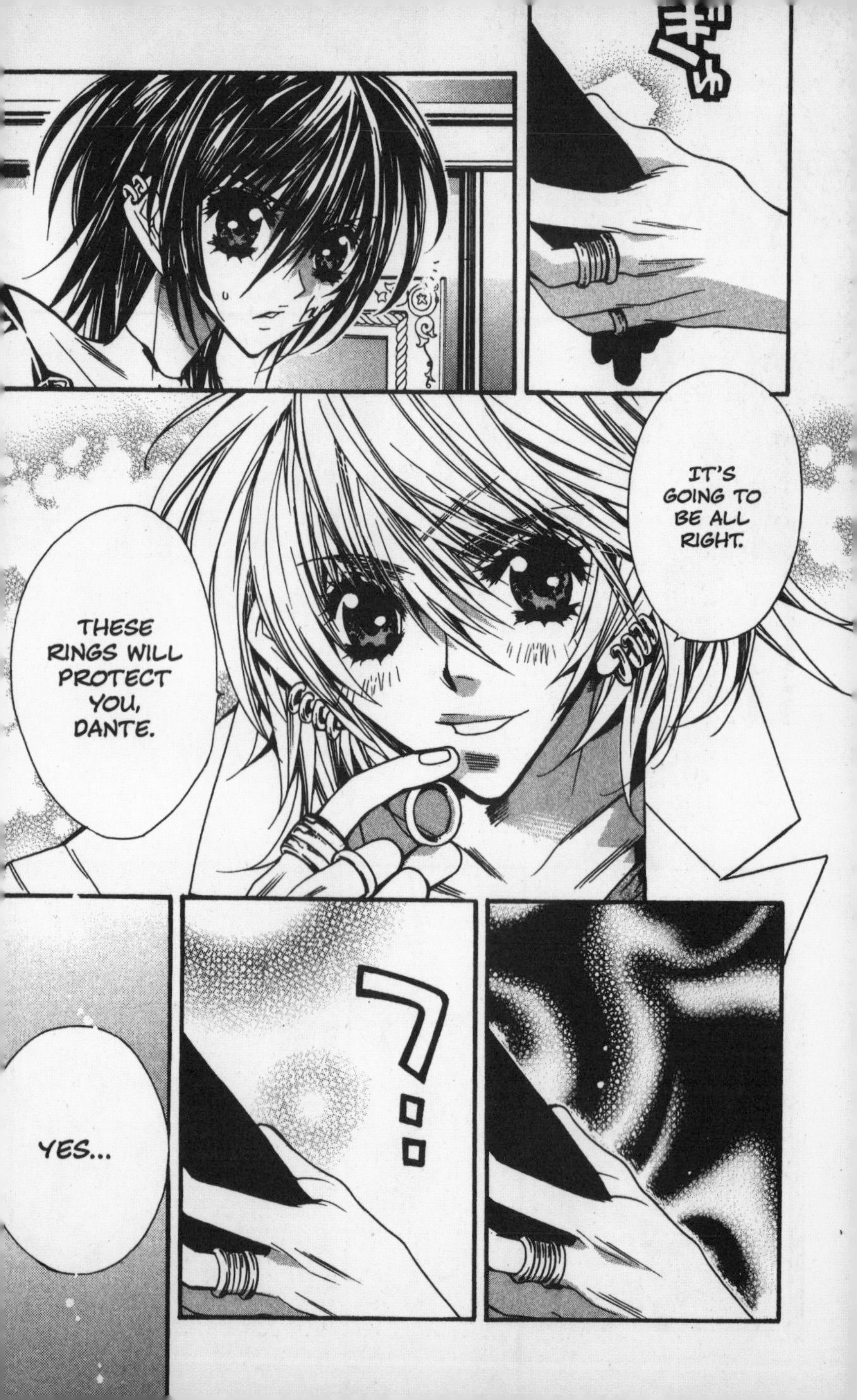
IT'S GOING TO BE ALL RIGHT.
THESE RINGS WILL PROTECT YOU, DANTE.
YES...

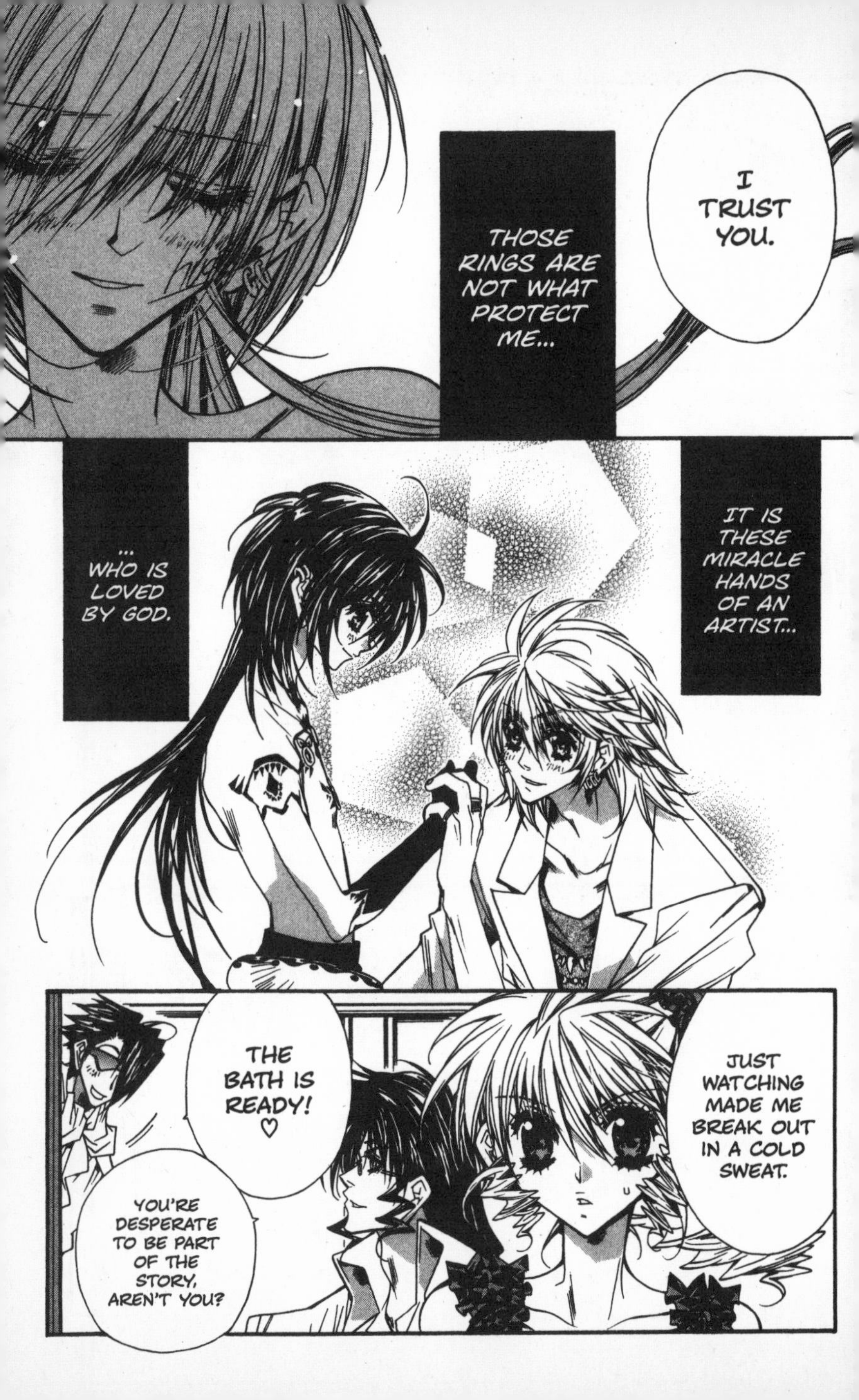

I TRUST YOU.
THOSE RINGS ARE NOT WHAT PROTECT ME...
IT IS THESE MIRACLE HANDS OF AN ARTIST...
... WHO IS LOVED BY GOD.
JUST WATCHING MADE ME BREAK OUT IN A COLD SWEAT.
THE BATH IS READY! ♡
YOU'RE DESPERATE TO BE PART OF THE STORY, AREN'T YOU?

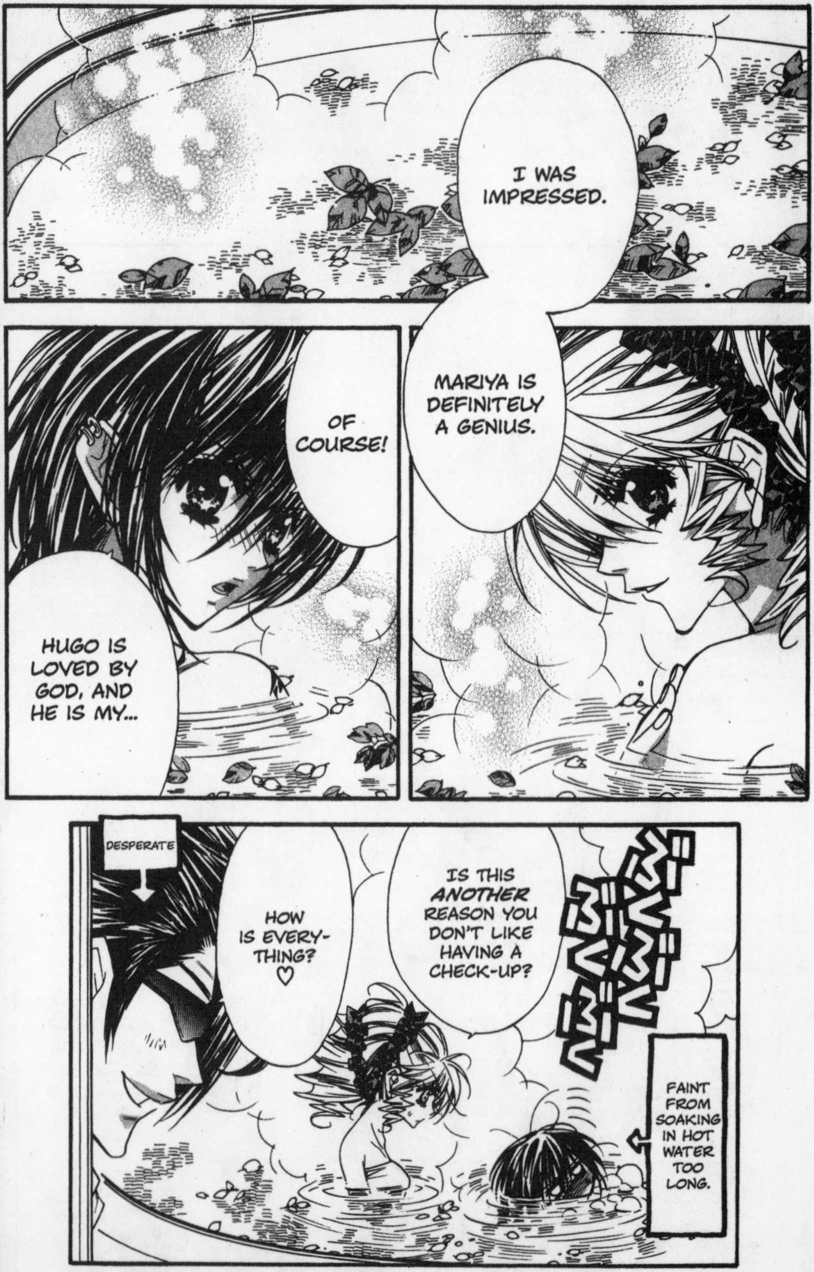
I WAS IMPRESSED.
MARIYA IS DEFINITELY A GENIUS.
OF COURSE!
HUGO IS LOVED BY GOD, AND HE IS MY...
IS THIS *ANOTHER* REASON YOU DON'T LIKE HAVING A CHECK-UP?
HOW IS EVERY-THING? ♡
DESPERATE
FAINT FROM SOAKING IN HOT WATER TOO LONG.

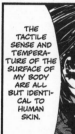

BONUS COMIC STRIP

VAMPIRE DOLL

REFLECTIONS

How Great Thou Art

Q.
PLEASE TELL US ABOUT MASTER MARIYA'S MAINTENANCE TECHNIQUE.
HUGO IS A GENIUS. IT IS AS IF I CAN FEEL HIS EXQUISITE SKILLS THROUGH HIS FINGER-TIPS.
THE TACTILE SENSE AND TEMPERA-TURE OF THE SURFACE OF MY BODY ARE ALL BUT IDENTI-CAL TO HUMAN SKIN.
WHEN HE TOUCHES IT, THIS INDESCRIB-ABLE, COMFORT-ING AIR CURRENT BEGINS TO STIR...
CONVECTIVE FLOW MERGES TOGETHER AND BECOMES RUSHING TORRENTS, DOMINATING MY BODY.
MOREOVER, WHEN HIS SOFT BREATH BRUSHES AGAINST MY SKIN...
SHOULD YOU BE LETTING HIM CONTINUE?
HEY! STOP! STOP RIGHT THERE!

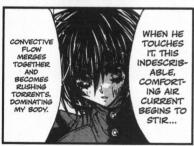

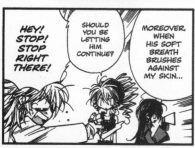

MARIYA "GOD'S HANDS" HUGO

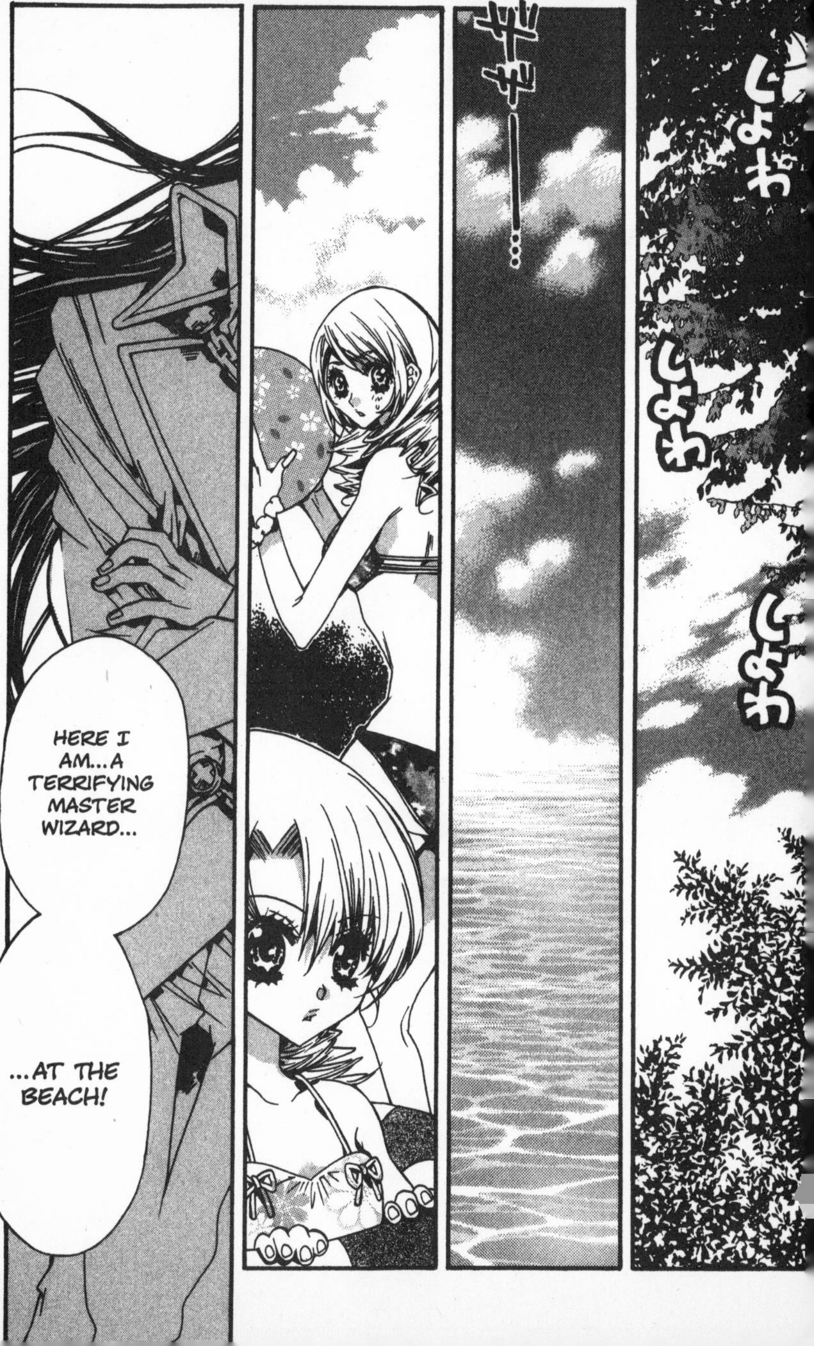

しょぉ
しょわ
しょわ
ザザー…
HERE I AM...A TERRIFYING MASTER WIZARD...
...AT THE BEACH!

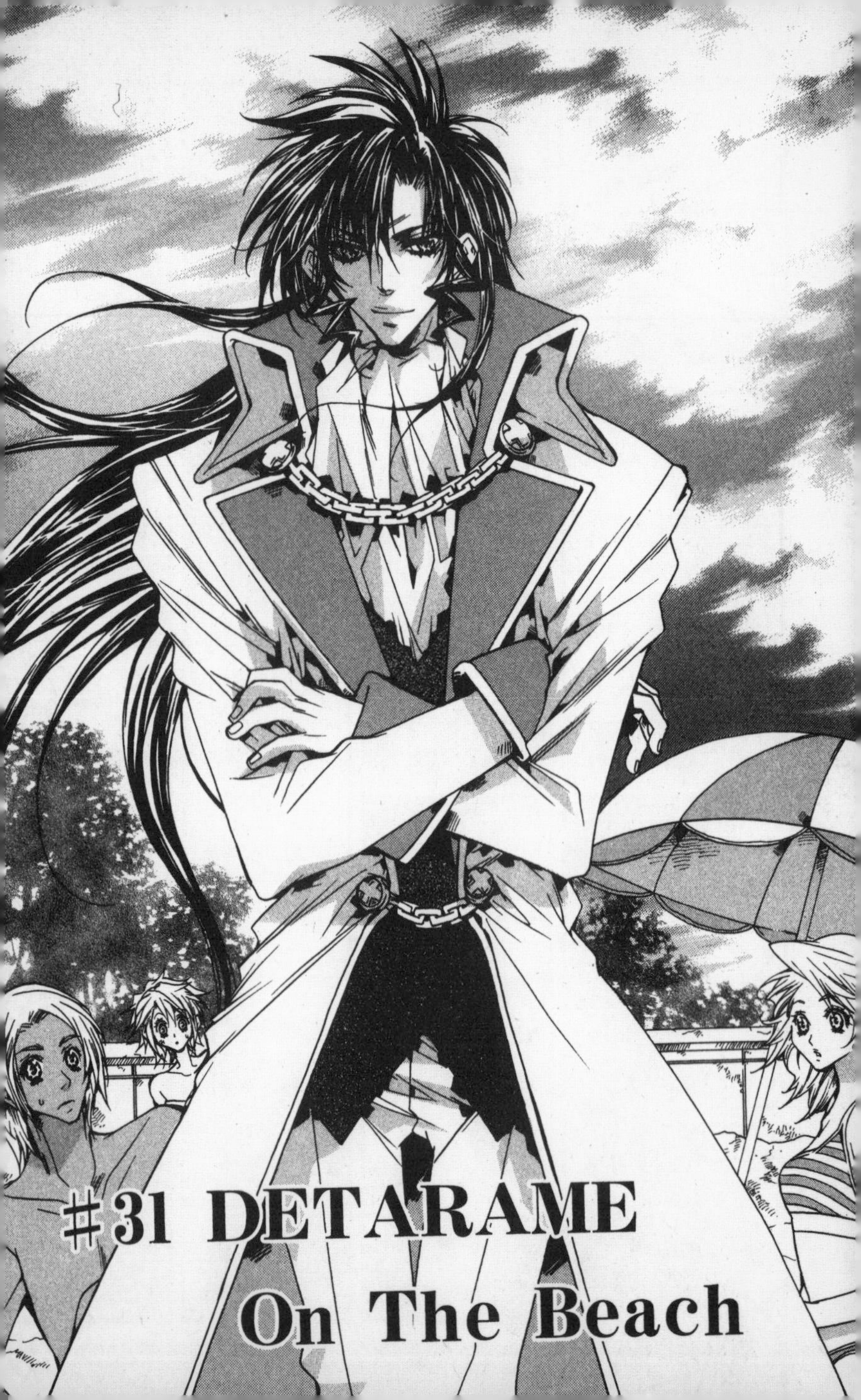
#31 DETARAME
On The Beach

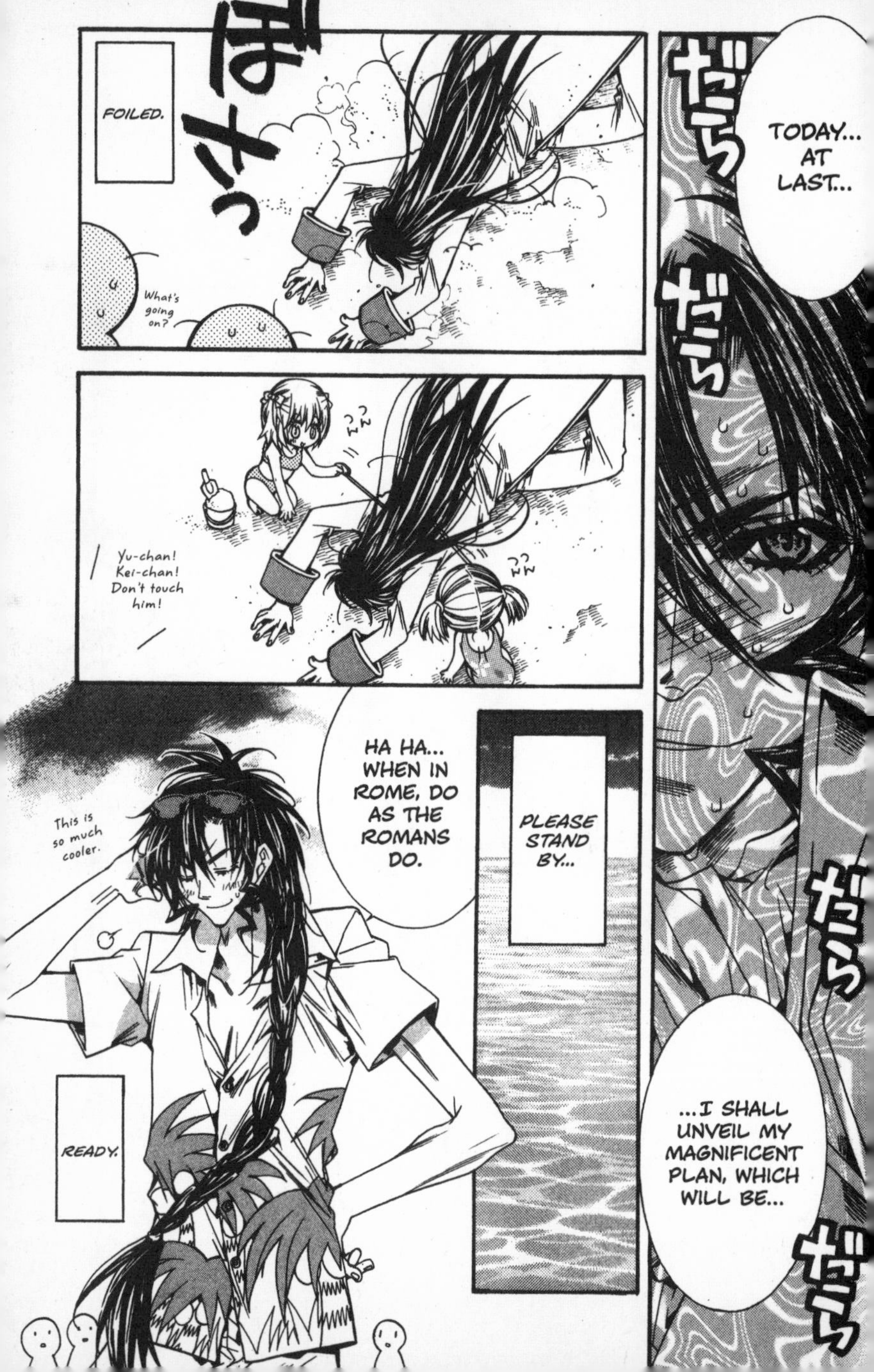
TODAY... AT LAST...
だら
だら
...I SHALL UNVEIL MY MAGNIFICENT PLAN, WHICH WILL BE...
だら
だら
ぼさっ
FOILED.
What's going on?
Yu-chan! Kei-chan! Don't touch him!
PLEASE STAND BY...
HA HA... WHEN IN ROME, DO AS THE ROMANS DO.
This is so much cooler.
READY.

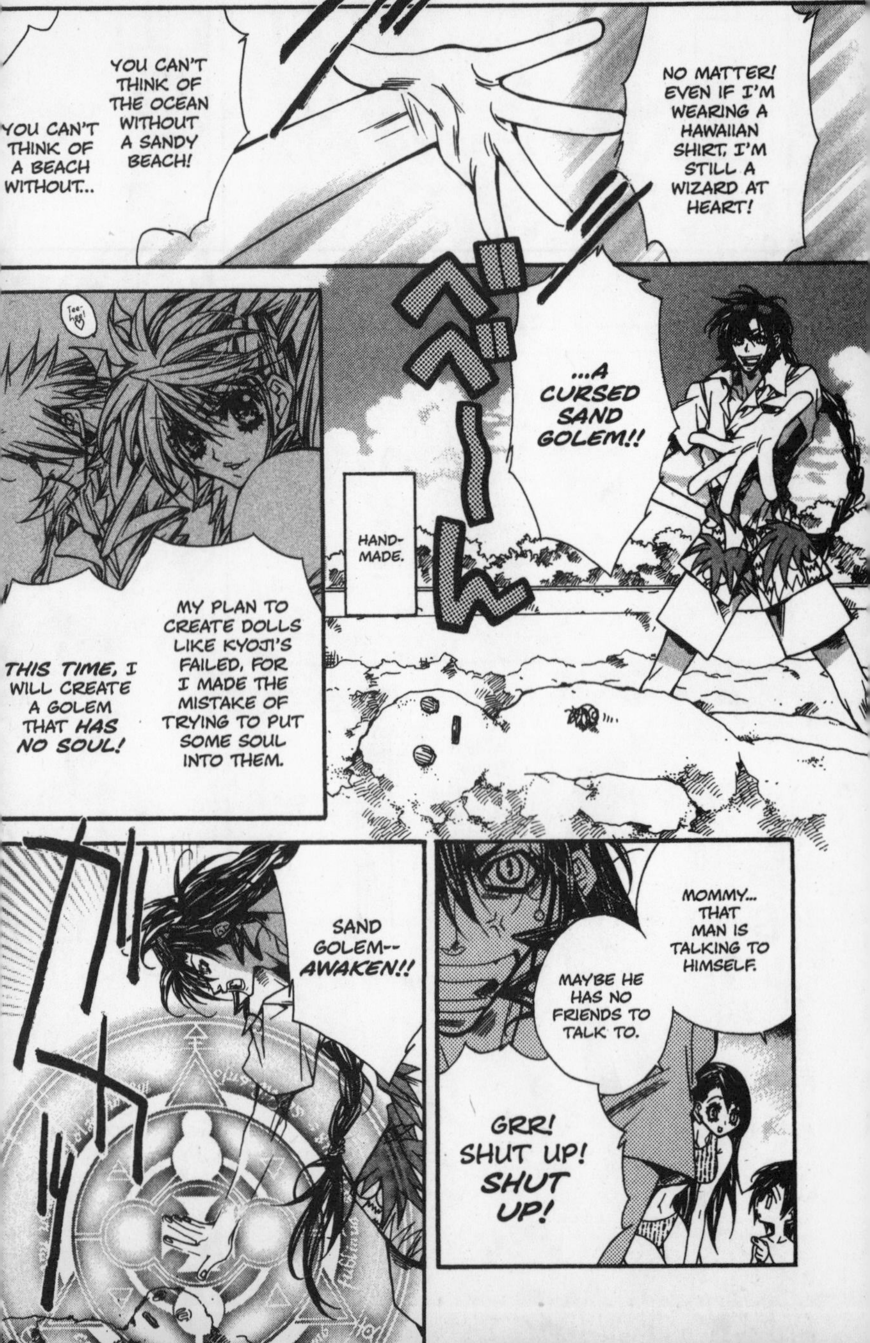
NO MATTER! EVEN IF I'M WEARING A HAWAIIAN SHIRT, I'M STILL A WIZARD AT HEART!
YOU CAN'T THINK OF THE OCEAN WITHOUT A SANDY BEACH!
YOU CAN'T THINK OF A BEACH WITHOUT...
...A CURSED SAND GOLEM!!
べべーん
HAND-MADE.
Tee-hee! ♡
MY PLAN TO CREATE DOLLS LIKE KYOJI'S FAILED, FOR I MADE THE MISTAKE OF TRYING TO PUT SOME SOUL INTO THEM.
THIS TIME, I WILL CREATE A GOLEM THAT HAS NO SOUL!
MOMMY... THAT MAN IS TALKING TO HIMSELF.
MAYBE HE HAS NO FRIENDS TO TALK TO.
GRR! SHUT UP! SHUT UP!
SAND GOLEM-- AWAKEN!!
カァッ

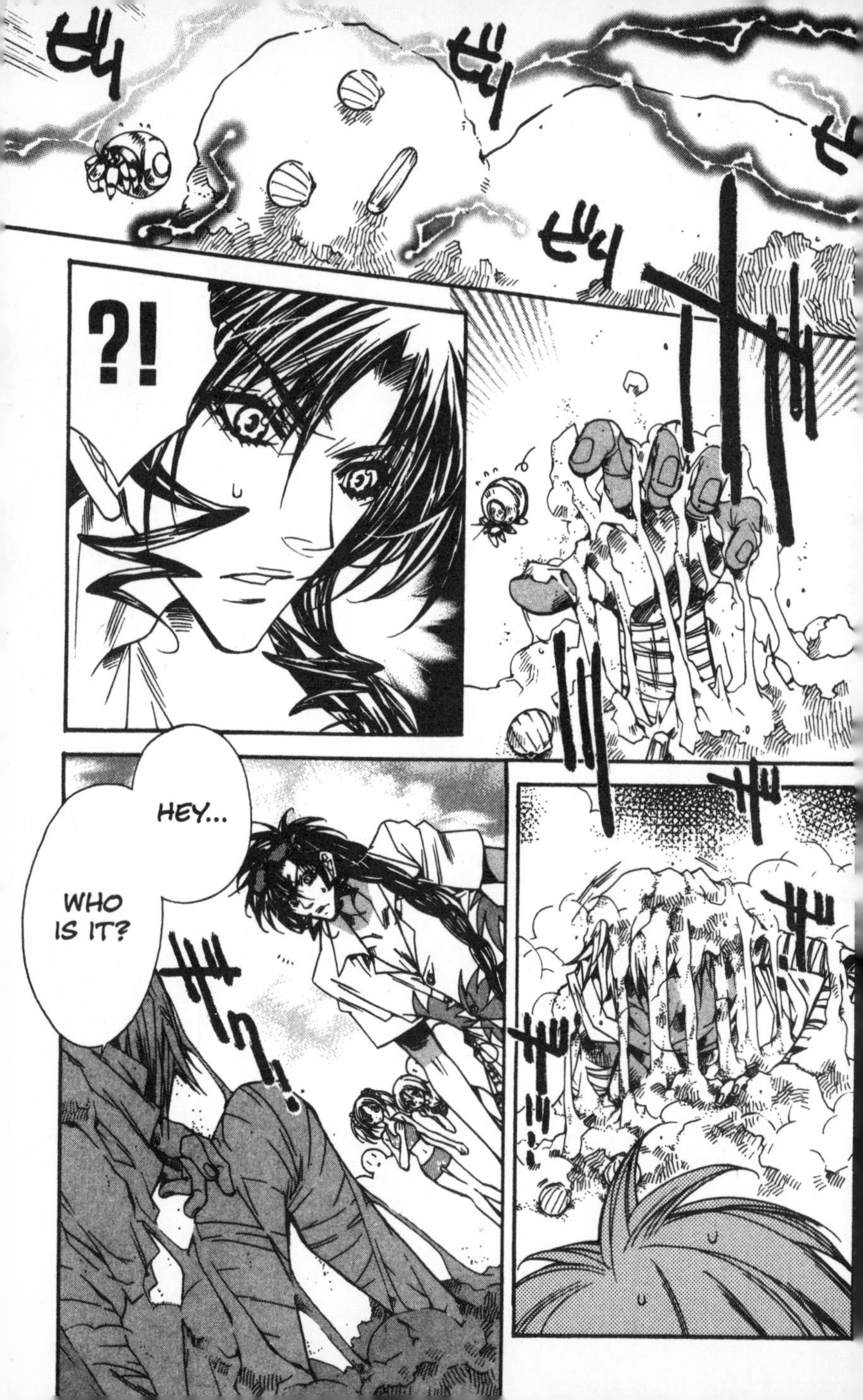
?!
HEY...
WHO IS IT?

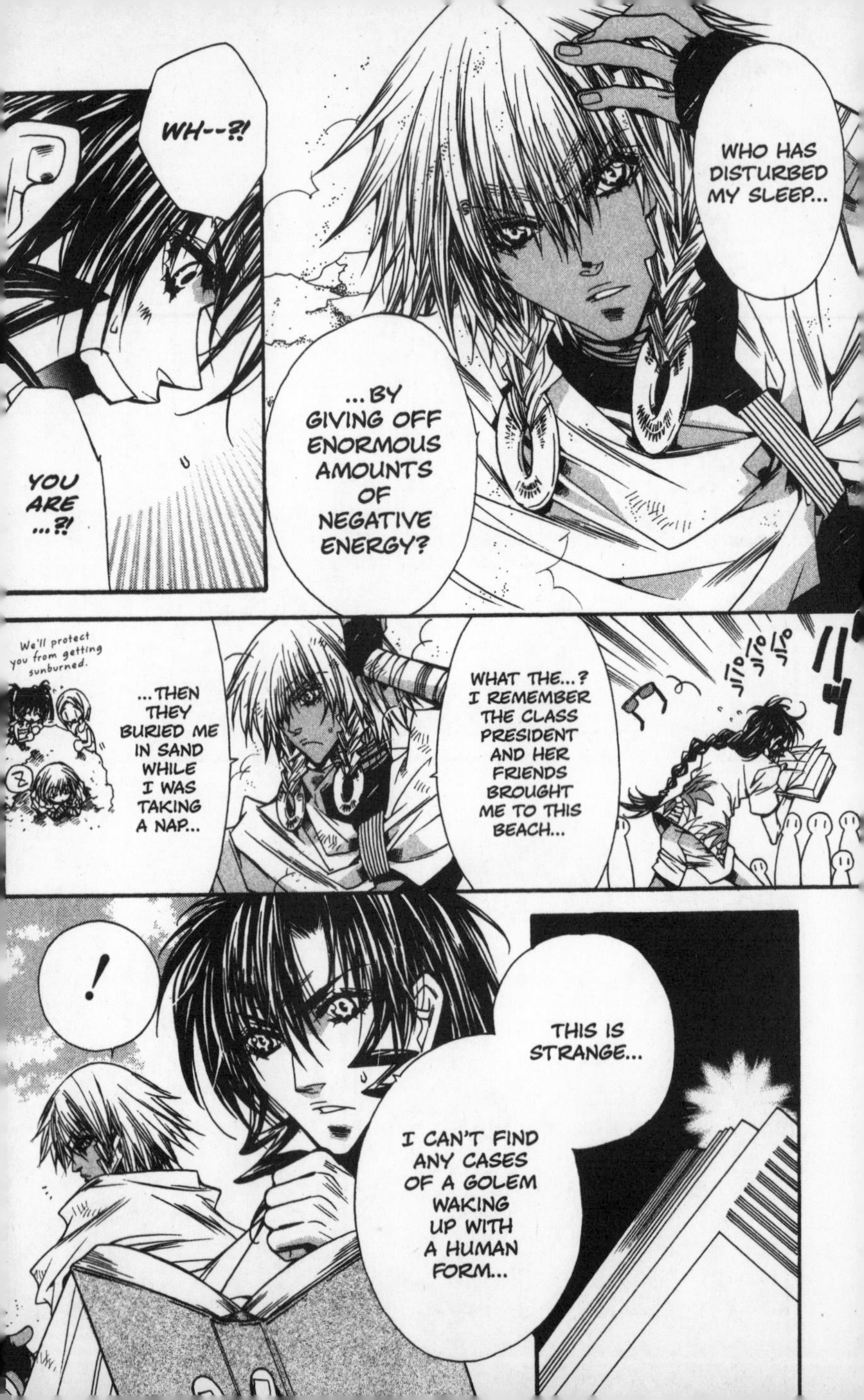
WHO HAS DISTURBED MY SLEEP...
...BY GIVING OFF ENORMOUS AMOUNTS OF NEGATIVE ENERGY?
WH--?!
YOU ARE ...?!
WHAT THE...? I REMEMBER THE CLASS PRESIDENT AND HER FRIENDS BROUGHT ME TO THIS BEACH...
...THEN THEY BURIED ME IN SAND WHILE I WAS TAKING A NAP...
We'll protect you from getting sunburned.
THIS IS STRANGE...
I CAN'T FIND ANY CASES OF A GOLEM WAKING UP WITH A HUMAN FORM...
!

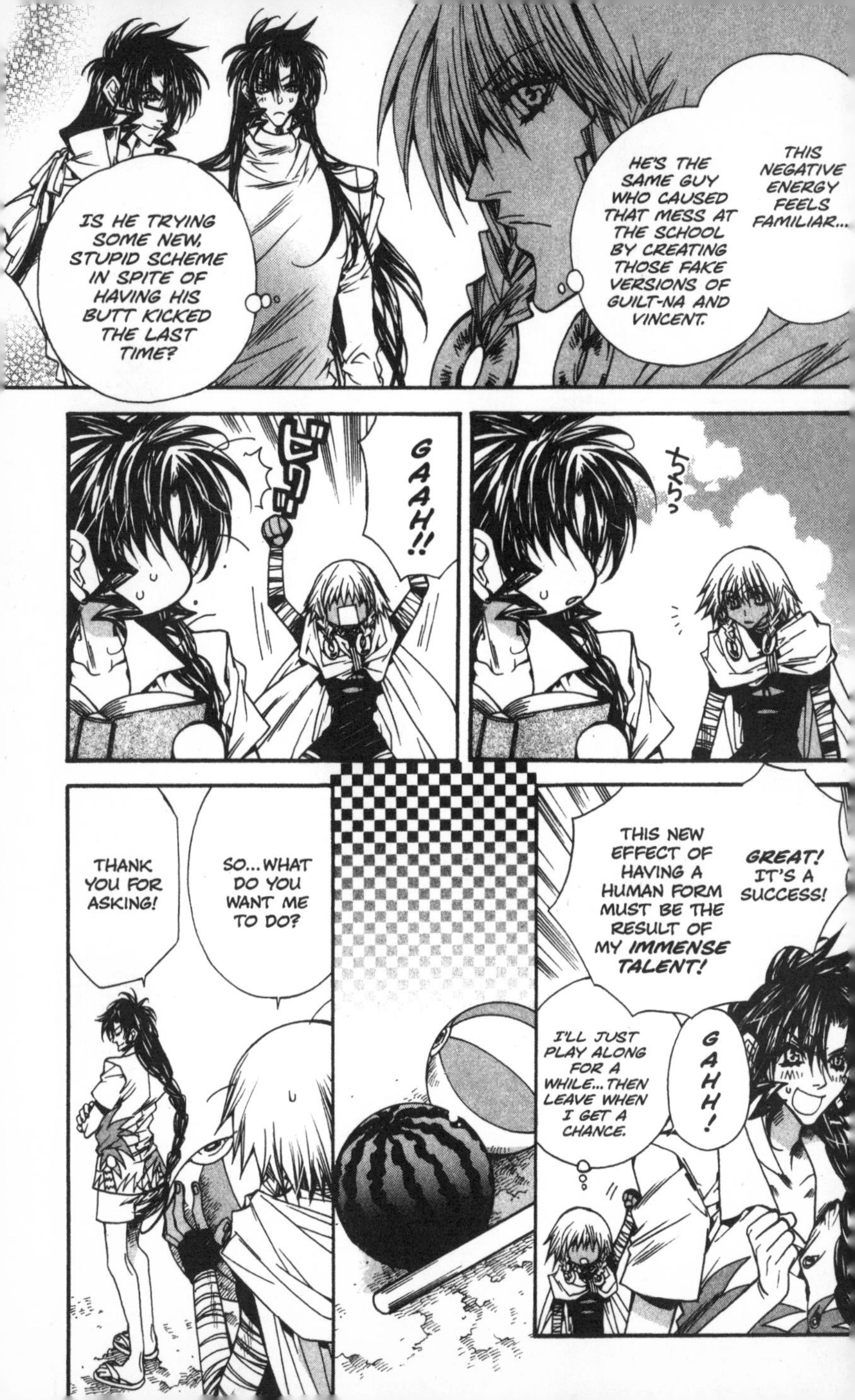
THIS NEGATIVE ENERGY FEELS FAMILIAR...
HE'S THE SAME GUY WHO CAUSED THAT MESS AT THE SCHOOL BY CREATING THOSE FAKE VERSIONS OF GUILT-NA AND VINCENT.
IS HE TRYING SOME NEW, STUPID SCHEME IN SPITE OF HAVING HIS BUTT KICKED THE LAST TIME?
GAAH!!
GREAT! IT'S A SUCCESS!
THIS NEW EFFECT OF HAVING A HUMAN FORM MUST BE THE RESULT OF MY IMMENSE TALENT!
GAHH!
I'LL JUST PLAY ALONG FOR A WHILE... THEN LEAVE WHEN I GET A CHANCE.
SO... WHAT DO YOU WANT ME TO DO?
THANK YOU FOR ASKING!

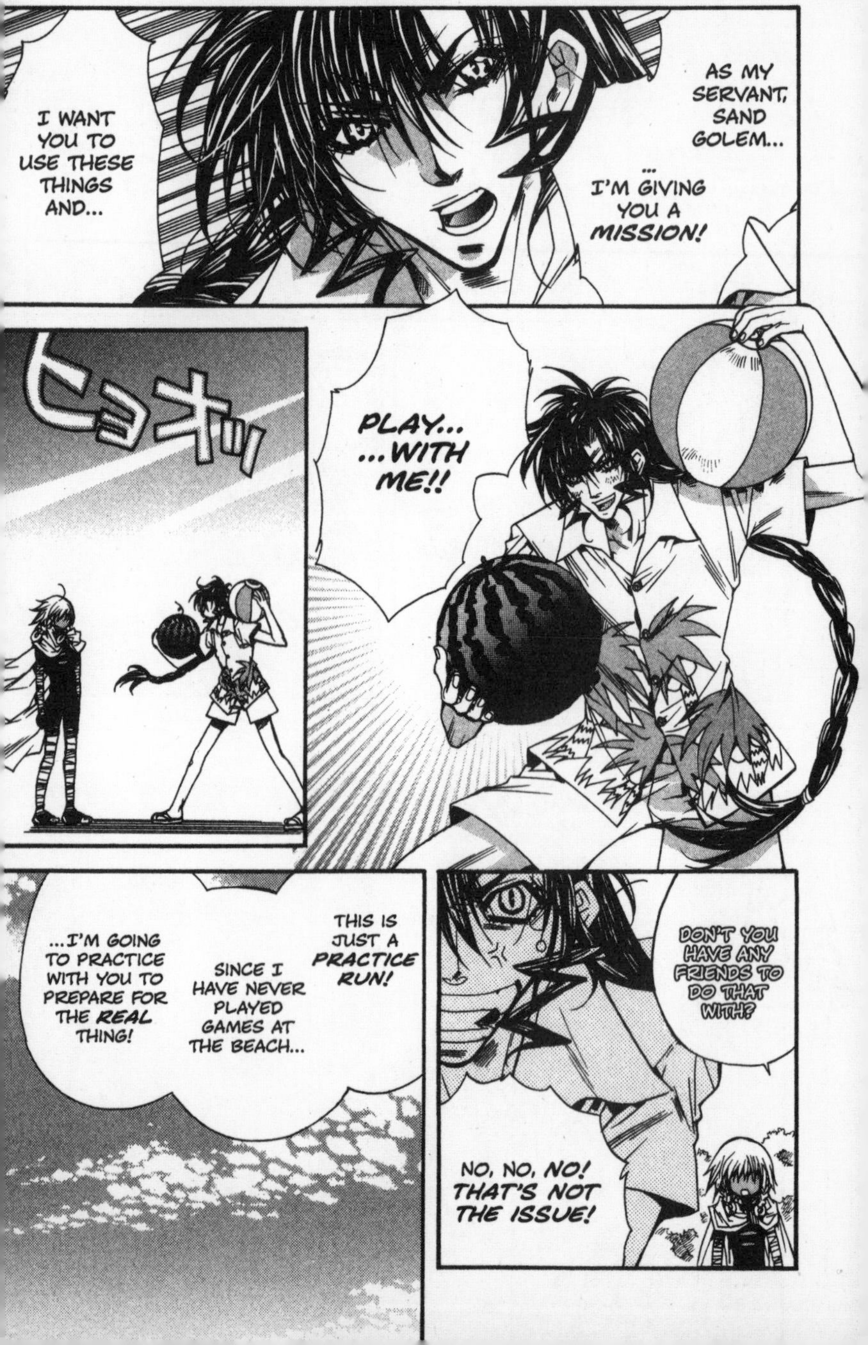
AS MY SERVANT, SAND GOLEM...
... I'M GIVING YOU A MISSION!
I WANT YOU TO USE THESE THINGS AND...
PLAY... ...WITH ME!!
ヒョオッ
DON'T YOU HAVE ANY FRIENDS TO DO THAT WITH?
NO, NO, NO! THAT'S NOT THE ISSUE!
THIS IS JUST A PRACTICE RUN!
SINCE I HAVE NEVER PLAYED GAMES AT THE BEACH...
...I'M GOING TO PRACTICE WITH YOU TO PREPARE FOR THE REAL THING!

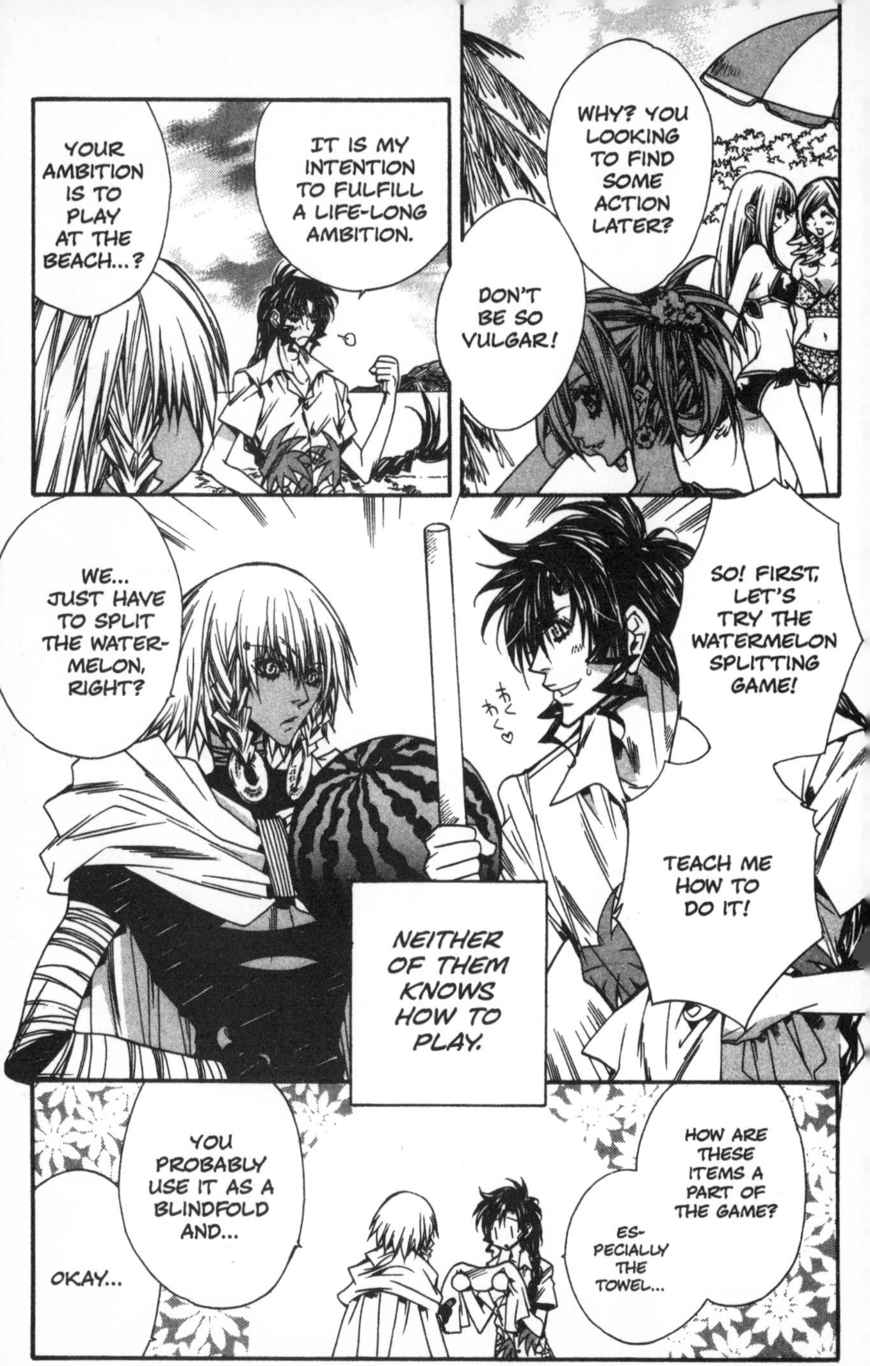
WHY? YOU LOOKING TO FIND SOME ACTION LATER?
DON'T BE SO VULGAR!
IT IS MY INTENTION TO FULFILL A LIFE-LONG AMBITION.
YOUR AMBITION IS TO PLAY AT THE BEACH...?
SO! FIRST, LET'S TRY THE WATERMELON SPLITTING GAME!
TEACH ME HOW TO DO IT!
わくわく♡
WE... JUST HAVE TO SPLIT THE WATER-MELON, RIGHT?
NEITHER OF THEM KNOWS HOW TO PLAY.
HOW ARE THESE ITEMS A PART OF THE GAME?
ES-PECIALLY THE TOWEL...
YOU PROBABLY USE IT AS A BLINDFOLD AND...
OKAY...

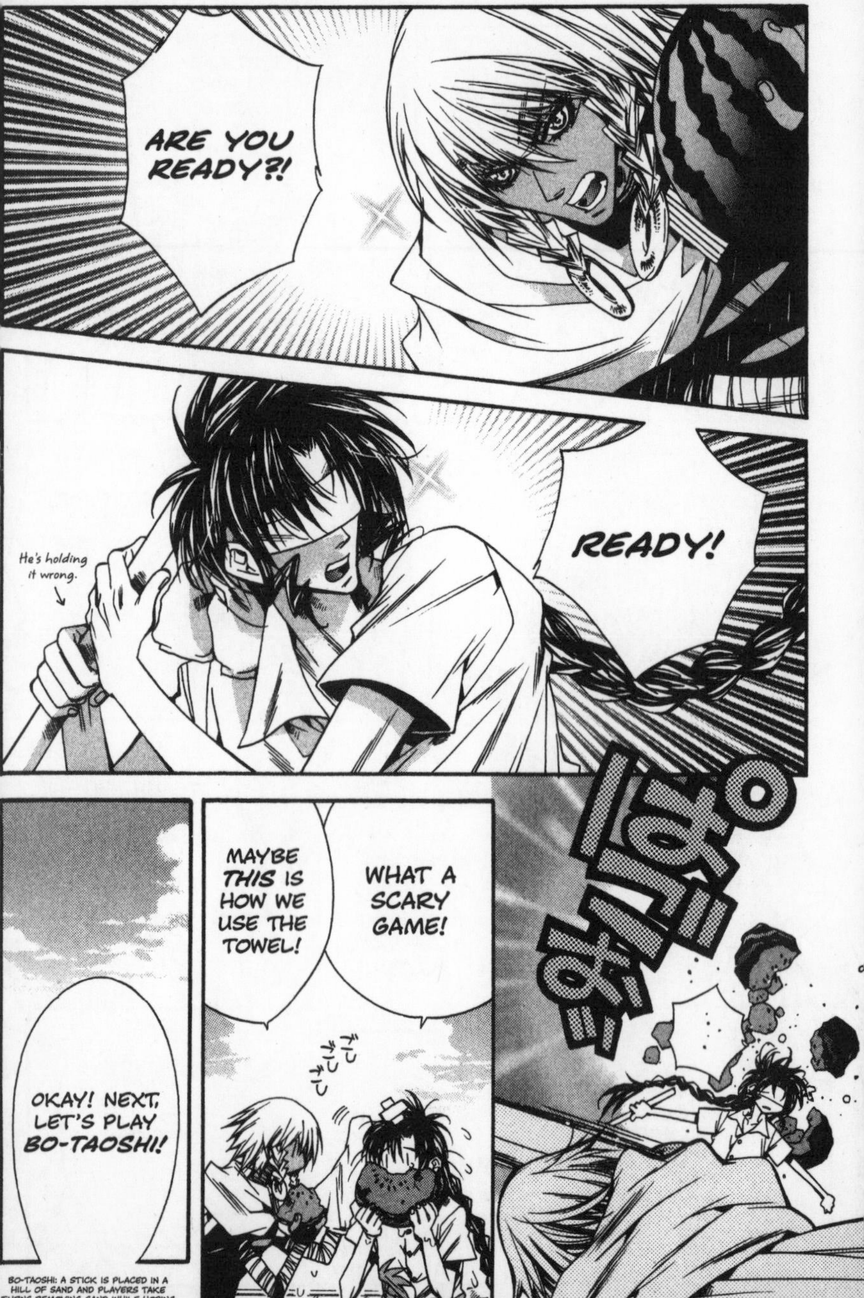
ARE YOU READY?!
READY!
He's holding it wrong.
WHAT A SCARY GAME!
MAYBE THIS IS HOW WE USE THE TOWEL!
OKAY! NEXT, LET'S PLAY BO-TAOSHI!

BO-TAOSHI: A STICK IS PLACED IN A HILL OF SAND AND PLAYERS TAKE TURNS REMOVING SAND WHILE HOPING THE STICK DOESN'T FALL OVER.

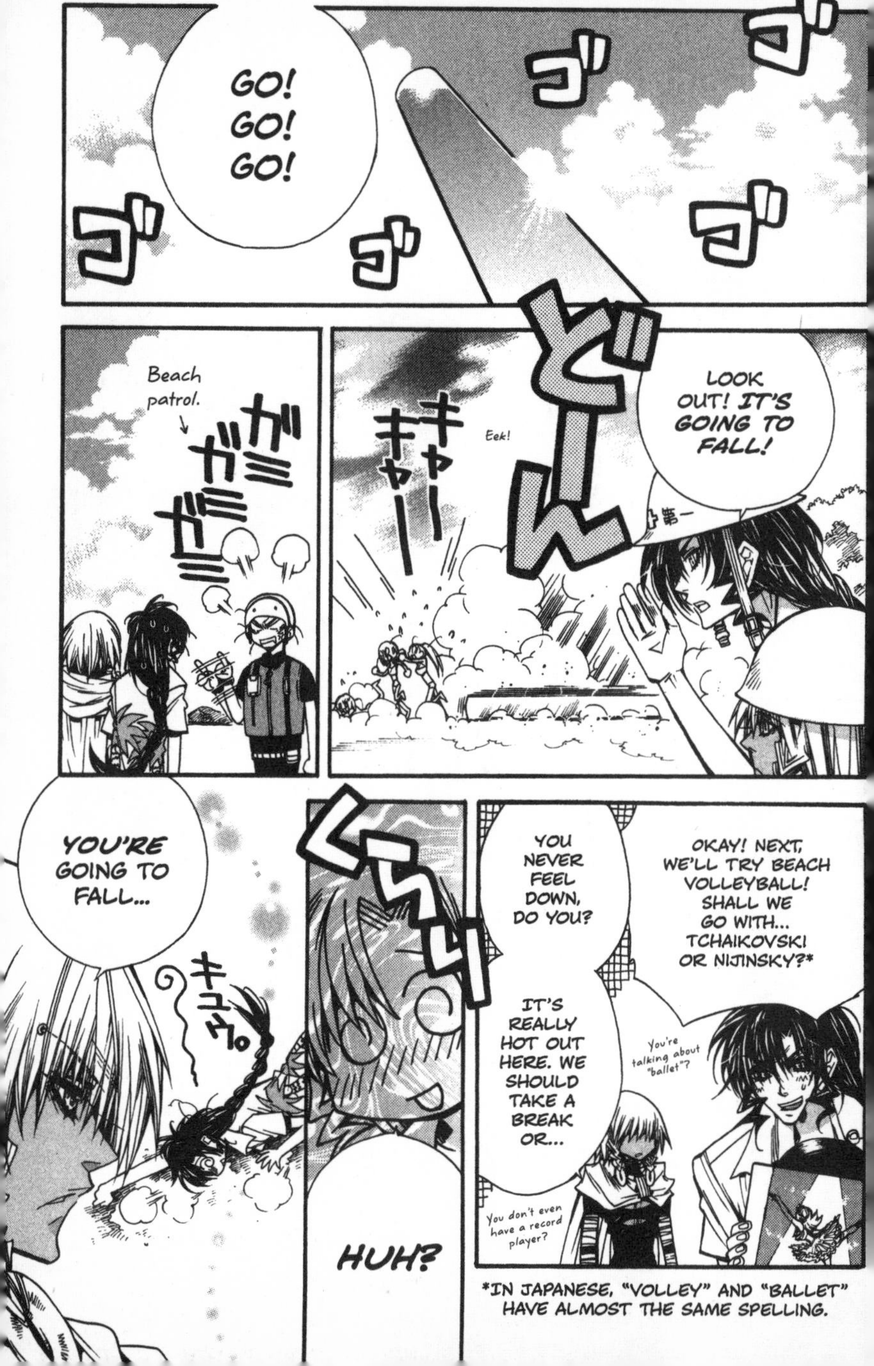
ゴ
ゴ
ゴ
GO! GO! GO!
ゴ
ゴ
どーん
LOOK OUT! IT'S GOING TO FALL!
キャーキャー
Eek!
Beach patrol.
ガミガミガミ
OKAY! NEXT, WE'LL TRY BEACH VOLLEYBALL! SHALL WE GO WITH... TCHAIKOVSKI OR NIJINSKY?*
You're talking about "ballet"?
YOU NEVER FEEL DOWN, DO YOU?
IT'S REALLY HOT OUT HERE. WE SHOULD TAKE A BREAK OR...
You don't even have a record player?
HUH?
YOU'RE GOING TO FALL...

*IN JAPANESE, "VOLLEY" AND "BALLET" HAVE ALMOST THE SAME SPELLING.

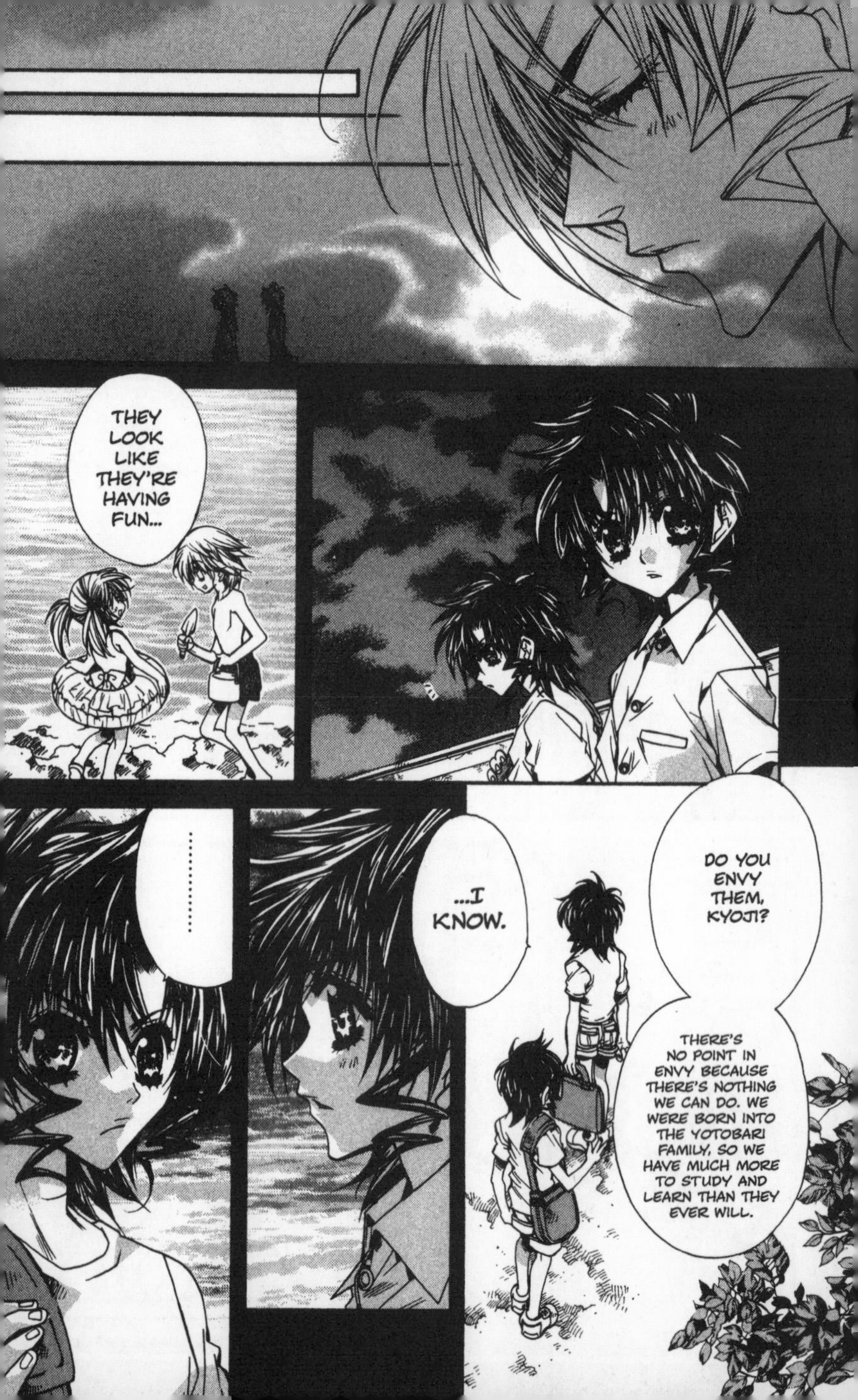
THEY LOOK LIKE THEY'RE HAVING FUN...
DO YOU ENVY THEM, KYOJI?
THERE'S NO POINT IN ENVY BECAUSE THERE'S NOTHING WE CAN DO. WE WERE BORN INTO THE YOTOBARI FAMILY, SO WE HAVE MUCH MORE TO STUDY AND LEARN THAN THEY EVER WILL.
...I KNOW.
....

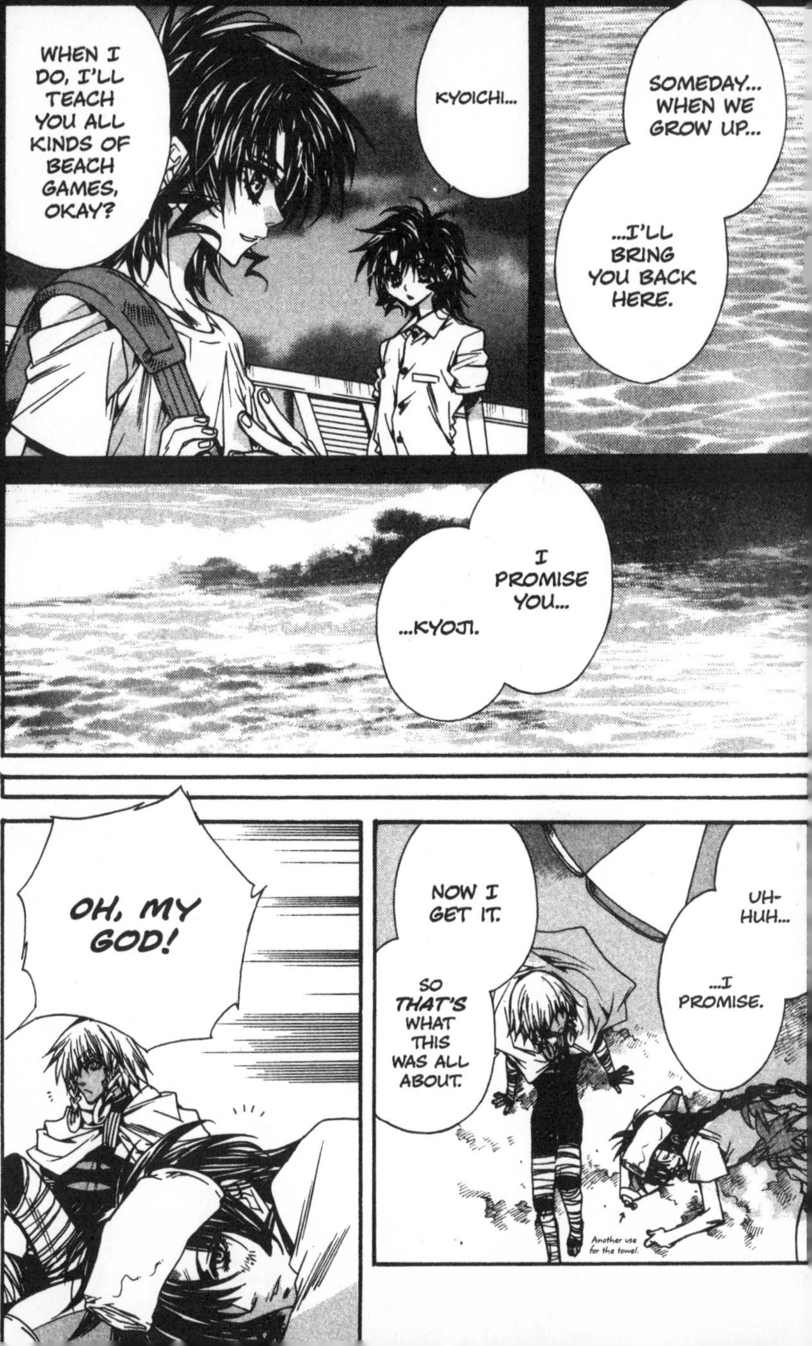
SOMEDAY... WHEN WE GROW UP...
...I'LL BRING YOU BACK HERE.
KYOICHI...
WHEN I DO, I'LL TEACH YOU ALL KINDS OF BEACH GAMES, OKAY?
I PROMISE YOU...
...KYOJI.
UH-HUH...
...I PROMISE.
NOW I GET IT.
SO *THAT'S* WHAT THIS WAS ALL ABOUT.
Another use for the towel.
OH, MY GOD!

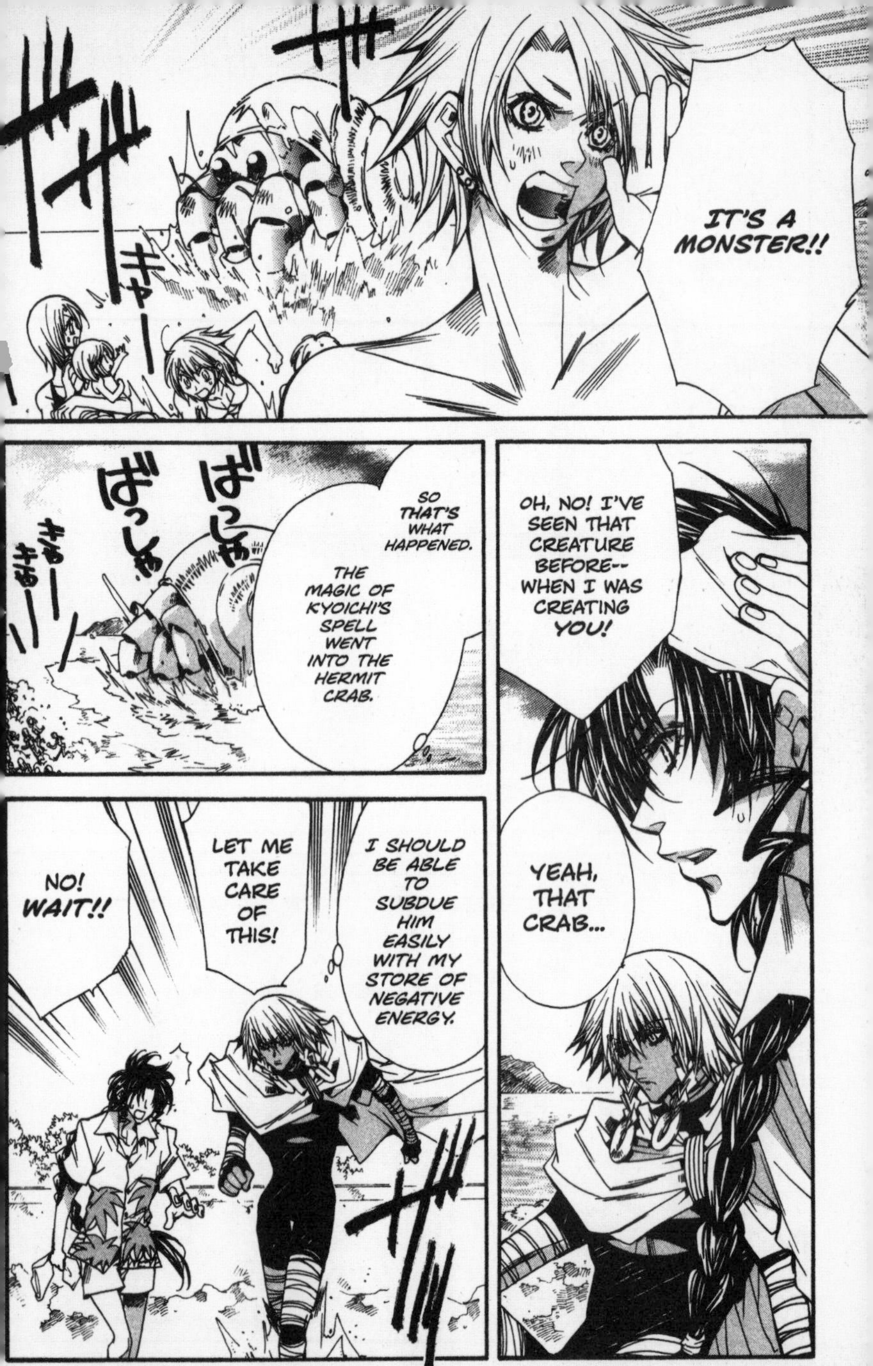
ザザ
ザザ
IT'S A MONSTER!!
キャー
OH, NO! I'VE SEEN THAT CREATURE BEFORE-- WHEN I WAS CREATING YOU!
YEAH, THAT CRAB...
ばっしゃ
ばっしゃ
きゃーきゃー
SO THAT'S WHAT HAPPENED.
THE MAGIC OF KYOICHI'S SPELL WENT INTO THE HERMIT CRAB.
I SHOULD BE ABLE TO SUBDUE HIM EASILY WITH MY STORE OF NEGATIVE ENERGY.
LET ME TAKE CARE OF THIS!
NO! WAIT!!

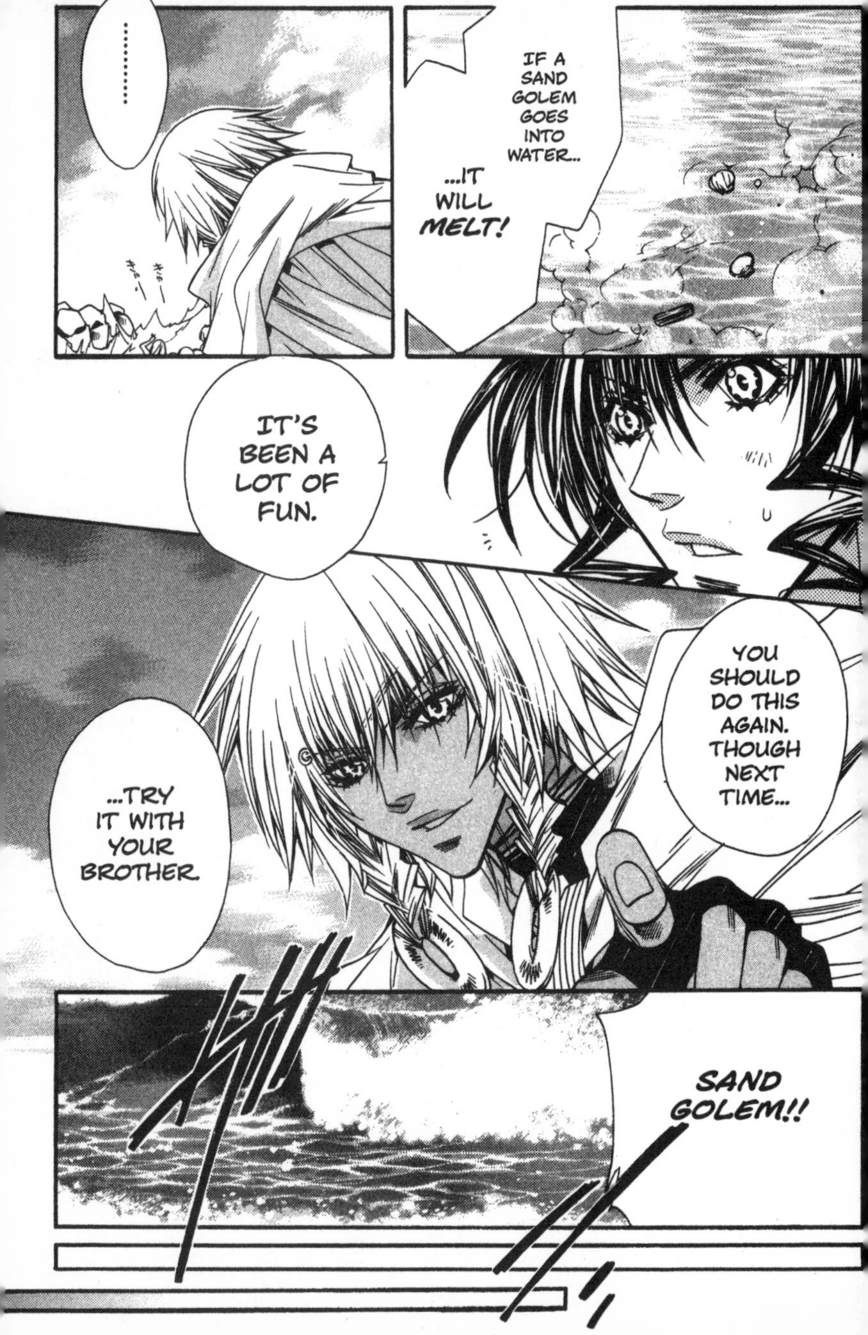
IF A SAND GOLEM GOES INTO WATER...
...IT WILL MELT!
....
IT'S BEEN A LOT OF FUN.
YOU SHOULD DO THIS AGAIN. THOUGH NEXT TIME...
...TRY IT WITH YOUR BROTHER.
SAND GOLEM!!

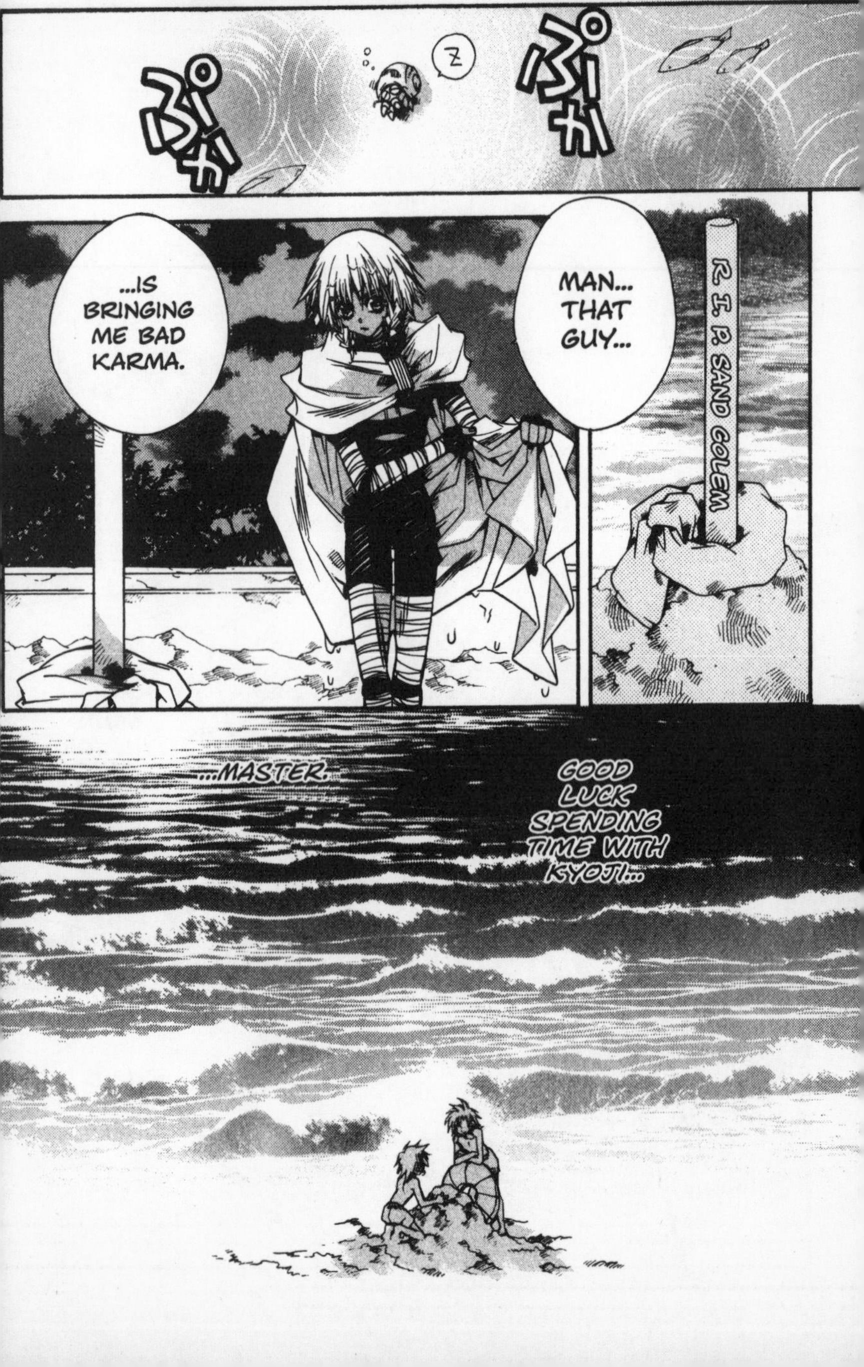
ぷか
ぷか
Z
R.I.P. SAND GOLEM
MAN... THAT GUY...
...IS BRINGING ME BAD KARMA.
GOOD LUCK SPENDING TIME WITH KYOJI...
...MASTER.

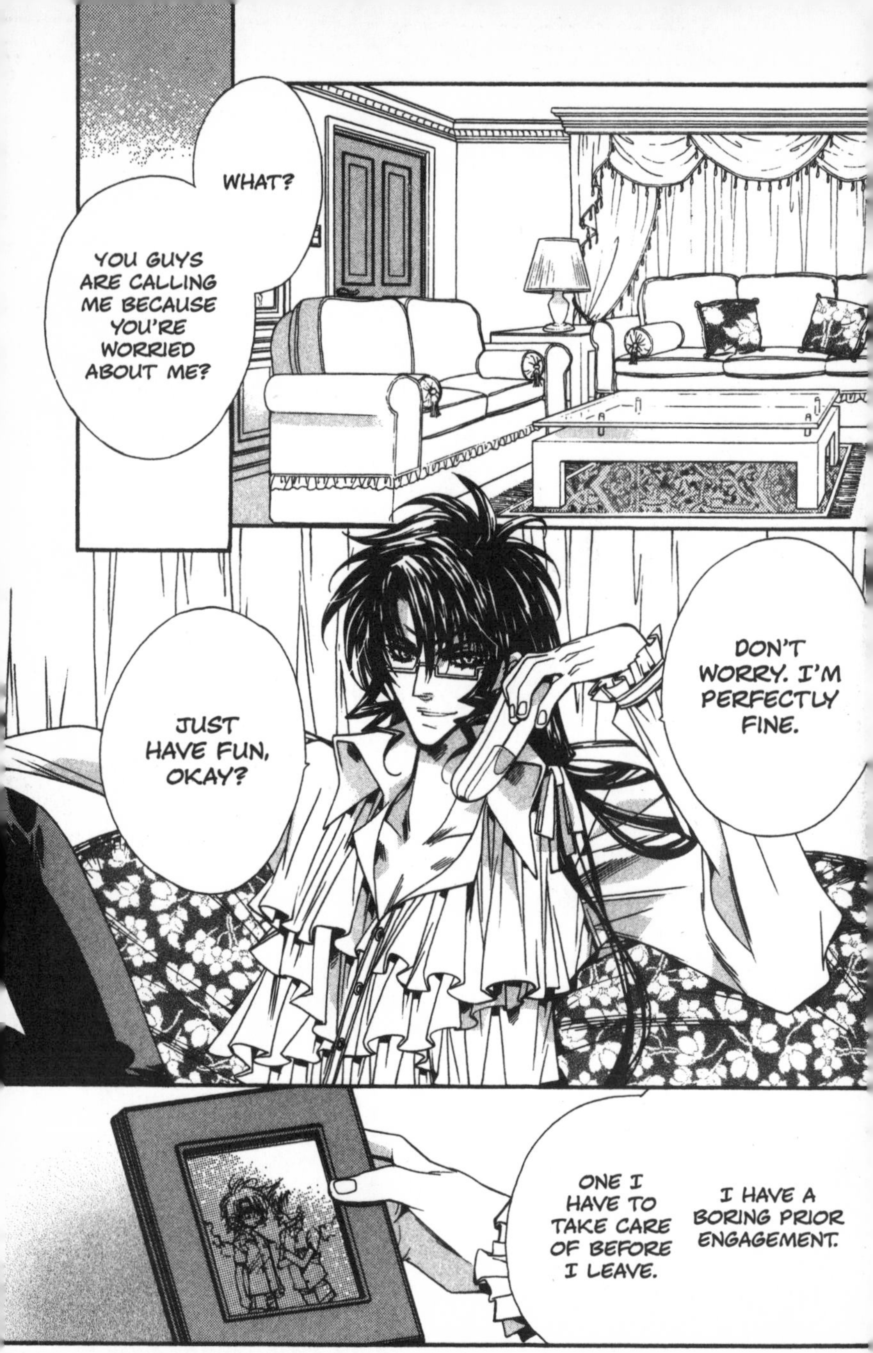
WHAT?
YOU GUYS ARE CALLING ME BECAUSE YOU'RE WORRIED ABOUT ME?
DON'T WORRY. I'M PERFECTLY FINE.
JUST HAVE FUN, OKAY?
I HAVE A BORING PRIOR ENGAGEMENT.
ONE I HAVE TO TAKE CARE OF BEFORE I LEAVE.

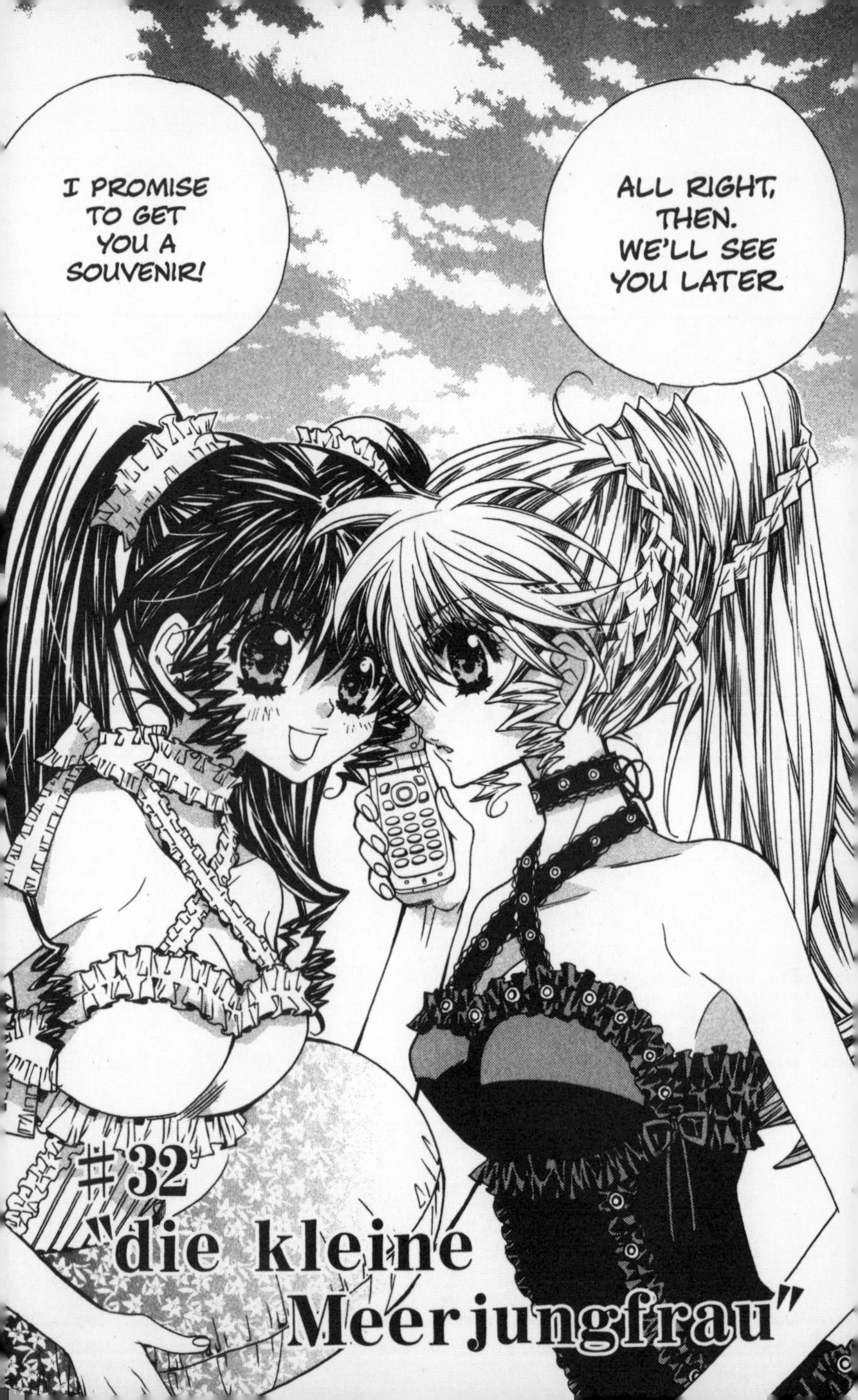
ALL RIGHT, THEN. WE'LL SEE YOU LATER
I PROMISE TO GET YOU A SOUVENIR!
#32 "die kleine Meerjungfrau"

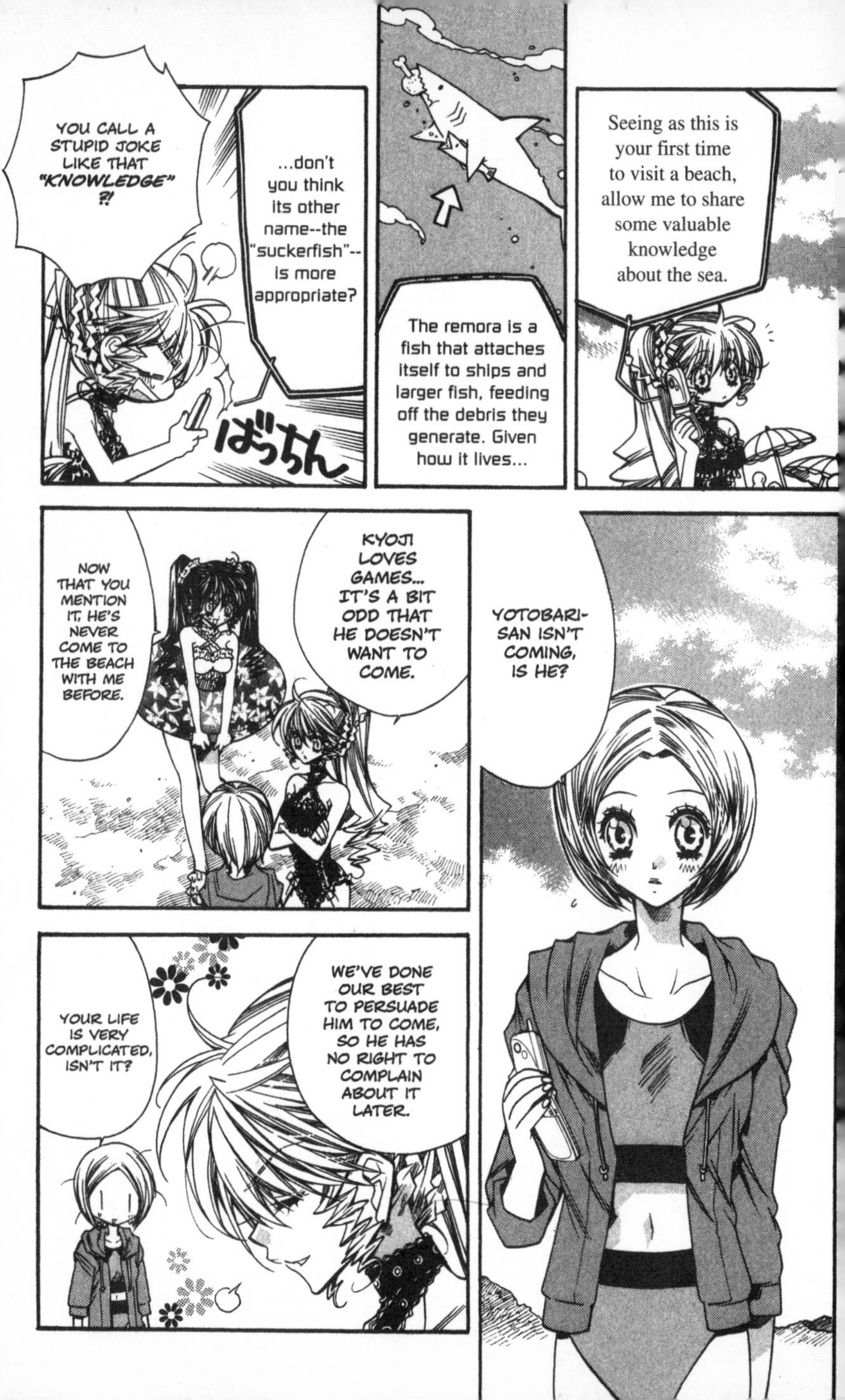
Seeing as this is your first time to visit a beach, allow me to share some valuable knowledge about the sea.
The remora is a fish that attaches itself to ships and larger fish, feeding off the debris they generate. Given how it lives...
...don't you think its other name--the "suckerfish"--is more appropriate?
ばっちん
YOU CALL A STUPID JOKE LIKE THAT "KNOWLEDGE" ?!
YOTOBARI-SAN ISN'T COMING, IS HE?
KYOJI LOVES GAMES... IT'S A BIT ODD THAT HE DOESN'T WANT TO COME.
NOW THAT YOU MENTION IT, HE'S NEVER COME TO THE BEACH WITH ME BEFORE.
WE'VE DONE OUR BEST TO PERSUADE HIM TO COME, SO HE HAS NO RIGHT TO COMPLAIN ABOUT IT LATER.
YOUR LIFE IS VERY COMPLICATED, ISN'T IT?

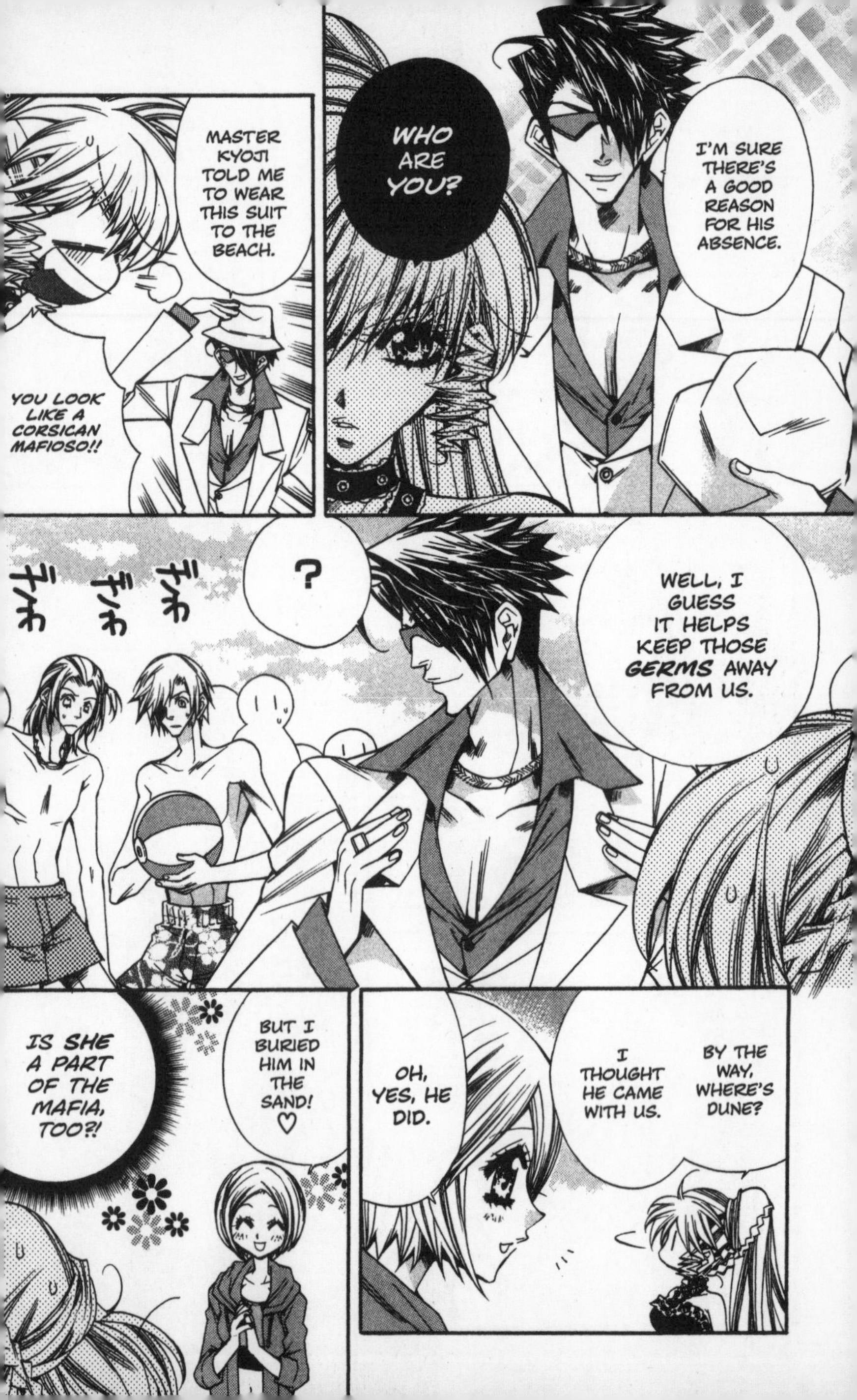
I'M SURE THERE'S A GOOD REASON FOR HIS ABSENCE.
WHO ARE YOU?
MASTER KYOJI TOLD ME TO WEAR THIS SUIT TO THE BEACH.
YOU LOOK LIKE A CORSICAN MAFIOSO!!
WELL, I GUESS IT HELPS KEEP THOSE GERMS AWAY FROM US.
?
ざわ ざわ ざわ
BY THE WAY, WHERE'S DUNE?
I THOUGHT HE CAME WITH US.
OH, YES, HE DID.
BUT I BURIED HIM IN THE SAND! ♡
IS SHE A PART OF THE MAFIA, TOO?!

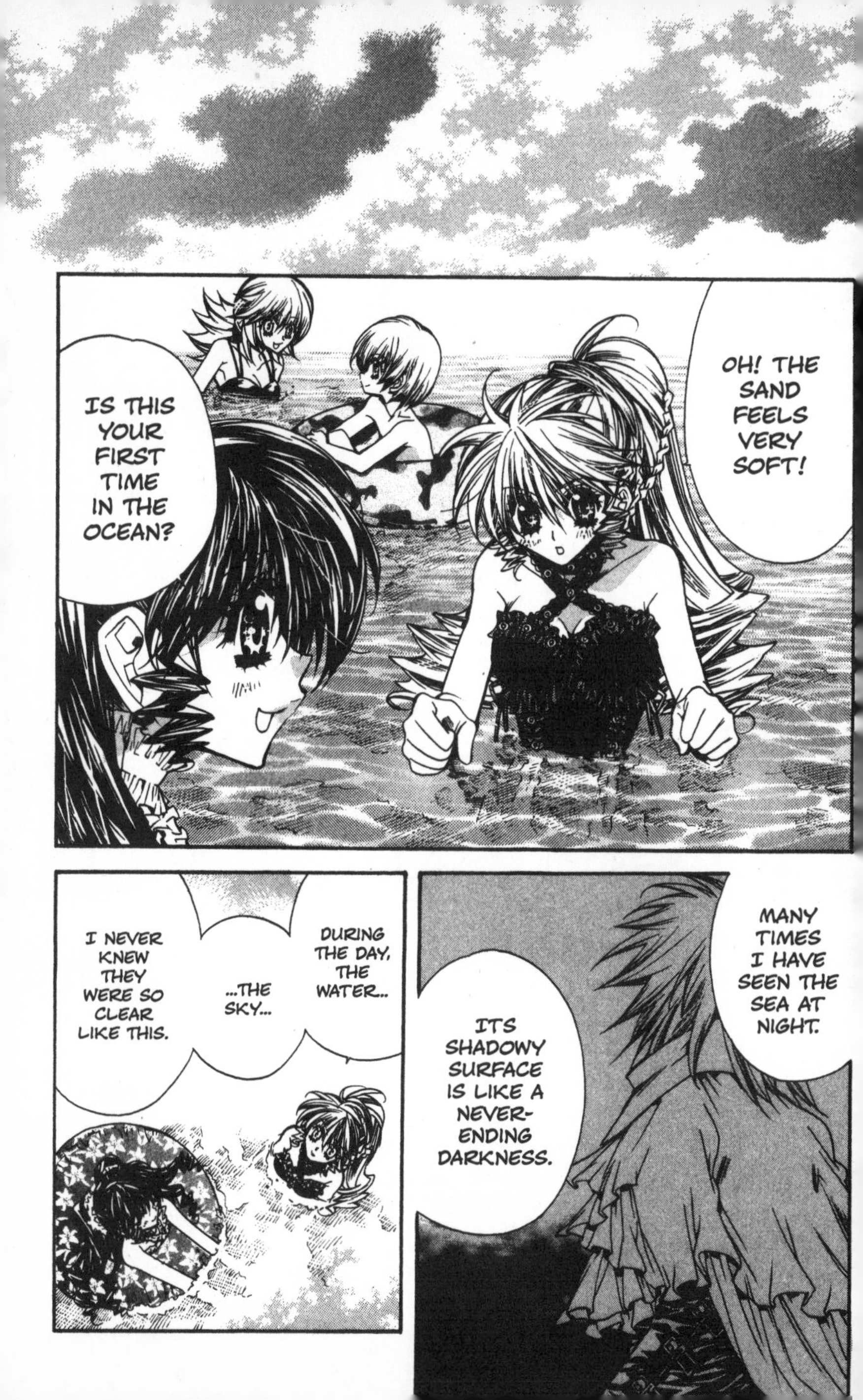
OH! THE SAND FEELS VERY SOFT!
IS THIS YOUR FIRST TIME IN THE OCEAN?
MANY TIMES I HAVE SEEN THE SEA AT NIGHT.
ITS SHADOWY SURFACE IS LIKE A NEVER-ENDING DARKNESS.
DURING THE DAY, THE WATER...
...THE SKY...
I NEVER KNEW THEY WERE SO CLEAR LIKE THIS.

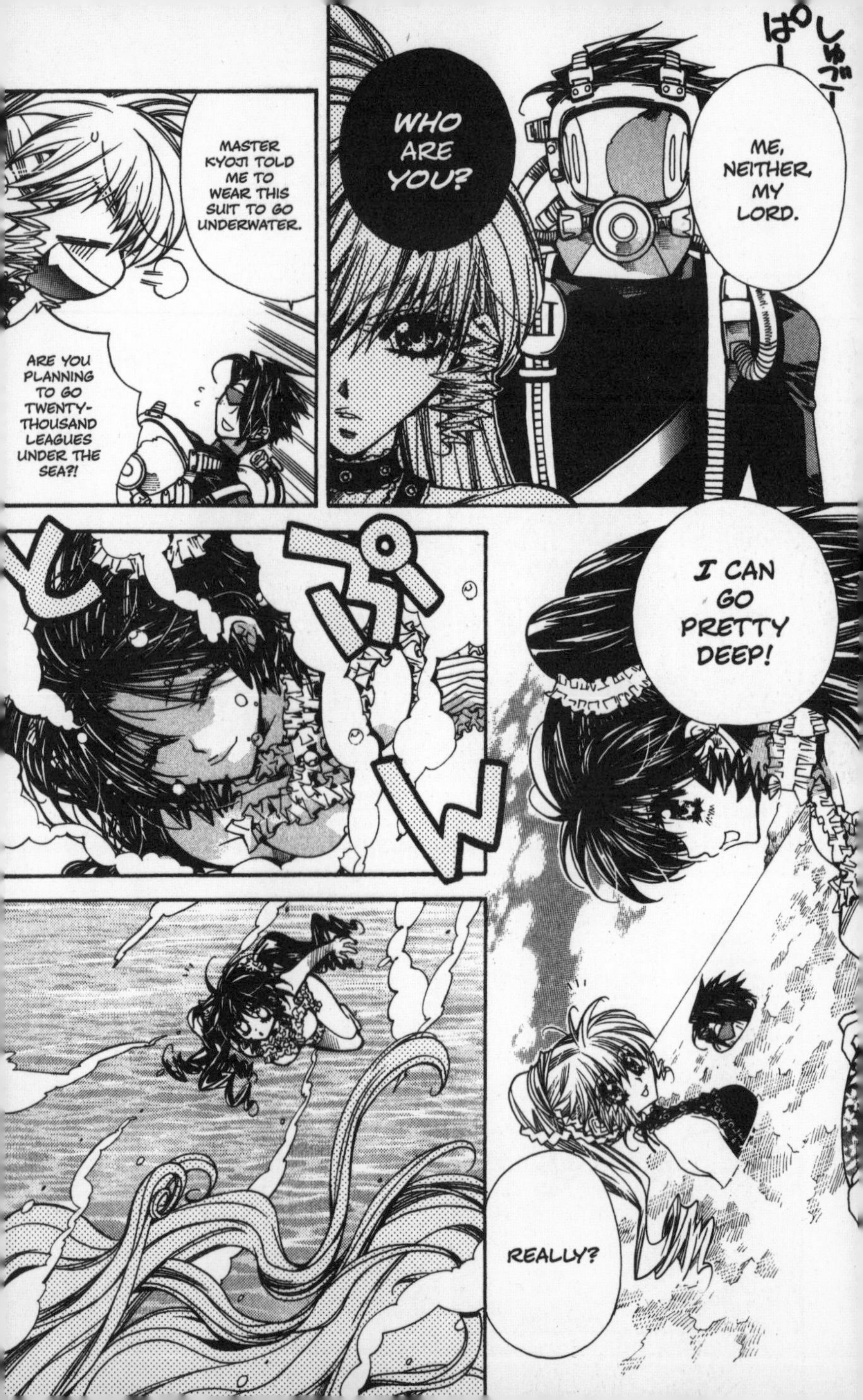
しゅブー
ぱー
ME, NEITHER, MY LORD.
WHO ARE YOU?
MASTER KYOJI TOLD ME TO WEAR THIS SUIT TO GO UNDERWATER.
ARE YOU PLANNING TO GO TWENTY-THOUSAND LEAGUES UNDER THE SEA?!
I CAN GO PRETTY DEEP!
REALLY?
とぷん

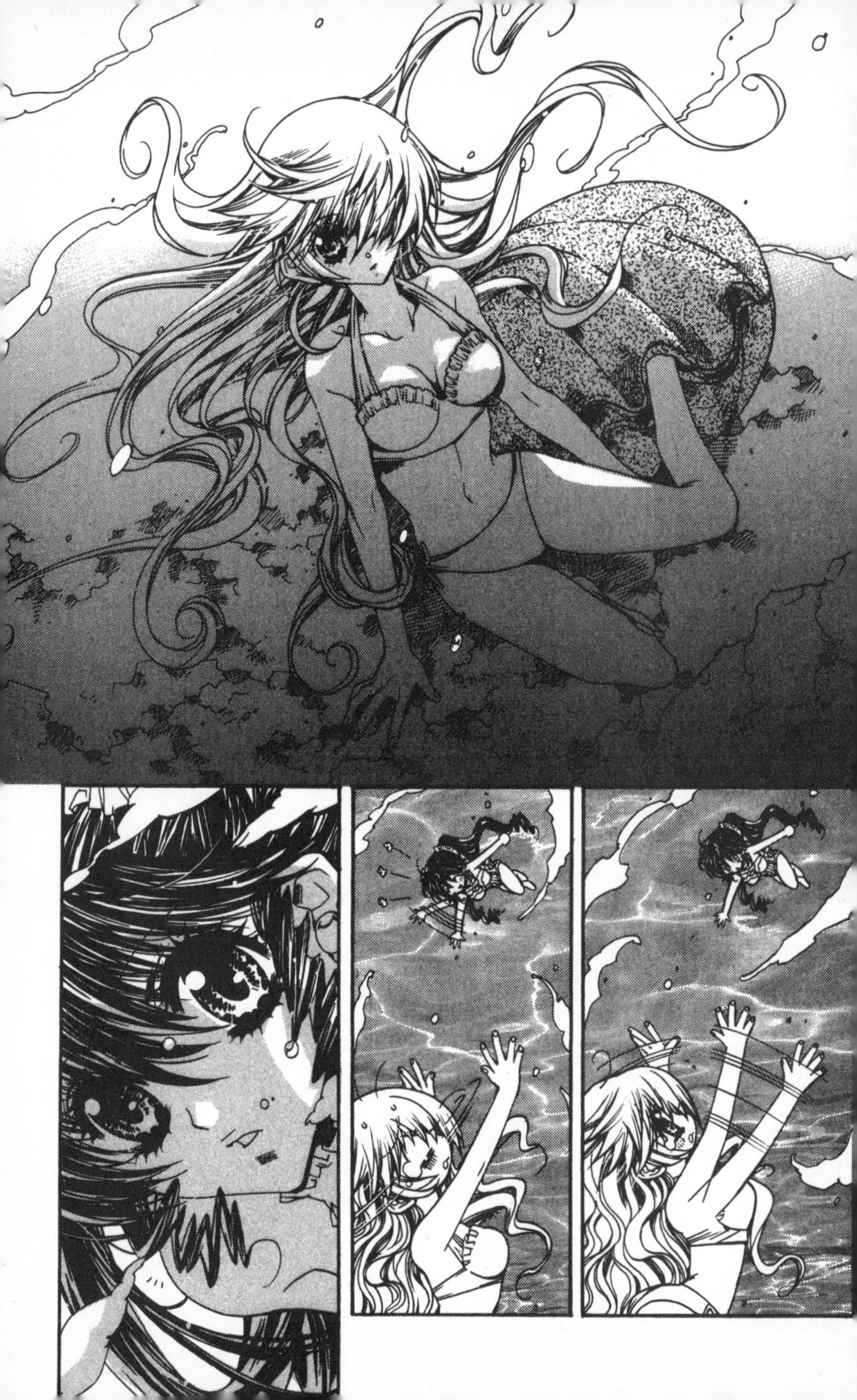

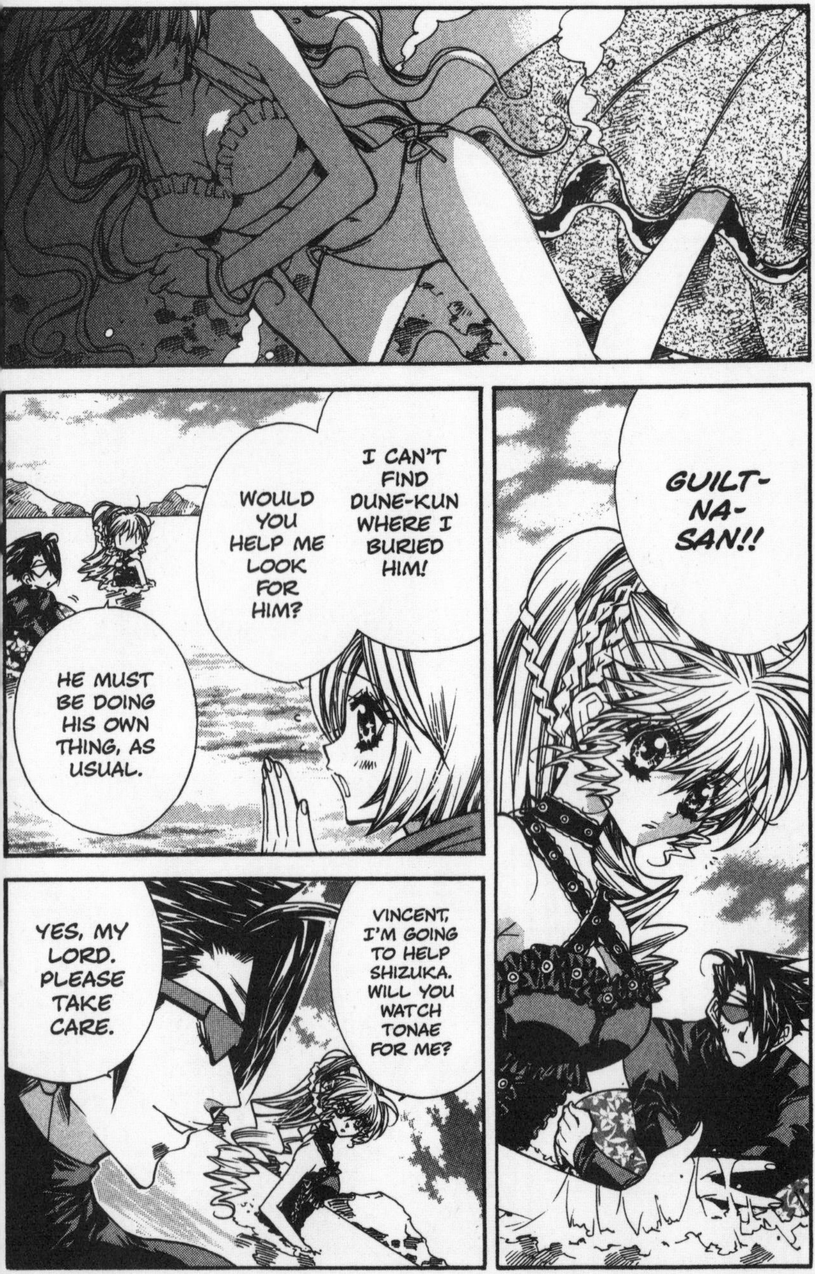
GUILT-NA-SAN!!
I CAN'T FIND DUNE-KUN WHERE I BURIED HIM!
WOULD YOU HELP ME LOOK FOR HIM?
HE MUST BE DOING HIS OWN THING, AS USUAL.
VINCENT, I'M GOING TO HELP SHIZUKA. WILL YOU WATCH TONAE FOR ME?
YES, MY LORD. PLEASE TAKE CARE.

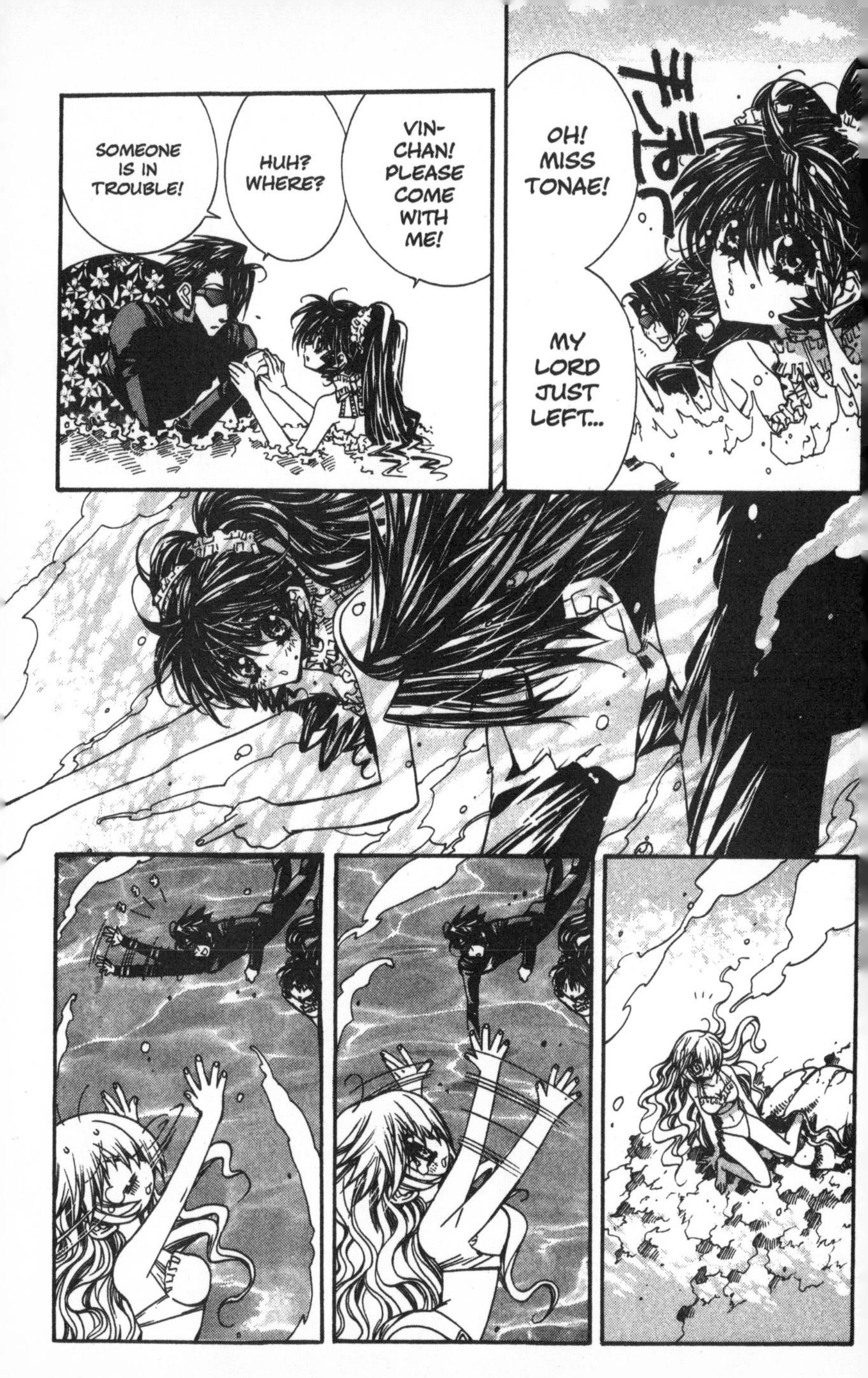
OH! MISS TONAE!
MY LORD JUST LEFT...
VIN-CHAN! PLEASE COME WITH ME!
HUH? WHERE?
SOMEONE IS IN TROUBLE!

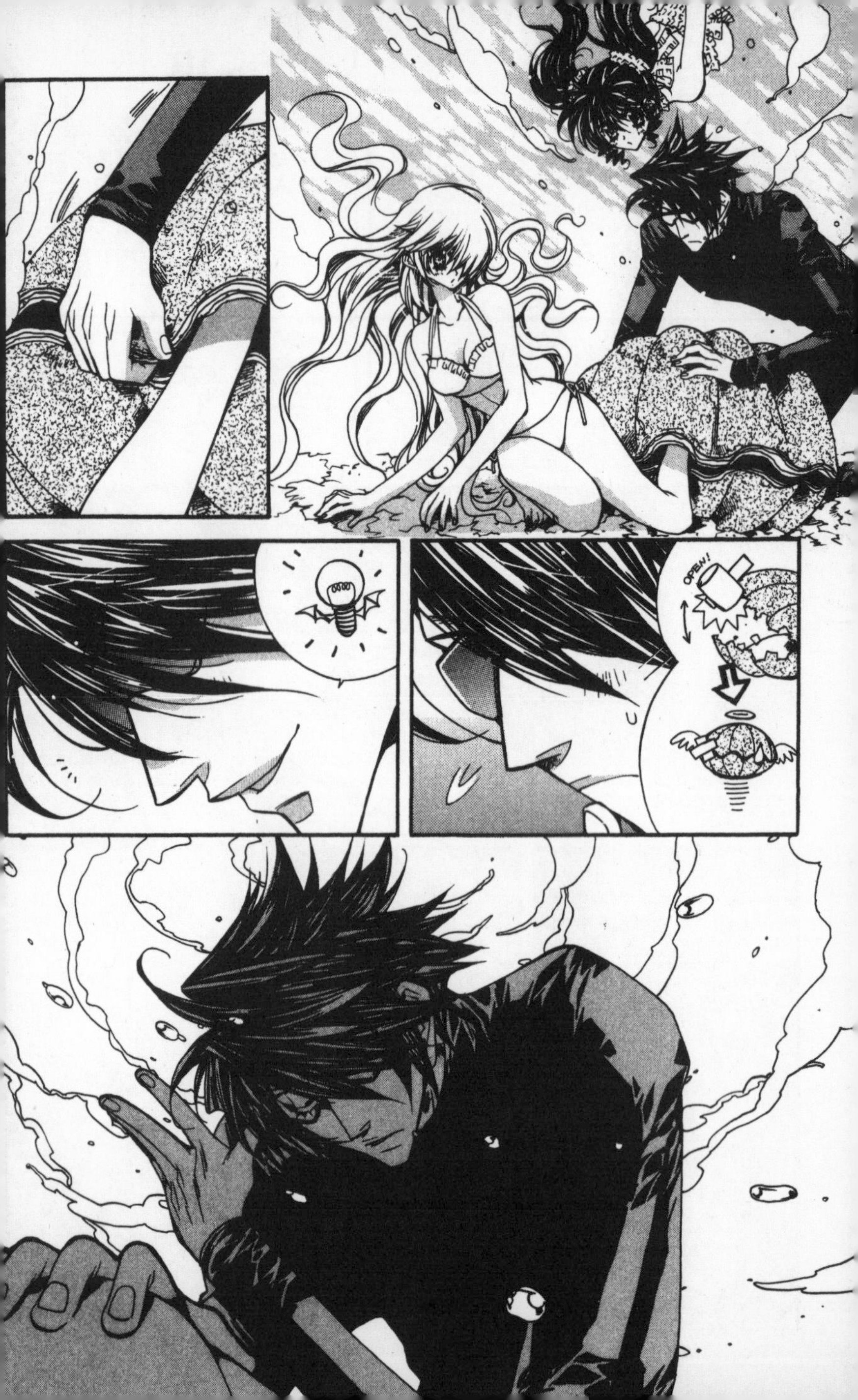
OPEN!

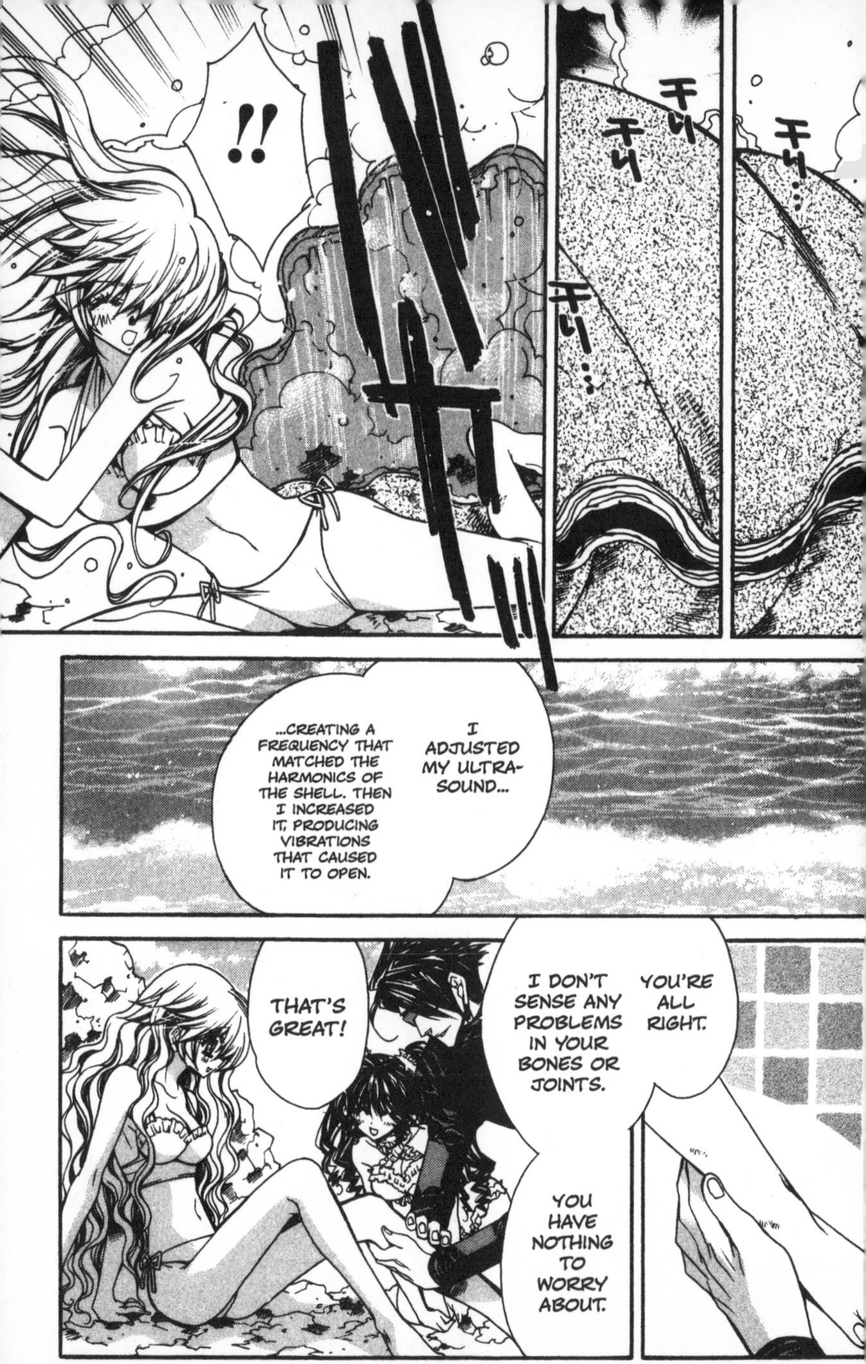

チリ…
チリ
チリ
チリ…
!!
I ADJUSTED MY ULTRA-SOUND...
...CREATING A FREQUENCY THAT MATCHED THE HARMONICS OF THE SHELL. THEN I INCREASED IT, PRODUCING VIBRATIONS THAT CAUSED IT TO OPEN.
YOU'RE ALL RIGHT.
I DON'T SENSE ANY PROBLEMS IN YOUR BONES OR JOINTS.
YOU HAVE NOTHING TO WORRY ABOUT.
THAT'S GREAT!

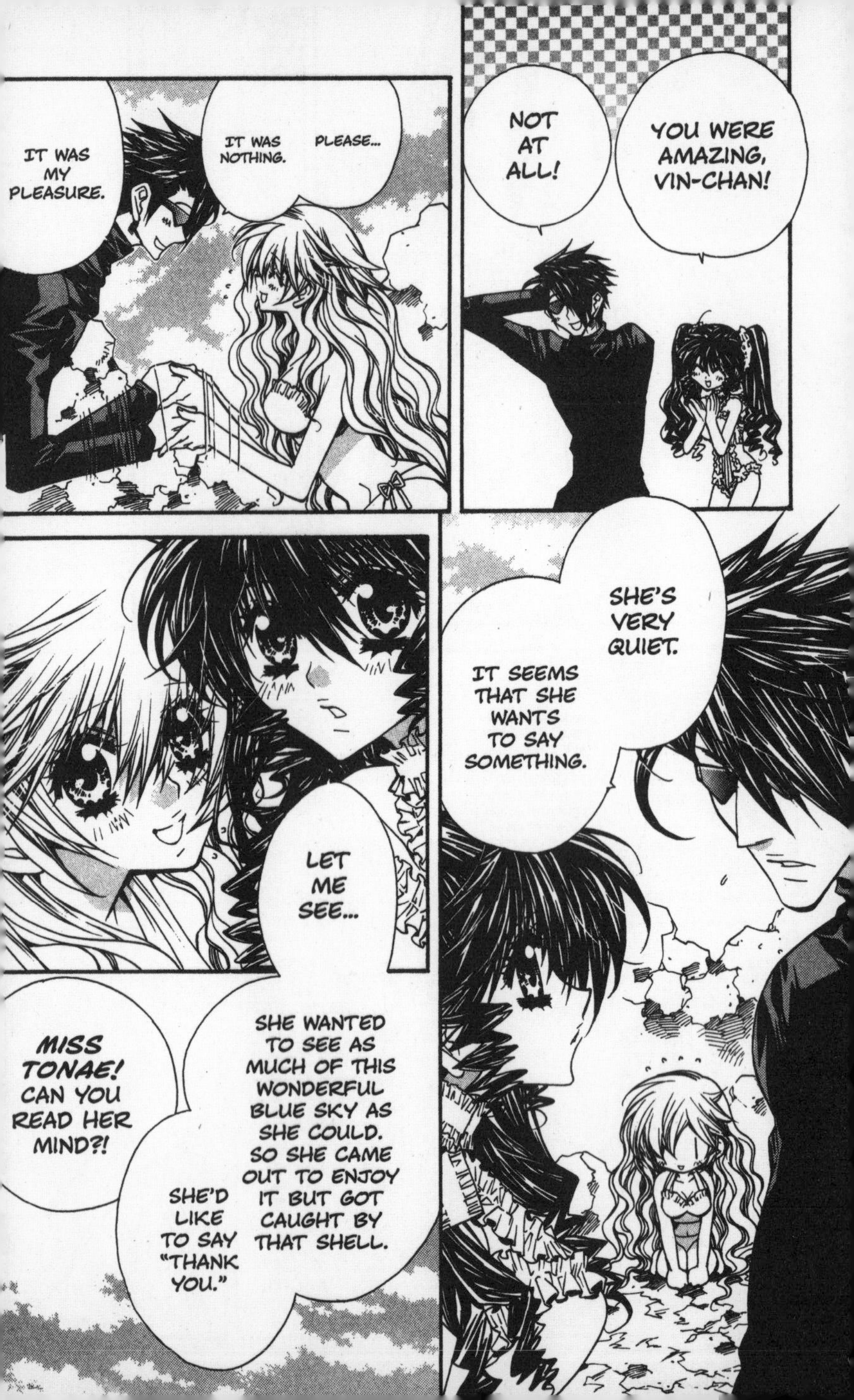
YOU WERE AMAZING, VIN-CHAN!
NOT AT ALL!
PLEASE...
IT WAS NOTHING.
IT WAS MY PLEASURE.
SHE'S VERY QUIET.
IT SEEMS THAT SHE WANTS TO SAY SOMETHING.
LET ME SEE...
SHE WANTED TO SEE AS MUCH OF THIS WONDERFUL BLUE SKY AS SHE COULD. SO SHE CAME OUT TO ENJOY IT BUT GOT CAUGHT BY THAT SHELL.
SHE'D LIKE TO SAY "THANK YOU."
MISS TONAE! CAN YOU READ HER MIND?!

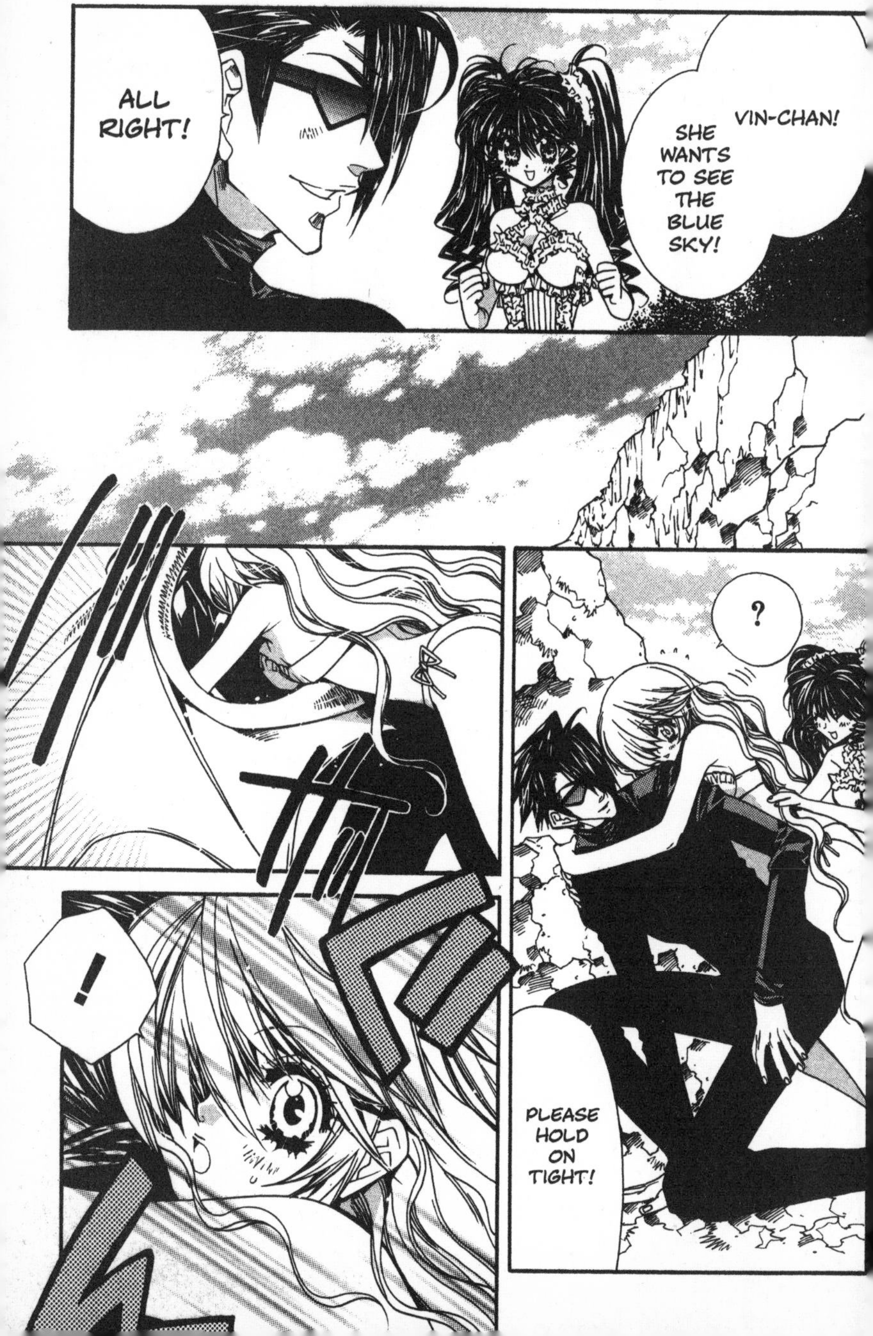
VIN-CHAN!
SHE WANTS TO SEE THE BLUE SKY!
ALL RIGHT!
?
PLEASE HOLD ON TIGHT!
!

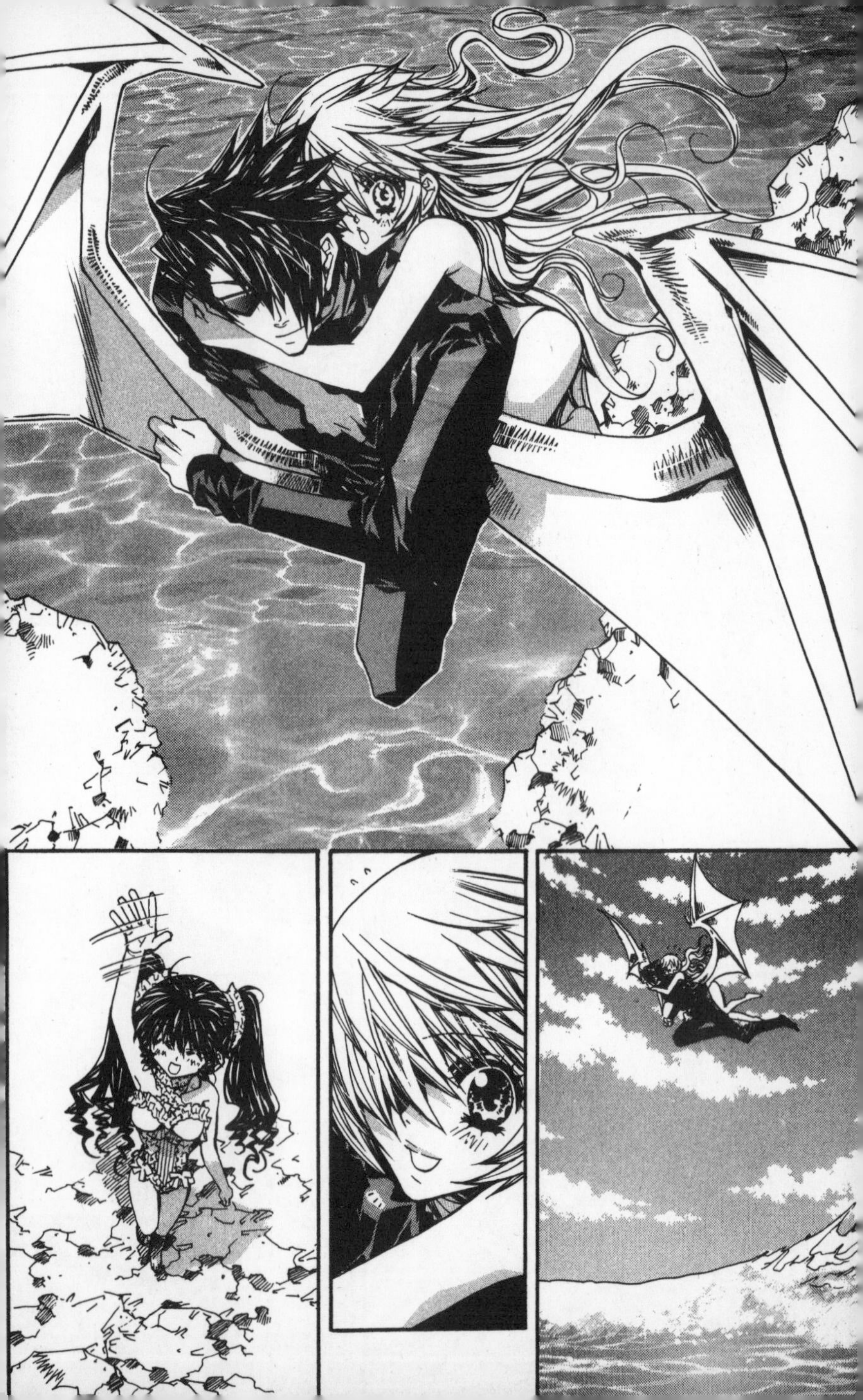

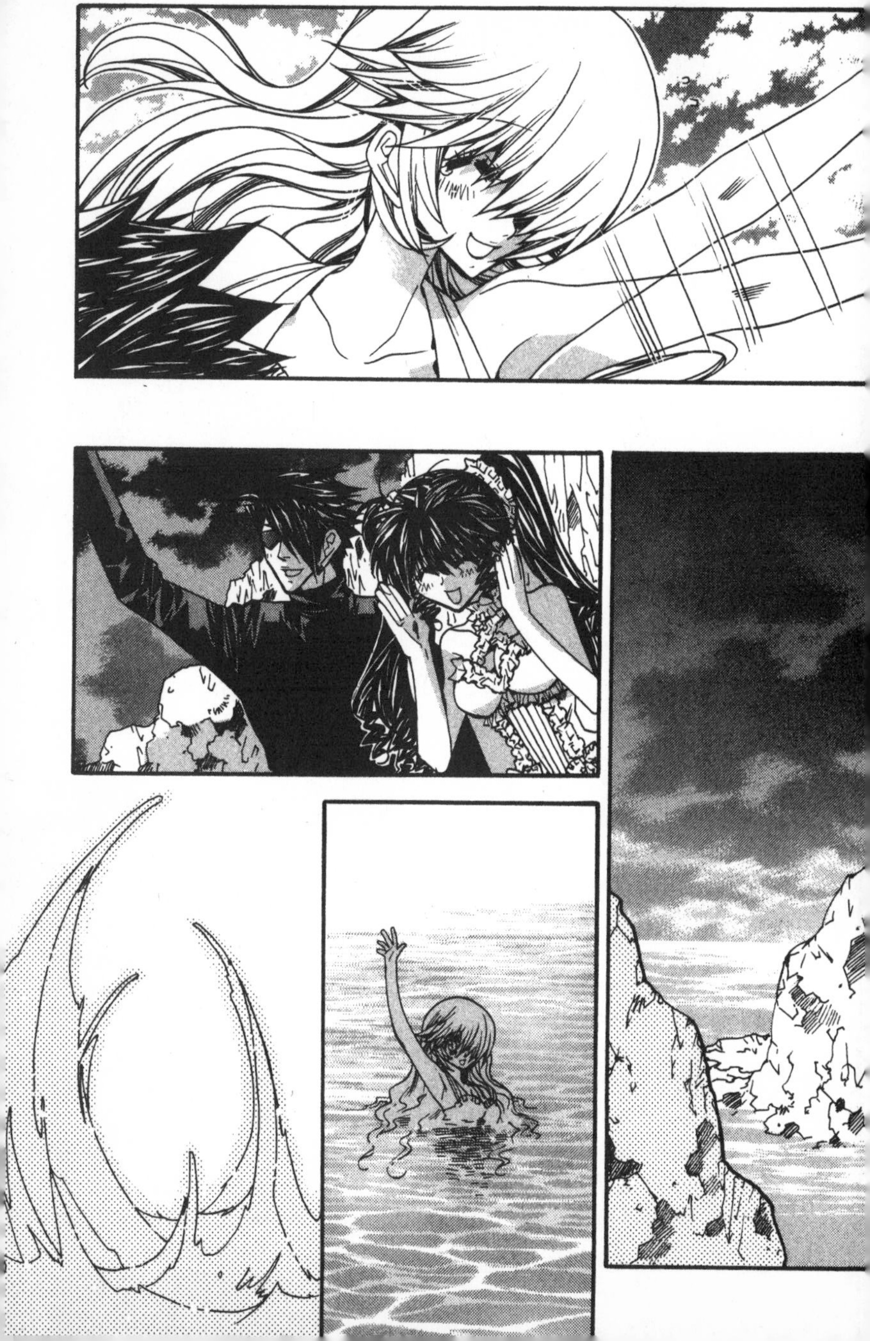

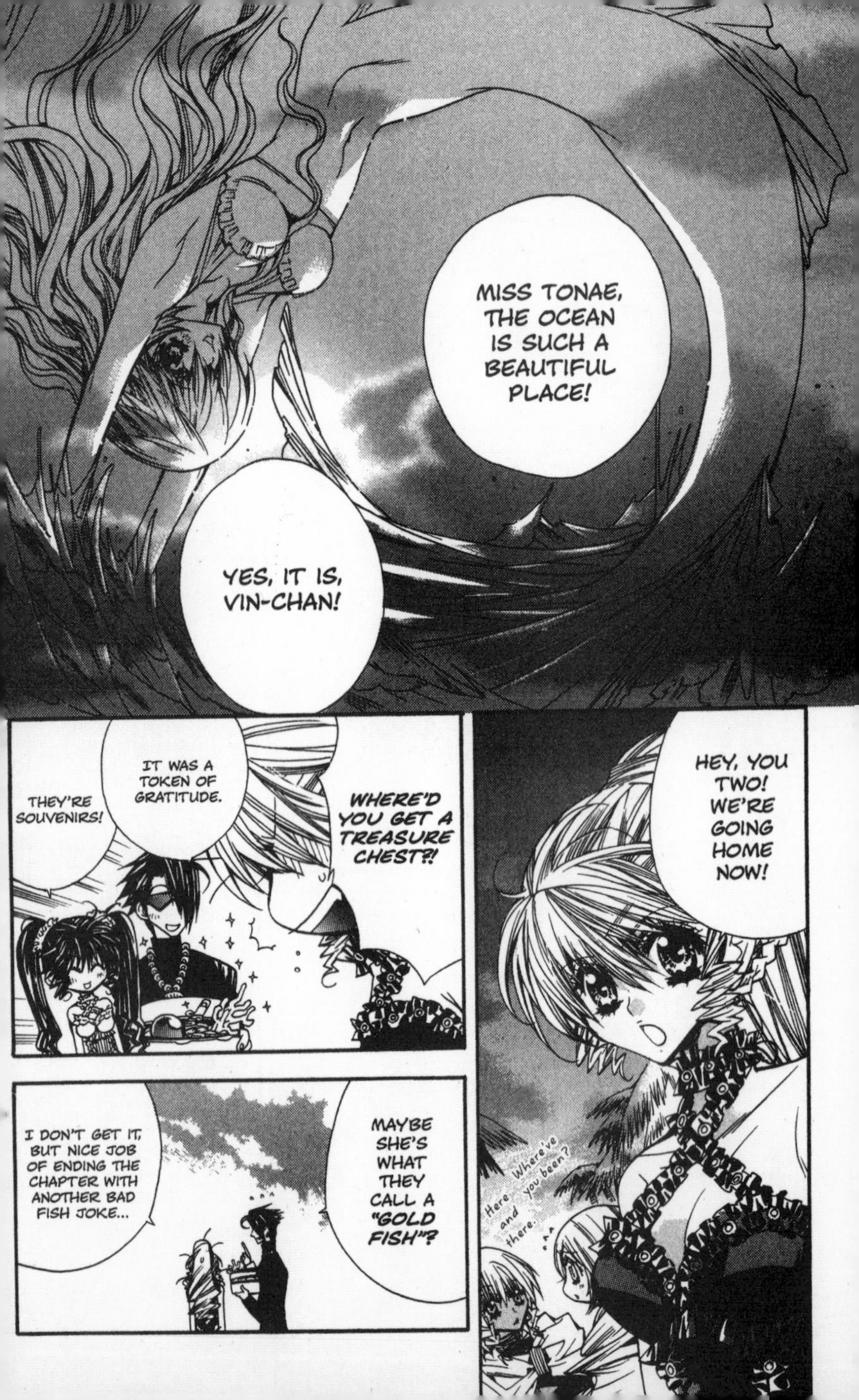
MISS TONAE, THE OCEAN IS SUCH A BEAUTIFUL PLACE!
YES, IT IS, VIN-CHAN!
HEY, YOU TWO! WE'RE GOING HOME NOW!
Where've you been?
Here and there.
WHERE'D YOU GET A TREASURE CHEST?!
IT WAS A TOKEN OF GRATITUDE.
THEY'RE SOUVENIRS!
MAYBE SHE'S WHAT THEY CALL A "GOLD FISH"?
I DON'T GET IT, BUT NICE JOB OF ENDING THE CHAPTER WITH ANOTHER BAD FISH JOKE...

BONUS COMIC STRIP

VAMPIRE DOLL REFLECTIONS

die kleine Meerjuligfrau

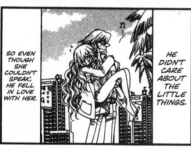

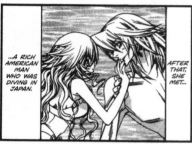

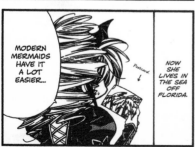

Q.

PLEASE TELL US WHAT HAPPENED TO THE MERMAID.

AFTER THAT, SHE MET...
...A RICH AMERICAN MAN WHO WAS DIVING IN JAPAN.
HE DIDN'T CARE ABOUT THE LITTLE THINGS.
SO EVEN THOUGH SHE COULDN'T SPEAK, HE FELL IN LOVE WITH HER.
NOW SHE LIVES IN THE SEA OFF FLORIDA.
Postcard.
MODERN MERMAIDS HAVE IT A LOT EASIER...

KYOICHI "HAWAIIAN SHIRT" YOTOBARI

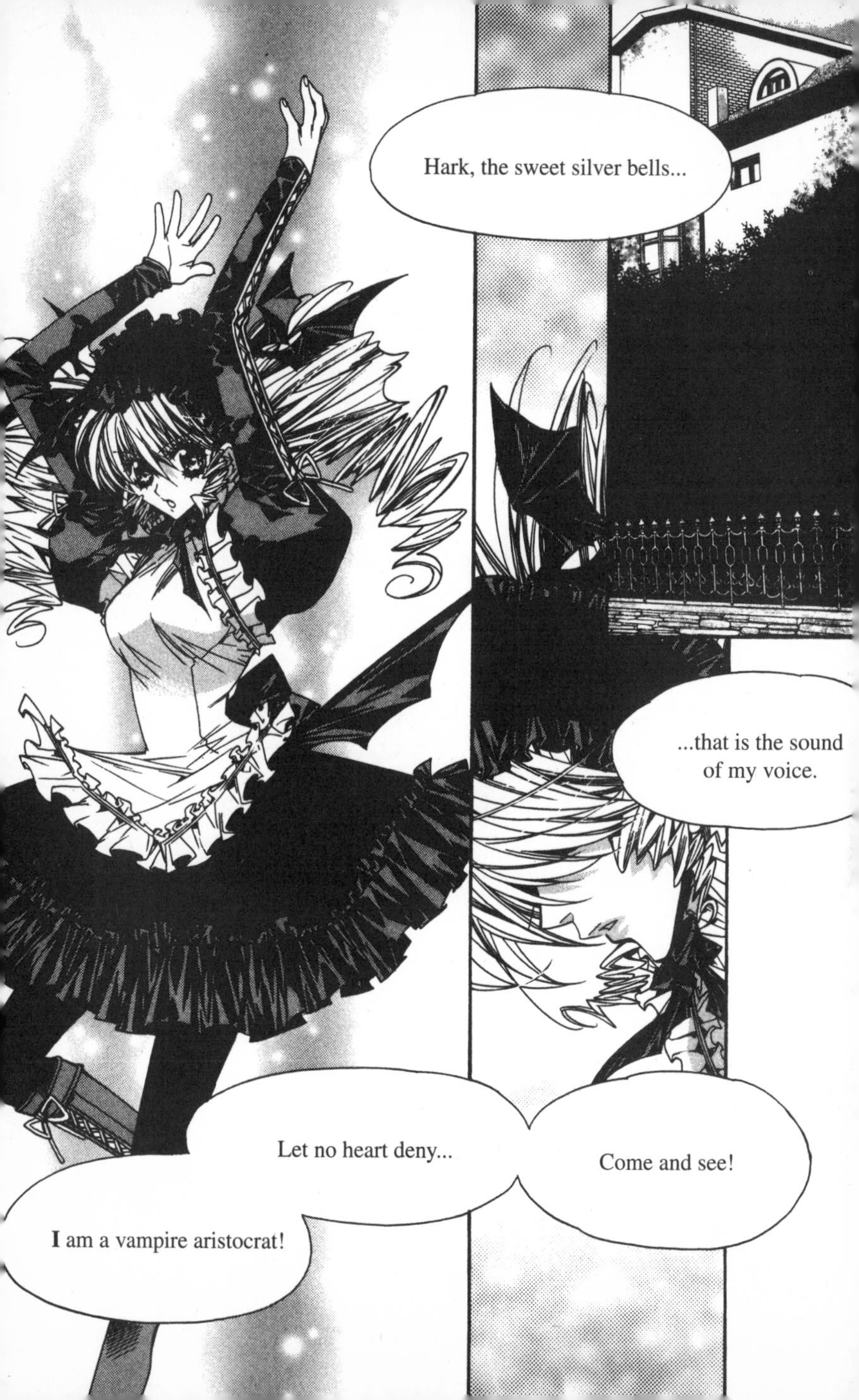
Hark, the sweet silver bells...
...that is the sound of my voice.
Come and see!
Let no heart deny...
I am a vampire aristocrat!

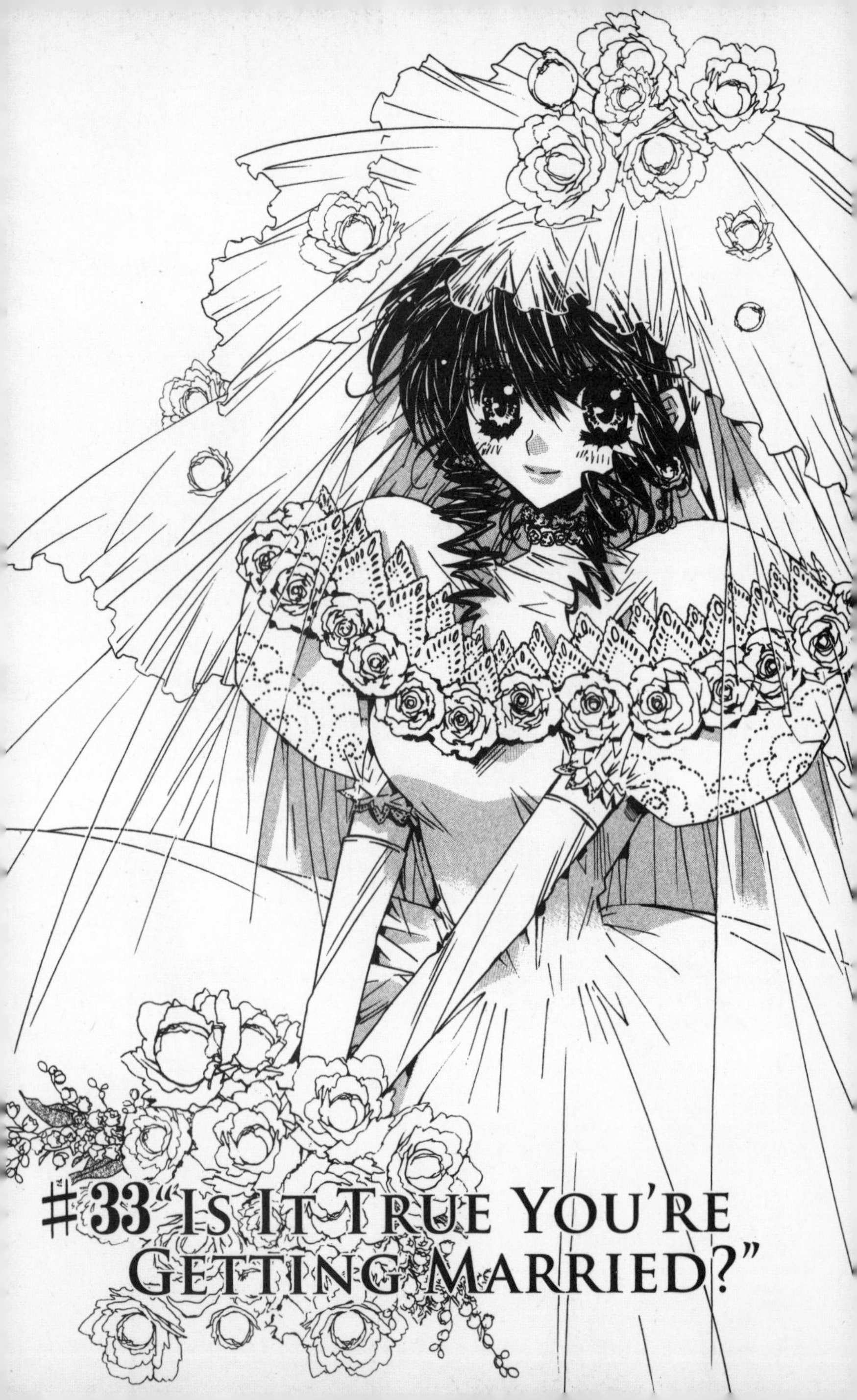

#33 "Is It True You're Getting Married?"

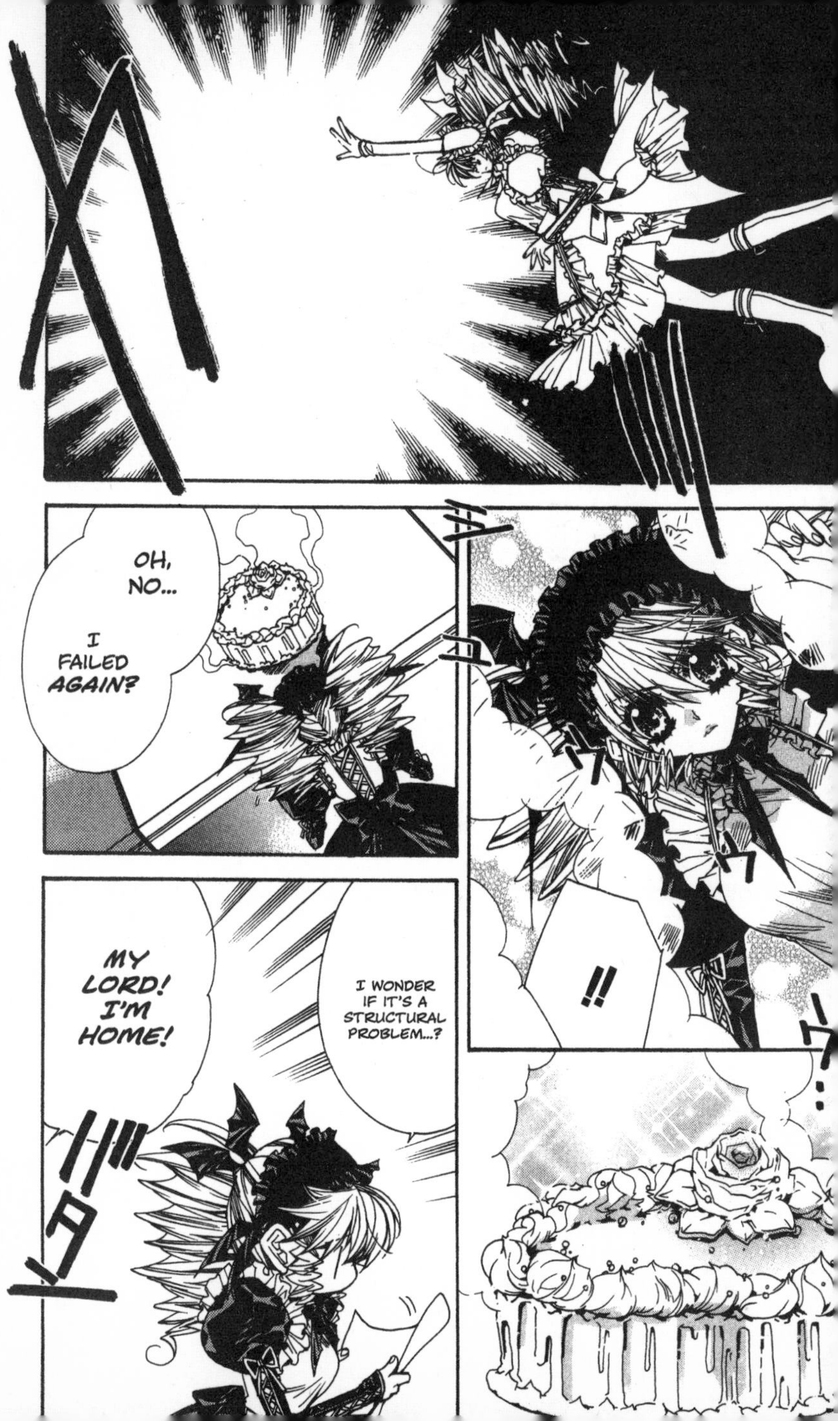
!!
OH, NO...
I FAILED AGAIN?
I WONDER IF IT'S A STRUCTURAL PROBLEM...?
MY LORD! I'M HOME!

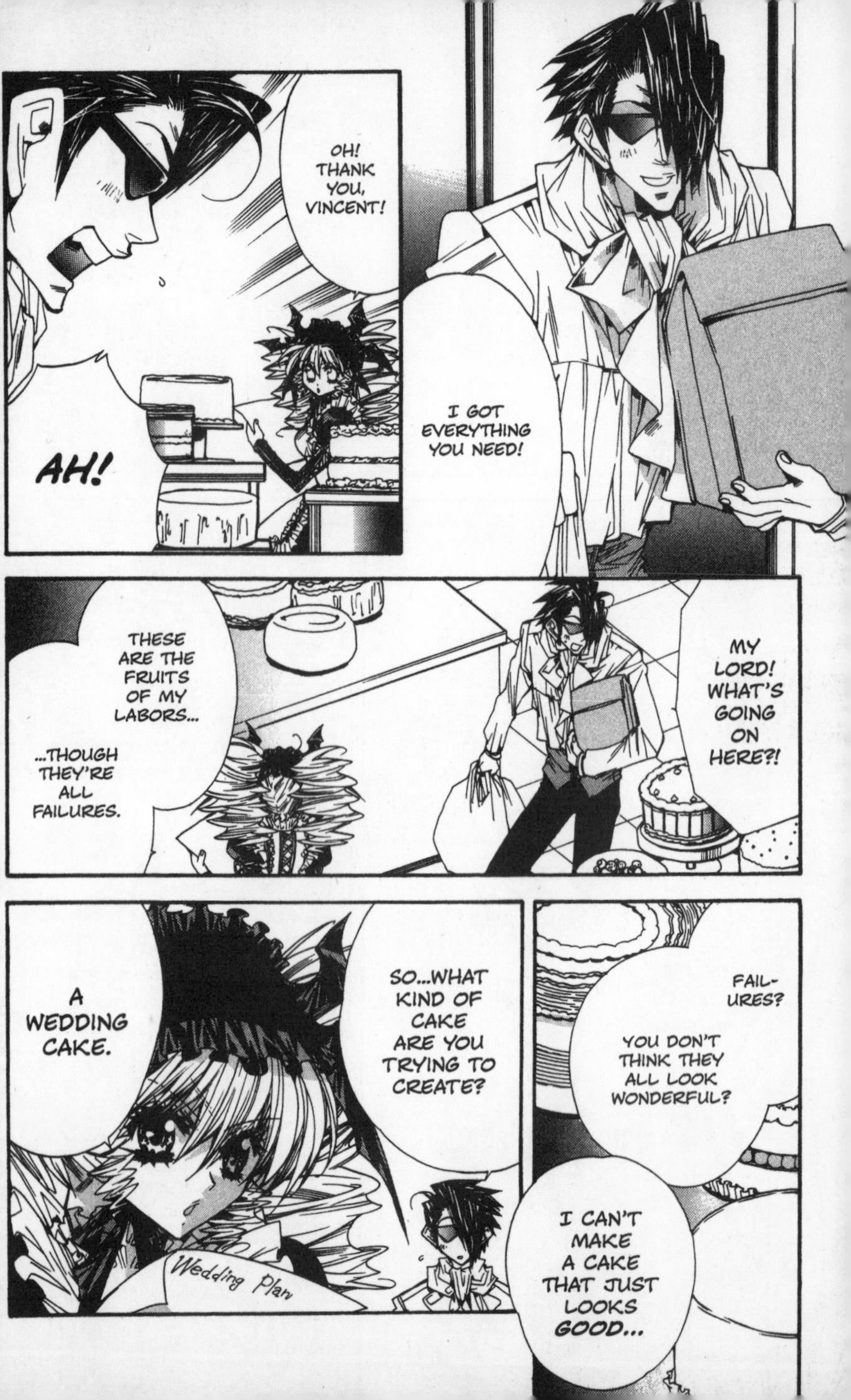
I GOT EVERYTHING YOU NEED!
OH! THANK YOU, VINCENT!
AH!
MY LORD! WHAT'S GOING ON HERE?!
THESE ARE THE FRUITS OF MY LABORS...
...THOUGH THEY'RE ALL FAILURES.
FAIL-URES?
YOU DON'T THINK THEY ALL LOOK WONDERFUL?
I CAN'T MAKE A CAKE THAT JUST LOOKS GOOD...
SO...WHAT KIND OF CAKE ARE YOU TRYING TO CREATE?
A WEDDING CAKE.
Wedding Plan

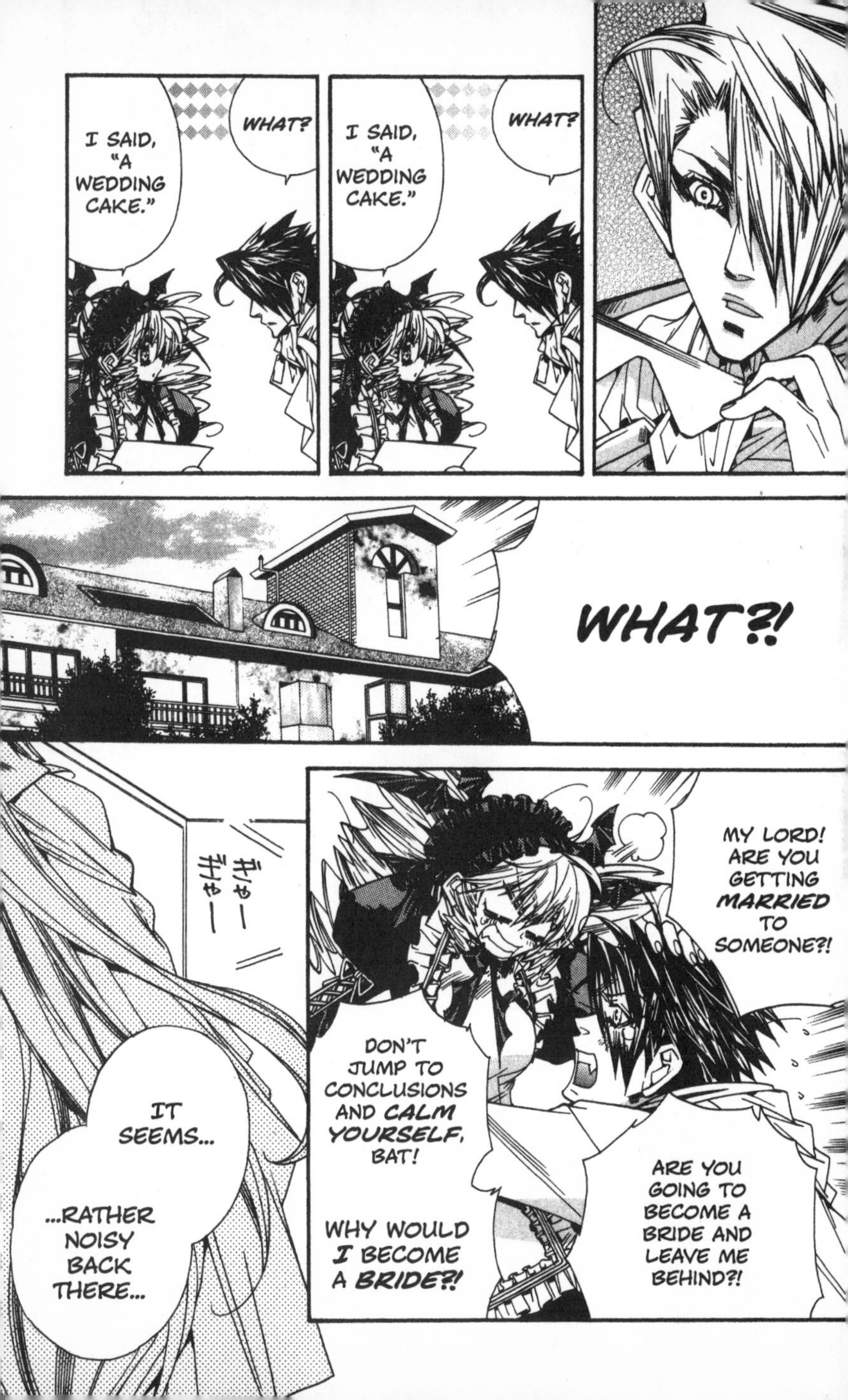
WHAT?
I SAID, "A WEDDING CAKE."
WHAT?
I SAID, "A WEDDING CAKE."
WHAT?!
MY LORD! ARE YOU GETTING MARRIED TO SOMEONE?!
ARE YOU GOING TO BECOME A BRIDE AND LEAVE ME BEHIND?!
DON'T JUMP TO CONCLUSIONS AND CALM YOURSELF, BAT!
WHY WOULD I BECOME A BRIDE?!
ギャーギャー
IT SEEMS...
...RATHER NOISY BACK THERE...

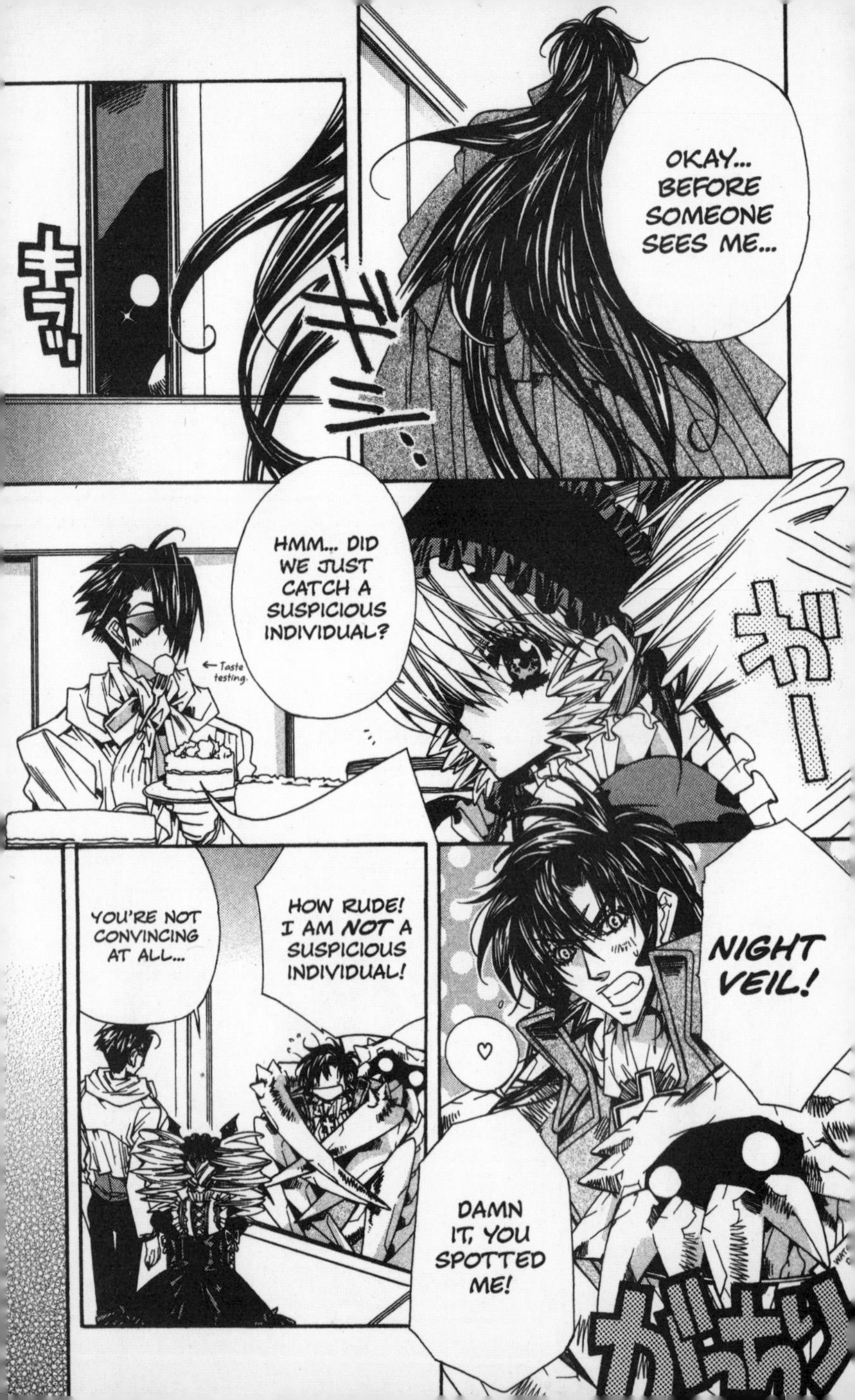
OKAY... BEFORE SOMEONE SEES ME...
HMM... DID WE JUST CATCH A SUSPICIOUS INDIVIDUAL?
← Taste testing.
NIGHT VEIL!
♡
DAMN IT, YOU SPOTTED ME!
HOW RUDE! I AM *NOT* A SUSPICIOUS INDIVIDUAL!
YOU'RE NOT CONVINCING AT ALL...

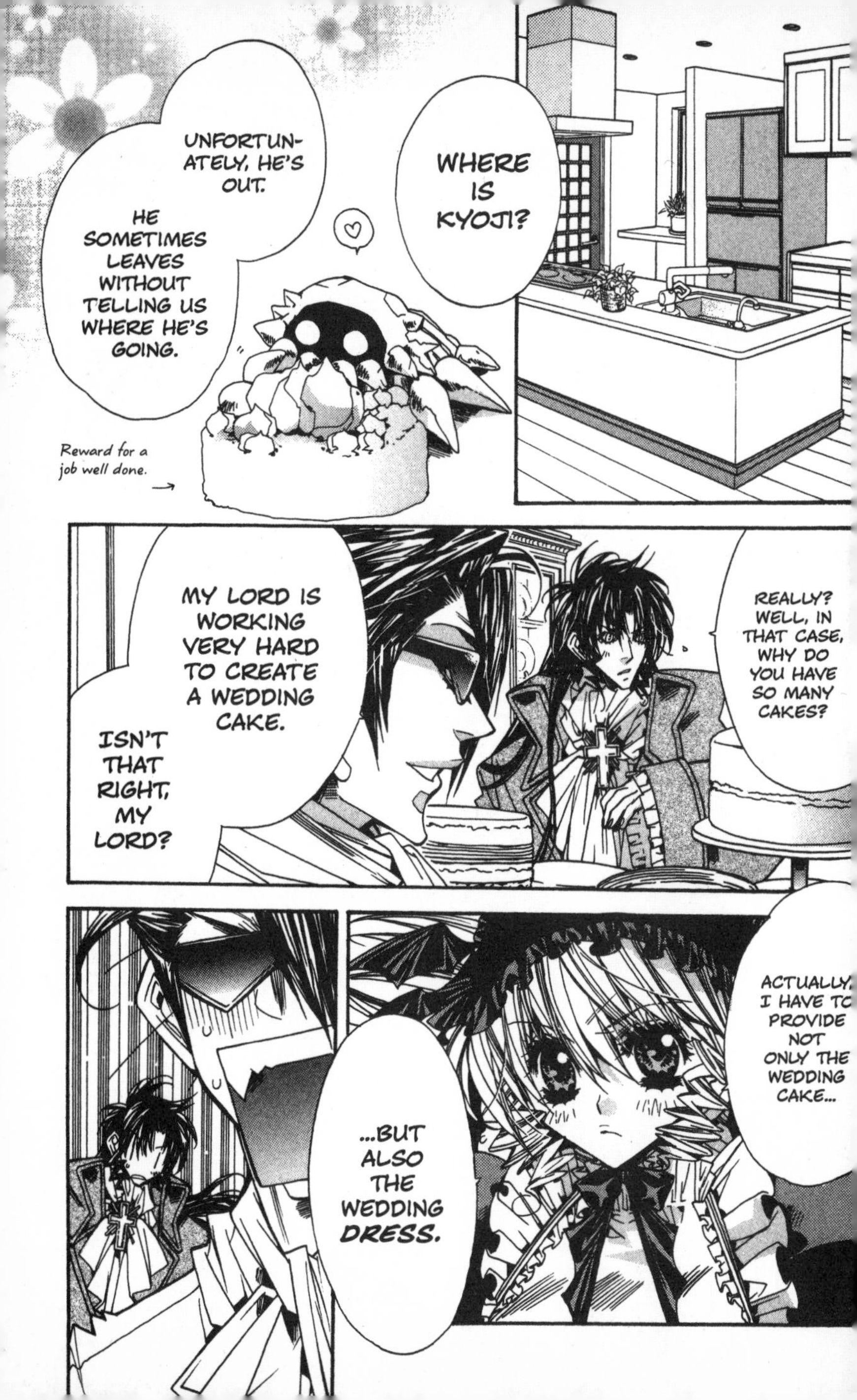
WHERE IS KYOJI?
UNFORTUNATELY, HE'S OUT.
HE SOMETIMES LEAVES WITHOUT TELLING US WHERE HE'S GOING.
Reward for a job well done.
REALLY? WELL, IN THAT CASE, WHY DO YOU HAVE SO MANY CAKES?
MY LORD IS WORKING VERY HARD TO CREATE A WEDDING CAKE.
ISN'T THAT RIGHT, MY LORD?
ACTUALLY, I HAVE TO PROVIDE NOT ONLY THE WEDDING CAKE...
...BUT ALSO THE WEDDING DRESS.

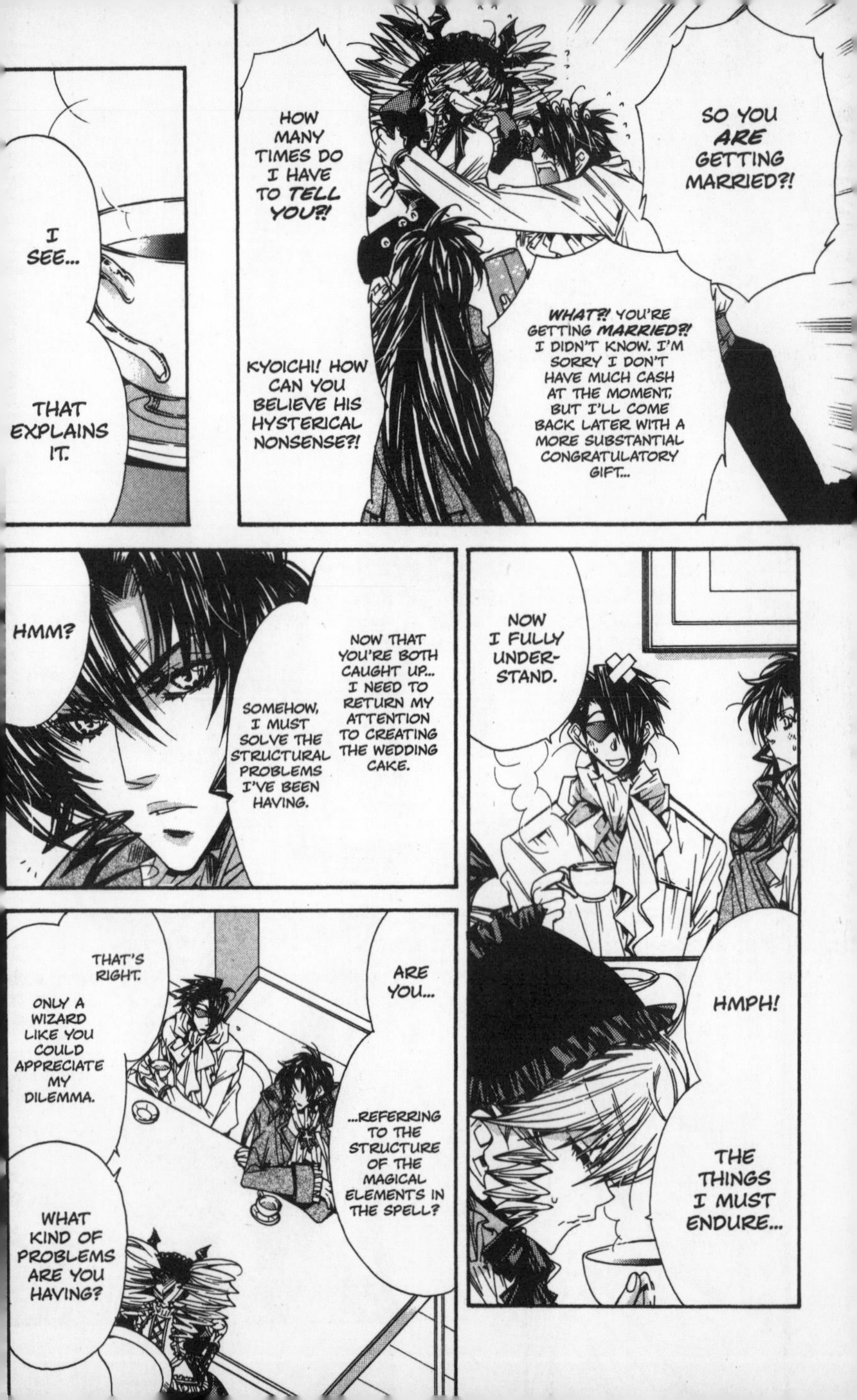
SO YOU ARE GETTING MARRIED?!
HOW MANY TIMES DO I HAVE TO TELL YOU?!
WHAT?! YOU'RE GETTING MARRIED?! I DIDN'T KNOW. I'M SORRY I DON'T HAVE MUCH CASH AT THE MOMENT, BUT I'LL COME BACK LATER WITH A MORE SUBSTANTIAL CONGRATULATORY GIFT...
KYOICHI! HOW CAN YOU BELIEVE HIS HYSTERICAL NONSENSE?!
I SEE...
THAT EXPLAINS IT.
NOW I FULLY UNDER-STAND.
HMPH!
THE THINGS I MUST ENDURE...
NOW THAT YOU'RE BOTH CAUGHT UP... I NEED TO RETURN MY ATTENTION TO CREATING THE WEDDING CAKE.
SOMEHOW, I MUST SOLVE THE STRUCTURAL PROBLEMS I'VE BEEN HAVING.
HMM?
ARE YOU...
...REFERRING TO THE STRUCTURE OF THE MAGICAL ELEMENTS IN THE SPELL?
THAT'S RIGHT.
ONLY A WIZARD LIKE YOU COULD APPRECIATE MY DILEMMA.
WHAT KIND OF PROBLEMS ARE YOU HAVING?

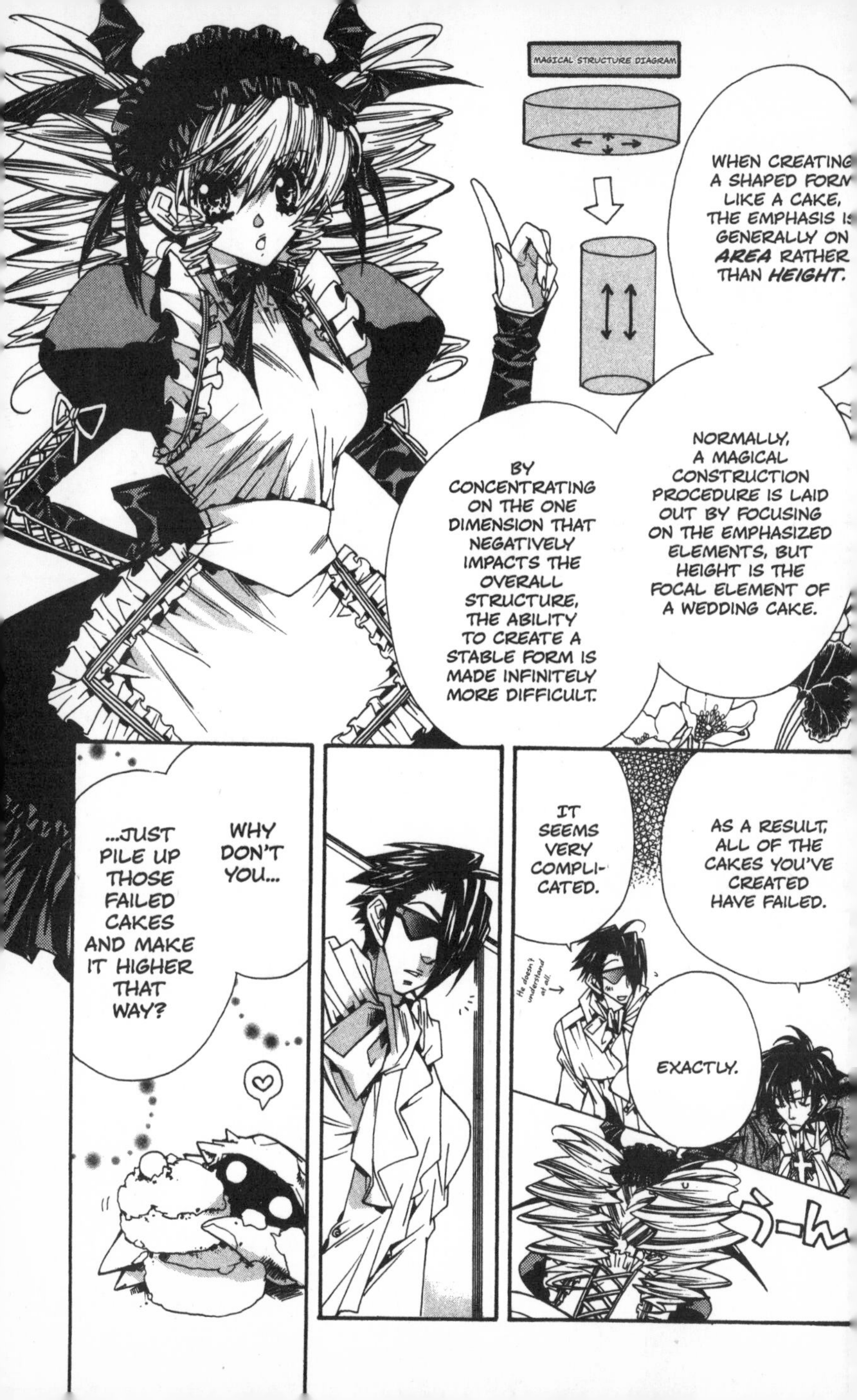
MAGICAL STRUCTURE DIAGRAM
WHEN CREATING A SHAPED FORM LIKE A CAKE, THE EMPHASIS IS GENERALLY ON *AREA* RATHER THAN *HEIGHT*.
NORMALLY, A MAGICAL CONSTRUCTION PROCEDURE IS LAID OUT BY FOCUSING ON THE EMPHASIZED ELEMENTS, BUT HEIGHT IS THE FOCAL ELEMENT OF A WEDDING CAKE.
BY CONCENTRATING ON THE ONE DIMENSION THAT NEGATIVELY IMPACTS THE OVERALL STRUCTURE, THE ABILITY TO CREATE A STABLE FORM IS MADE INFINITELY MORE DIFFICULT.
AS A RESULT, ALL OF THE CAKES YOU'VE CREATED HAVE FAILED.
IT SEEMS VERY COMPLICATED.
He doesn't understand at all.
EXACTLY.
うーん
WHY DON'T YOU...
...JUST PILE UP THOSE FAILED CAKES AND MAKE IT HIGHER THAT WAY?

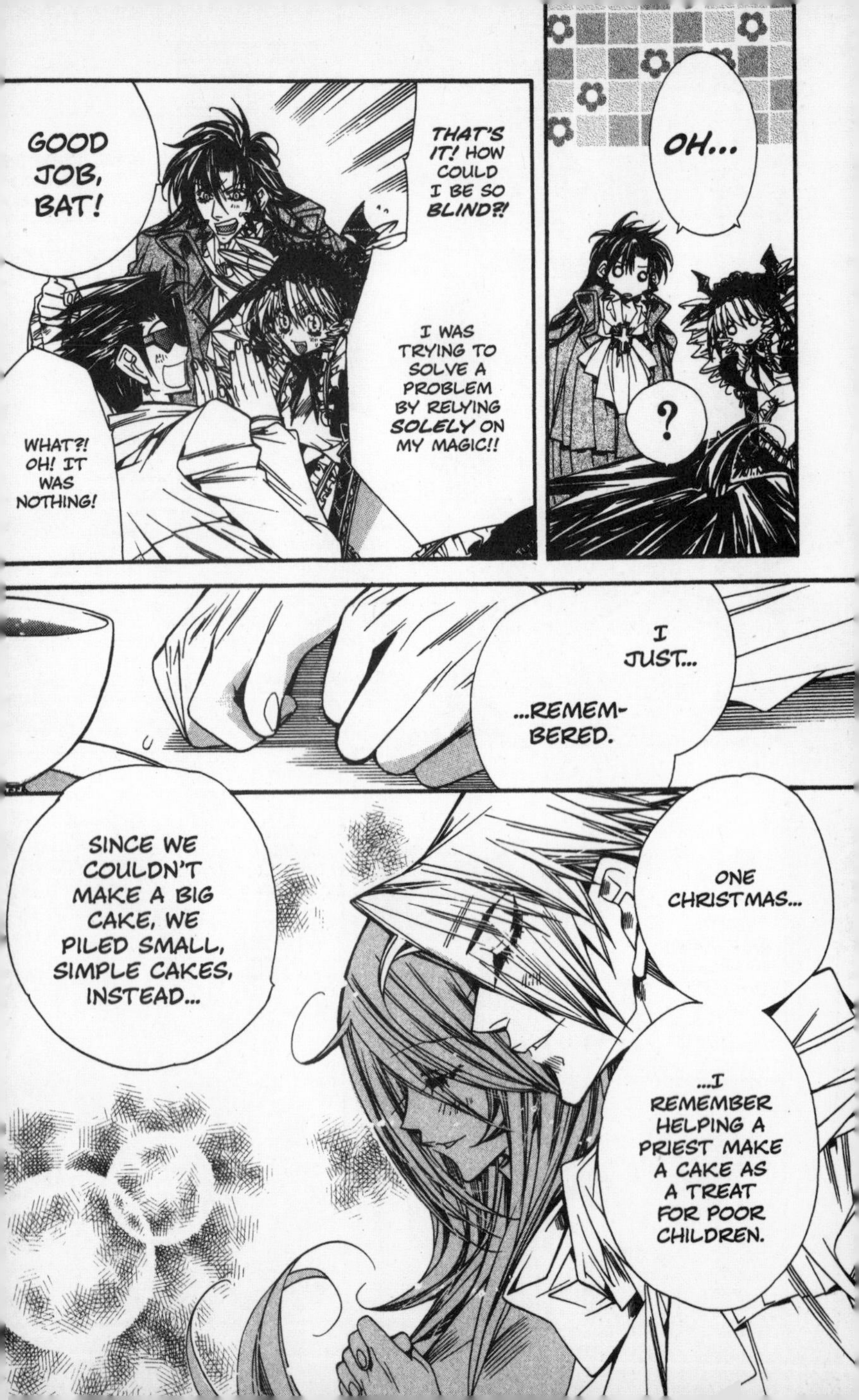
OH...
?
THAT'S IT! HOW COULD I BE SO BLIND?!
GOOD JOB, BAT!
I WAS TRYING TO SOLVE A PROBLEM BY RELYING SOLELY ON MY MAGIC!!
WHAT?! OH! IT WAS NOTHING!
I JUST...
...REMEMBERED.
ONE CHRISTMAS...
...I REMEMBER HELPING A PRIEST MAKE A CAKE AS A TREAT FOR POOR CHILDREN.
SINCE WE COULDN'T MAKE A BIG CAKE, WE PILED SMALL, SIMPLE CAKES, INSTEAD...

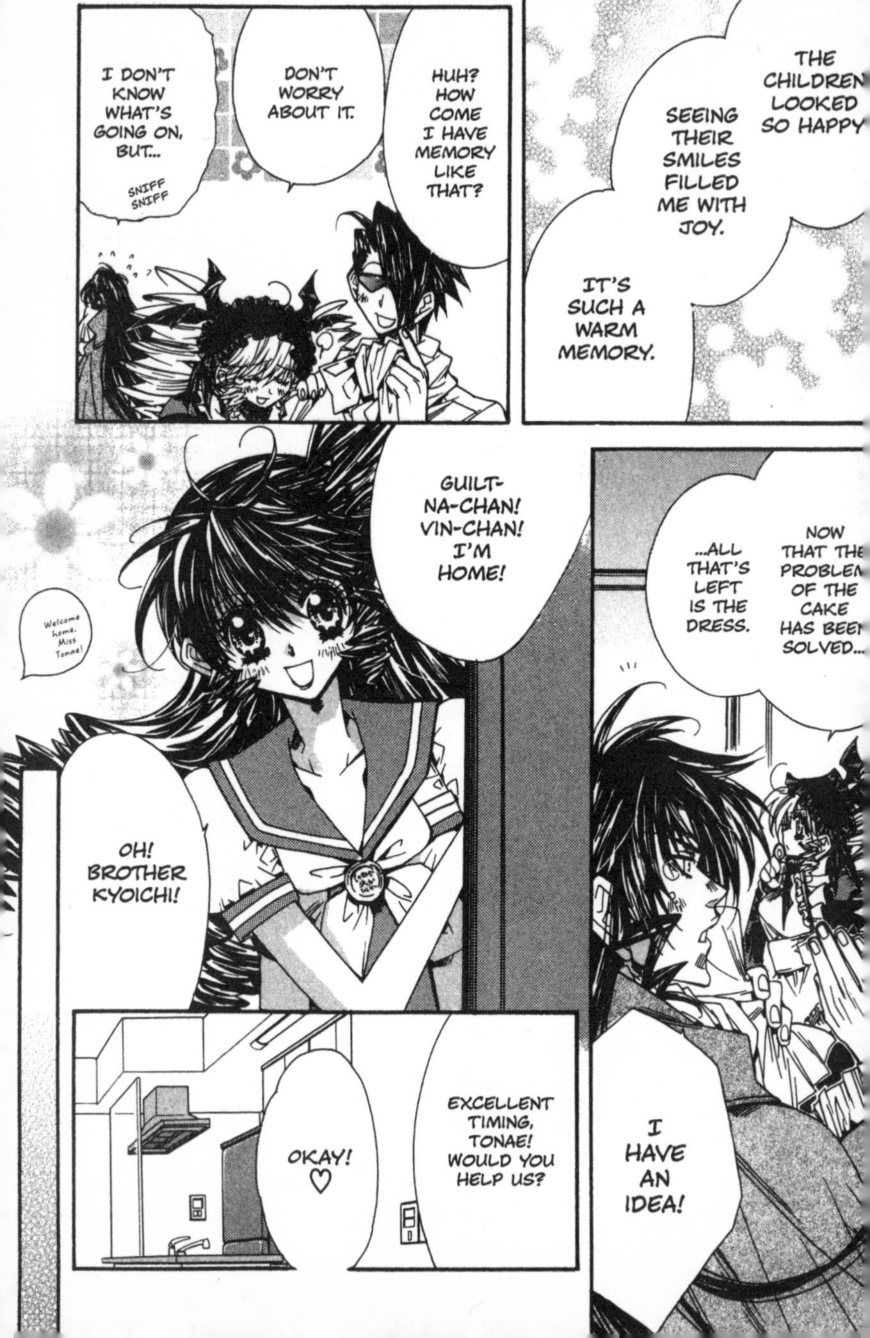
THE CHILDREN LOOKED SO HAPPY.
SEEING THEIR SMILES FILLED ME WITH JOY.
IT'S SUCH A WARM MEMORY.
HUH? HOW COME I HAVE MEMORY LIKE THAT?
DON'T WORRY ABOUT IT.
I DON'T KNOW WHAT'S GOING ON, BUT...
SNIFF SNIFF
NOW THAT THE PROBLEM OF THE CAKE HAS BEEN SOLVED...
...ALL THAT'S LEFT IS THE DRESS.
I HAVE AN IDEA!
GUILT-NA-CHAN! VIN-CHAN! I'M HOME!
Welcome home, Miss Tonae!
OH! BROTHER KYOICHI!
EXCELLENT TIMING, TONAE! WOULD YOU HELP US?
OKAY! ♡

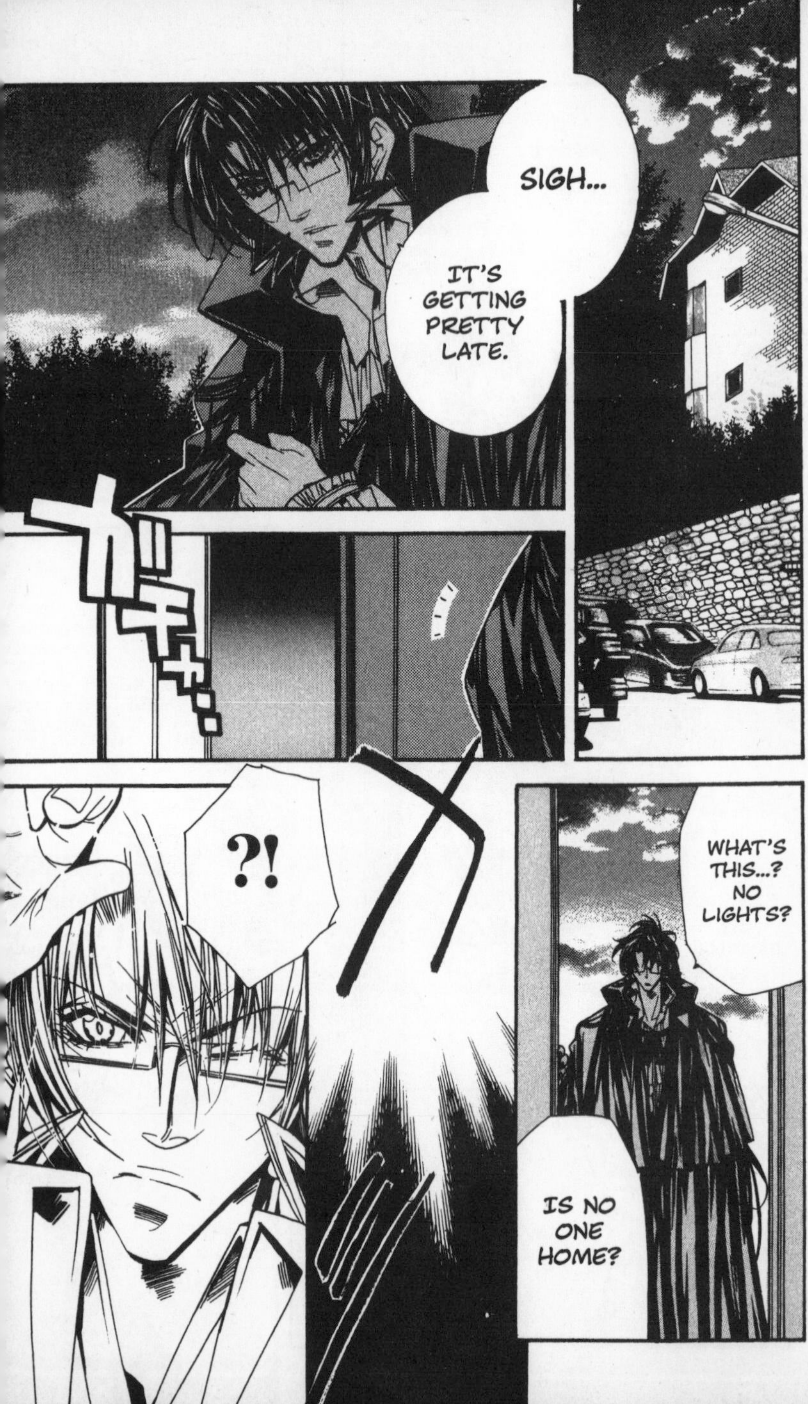
SIGH...
IT'S GETTING PRETTY LATE.
ガチャ...
WHAT'S THIS...? NO LIGHTS?
IS NO ONE HOME?
?!

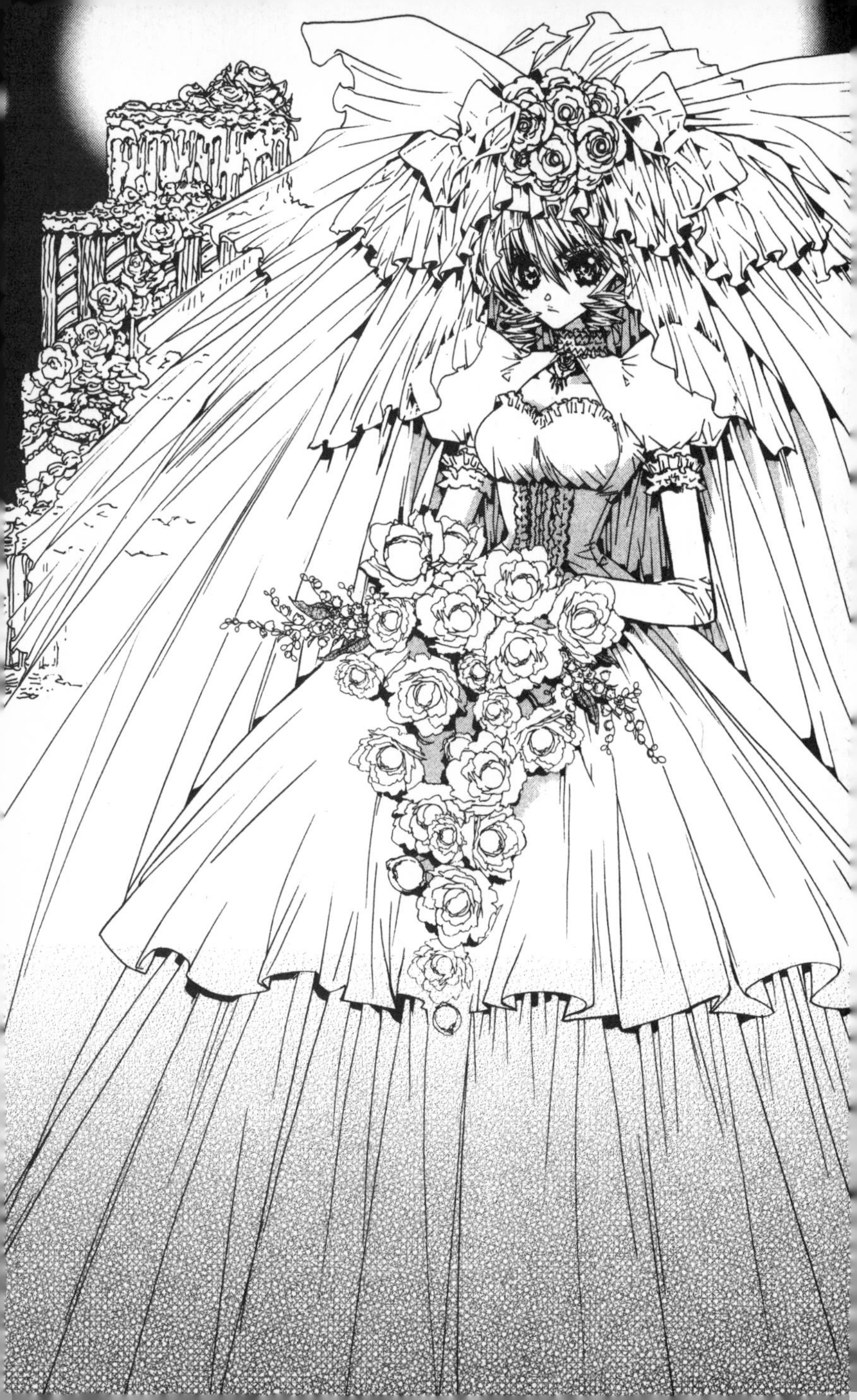

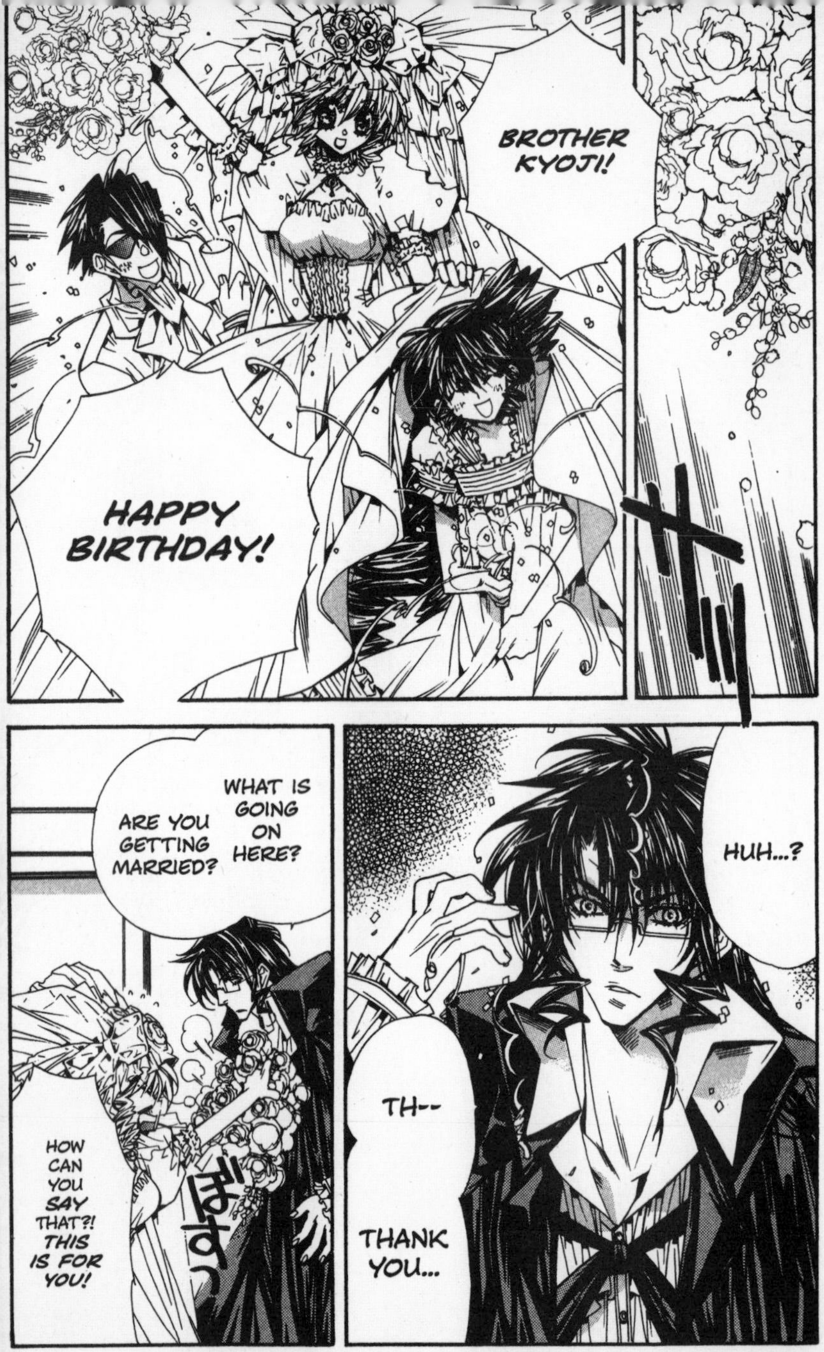
BROTHER KYOJI!
HAPPY BIRTHDAY!
HUH...?
TH--
THANK YOU...
WHAT IS GOING ON HERE?
ARE YOU GETTING MARRIED?
ぼすっ
HOW CAN YOU SAY THAT?! THIS IS FOR YOU!

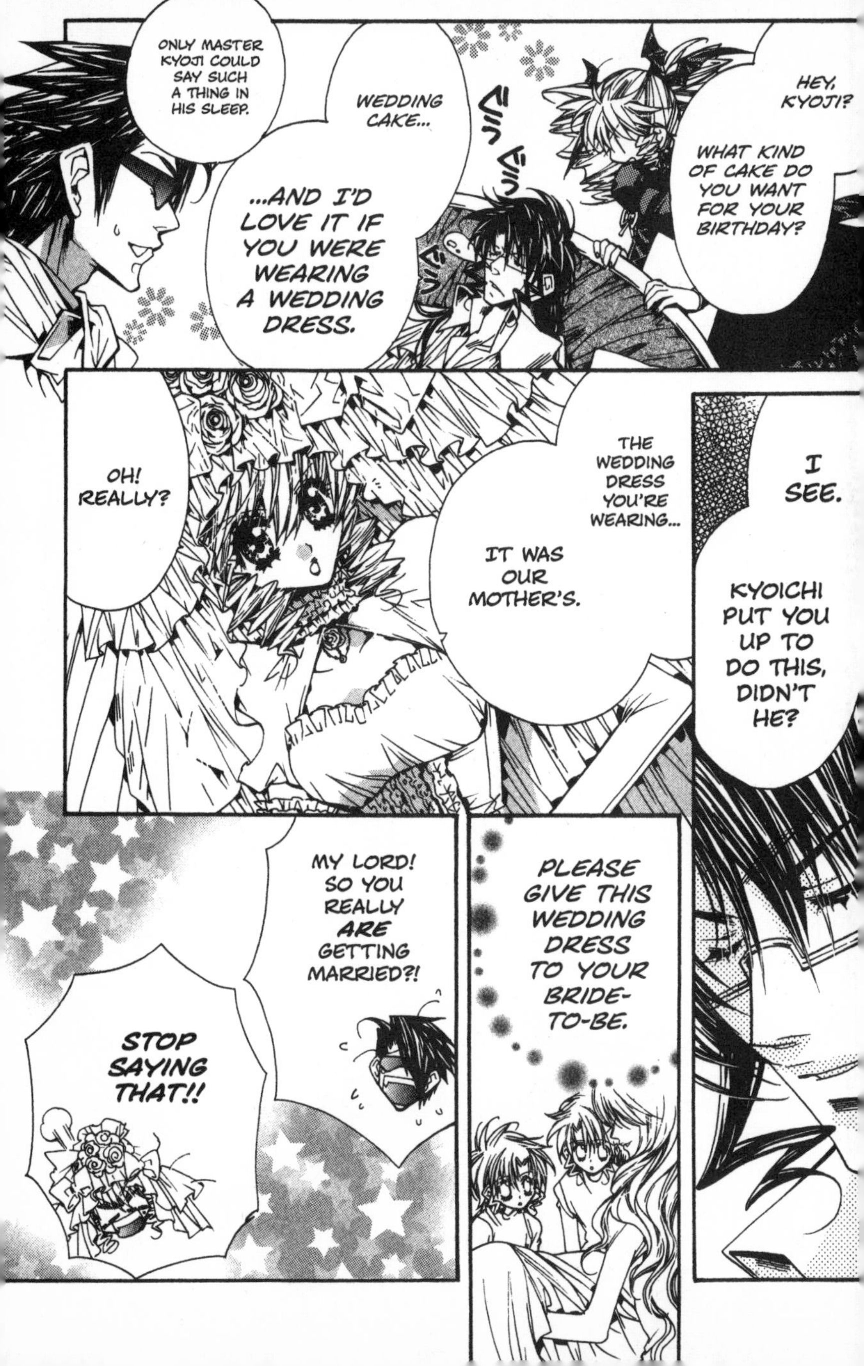
HEY, KYOJI?
WHAT KIND OF CAKE DO YOU WANT FOR YOUR BIRTHDAY?
WEDDING CAKE...
...AND I'D LOVE IT IF YOU WERE WEARING A WEDDING DRESS.
ONLY MASTER KYOJI COULD SAY SUCH A THING IN HIS SLEEP.
I SEE.
KYOICHI PUT YOU UP TO DO THIS, DIDN'T HE?
THE WEDDING DRESS YOU'RE WEARING...
IT WAS OUR MOTHER'S.
OH! REALLY?
PLEASE GIVE THIS WEDDING DRESS TO YOUR BRIDE-TO-BE.
MY LORD! SO YOU REALLY ARE GETTING MARRIED?!
STOP SAYING THAT!!

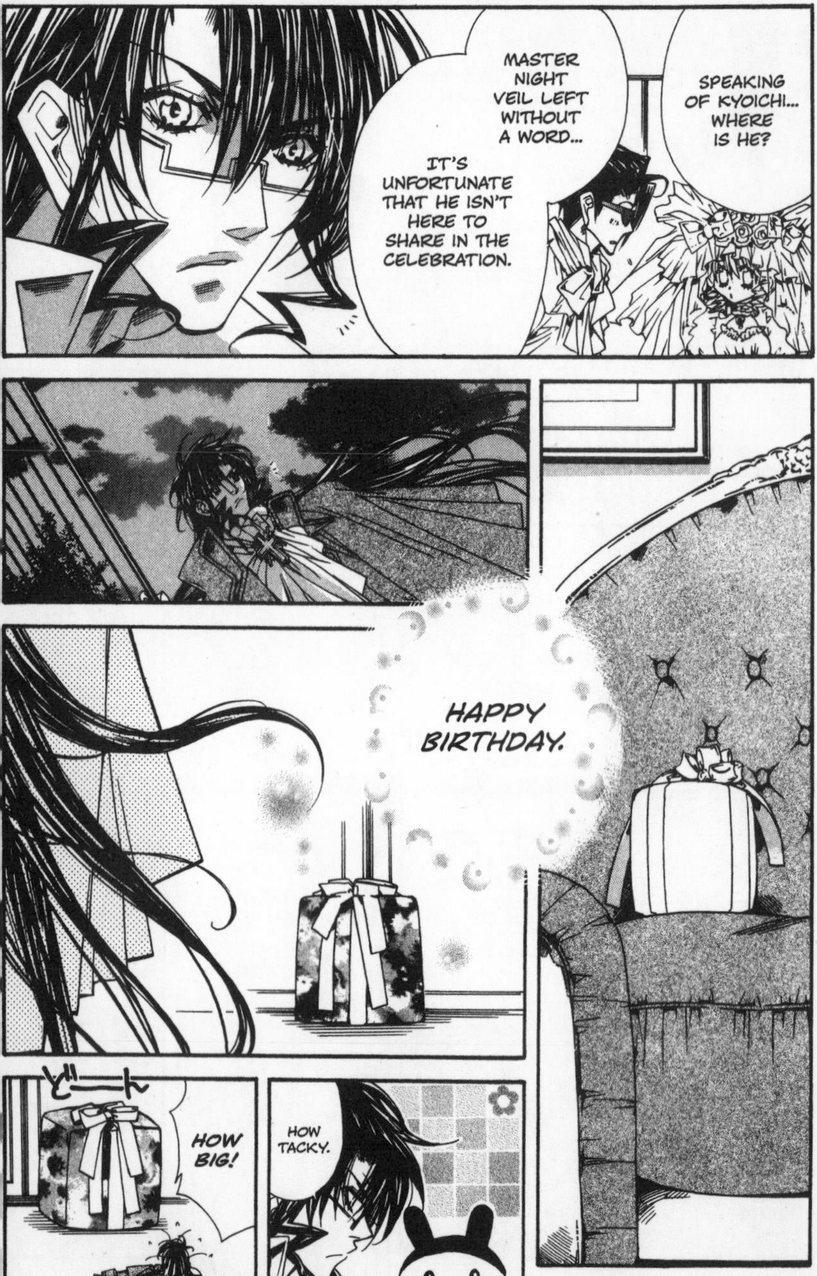
SPEAKING OF KYOICHI... WHERE IS HE?
MASTER NIGHT VEIL LEFT WITHOUT A WORD...
IT'S UNFORTUNATE THAT HE ISN'T HERE TO SHARE IN THE CELEBRATION.
HAPPY BIRTHDAY.
HOW TACKY.
HOW BIG!
どーーん

BONUS COMIC STRIP

VAMPIRE DOLL REFLECTIONS

Is It True You're Getting Married?

Q.
WHAT DID KYOJI GIVE KYOICHI?
IT'S SWEET, SOFT, COLD, AND BIG!
AN ICE CREAM CAKE?
IT HAS DAPPLED GREEN AND BLACK COLORING AND IS STICKY. SOMETIMES IT WILL WHISTLE IF YOU HANG IT ON A WALL.
Imagination running wild.
MASTER NIGHT VEIL WAS ATTACKED BY YOUR GIFT LAST NIGHT!
REALLY? BUT I TRAINED IT...
I HAVE A FEELING I'LL BE HAVING NIGHTMARES TONIGHT...

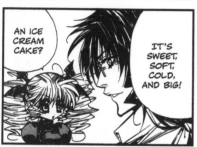

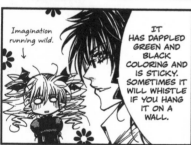

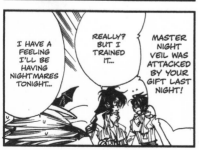

KYOJI "MY DEAR BROTHER" YOTOBARI

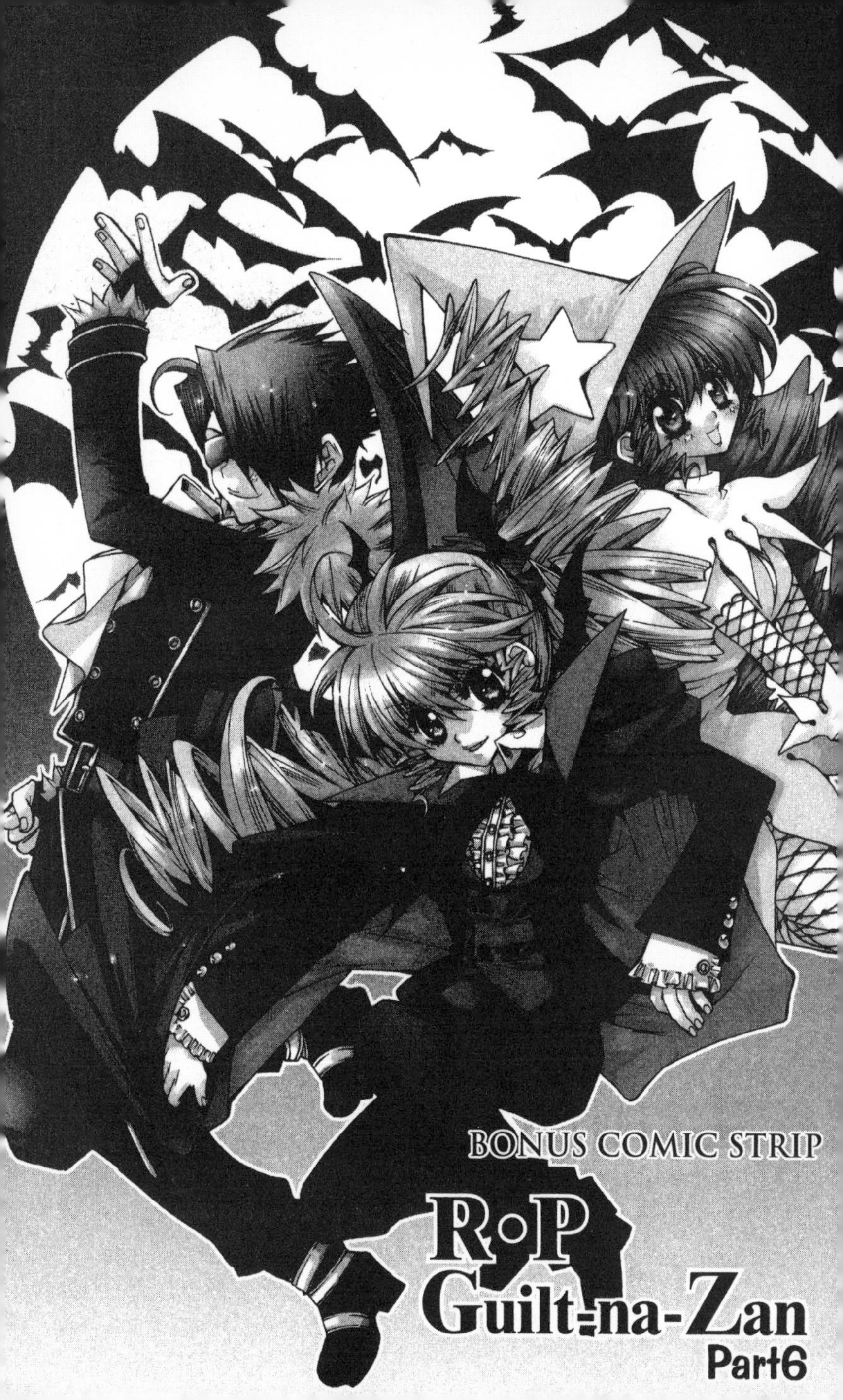
BONUS COMIC STRIP
R•P
Guilt-na-Zan
Part6

GUILT-NA-ZAN BONUS COMIC STRIPS
ROLE PLAYING GUILT-NA-ZAN

MAIN CHARACTERS

STORY SO FAR:

EMPEROR KYOJI HAS TRANSFORMED GUILT-NA-ZAN INTO A GIRL, SENDING GUILT-NA-ZAN ON A QUEST TO REGAIN HIS TRUE FORM. ALONG THE WAY, HE HAS GAINED TRAVELING COMPANIONS AND UNCOVERED MYSTERIES TO AID IN HIS JOURNEY...

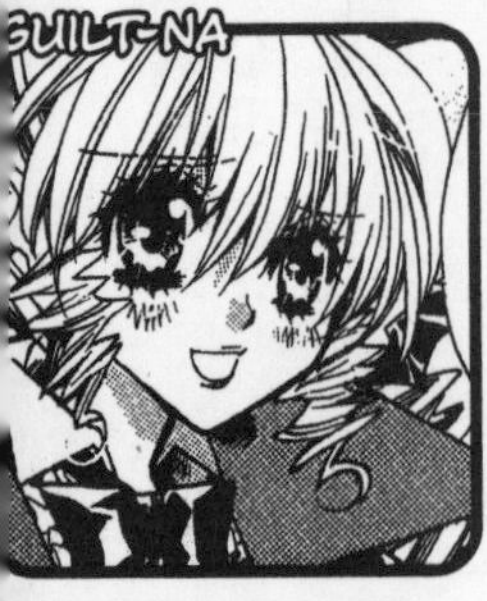
GUILT-NA

TRANSFORMED INTO A GIRL BY EMPEROR KYOJI, GUILT-NA FIGHTS HARD IN ORDER TO RETURN TO HIS ORIGINAL BODY.

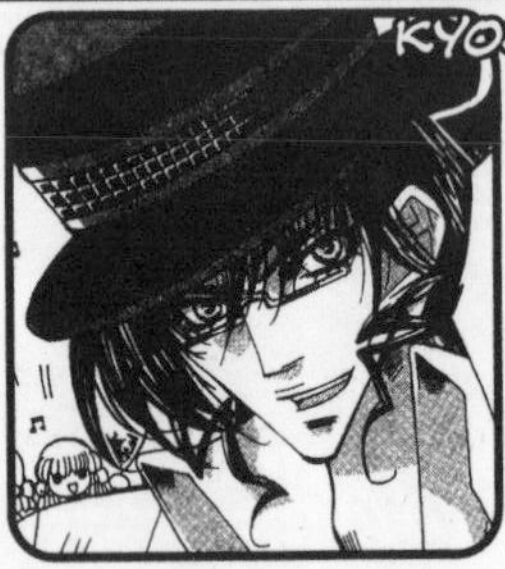
KYOJI

THIS OMNIPRESENT SOURCE OF EVIL IS VERY DIFFICULT TO DEFEAT, WHICH DISCOURAGES PEOPLE FROM FIGHTING HIM.

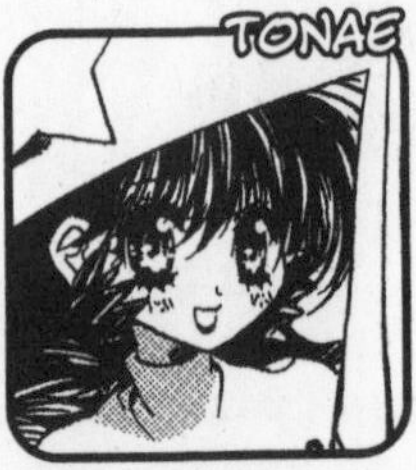
TONAE

SHE IS A POWERFUL WITCH WHOSE ABILITIES INCLUDE TURNING ROTTEN RICE BALLS INTO FRESH ONES.

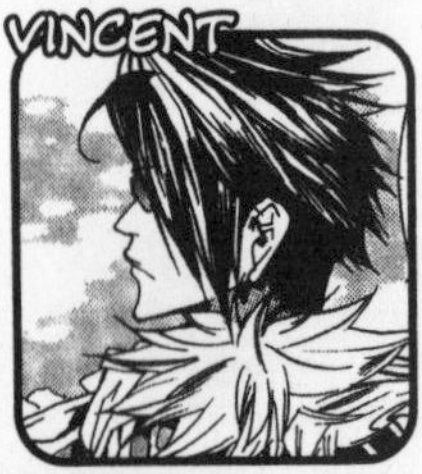
VINCENT

HE IS A BAT WHO SERVES GUILT-NA-ZAN. AS A HEALER, NOT MUCH IS EXPECTED OF HIM IN BATTLE.

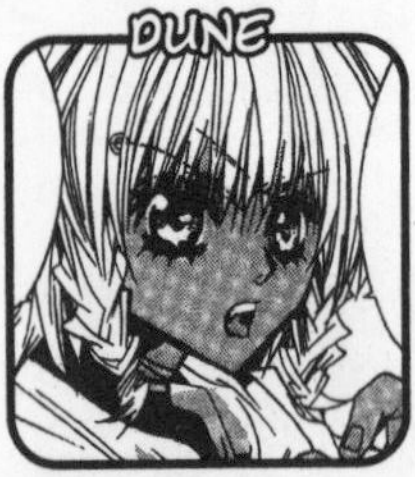
DUNE

A BANDIT WHO SUCKS NEGATIVE ENERGY TO USE AS HIS OWN, HE'S USEFUL IN AND OUT OF BATTLE AND MAKES A PERFECT STRAIGHT-MAN.

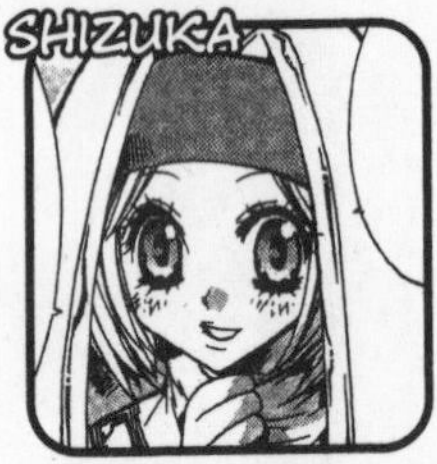
SHIZUKA

THIS MONK IS THE KEY TO REACHING THE DESTINATION WITHOUT SIDETRACKING THE GROUP.

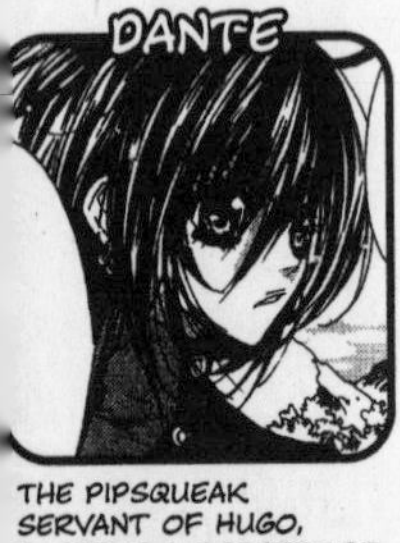
DANTE

THE PIPSQUEAK SERVANT OF HUGO, DANTE IS A BERSERKER AND VERY STRONG.

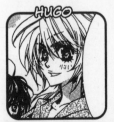

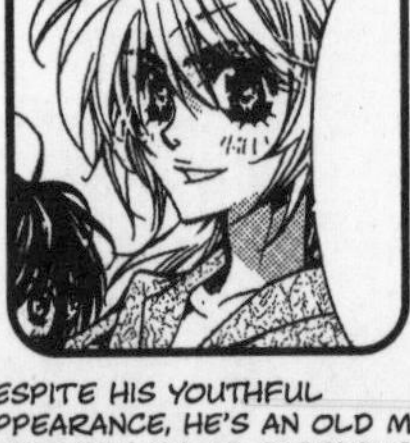
HUGO

DESPITE HIS YOUTHFUL APPEARANCE, HE'S AN OLD MAN. HE'S VERY KNOWLEDGEABLE, BUT HE'S ALSO SENILE.

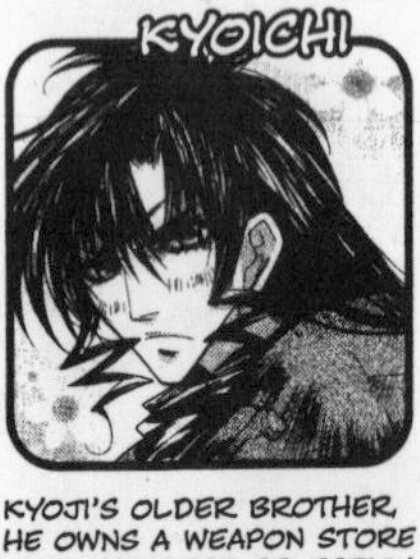
KYOICHI

KYOJI'S OLDER BROTHER, HE OWNS A WEAPON STORE WITH THE BEST SELECTION OF HAUNTED WEAPONS.

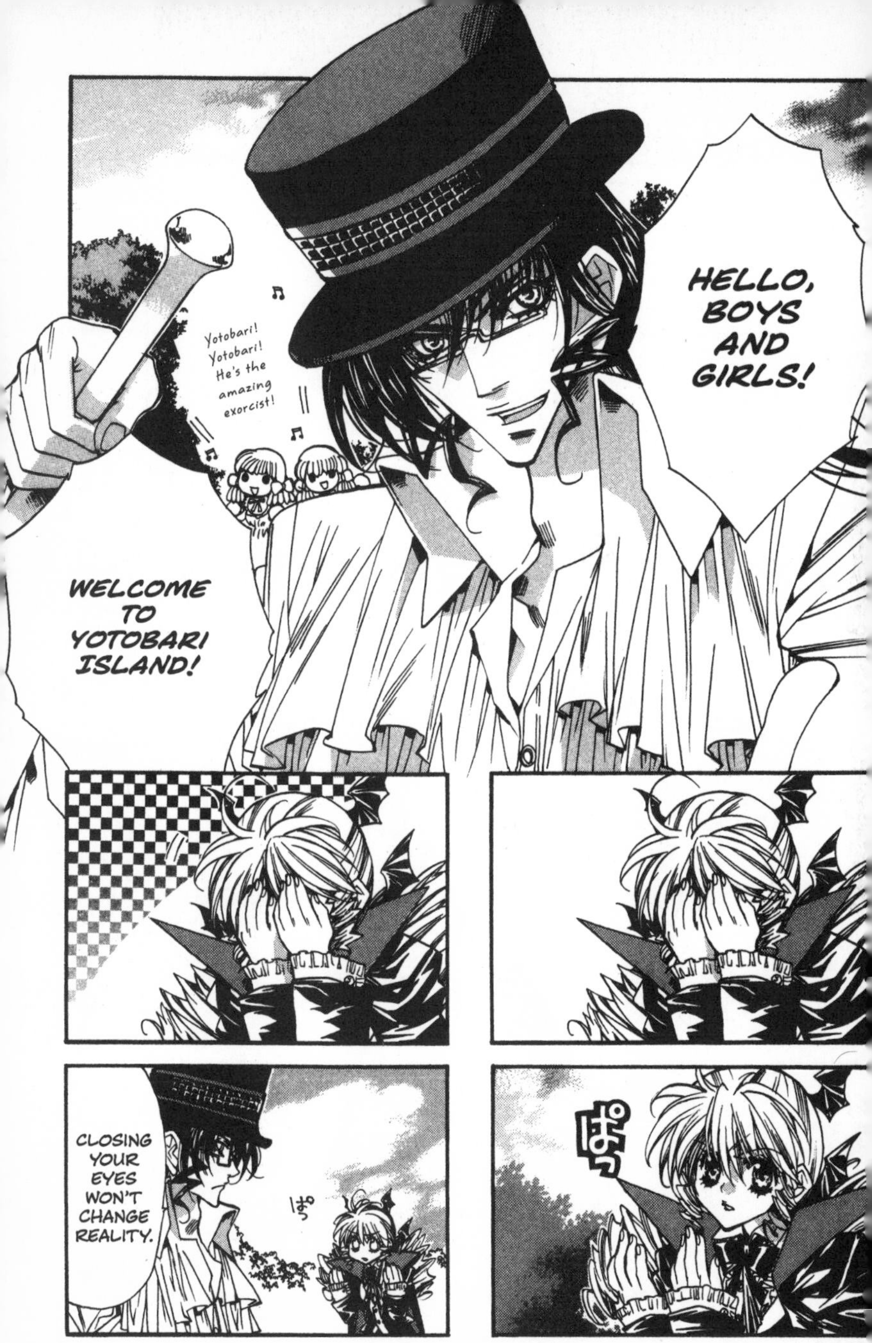
HELLO, BOYS AND GIRLS!
Yotobari! Yotobari! He's the amazing exorcist!
WELCOME TO YOTOBARI ISLAND!
ぱっ
CLOSING YOUR EYES WON'T CHANGE REALITY.
ぱっ

Sphinxes Don't Cry

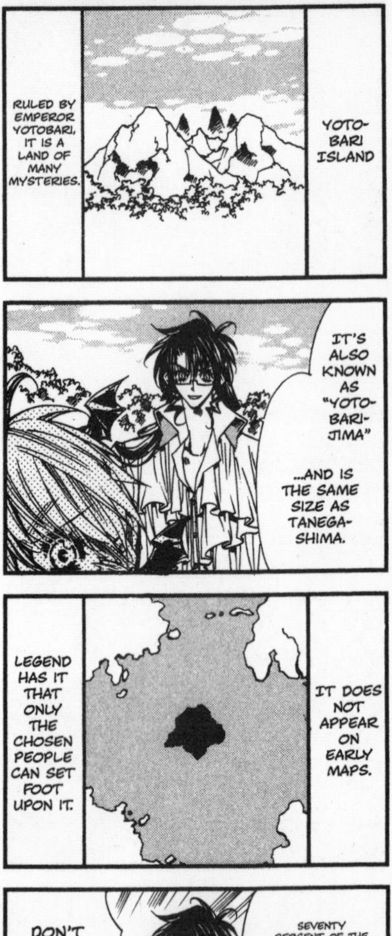
YOTO-BARI ISLAND
RULED BY EMPEROR YOTOBARI, IT IS A LAND OF MANY MYSTERIES.
IT'S ALSO KNOWN AS "YOTO-BARI-JIMA"
...AND IS THE SAME SIZE AS TANEGA-SHIMA.
IT DOES NOT APPEAR ON EARLY MAPS.
LEGEND HAS IT THAT ONLY THE CHOSEN PEOPLE CAN SET FOOT UPON IT.
SEVENTY PERCENT OF THE POPULATION HAS THE LAST NAME "YOTOBARI." OUR INDIGENOUS PRODUCT IS FRILLY CLOTHES.
IN SPRING, CHERRY TREES BLOOM EVERYWHERE.
DON'T KILL THE MOOD!

Stay With You

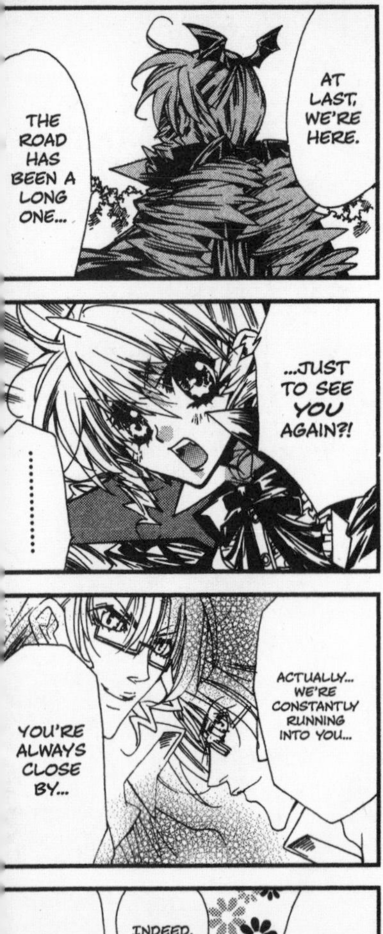
AT LAST, WE'RE HERE.
THE ROAD HAS BEEN A LONG ONE...
...JUST TO SEE YOU AGAIN?!
....
ACTUALLY... WE'RE CONSTANTLY RUNNING INTO YOU...
YOU'RE ALWAYS CLOSE BY...
BESIDE US THROUGH THICK AND THIN...
INDEED.
PLEASE DON'T BE MANIPULATED, GUILT-NA-SAN...

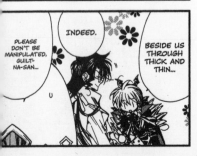

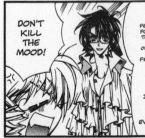

GUILT-NA-ZAN BONUS COMIC STRIPS!

The Last Obstacle

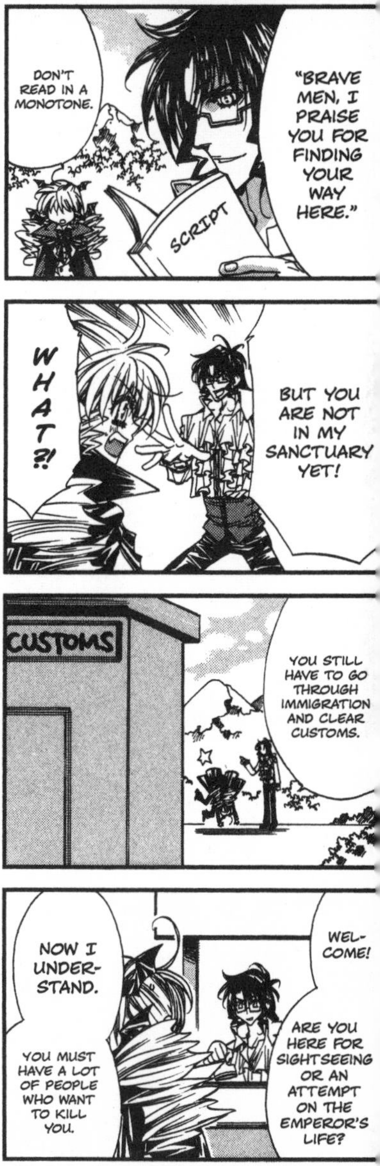
"BRAVE MEN, I PRAISE YOU FOR FINDING YOUR WAY HERE."
SCRIPT
DON'T READ IN A MONOTONE.
BUT YOU ARE NOT IN MY SANCTUARY YET!
WHAT?!
YOU STILL HAVE TO GO THROUGH IMMIGRATION AND CLEAR CUSTOMS.
CUSTOMS
WEL-COME!
ARE YOU HERE FOR SIGHTSEEING OR AN ATTEMPT ON THE EMPEROR'S LIFE?
NOW I UNDER-STAND.
YOU MUST HAVE A LOT OF PEOPLE WHO WANT TO KILL YOU.

Happy Tourists

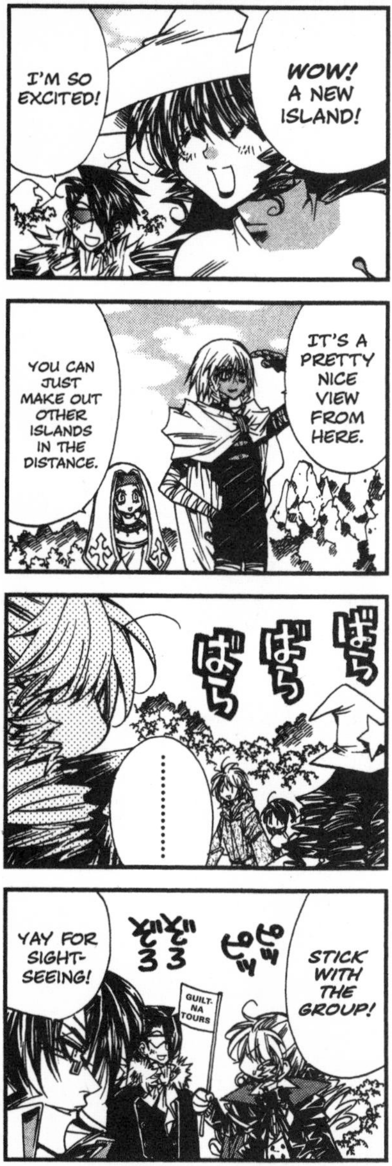
WOW! A NEW ISLAND!
I'M SO EXCITED!
IT'S A PRETTY NICE VIEW FROM HERE.
YOU CAN JUST MAKE OUT OTHER ISLANDS IN THE DISTANCE.
ばら
ばら
ばら
……
STICK WITH THE GROUP!
ピッ ピッ
ぞろぞろ
GUILT-NA TOURS
YAY FOR SIGHT-SEEING!

Being Old

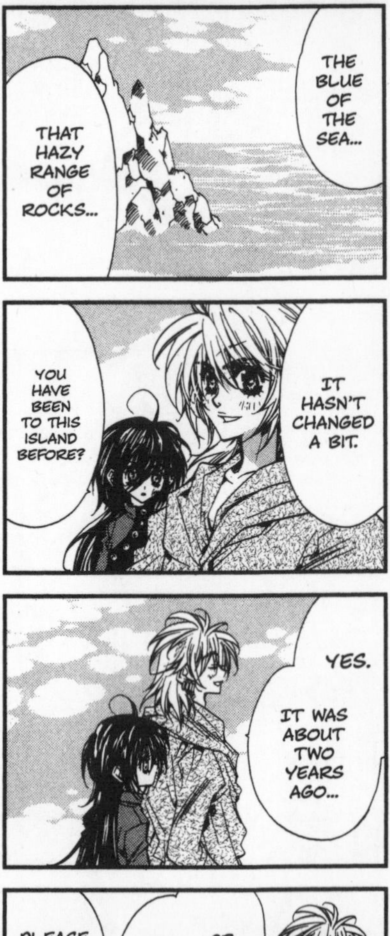
THE BLUE OF THE SEA...
THAT HAZY RANGE OF ROCKS...
IT HASN'T CHANGED A BIT.
YOU HAVE BEEN TO THIS ISLAND BEFORE?
YES.
IT WAS ABOUT TWO YEARS AGO...
OR...
...WAS IT 200 YEARS AGO?
PLEASE DON'T TALK LIKE THAT.

Height

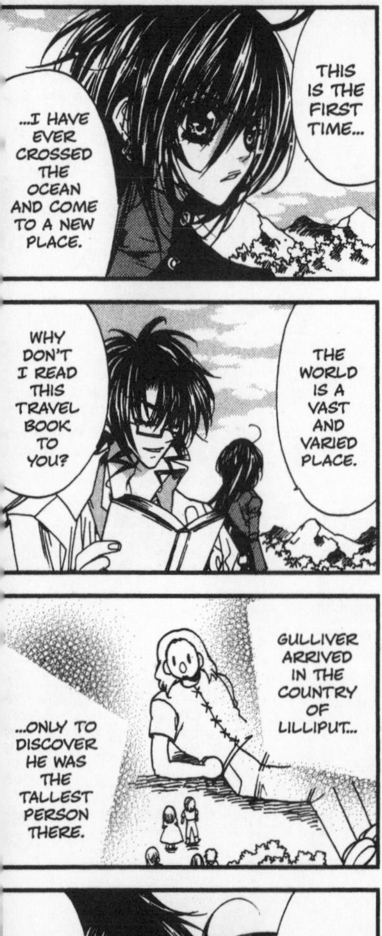
THIS IS THE FIRST TIME...
...I HAVE EVER CROSSED THE OCEAN AND COME TO A NEW PLACE.
THE WORLD IS A VAST AND VARIED PLACE.
WHY DON'T I READ THIS TRAVEL BOOK TO YOU?
GULLIVER ARRIVED IN THE COUNTRY OF LILLIPUT...
...ONLY TO DISCOVER HE WAS THE TALLEST PERSON THERE.
PLEASE TELL ME MORE!
A TAD OBSESSED WITH HEIGHT, ARE WE?

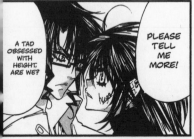

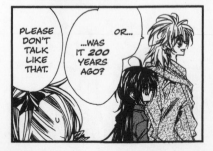

GUILT-NA-ZAN BONUS COMIC STRIPS!

Stereotypical Plot Twist

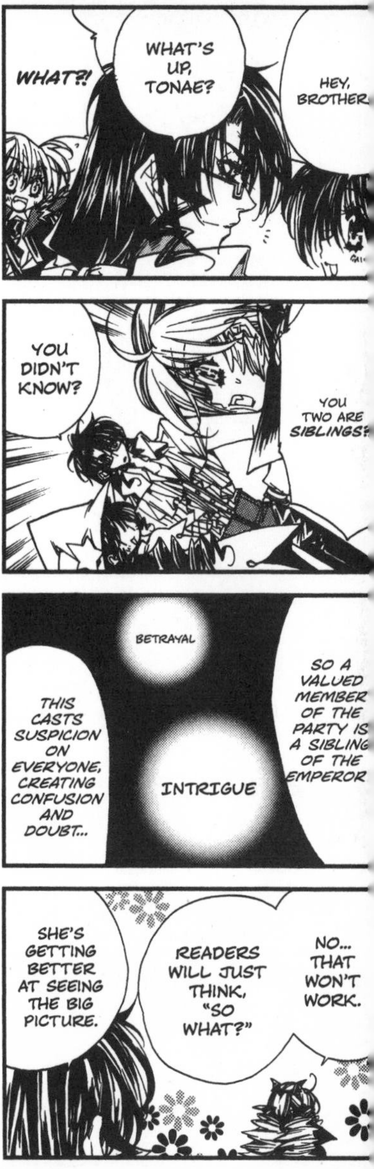
HEY, BROTHER
WHAT'S UP, TONAE?
WHAT?!
YOU TWO ARE SIBLINGS?
YOU DIDN'T KNOW?
SO A VALUED MEMBER OF THE PARTY IS A SIBLING OF THE EMPEROR
BETRAYAL
INTRIGUE
THIS CASTS SUSPICION ON EVERYONE, CREATING CONFUSION AND DOUBT...
NO... THAT WON'T WORK.
READERS WILL JUST THINK, "SO WHAT?"
SHE'S GETTING BETTER AT SEEING THE BIG PICTURE.

An Island Called...

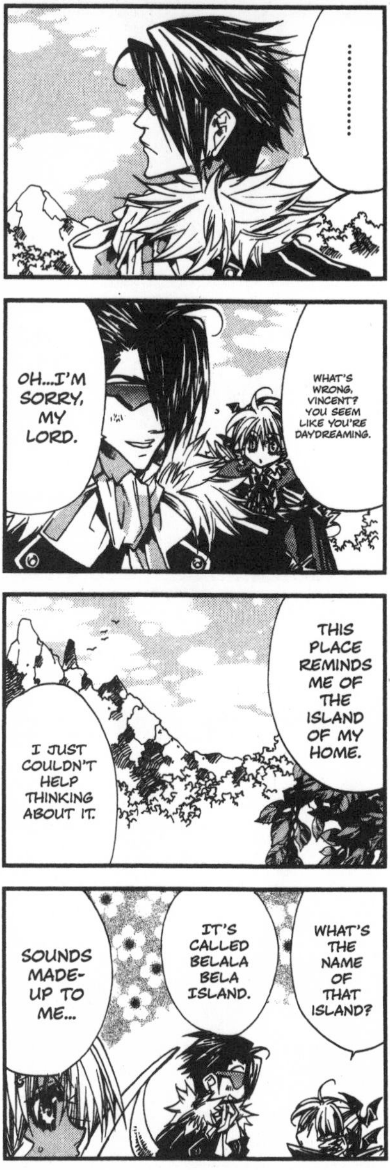
....
WHAT'S WRONG, VINCENT? YOU SEEM LIKE YOU'RE DAYDREAMING.
OH...I'M SORRY, MY LORD.
THIS PLACE REMINDS ME OF THE ISLAND OF MY HOME.
I JUST COULDN'T HELP THINKING ABOUT IT.
WHAT'S THE NAME OF THAT ISLAND?
IT'S CALLED BELALA BELA ISLAND.
SOUNDS MADE-UP TO ME...

Dorothy Doodling

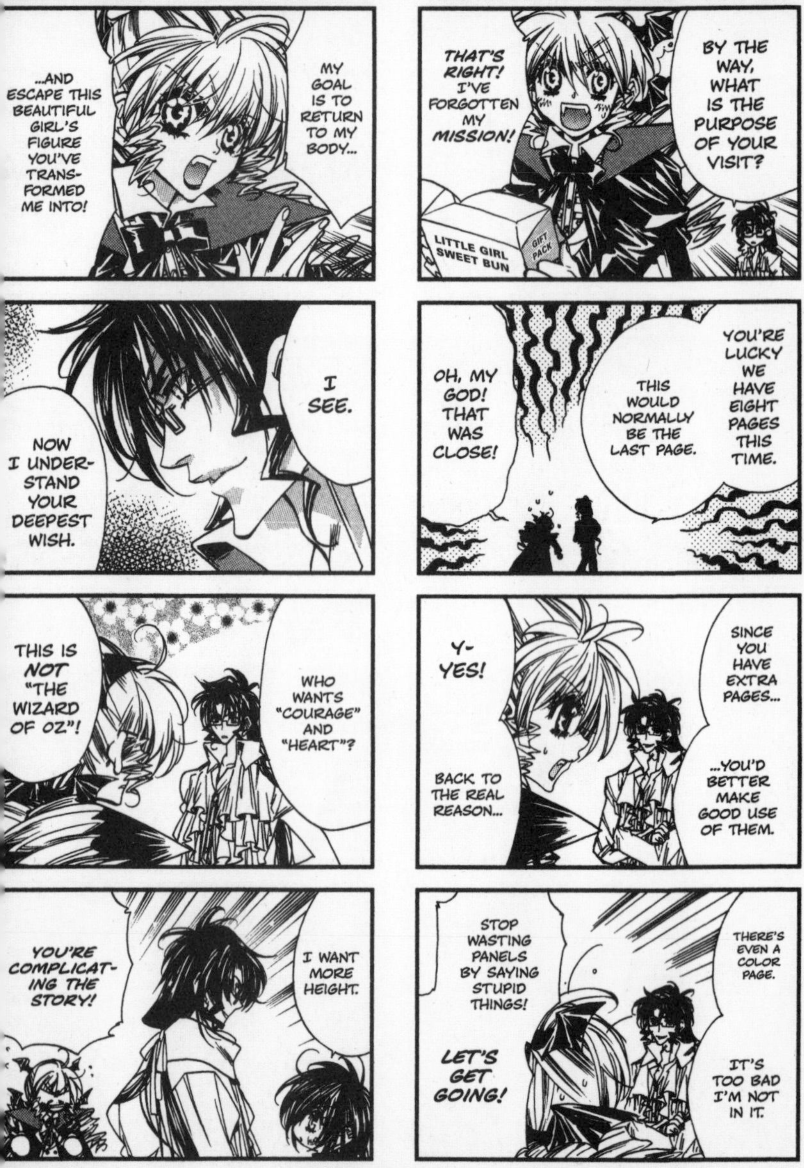
BY THE WAY, WHAT IS THE PURPOSE OF YOUR VISIT?
THAT'S RIGHT! I'VE FORGOTTEN MY MISSION!
LITTLE GIRL SWEET BUN
GIFT PACK
YOU'RE LUCKY WE HAVE EIGHT PAGES THIS TIME.
THIS WOULD NORMALLY BE THE LAST PAGE.
OH, MY GOD! THAT WAS CLOSE!
SINCE YOU HAVE EXTRA PAGES...
...YOU'D BETTER MAKE GOOD USE OF THEM.
Y-YES!
BACK TO THE REAL REASON...
THERE'S EVEN A COLOR PAGE.
IT'S TOO BAD I'M NOT IN IT.
STOP WASTING PANELS BY SAYING STUPID THINGS!
LET'S GET GOING!
MY GOAL IS TO RETURN TO MY BODY...
...AND ESCAPE THIS BEAUTIFUL GIRL'S FIGURE YOU'VE TRANSFORMED ME INTO!
I SEE.
NOW I UNDERSTAND YOUR DEEPEST WISH.
WHO WANTS "COURAGE" AND "HEART"?
THIS IS NOT "THE WIZARD OF OZ"!
I WANT MORE HEIGHT.
YOU'RE COMPLICATING THE STORY!

GUILT-NA-ZAN BONUS COMIC STRIPS!

Although It's Not Wrong...

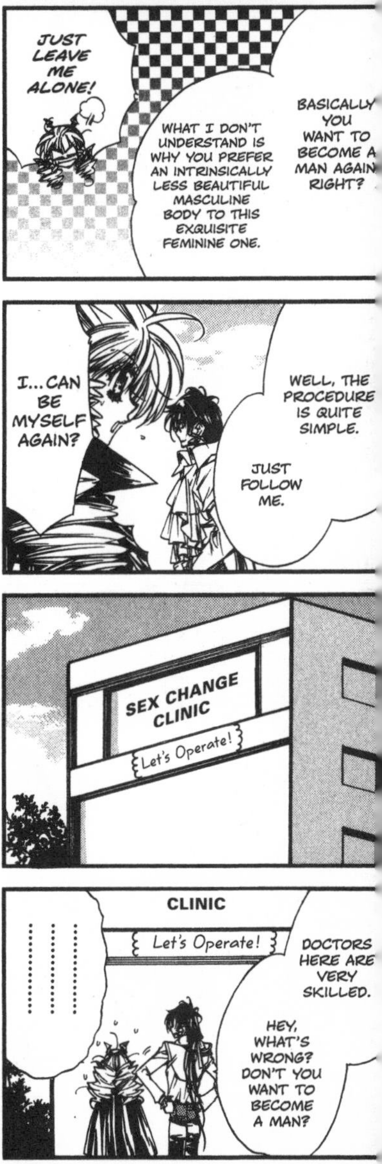
BASICALLY YOU WANT TO BECOME A MAN AGAIN RIGHT?
WHAT I DON'T UNDERSTAND IS WHY YOU PREFER AN INTRINSICALLY LESS BEAUTIFUL MASCULINE BODY TO THIS EXQUISITE FEMININE ONE.
JUST LEAVE ME ALONE!
WELL, THE PROCEDURE IS QUITE SIMPLE.
JUST FOLLOW ME.
I...CAN BE MYSELF AGAIN?
SEX CHANGE CLINIC
Let's Operate!
DOCTORS HERE ARE VERY SKILLED.
HEY, WHAT'S WRONG? DON'T YOU WANT TO BECOME A MAN?
CLINIC
Let's Operate!
......

Travel Video

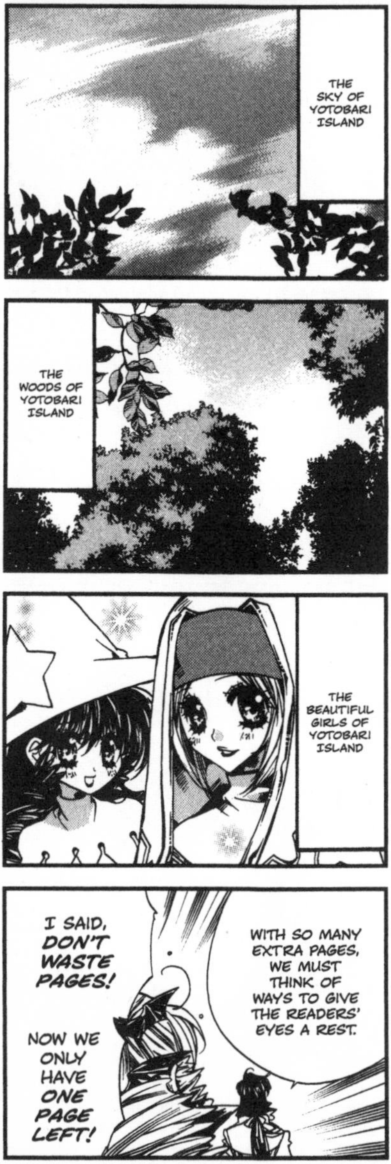
THE SKY OF YOTOBARI ISLAND
THE WOODS OF YOTOBARI ISLAND
THE BEAUTIFUL GIRLS OF YOTOBARI ISLAND
WITH SO MANY EXTRA PAGES, WE MUST THINK OF WAYS TO GIVE THE READERS' EYES A REST.
I SAID, *DON'T WASTE PAGES!*
NOW WE ONLY HAVE *ONE PAGE LEFT!*

Narrator

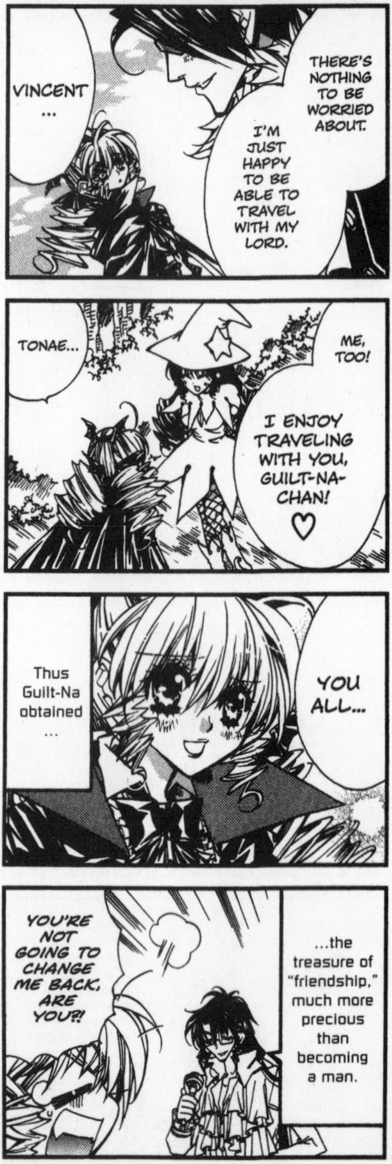
THERE'S NOTHING TO BE WORRIED ABOUT.
I'M JUST HAPPY TO BE ABLE TO TRAVEL WITH MY LORD.
VINCENT ...
ME, TOO!
I ENJOY TRAVELING WITH YOU, GUILT-NA-CHAN! ♡
TONAE...
YOU ALL...
Thus Guilt-Na obtained ...
...the treasure of "friendship," much more precious than becoming a man.
YOU'RE NOT GOING TO CHANGE ME BACK, ARE YOU?!

Together Again?

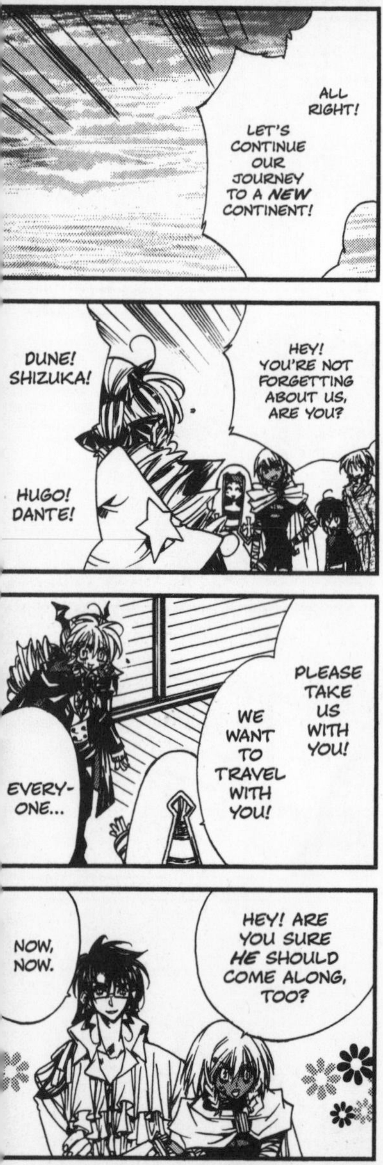
ALL RIGHT!
LET'S CONTINUE OUR JOURNEY TO A *NEW* CONTINENT!
HEY! YOU'RE NOT FORGETTING ABOUT US, ARE YOU?
DUNE! SHIZUKA!
HUGO! DANTE!
PLEASE TAKE US WITH YOU!
WE WANT TO TRAVEL WITH YOU!
EVERY-ONE...
HEY! ARE YOU SURE *HE* SHOULD COME ALONG, TOO?
NOW, NOW.

BONUS COMIC STRIP

R•P• Guilt-na-Zan Part 7

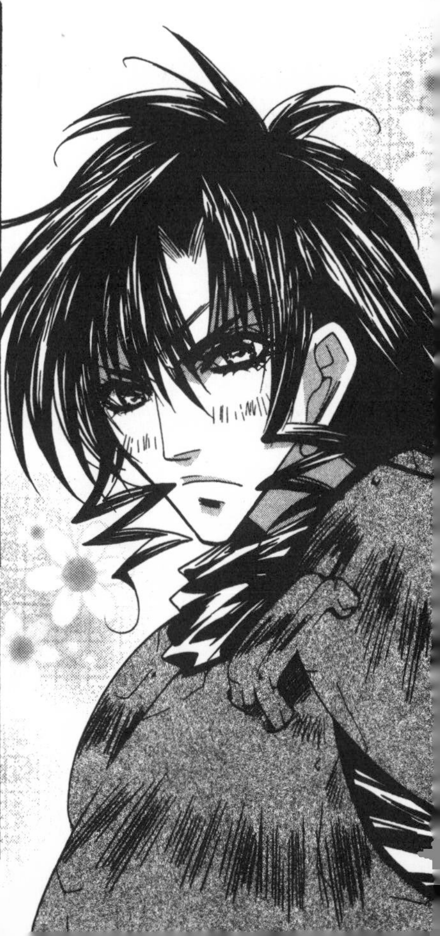

Visions

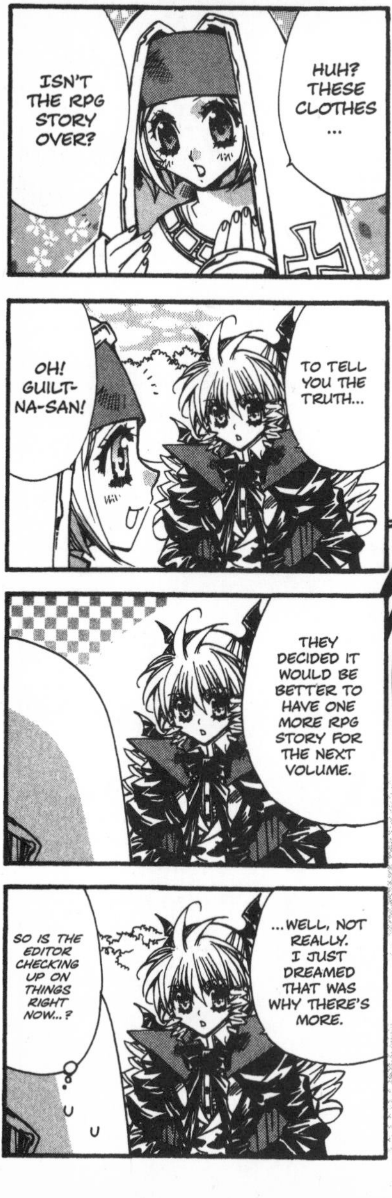
HUH? THESE CLOTHES ...
ISN'T THE RPG STORY OVER?
TO TELL YOU THE TRUTH...
OH! GUILT-NA-SAN!
THEY DECIDED IT WOULD BE BETTER TO HAVE ONE MORE RPG STORY FOR THE NEXT VOLUME.
...WELL, NOT REALLY. I JUST DREAMED THAT WAS WHY THERE'S MORE.
SO IS THE EDITOR CHECKING UP ON THINGS RIGHT NOW...?

"Wake Up" Says the Voice

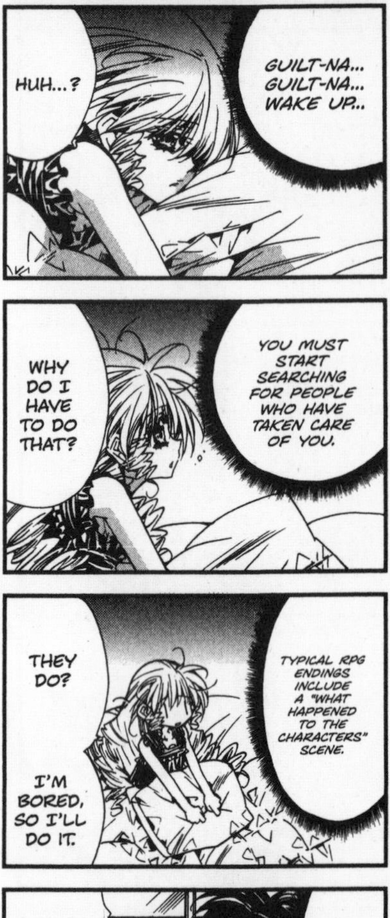
GUILT-NA... GUILT-NA... WAKE UP...
HUH...?
YOU MUST START SEARCHING FOR PEOPLE WHO HAVE TAKEN CARE OF YOU.
WHY DO I HAVE TO DO THAT?
TYPICAL RPG ENDINGS INCLUDE A "WHAT HAPPENED TO THE CHARACTERS" SCENE.
THEY DO?
I'M BORED, SO I'LL DO IT.
BE SURE TO VISIT ME, TOO.
I'M ALREADY HERE!

Magic Item

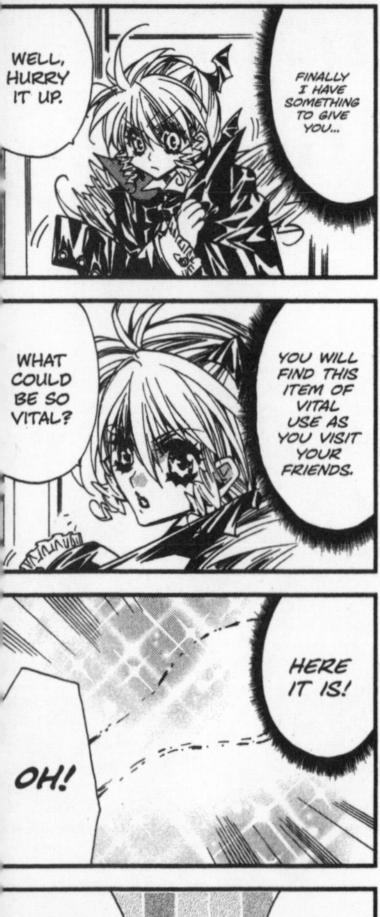
FINALLY I HAVE SOMETHING TO GIVE YOU...
WELL, HURRY IT UP.
YOU WILL FIND THIS ITEM OF VITAL USE AS YOU VISIT YOUR FRIENDS.
WHAT COULD BE SO VITAL?
HERE IT IS!
OH!
I WAS TOLD TO BRING IT WITH ME.
HAPPY LITTLE GIRL
YOU'D HAVE TO VISIT THEM DURING A FEAST TO MAKE THAT USEFUL.

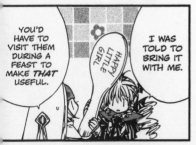

It's a giant rice paddle.

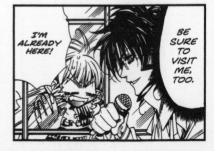

GUILT-NA-ZAN BONUS COMIC STRIPS!

What Happened to Shizuka

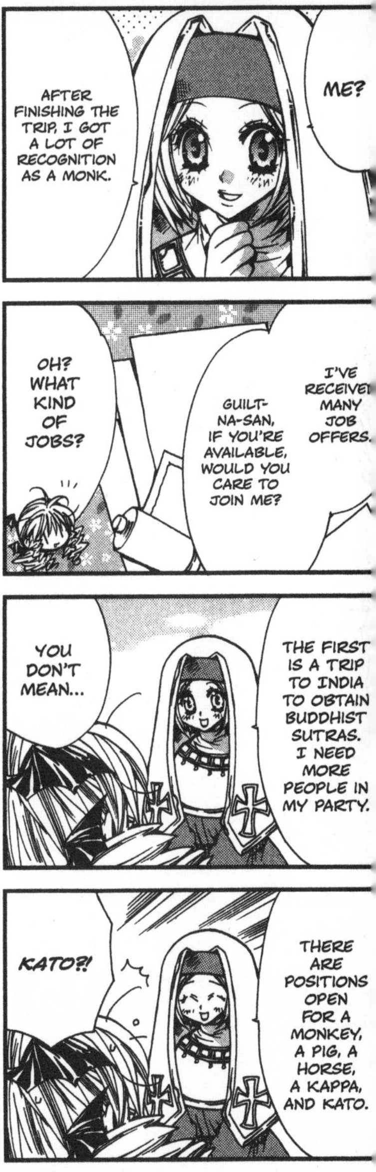
ME?
AFTER FINISHING THE TRIP, I GOT A LOT OF RECOGNITION AS A MONK.
I'VE RECEIVE MANY JOB OFFERS.
GUILT-NA-SAN, IF YOU'RE AVAILABLE, WOULD YOU CARE TO JOIN ME?
OH? WHAT KIND OF JOBS?
THE FIRST IS A TRIP TO INDIA TO OBTAIN BUDDHIST SUTRAS. I NEED MORE PEOPLE IN MY PARTY.
YOU DON'T MEAN...
THERE ARE POSITIONS OPEN FOR A MONKEY, A PIG, A HORSE, A KAPPA, AND KATO.
KATO?!

*Kato is a bald comedian.

What Happened to Dune

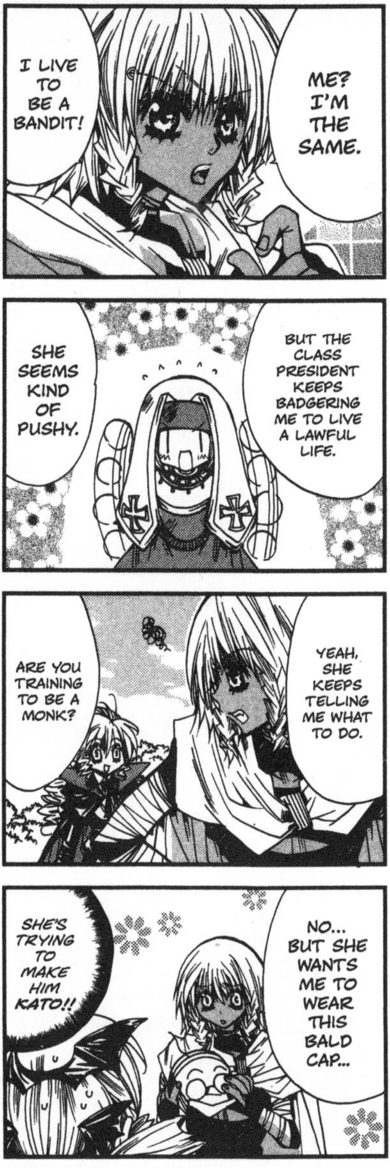
ME? I'M THE SAME.
I LIVE TO BE A BANDIT!
BUT THE CLASS PRESIDENT KEEPS BADGERING ME TO LIVE A LAWFUL LIFE.
SHE SEEMS KIND OF PUSHY.
YEAH, SHE KEEPS TELLING ME WHAT TO DO.
ARE YOU TRAINING TO BE A MONK?
NO... BUT SHE WANTS ME TO WEAR THIS BALD CAP...
SHE'S TRYING TO MAKE HIM KATO!!

What Happened to Vincent

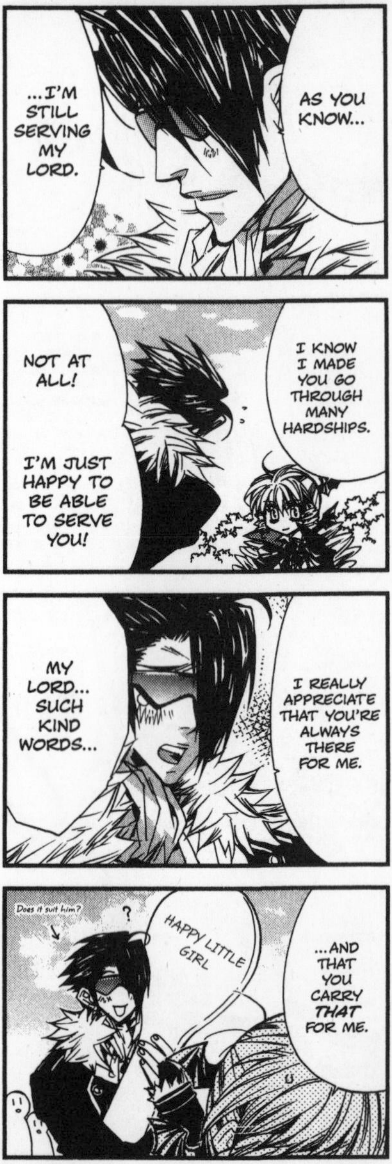
AS YOU KNOW...
...I'M STILL SERVING MY LORD.
I KNOW I MADE YOU GO THROUGH MANY HARDSHIPS.
NOT AT ALL!
I'M JUST HAPPY TO BE ABLE TO SERVE YOU!
I REALLY APPRECIATE THAT YOU'RE ALWAYS THERE FOR ME.
MY LORD... SUCH KIND WORDS...
...AND THAT YOU CARRY *THAT* FOR ME.
HAPPY LITTLE GIRL
?
Does it suit him?

What Happened to Tonae

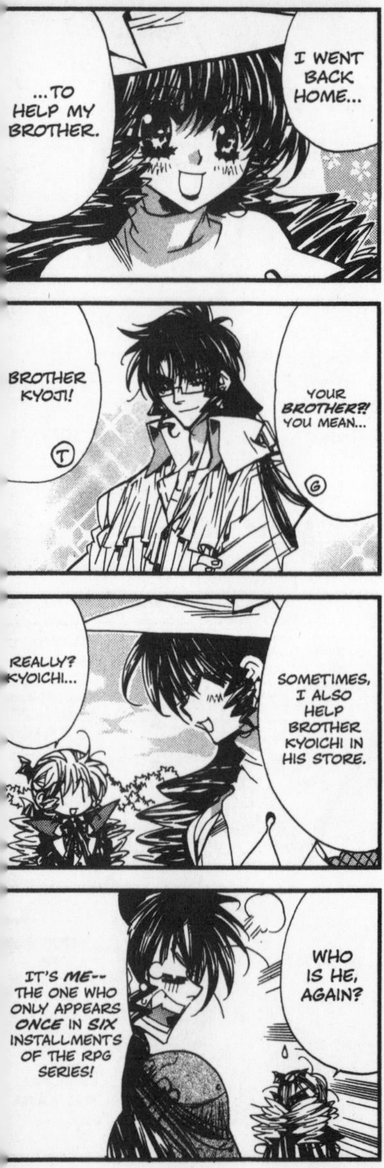
I WENT BACK HOME...
...TO HELP MY BROTHER.
YOUR *BROTHER?!* YOU MEAN...
G
BROTHER KYOJI!
T
SOMETIMES, I ALSO HELP BROTHER KYOICHI IN HIS STORE.
REALLY? KYOICHI...
WHO IS HE, AGAIN?
IT'S *ME*-- THE ONE WHO ONLY APPEARS *ONCE* IN *SIX* INSTALLMENTS OF THE RPG SERIES!

GUILT-NA-ZAN BONUS COMIC STRIPS!

What Happened to Night Veil

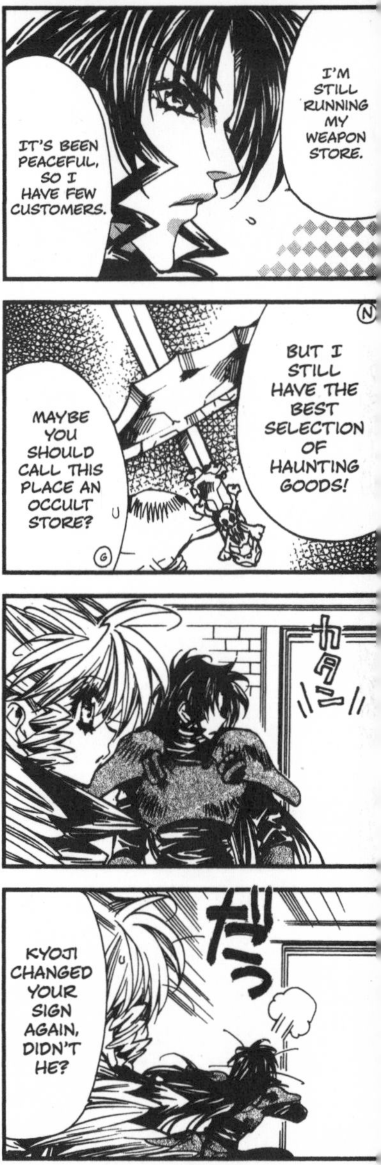

I'M STILL RUNNING MY WEAPON STORE.
IT'S BEEN PEACEFUL, SO I HAVE FEW CUSTOMERS.
BUT I STILL HAVE THE BEST SELECTION OF HAUNTING GOODS!
MAYBE YOU SHOULD CALL THIS PLACE AN OCCULT STORE?
カタン
だっ
KYOJI CHANGED YOUR SIGN AGAIN, DIDN'T HE?

What Happened to Kyoji

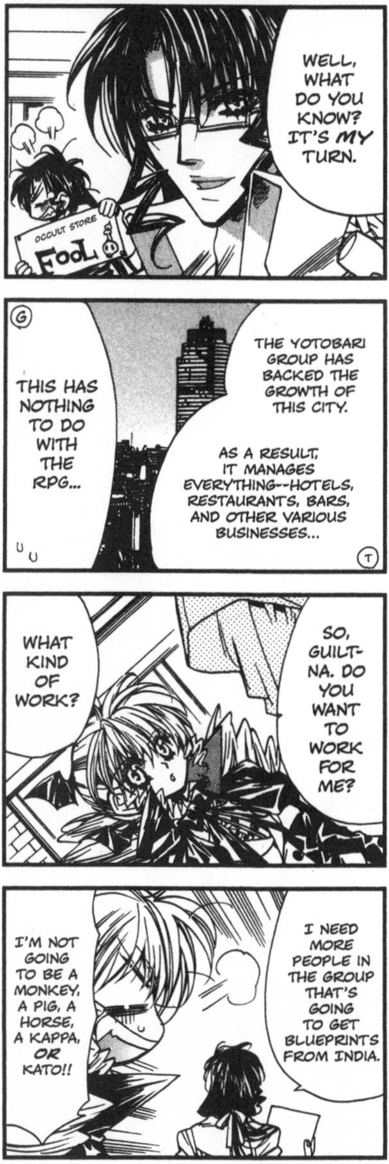

WELL, WHAT DO YOU KNOW? IT'S MY TURN.
OCCULT STORE
FOOL
THE YOTOBARI GROUP HAS BACKED THE GROWTH OF THIS CITY.
AS A RESULT, IT MANAGES EVERYTHING--HOTELS, RESTAURANTS, BARS, AND OTHER VARIOUS BUSINESSES...
THIS HAS NOTHING TO DO WITH THE RPG...
SO, GUILT-NA. DO YOU WANT TO WORK FOR ME?
WHAT KIND OF WORK?
I NEED MORE PEOPLE IN THE GROUP THAT'S GOING TO GET BLUEPRINTS FROM INDIA.
I'M NOT GOING TO BE A MONKEY, A PIG, A HORSE, A KAPPA, OR KATO!!

What Happened to Hugo

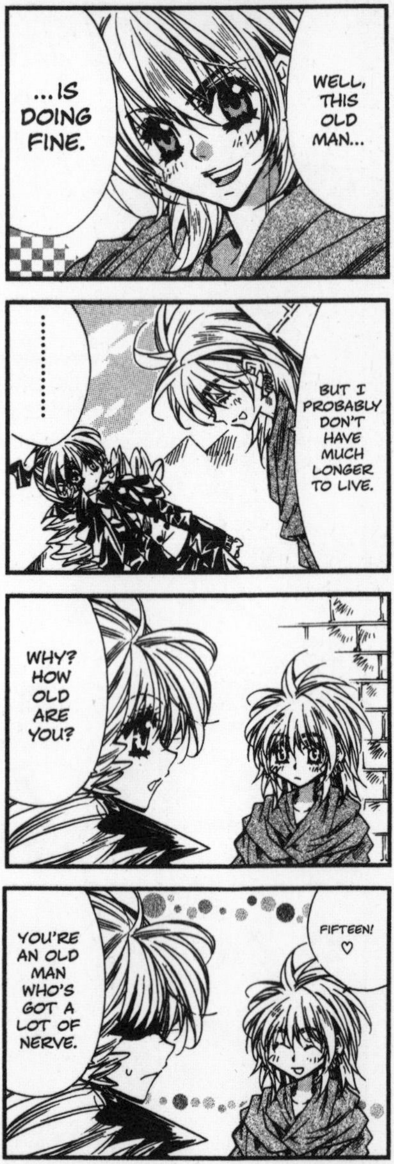
WELL, THIS OLD MAN...
...IS DOING FINE.
BUT I PROBABLY DON'T HAVE MUCH LONGER TO LIVE.
....
WHY? HOW OLD ARE YOU?
FIFTEEN! ♡
YOU'RE AN OLD MAN WHO'S GOT A LOT OF NERVE.

What Happened to Dante

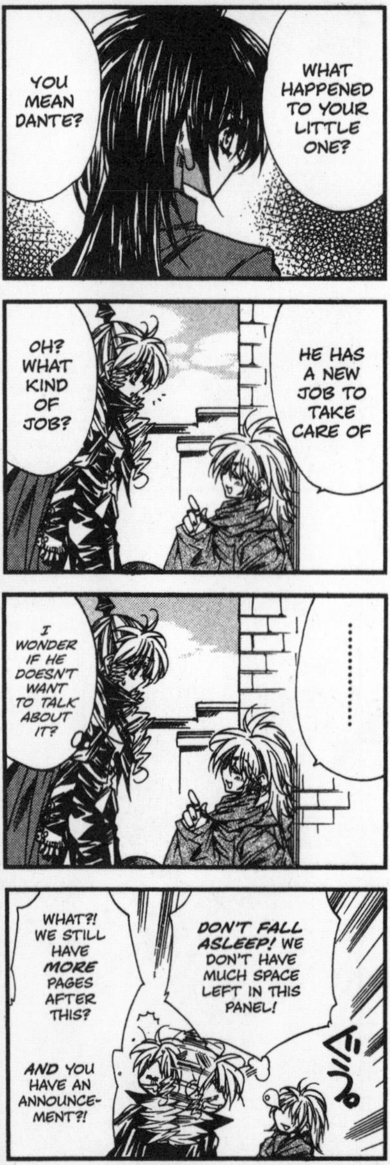
WHAT HAPPENED TO YOUR LITTLE ONE?
YOU MEAN DANTE?
HE HAS A NEW JOB TO TAKE CARE OF
OH? WHAT KIND OF JOB?
....
I WONDER IF HE DOESN'T WANT TO TALK ABOUT IT?
DON'T FALL ASLEEP! WE DON'T HAVE MUCH SPACE LEFT IN THIS PANEL!
WHAT?! WE STILL HAVE MORE PAGES AFTER THIS?
AND YOU HAVE AN ANNOUNCEMENT?!

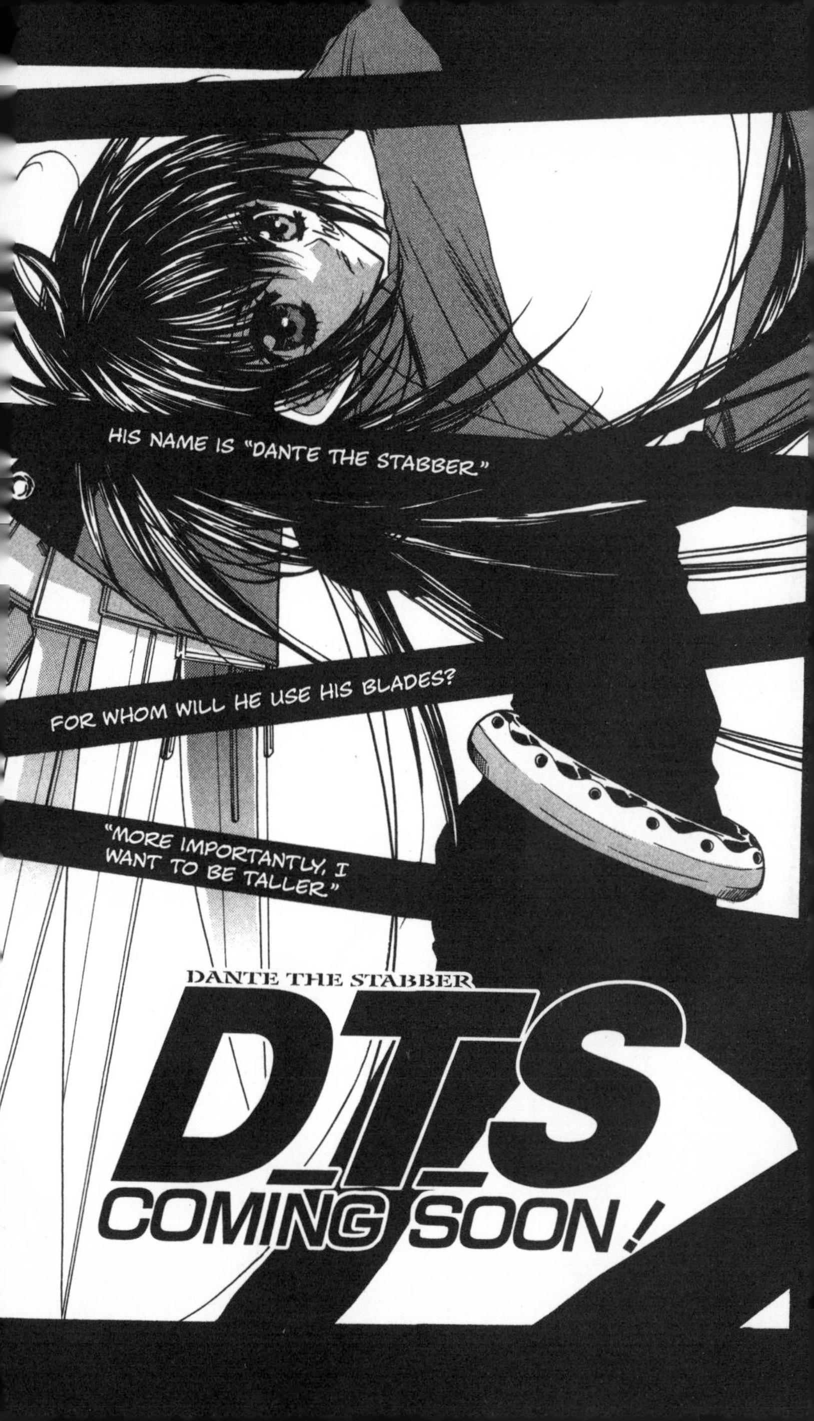
HIS NAME IS "DANTE THE STABBER"
FOR WHOM WILL HE USE HIS BLADES?
"MORE IMPORTANTLY, I WANT TO BE TALLER"
DANTE THE STABBER
D.T.S
COMING SOON!

GUILTNA "TRUE HERO" DOLL

BONUS COMIC STRIP

D_T_S

(Dante the Stabber)

Part 1

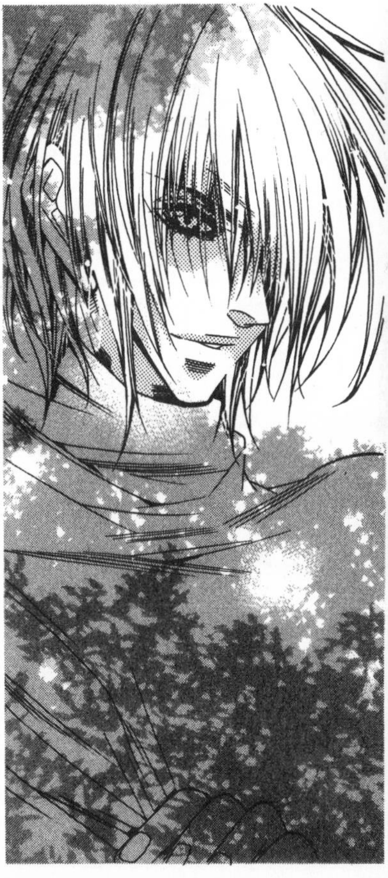

Specs

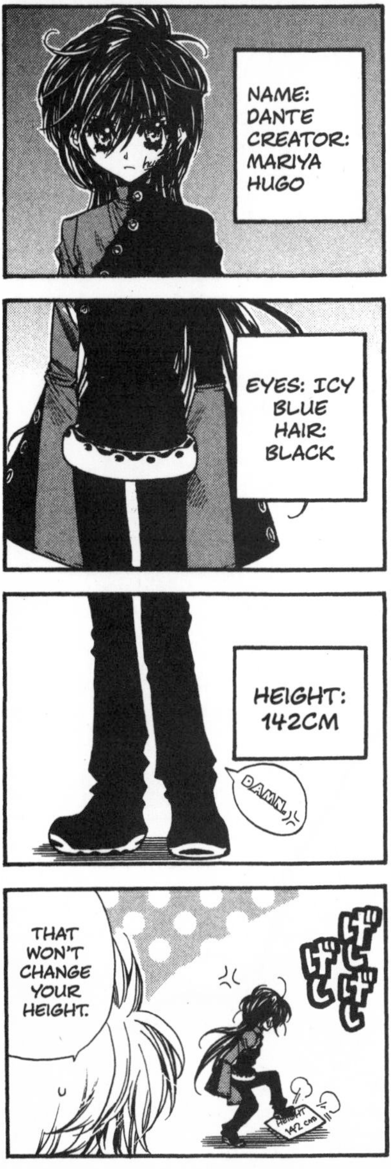
NAME: DANTE CREATOR: MARIYA HUGO
EYES: ICY BLUE HAIR: BLACK
HEIGHT: 142CM
DAMN.
THAT WON'T CHANGE YOUR HEIGHT.
げしげし
げし
HEIGHT 142 cm

Benefit

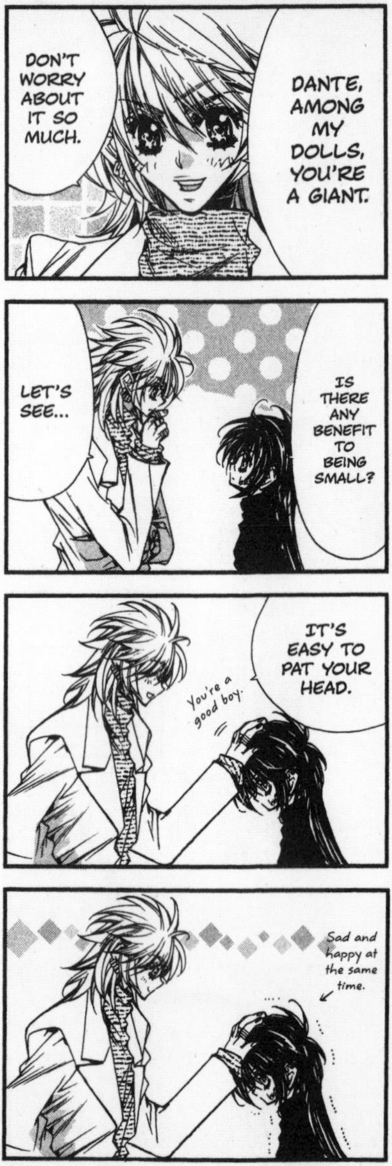
DANTE, AMONG MY DOLLS, YOU'RE A GIANT.
DON'T WORRY ABOUT IT SO MUCH.
IS THERE ANY BENEFIT TO BEING SMALL?
LET'S SEE...
IT'S EASY TO PAT YOUR HEAD.
You're a good boy.
Sad and happy at the same time.

Touching Memory

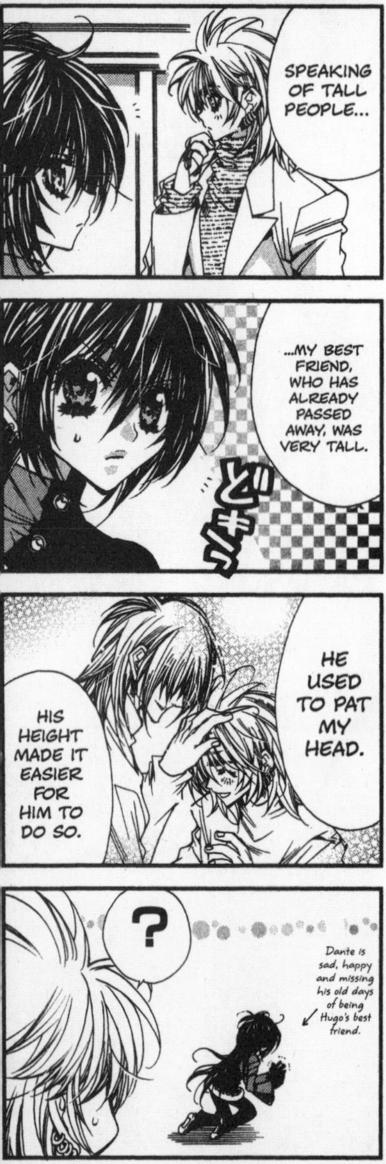
SPEAKING OF TALL PEOPLE...
...MY BEST FRIEND, WHO HAS ALREADY PASSED AWAY, WAS VERY TALL.
どキッ
HE USED TO PAT MY HEAD.
HIS HEIGHT MADE IT EASIER FOR HIM TO DO SO.
?
Dante is sad, happy and missing his old days of being Hugo's best friend.

GUILT-NA-ZAN BONUS COMIC STRIPS!

Perspective

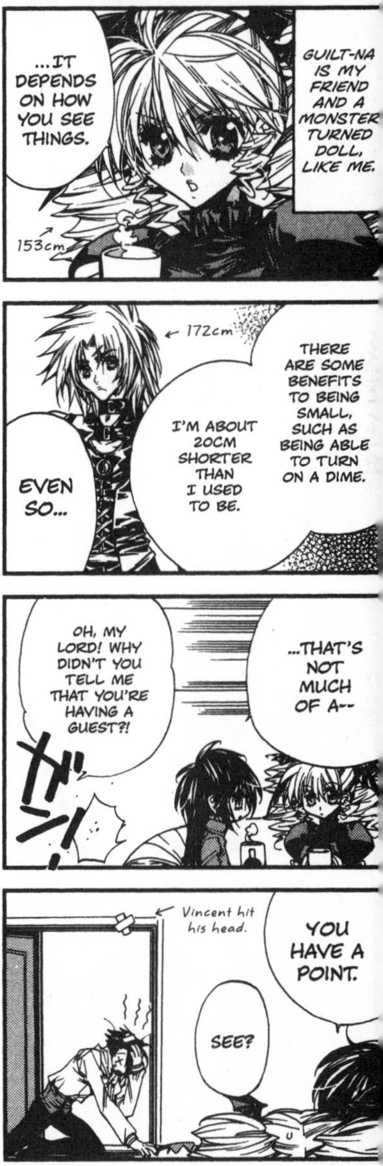
GUILT-NA IS MY FRIEND AND A MONSTER TURNED DOLL, LIKE ME.
...IT DEPENDS ON HOW YOU SEE THINGS.
153cm
172cm
THERE ARE SOME BENEFITS TO BEING SMALL, SUCH AS BEING ABLE TO TURN ON A DIME.
I'M ABOUT 20CM SHORTER THAN I USED TO BE.
EVEN SO...
...THAT'S NOT MUCH OF A--
OH, MY LORD! WHY DIDN'T YOU TELL ME THAT YOU'RE HAVING A GUEST?!
ガン!
YOU HAVE A POINT.
Vincent hit his head.
SEE?

Most People

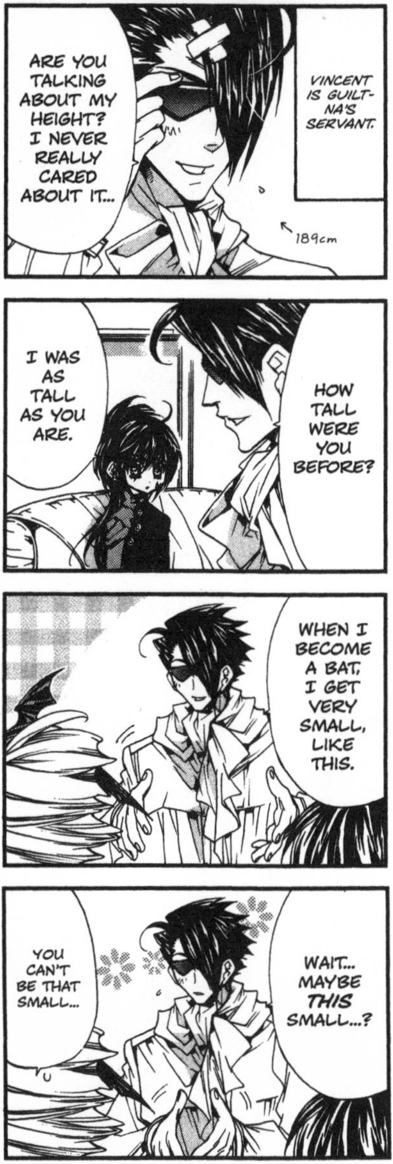
VINCENT IS GUILT-NA'S SERVANT.
ARE YOU TALKING ABOUT MY HEIGHT? I NEVER REALLY CARED ABOUT IT...
189cm
HOW TALL WERE YOU BEFORE?
I WAS AS TALL AS YOU ARE.
WHEN I BECOME A BAT, I GET VERY SMALL, LIKE THIS.
WAIT... MAYBE THIS SMALL...?
YOU CAN'T BE THAT SMALL...

Nickname

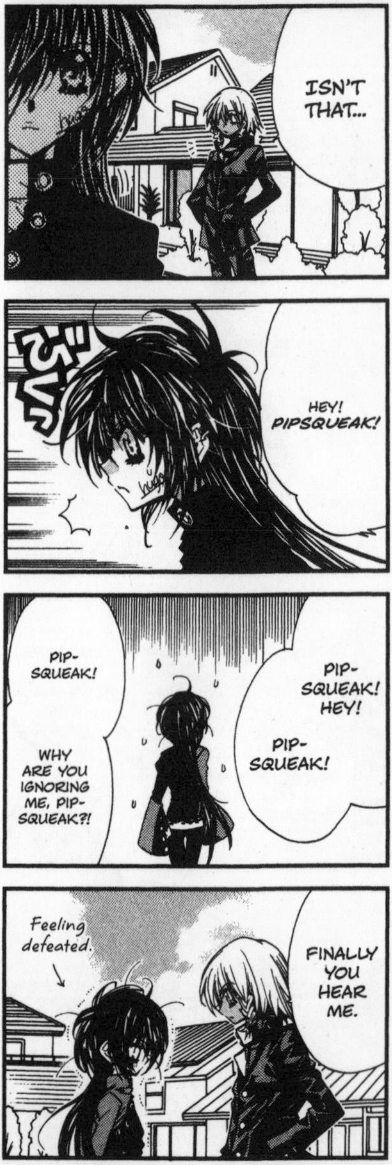
ISN'T THAT...
びくっ
HEY! PIPSQUEAK!
PIP-SQUEAK! HEY!
PIP-SQUEAK!
PIP-SQUEAK!
WHY ARE YOU IGNORING ME, PIP-SQUEAK?!
FINALLY YOU HEAR ME.
Feeling defeated.

Becoming Bigger

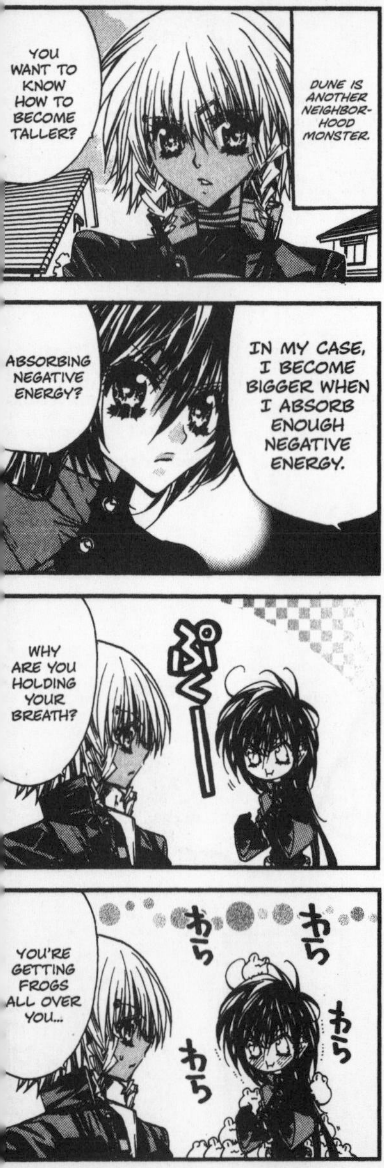
DUNE IS ANOTHER NEIGHBOR-HOOD MONSTER.
YOU WANT TO KNOW HOW TO BECOME TALLER?
IN MY CASE, I BECOME BIGGER WHEN I ABSORB ENOUGH NEGATIVE ENERGY.
ABSORBING NEGATIVE ENERGY?
ぷくー
WHY ARE YOU HOLDING YOUR BREATH?
わら
わら
わら
わら
YOU'RE GETTING FROGS ALL OVER YOU...

GUILT-NA-ZAN BONUS COMIC STRIPS!

The Macro Theory

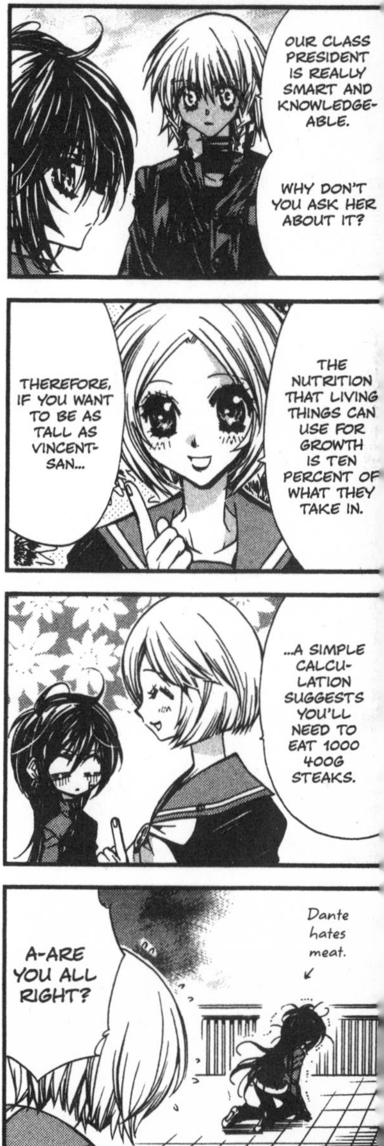
OUR CLASS PRESIDENT IS REALLY SMART AND KNOWLEDGE-ABLE.
WHY DON'T YOU ASK HER ABOUT IT?
THE NUTRITION THAT LIVING THINGS CAN USE FOR GROWTH IS TEN PERCENT OF WHAT THEY TAKE IN.
THEREFORE, IF YOU WANT TO BE AS TALL AS VINCENT-SAN...
...A SIMPLE CALCU-LATION SUGGESTS YOU'LL NEED TO EAT 1000 400G STEAKS.
Dante hates meat.
A-ARE YOU ALL RIGHT?

Tamaki-chan

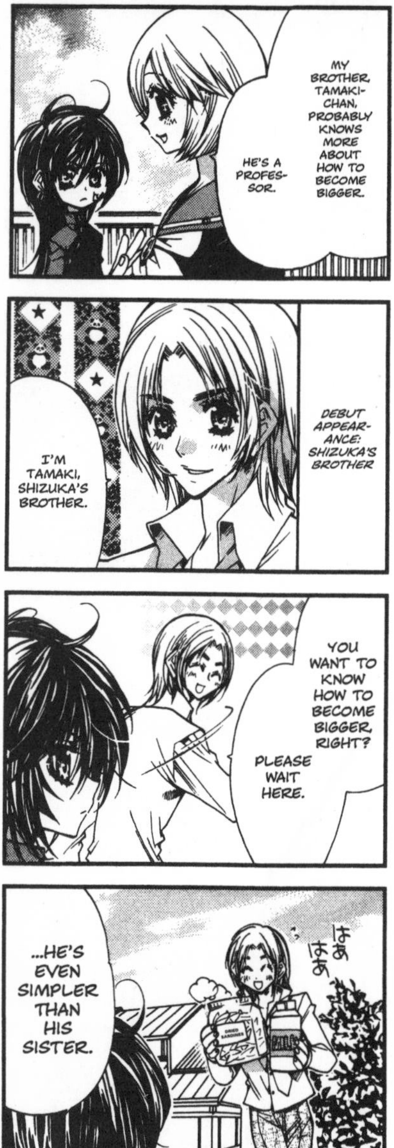
MY BROTHER, TAMAKI-CHAN, PROBABLY KNOWS MORE ABOUT HOW TO BECOME BIGGER.
HE'S A PROFES-SOR.
DEBUT APPEAR-ANCE: SHIZUKA'S BROTHER
I'M TAMAKI, SHIZUKA'S BROTHER.
YOU WANT TO KNOW HOW TO BECOME BIGGER, RIGHT?
PLEASE WAIT HERE.
はあ はあ
...HE'S EVEN SIMPLER THAN HIS SISTER.

Always

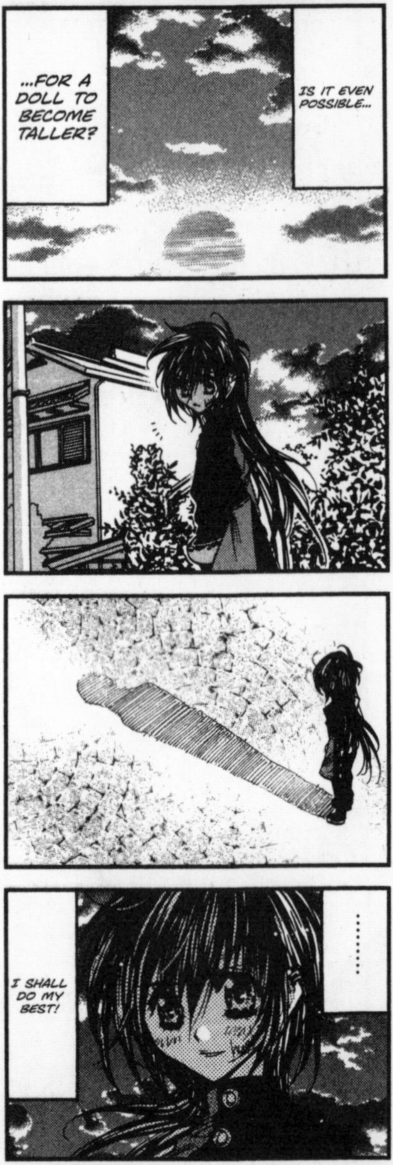

IS IT EVEN POSSIBLE...
...FOR A DOLL TO BECOME TALLER?
......
I SHALL DO MY BEST!

Sad and Happy, Again

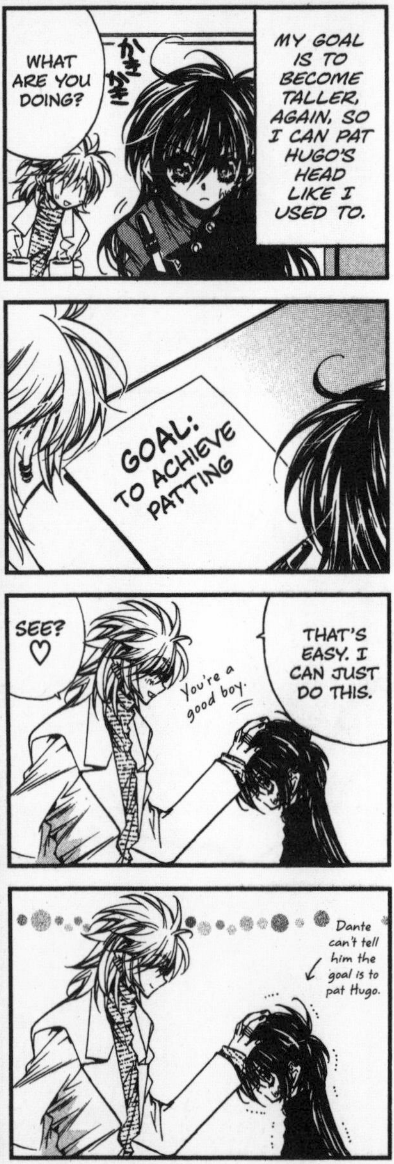

MY GOAL IS TO BECOME TALLER, AGAIN, SO I CAN PAT HUGO'S HEAD LIKE I USED TO.
かきかき
WHAT ARE YOU DOING?
GOAL: TO ACHIEVE PATTING
THAT'S EASY. I CAN JUST DO THIS.
You're a good boy.
SEE? ♡
Dante can't tell him the goal is to pat Hugo.

Bonus Comic Strip

D_T_S

(Dante the Stabber)

Part2

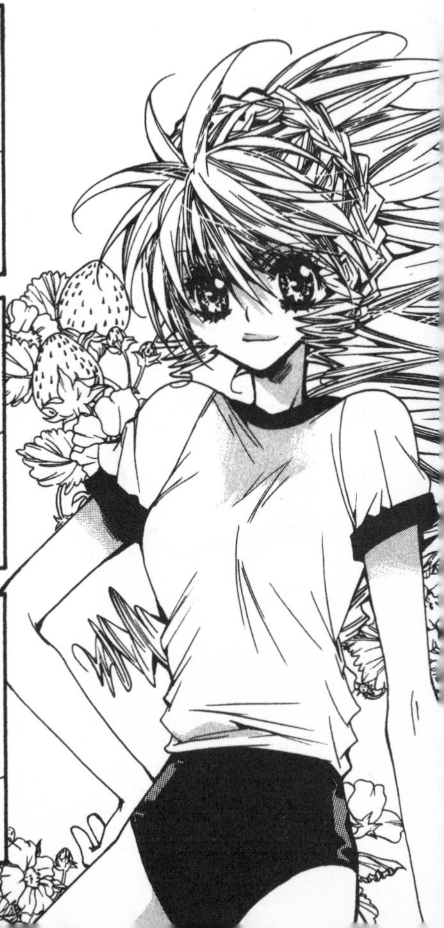

Quick Response

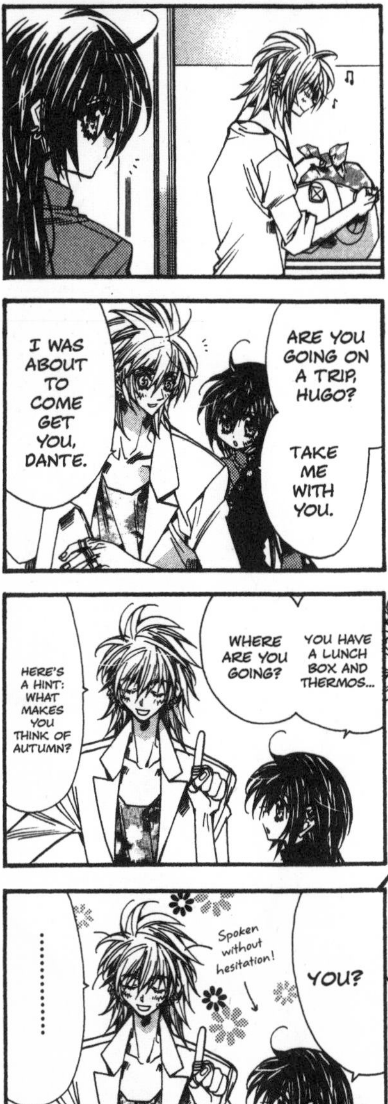

♫
ARE YOU GOING ON A TRIP, HUGO?
TAKE ME WITH YOU.
I WAS ABOUT TO COME GET YOU, DANTE.
YOU HAVE A LUNCH BOX AND THERMOS...
WHERE ARE YOU GOING?
HERE'S A HINT: WHAT MAKES YOU THINK OF AUTUMN?
YOU?
Spoken without hesitation!
....

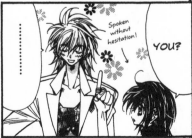

Opening Ceremony

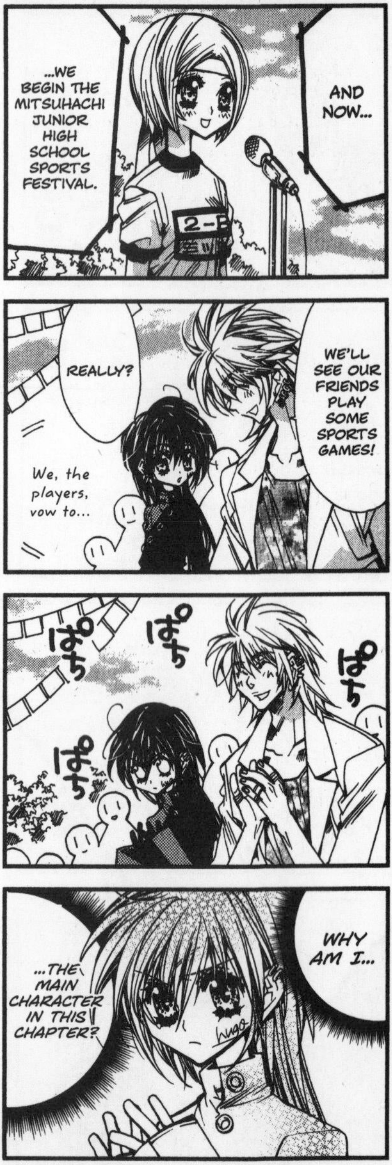
AND NOW...
...WE BEGIN THE MITSUHACHI JUNIOR HIGH SCHOOL SPORTS FESTIVAL.
WE'LL SEE OUR FRIENDS PLAY SOME SPORTS GAMES!
REALLY?
We, the players, vow to...
ぱち
ぱち
ぱち
ぱち
WHY AM I...
...THE MAIN CHARACTER IN THIS CHAPTER?

Scavenger Hunt Race

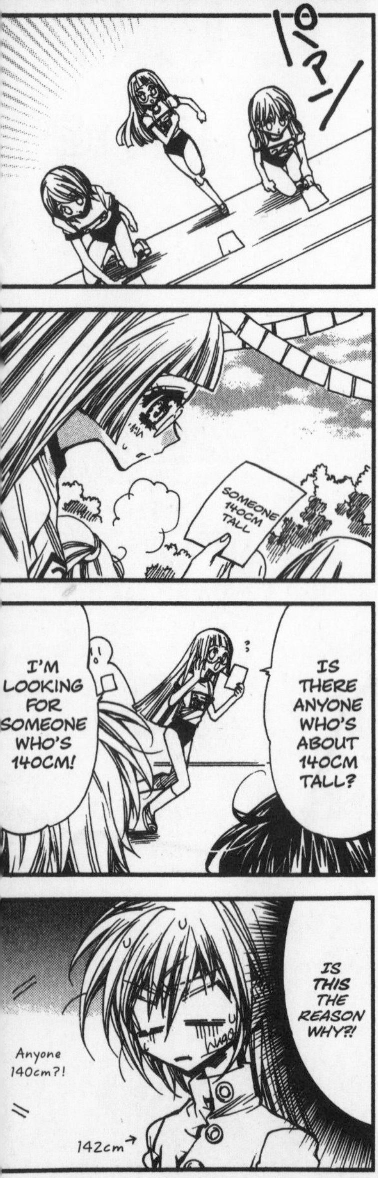
パァン
SOMEONE 140CM TALL
IS THERE ANYONE WHO'S ABOUT 140CM TALL?
I'M LOOKING FOR SOMEONE WHO'S 140CM!
IS THIS THE REASON WHY?!
Anyone 140cm?!
142cm

GUILT-NA-ZAN BONUS COMIC STRIPS!

M.V.P.

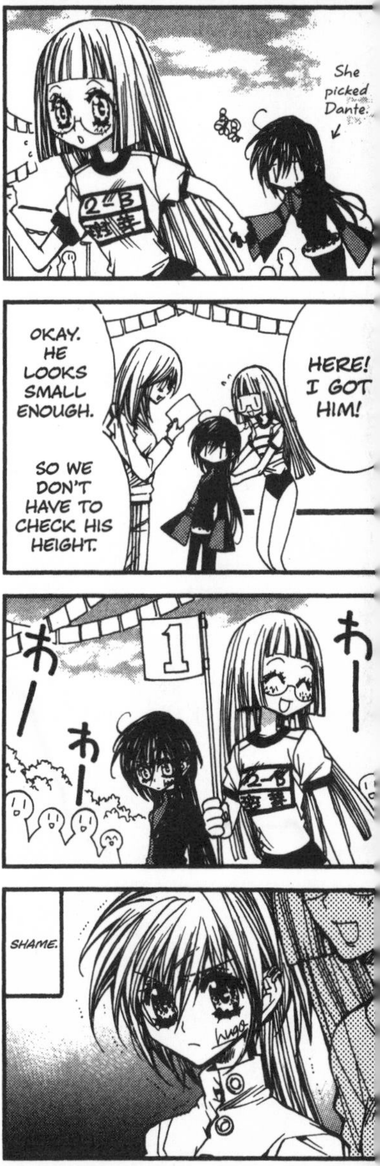
She picked Dante.
HERE! I GOT HIM!
OKAY. HE LOOKS SMALL ENOUGH.
SO WE DON'T HAVE TO CHECK HIS HEIGHT.
1
わー
わー
わー
SHAME.

Simplicity

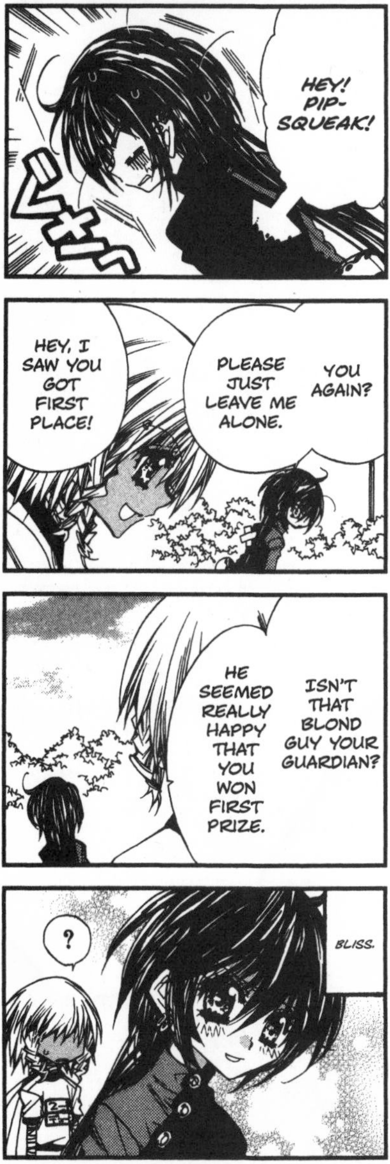
HEY! PIP-SQUEAK!
YOU AGAIN?
PLEASE JUST LEAVE ME ALONE.
HEY, I SAW YOU GOT FIRST PLACE!
ISN'T THAT BLOND GUY YOUR GUARDIAN?
HE SEEMED REALLY HAPPY THAT YOU WON FIRST PRIZE.
BLISS.
?

Being Busy

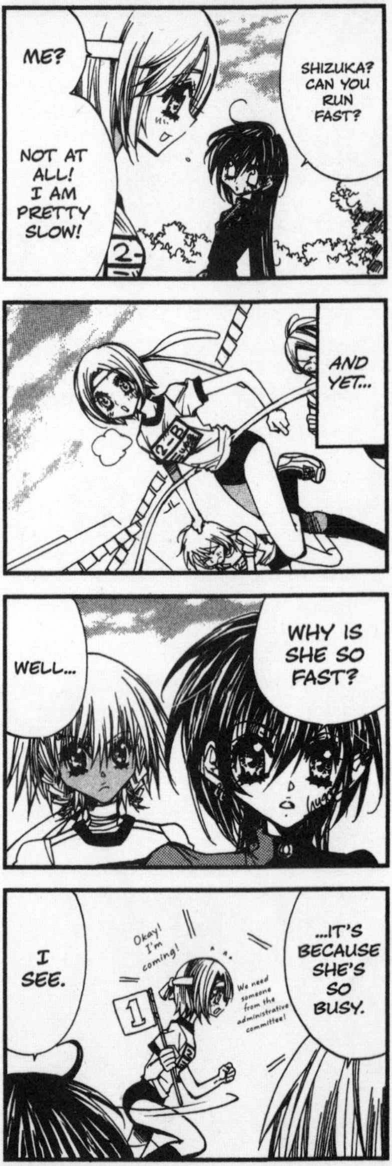
SHIZUKA? CAN YOU RUN FAST?
ME?
NOT AT ALL! I AM PRETTY SLOW!
AND YET...
WHY IS SHE SO FAST?
WELL...
...IT'S BECAUSE SHE'S SO BUSY.
We need someone from the administrative committee!
Okay! I'm coming!
I SEE.

Greedy Pig

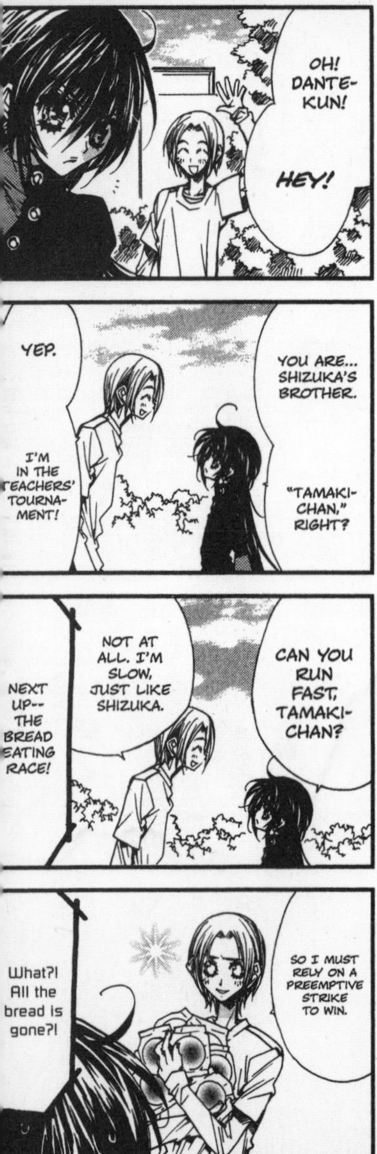
OH! DANTE-KUN!
HEY!
YOU ARE... SHIZUKA'S BROTHER.
"TAMAKI-CHAN," RIGHT?
YEP.
I'M IN THE TEACHERS' TOURNAMENT!
CAN YOU RUN FAST, TAMAKI-CHAN?
NOT AT ALL. I'M SLOW, JUST LIKE SHIZUKA.
NEXT UP-- THE BREAD EATING RACE!
SO I MUST RELY ON A PREEMPTIVE STRIKE TO WIN.
What?! All the bread is gone?!

GUILT-NA-ZAN BONUS COMIC STRIPS!

Greedy Monster

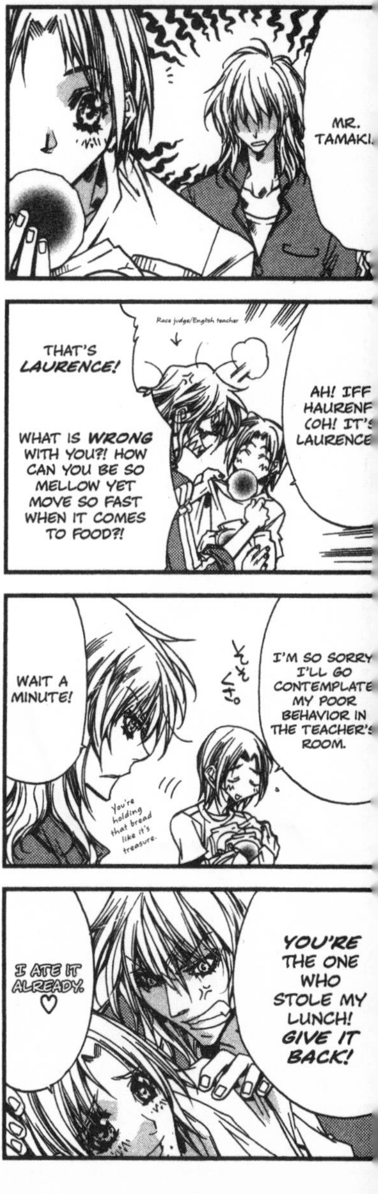

MR. TAMAKI.
AH! IFF HAURENF (OH! IT'S LAURENCE
Race judge/English teacher
THAT'S LAURENCE!
WHAT IS WRONG WITH YOU?! HOW CAN YOU BE SO MELLOW YET MOVE SO FAST WHEN IT COMES TO FOOD?!
I'M SO SORRY I'LL GO CONTEMPLATE MY POOR BEHAVIOR IN THE TEACHER'S ROOM.
WAIT A MINUTE!
You're holding that bread like it's treasure.
YOU'RE THE ONE WHO STOLE MY LUNCH! GIVE IT BACK!
I ATE IT ALREADY. ♡

Appearance

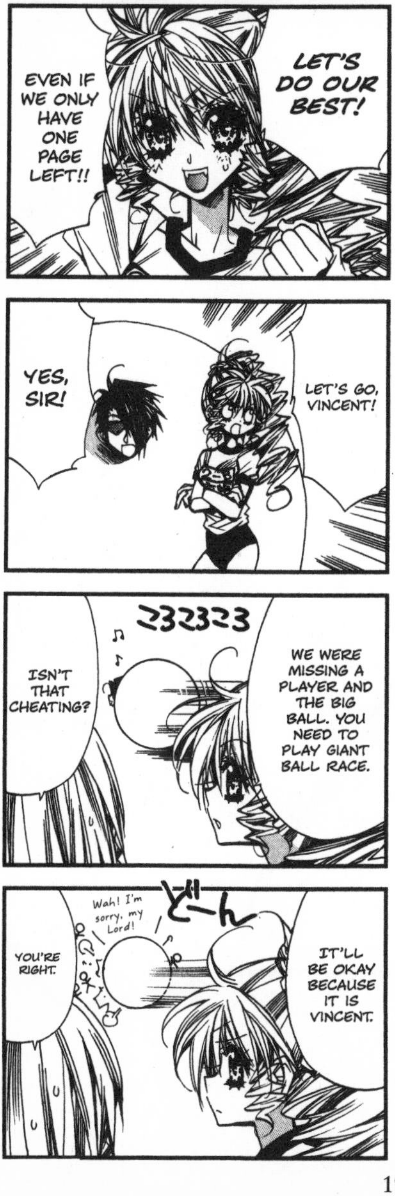

LET'S DO OUR BEST!
EVEN IF WE ONLY HAVE ONE PAGE LEFT!!
LET'S GO, VINCENT!
YES, SIR!
WE WERE MISSING A PLAYER AND THE BIG BALL. YOU NEED TO PLAY GIANT BALL RACE.
ISN'T THAT CHEATING?
IT'LL BE OKAY BECAUSE IT IS VINCENT.
どーん
Wah! I'm sorry, my Lord!
YOU'RE RIGHT.

Ball Games

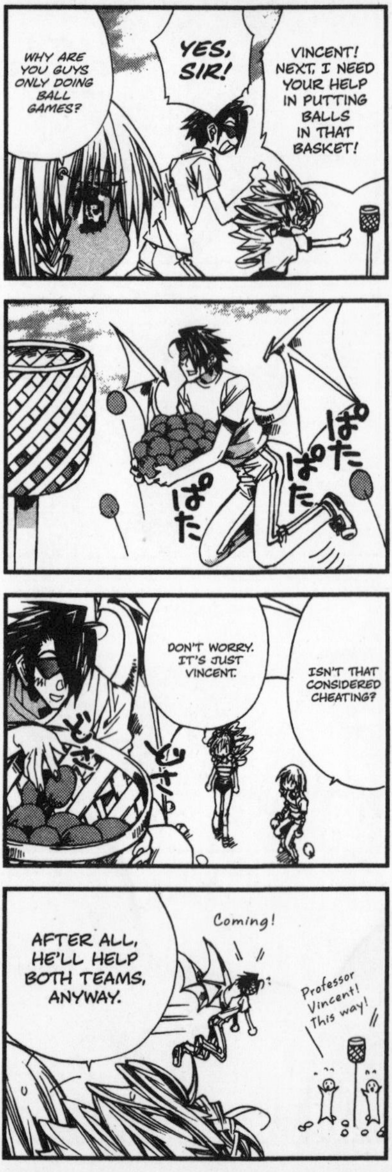
VINCENT! NEXT, I NEED YOUR HELP IN PUTTING BALLS IN THAT BASKET!
YES, SIR!
WHY ARE YOU GUYS ONLY DOING BALL GAMES?
ぱたぱた
ぱたぱた
ISN'T THAT CONSIDERED CHEATING?
DON'T WORRY. IT'S JUST VINCENT.
どさっ
どさっ
Professor Vincent! This way!
Coming!
AFTER ALL, HE'LL HELP BOTH TEAMS, ANYWAY.

Nutritious Lunch

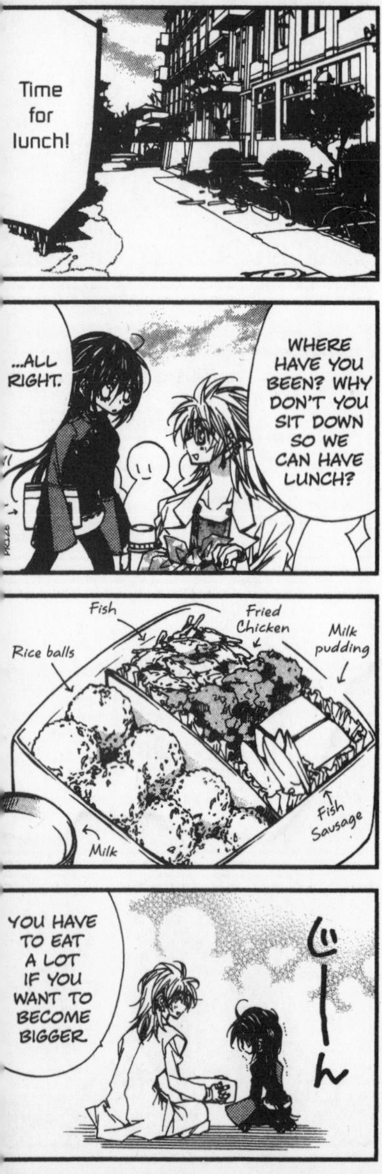
Time for lunch!
WHERE HAVE YOU BEEN? WHY DON'T YOU SIT DOWN SO WE CAN HAVE LUNCH?
...ALL RIGHT.
Milk pudding
Fried Chicken
Fish
Rice balls
Fish Sausage
Milk
じーーん
YOU HAVE TO EAT A LOT IF YOU WANT TO BECOME BIGGER

POSTSCRIPT

Postscript, Part 1

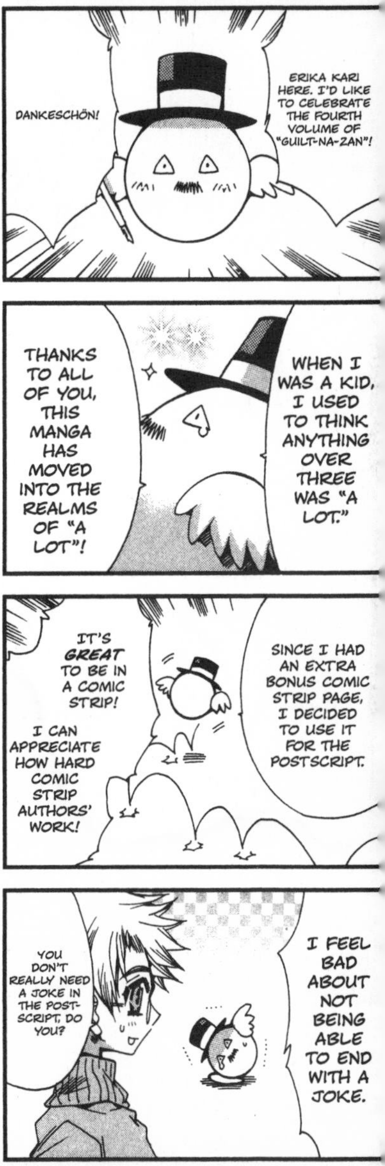
ERIKA KARI HERE. I'D LIKE TO CELEBRATE THE FOURTH VOLUME OF "GUILT-NA-ZAN"!
DANKESCHÖN!
WHEN I WAS A KID, I USED TO THINK ANYTHING OVER THREE WAS "A LOT."
THANKS TO ALL OF YOU, THIS MANGA HAS MOVED INTO THE REALMS OF "A LOT"!
SINCE I HAD AN EXTRA BONUS COMIC STRIP PAGE, I DECIDED TO USE IT FOR THE POSTSCRIPT.
IT'S GREAT TO BE IN A COMIC STRIP!
I CAN APPRECIATE HOW HARD COMIC STRIP AUTHORS' WORK!
I FEEL BAD ABOUT NOT BEING ABLE TO END WITH A JOKE.
YOU DON'T REALLY NEED A JOKE IN THE POST-SCRIPT, DO YOU?

Postscript, Part 2

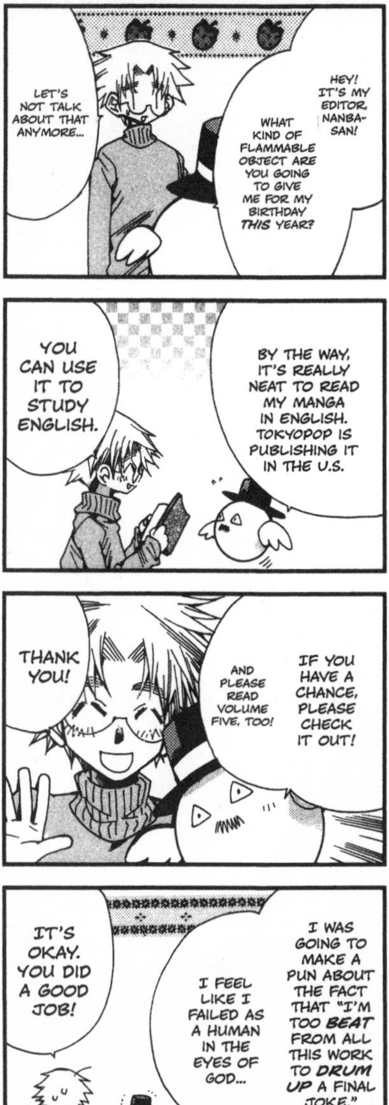
HEY! IT'S MY EDITOR, NANBA-SAN!
WHAT KIND OF FLAMMABLE OBJECT ARE YOU GOING TO GIVE ME FOR MY BIRTHDAY THIS YEAR?
LET'S NOT TALK ABOUT THAT ANYMORE...
BY THE WAY, IT'S REALLY NEAT TO READ MY MANGA IN ENGLISH. TOKYOPOP IS PUBLISHING IT IN THE U.S.
YOU CAN USE IT TO STUDY ENGLISH.
IF YOU HAVE A CHANCE, PLEASE CHECK IT OUT!
AND PLEASE READ VOLUME FIVE, TOO!
THANK YOU!
I WAS GOING TO MAKE A PUN ABOUT THE FACT THAT "I'M TOO BEAT FROM ALL THIS WORK TO DRUM UP A FINAL JOKE."
I FEEL LIKE I FAILED AS A HUMAN IN THE EYES OF GOD...
IT'S OKAY. YOU DID A GOOD JOB!

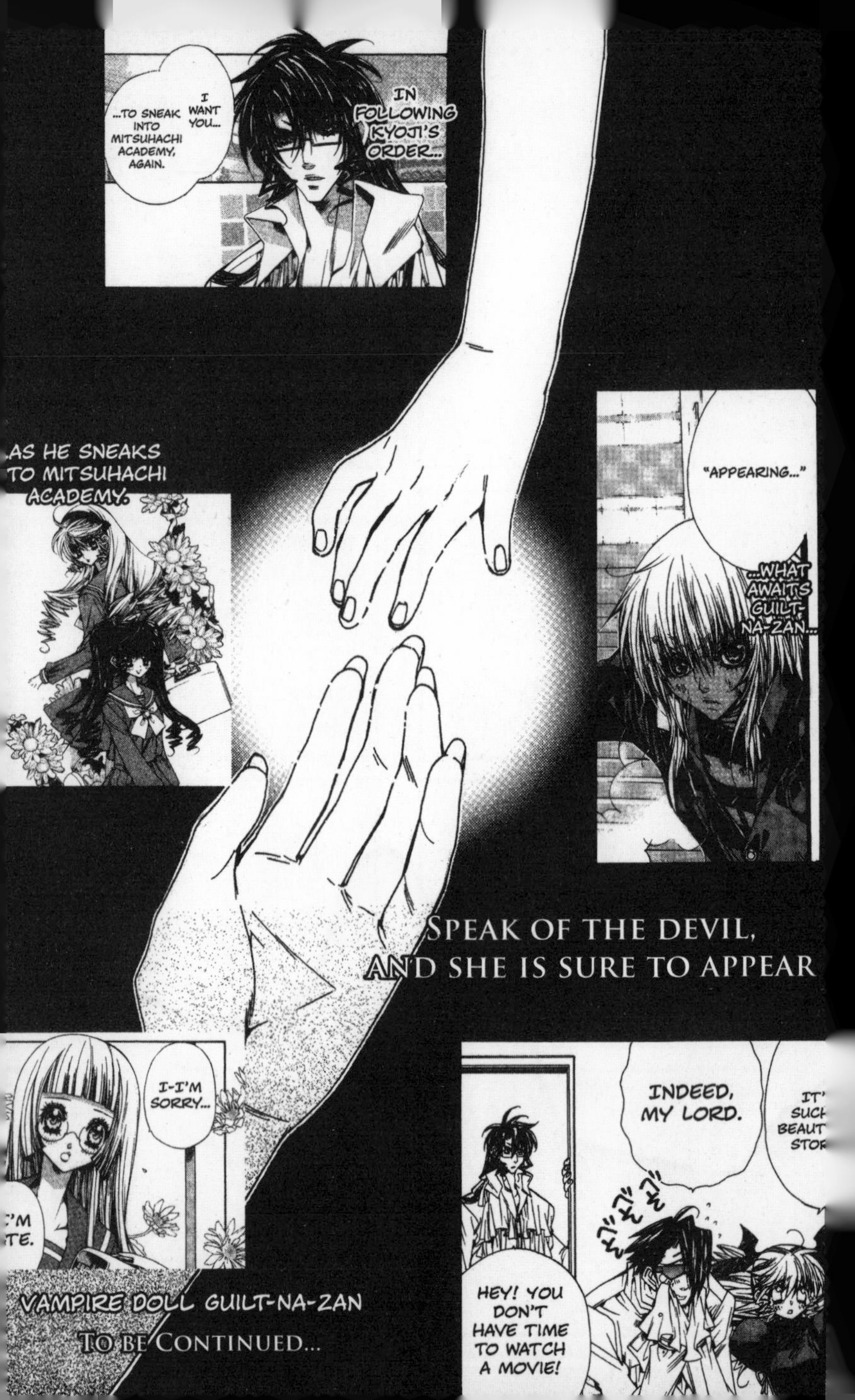
IN FOLLOWING KYOJI'S ORDER...
I WANT YOU...
...TO SNEAK INTO MITSUHACHI ACADEMY, AGAIN.
"APPEARING..."
...WHAT AWAITS GUILT-NA-ZAN...
AS HE SNEAKS TO MITSUHACHI ACADEMY.
SPEAK OF THE DEVIL, AND SHE IS SURE TO APPEAR
INDEED, MY LORD.
HEY! YOU DON'T HAVE TIME TO WATCH A MOVIE!
I-I'M SORRY...
VAMPIRE DOLL GUILT-NA-ZAN
TO BE CONTINUED...

Fruits Basket™
By Natsuki Takaya
Volume 18

The next volume of the bestselling series is here!

Everyone knows Isuzu is in the hospital...or is she? While everyone is searching for her, Isuzu is hatching a scheme that may allow her to break the curse!

The #1 selling shojo manga in America!

ROMANCE   T TEEN AGE 13+

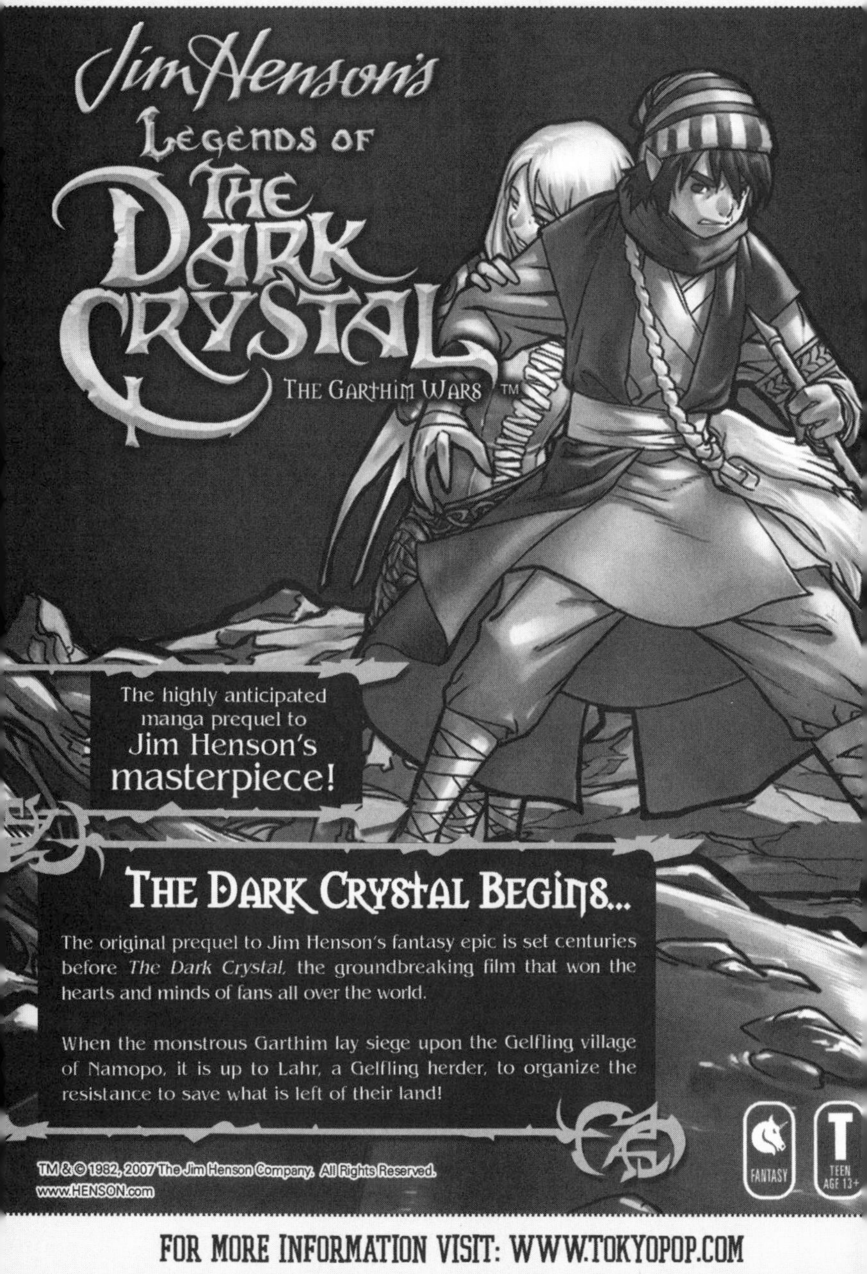
Jim Henson's
Legends of
The Dark Crystal
The Garthim Wars ™
The highly anticipated manga prequel to Jim Henson's masterpiece!
The Dark Crystal Begins...
The original prequel to Jim Henson's fantasy epic is set centuries before *The Dark Crystal,* the groundbreaking film that won the hearts and minds of fans all over the world.
When the monstrous Garthim lay siege upon the Gelfling village of Namopo, it is up to Lahr, a Gelfling herder, to organize the resistance to save what is left of their land!
FANTASY
T
TEEN AGE 13+
TM & © 1982, 2007 The Jim Henson Company. All Rights Reserved.
www.HENSON.com

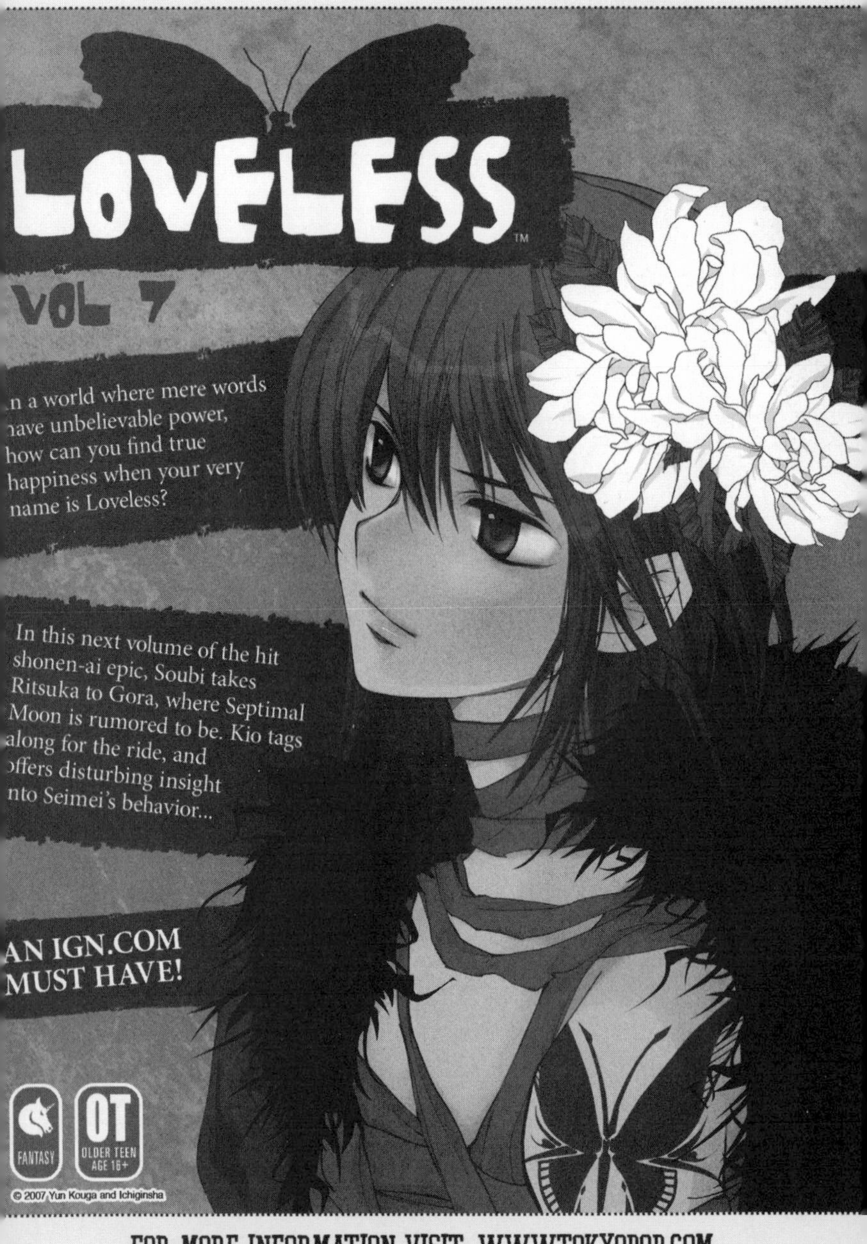
LOVELESS™
VOL 7
n a world where mere words
ave unbelievable power,
how can you find true
happiness when your very
name is Loveless?
In this next volume of the hit
shonen-ai epic, Soubi takes
Ritsuka to Gora, where Septimal
Moon is rumored to be. Kio tags
along for the ride, and
ffers disturbing insight
nto Seimei's behavior...
AN IGN.COM
MUST HAVE!
FANTASY
OT
OLDER TEEN
AGE 16+
© 2007 Yun Kouga and Ichiginsha

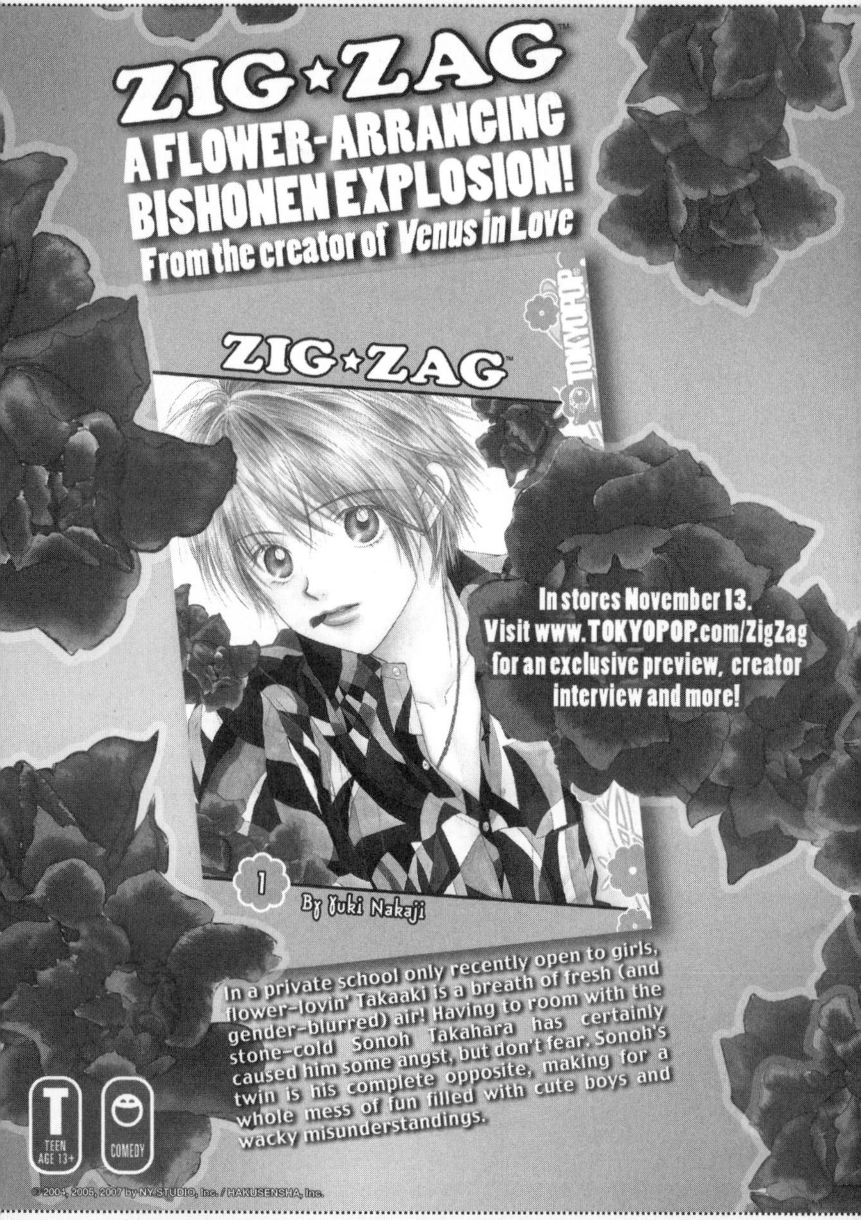
ZIG★ZAG™
A FLOWER-ARRANGING BISHONEN EXPLOSION!
From the creator of Venus in Love
TOKYOPOP
ZIG★ZAG™
1
By Yuki Nakaji
In stores November 13.
Visit www.TOKYOPOP.com/ZigZag for an exclusive preview, creator interview and more!
In a private school only recently open to girls, flower-lovin' Takaaki is a breath of fresh (and gender-blurred) air! Having to room with the stone-cold Sonoh Takahara has certainly caused him some angst, but don't fear. Sonoh's twin is his complete opposite, making for a whole mess of fun filled with cute boys and wacky misunderstandings.
T TEEN AGE 13+
COMEDY
© 2004, 2005, 2007 by NY STUDIO, Inc. / HAKUSENSHA, Inc.

STOP!

This is the back of the book.
You wouldn't want to spoil a great ending!

This book is printed "manga-style," in the authentic Japanese right-to-left format. Since none of the artwork has been flipped or altered, readers get to experience the story just as the creator intended. You've been asking for it, so TOKYOPOP® delivered: authentic, hot-off-the-press, and far more fun!

DIRECTIONS

If this is your first time reading manga-style, here's a quick guide to help you understand how it works.

It's easy... just start in the top right panel and follow the numbers. Have fun, and look for more 100% authentic manga from TOKYOPOP®!